EARLY
WARNING

EARLY WARNING

MICHAEL WALSH

PINNACLE BOOKS
KENSINGTON PUBLISHING CORP.
www.kensingtonbooks.com

PINNACLE BOOKS are published by

Kensington Publishing Corp.
119 West 40th Street
New York, NY 10018

All Kensington titles, imprints, and distributed lines are available at special quantity discounts for bulk purchases for sales promotions, premiums, fund-raising, educational, or institutional use.

Special book excerpts or customized printings can also be created to fit specific needs. For details, write or phone the office of the Kensington special sales manager: Kensington Publishing Corp., 119 West 40th Street, New York, NY 10018, attn: Special Sales Department; phone 1-800-221-2647.

This book is a work of fiction. Names, characters, businesses, organizations, places, events, and incidents either are the product of the author's imagination or are used fictitiously. Any resemblance to actual persons, living or dead, events, or locales is entirely coincidental.

ISBN-13: 978-0-7860-2043-0
ISBN-10: 0-7860-2043-1

First printing: September 2010

10 9 8 7 6 5 4 3 2 1

Printed in the United States of America

For JoAnn Cahill

PROLOGUE

London, England

Dressed entirely in black, Amanda Harrington stood silent as the chauffeur opened the Bentley's rear passenger door, and involuntarily flinched as she got in.

Nothing on the seat. Nothing on the center console. No note, no gifts, no flowers, no champagne, no chocolate. Good.

She relaxed a little as the liveried driver closed the door. The drugs had worn off after about a month—he had given her a far stronger dose than the attending physicians at Cromwell Hospital had at first thought—and they said it was a miracle that she hadn't died. It took another couple of months for her to be able to breathe without mechanical assistance, and still more time to regain the use of her limbs.

Then it was another few months at Bethlem Royal, where she underwent a battery of psychological tests and counseling, to make sure she was ready to take her place back in society, that the stress of reentry—and the possibility of encountering *him*—would not be too much for her still-fragile psyche to bear.

All of this was done in complete seclusion and secrecy. Of the events in France, the newspapers and the BBC had carried not a word; the British government had thrown the cloak of the Official Secrets Act around the whole episode, managed her affairs while she recovered, tended to her property in London as well as to a villa in Costa Rica that nobody even knew she owned. She didn't know who had ordered that courtesy, or why, but at this point she was simply grateful to be allowed to return home. Even with the shock of her terrible loss still as fresh as it had been nine months ago.

London in the summer was a dicey proposition, but today was as warm and welcoming as it got. Still, she felt a little chill wash over her as the car pulled up in front of her home, 4 Kensington Park Gardens in Holland Park.

"Your residence, madam," said the driver, opening the door and offering her an arm. Amanda accepted it gratefully.

The man—he was either Indian or Pakistani, which was far from unusual in London—gently but firmly helped her up the few steps to the front door of her home. "May I help you with your keys, madam?" he inquired.

"No, thank you, that's quite all right," she replied. Though she was still weak, she wanted to be able to do something for herself, and entering her own home under her own steam was a good place to start.

"You're quite sure?" The man was very kind, and he had a pleasing twinkle in his eye, as if her infirmity was a secret that only the two of them shared.

"Yes, quite sure," she said, trying to smile but failing. She put the key in the lock and turned it. It opened with the same satisfying *thunk* she was so used to, and for a brief moment all seemed right with the world. The door swung open, and the front hall lay before her.

As the driver fetched her luggage, Amanda stood in the doorway, breathing in the familiar smells. It seemed that she had been gone for ages, and that she had just left, on his order, bringing with her what he had called so vulgarly the "insurance policy . . ."

No—she didn't want to think about that. Not yet. Not now. Maybe not ever.

The driver was standing behind her, her belongings in his hands. "Madam?" he prompted.

Amanda stood aside to let him pass, and he went into the hallway. "Set them down there, thank you," she said.

"You're sure?"

She managed to muster a weak smile of confidence. "Yes, thank you. That will be all."

They stood in the doorway for an awkward moment, and this time it was he who stepped aside to allow her entry. Then he moved past her, onto the top step, nodded, and turned to go.

"I'm terribly afraid I've completely forgotten my manners," said Amanda suddenly, fumbling in her purse. But the driver waved her off without a word: he was not accepting gratuities today. "In that case," said Amanda, "please tell me your name."

"Achmed," said the man, with a slight bow.

"Thank you, Achmed," said Amanda. And then he was gone.

Inside the house, Amanda fixed the lock once more but made no further move to enter her home. Instead, she stood stock-still, as if listening for voices. But the only sound she could hear was that of her own shallow breathing.

She turned right, into the parlor. If there was going to be anything, she hoped it would be here, right in the first room, to spare her any further suspense. But the room was as she had left it, the piano still in the corner, the books still on the shelves, even the decanters still on the sideboard. She felt like pouring herself a drink, but the doctors had warned her not to, not for a while anyway. Perhaps tomorrow. Or next week. Or never.

Again, she listened. Again, nothing.

Amanda returned to the hall and started up the steps. She

left the luggage in the hallway. There was plenty of time to retrieve it, and besides she had closets full of clothing upstairs. It suddenly occurred to her to wonder how she had come to have any luggage at all, since she had brought almost nothing to France, but someone must have provided her with some of her things during her long hospital stay.

Maybe him. God, she hoped not.

She ascended the long flight of stairs up to the first floor.

Nothing but silence greeted her at the stop of the stairs. The guest rooms yawned tidy but empty. There wasn't a speck of dust anywhere, nothing to betray her long absence.

She went up another flight of stairs, to her floor, her personal floor. The one that had been *their* floor together.

The door to the child's room was shut, and she decided not to enter it. Too many bad memories there. She sniffed the air: faintly, just faintly, she believed she could make out the smell of Indian food, one of their last meals together here.

She turned back to her bedroom. The bed was made, her things exactly where she had left them. Cautiously, she kicked off her shoes and scrunched her toes against the carpet. Then she lay down, across the bed, staring at the ceiling, glad she was home at last and yet wishing she were anywhere but here, feeling every inch a bereaved mother, every inch an orphan and every inch a widow.

How long she lay like that she could not tell, but eventually she was awakened by the soft tones of a mobile phone, ringing somewhere in the house. Somewhere nearby.

That was impossible. Her legendary battery of mobiles, BlackBerrys, and PDAs had been lost in France and not replaced. She lay there, not wishing to rise, hoping that the sound was merely an illusion, an after-effect of her ordeal, a side effect of her treatments.

The sound stopped. She breathed in. And then the ringing started again.

There must be a phone in the house she had forgotten about. One that she had left plugged in. One whose service somehow hadn't been canceled.

No, it was impossible. But something was still ringing.

Amanda rose and moved toward the bedroom door. The sound grew louder.

She stepped into the hall: louder still. She prayed to a God she didn't quite believe in that it was not coming from down the hall. From *her* room. But it was.

No. She had free will. She had free choice. She didn't have to answer it.

The ring tone stopped, then started up again almost immediately. This time there was no denying it: somebody was calling her.

A crazy thought struck her. Maybe it was *her*. Her child. No matter what those doctors had tried to tell her, tried to beat out of her, tried to beat into her, no matter how much she understood rationally that the whole thing had been a delusion, deep down she didn't believe them. She knew herself, knew her instincts, knew her inner voices.

She stopped, caught herself. No. Her lover was dead. *She* was gone. It was over.

And then the phone rang again and this time she knew she had no choice. She had to answer it. Had to go in *there*.

She opened the door. The room was just as she had left it nine months ago, a perfect dream room for a twelve-year-old girl, filled with fluffy pillows and stuffed animals. She could practically smell her presence, and if she squinted hard enough, could imagine that she saw the outlines of the girl's body still visible in the bedclothes. Then the phone rang again.

Now she heard the melody clearly: Schubert's *"Unfinished" Symphony*. She shuddered, moved in the direction of the sound, searching for it until she realized that it was staring right at her: on Emma's bed, lying atop the stack of pillows like the princess atop the pea.

It was still ringing as she picked it up, if you could call what phones did these days ringing. "Hello?" she said in a voice that she hoped was strong. She flinched at the silence, dreading whatever was at the other end of the line. Waiting, waiting . . .

And then he spoke: "Compassionate leave is over. It's time to get back to work."

Amanda Harrington collapsed unconscious onto the floor.

Either a universe that is all order,
or else a farrago thrown together at random,
yet somehow forming a universe.
—MARCUS AURELIUS, *Meditations*, Book IV

CHAPTER ONE

Budapest, Hungary

From Castle Hill, the view was straight east, across the Danube and into central Asia. Nobody thought of it that way anymore, of course, but two hundred years ago, before unification, the change in topography mirrored the change in the people and in the culture. On the right bank was Buda, rugged and hilly, while on the left lay the old city of Pest, gateway to the steppes of central Asia. From here it was practically a straight shot across Hungary to Nyiregyhaza, through the Carpathians and into the Ukraine, and thence to the Ural Mountains, and Siberia.

He had been here; Devlin knew it. If he sniffed the air, he could practically smell him. He had lost the trail in France, in that horrible refuge the monster kept in the old Abbey of Clairvaux, now a maximum-security French prison. Lost him thanks to Milverton's nearly lethal knife thrust through his shoulder, and Skorzeny's final, desperate kick. Milverton had been every bit as good as he had thought, and Skorzeny even more dangerous and clever. But the former was no longer with us; for the latter, it would be only a matter of time. Devlin had sworn that to the President of the United States, to himself and, most of all, to her.

The sound of voices, speaking softly in Hungarian, wafted across the still night air.

The Hilton Budapest was a near-ideal blending of the sacred and the profane, constructed in and around the ruins of a 13th-century Dominican Church and a baroque-era Jesuit college. The St. Matthias Church stood nearby, and behind it the Fisherman's Bastion, with its seven towers and filigreed walkways. In the dark, it was a perfect place to hide. Devlin stepped back into the shadows and waited.

Operational security was everything.

The voice drew closer. Two men walked within fifteen feet of him, lost in conversation, wreathed in cigarette smoke. The rest of the civilized world had gradually kicked the habit, but not in central Europe. Good. Cigarettes dulled the senses, and not only of taste or, depending on which hand the smoker used, touch, but also of hearing. The small sounds associated with smoking, on a night as quiet as this, seemed many decibels louder: the inhaling, the exhaling, the spitting. Devlin had long ago learned to turn anything to an advantage, and now he was going to allow a filthy habit to shelter him until the moment was right.

He had trailed one of them from Geneva, Switzerland, across the Alps, through Austria, where he had narrowly missed him in Vienna and finally here to Budapest. His name was Farid Belghazi, an Algerian-born French scientist attached to the *Organisation Européenne pour la Recherche Nucléaire*, better known as CERN, and among the projects he had been assigned to was the Large Hadron Collider, the proton-smashing experiment that was attempting nothing less than to re-create the conditions that obtained at the dawn of the universe: the Big Bang. In short, they were searching for the "God particle."

Belghazi was hardly after anything so grand, but as someone who had a top security clearance throughout the facility, his knowledge of the other research into high-energy particle physics that was going on near the French-Swiss border could be invaluable to civilization's professed enemies. In addition, CERN had been the birthplace of the World Wide Web, and was actively involved in GRID computing to power data analysis; a virtual supercomputer of networked workstations, all working on the same problem. If you were going to insinuate a spy into a sensitive agency, CERN was probably the next best target after NSA headquarters in Fort Meade, Maryland, itself. The National Security Agency had first picked up Belghazi's trail by flagging a series of phone calls and e-mails. As the lead operative of the Central Security Service's Branch 4, Devlin naturally had access to the information. Now he was going to find out what it all meant.

About ten meters ahead, Devlin shadowed the two men, keeping within the cover of the Fisherman's Bastion. Now he could hear the voices clearly. The pair was speaking Hungarian, one speaker a native, the other his man, Belghazi. Magyar was not one of Devlin's best languages, and he knew he could not hope to pass for a Hungarian unless the conversation was brusque and confined to a few sentences. He'd have to act fast before he aroused any suspicions.

In Devlin's experience, the direct approach was almost always the best. Fishing a pack of Marlboros out of his pocket, he stuck an unlighted cigarette in his mouth and stepped out of the shadows and into their path. "Have you got a light?" he mumbled, offering the pack around as was customary in this part of the world. Obligingly, the Hungarian instinctively extended a lighter. Although it was dark, he could see a light flash in Belghazi's eyes, but by then it was too late. Devlin grabbed the Hungarian by the wrist and yanked, sending him sprawling into the darkness behind them. Under the rules of engagement of a snatch-and-grab operation like this—rules that even applied to him—he was not allowed to terminate unknown civilians unless he was a) sure of hostile intent and b) had total deniability. Meanwhile, he had a more immediate problem.

Belghazi went for his knife, but Devlin was ready for it. He spun, his left hand chopping down hard on the knife thrust. At the same time, he crossed with his right and met the point of the Algerian's jaw, knocking him backward toward the road where, at that same moment, a small black Prius glided up soundlessly, its trunk already opened. In one motion, Devlin stuck a needle into the Algerian's neck and heaved him into the trunk; the drug would only incapacitate him, not render him unconscious. Without a trace of haste, he closed it as if he had just tossed in his suitcase. Then he walked around the car and got into the front passenger seat.

She was at the wheel, the car already moving as the door closed. The blond hair fell nearly to her shoulders. "What do we know?" she asked.

"Not much, but we'll soon know a lot more."

The Prius—still something of an anomaly in these precincts—made its way down the winding streets, heading for the *Erzsébet hid*—the Elisabeth Bridge—and Pest beyond. The safe house was there, disguised as a garage and tucked away in a service alley behind the row of glittering Western hotels that now lined the river.

The first sign that anything was amiss came on the bridge. "Trouble," said Maryam.

Devlin pulled out what to all outward appearances was an ordinary Nokia Surge, the kind with a rectangular screen that disguised a slide-out mini-keyboard and, indeed, it could function that way should anyone ask. This one, however, was also an infrared sensor/scanner that could monitor all electronic devices up to a range of fifty meters; in a few seconds they would know how many men were chasing them and even read and listen in on their communications.

"How many?"

Her eyes flicked to the rearview mirror, and then to the side mirrors. "Two Mercedes SUVs, tinted windows. One after another, behind us. They'll be on either side of us as soon as we leave the bridge.

"Weapons?"

"In the back."

Devlin looked down and saw a golf bag on the floor. He pulled it open to find an array of small arms, including a brace of Heckler & Koch Mark 23 Special Ops, a Beretta UGB autoloader shotgun, and a couple of Armalite semi-automatics. "They'll do," he said, handing her one of the HKs and sliding the shotgun, barrel down, between his legs.

They jumped off the Elisabeth Bridge and turned right on the Váci utca. There was no way they could outrun the Benzes, and compartmentalized security dictated that they go nowhere near the safe house. They were going to have to improvise, but they were both good at that—they had been doing it all their lives. The Prius dove into the maze of streets, the remnants of ancient cattle trails and goat paths that had somehow or other survived the grand visions of the Austro-Hungarian Empire at its zenith, and had been allowed to remain as they were practically since Attila had swept out of the East, bringing revolution, retribution, destruction, and death.

They would use the streets as their defense.

There was no way the Benzes could follow them closely. European drivers, Devlin knew, could race down narrow passageways with a bravado that more cautious Americans would never dare; it was not unusual for drivers to kiss mirrors as they passed each other, but rarely did they scrape a building or knock down a passing pedestrian or bicyclist.

Still, this was going to be a challenge, and all they needed was enough time to ditch the Prius and get the backup unit in place when they were ready to hop.

"How did they pick us up?" Maryam hissed as she drove. "I thought you said we had complete op sec."

"RoE," replied Devlin. "I should have taken the other guy out, but . . ." He didn't need to finish the sentence. Since the bombing of the Marine barracks in Beirut, every op had chafed at the ridiculous rules imposed on them, mostly by the State Department. Foggy Bottom had never met a country or even an enemy it didn't think it could bore to death in a great gaseous fog.

They whizzed along the narrow streets. In the old days, before the revolution of 1989, the streets would have been pretty much deserted at this hour, not only because communist governments deemed anyone out after hours as automatically suspicious but also because very few people could afford to own an automobile. With the fall of the Berlin Wall and the collapse of the Soviet Union that had all changed, but the late hour was working in their favor.

As Maryam drove—unpredictably, never following a pattern and sometimes reversing course in the middle of a street, and darting down one-way streets if circumstances allowed—Devlin punched in the safe house contact number. This was not the time for the flat-out emergency number, the one that signaled that the entire op had gone tits up and that an extraction team was necessary. Besides, under the terms of his incarnation as Branch 4's deadliest and most classified operative, his identity was to be kept secret at all times. The only people who even knew of his existence were the president, the secretary of defense, and the head of the NSA.

And now, of course, her. But that was by choice, not necessity or command.

The Nokia sent its signal. Even if they were monitoring the Prius's electronic transmissions, they would never be able to detect it. Devlin's infrequent field communications bounced through a row of encrypted cutouts, with a ping off Fort Meade, where they were re-encrypted via the Dual_ EC_DRBG, a pseudo-random number generator, and then redirected, so that whoever was on the receiving end would have no way of telling the signal's provenance. In the never-ending war between the hunter and the hunted, The Building's encryption technology was subjected to relentless and rigorous upgrades; sometimes it seemed that half the best minds in the Puzzle Palace were at work and making sure their own SIGINT was safe from predatory eyes and ears, while the other half penetrated the bad guys' innermost defenses. Whether anyone would ever win this game was moot, but once you were in it, you were in it to win it.

Still, the Mercedes-Benzes shadowed them, keeping to parallel streets when necessary, but always on their tail, as if they were electronically tracking them.

"Are you sure this car is clean?" barked Devlin.

"Stole it myself this morning, completely randomly," she replied. "There's no way they could have known about it."

"Then they were following you."

"Impossible. I just got in country."

"Then they picked you up at origination."

"Also impossible. I bought three tickets to three different destinations, each one in a different name. No ghosts."

"That you saw."

She shot him a quick, angry glance. "Are you challenging my professionalism?" she asked, zipping the Prius between two oncoming vehicles and splitting them perfectly.

"Absolutely not," he replied, and that was the truth. She was as good as they came. Where she had grown up, and what she'd had to endure, had made her so. "But you know the old saying: when you eliminate the impossible, whatever remains, however improbable, must be the truth."

"Wild Bill Donovan?"

"Sherlock Holmes, *The Sign of the Four* . . ."

"Hold on!"

The car careered to the left, nearly tipped, then righted it-self and regained traction. Behind them, the two Benzes gained.

"Slow down and let them pass us," said Devlin. Just as their pursuers were about to pull even, Maryam hit the brakes and the SUVs, their drivers caught by surprise, went zipping by. "Got 'em both," said Devlin. "Now lose 'em while I digest this."

Maryam wheeled left onto the Irányi utca, then made her way back north a couple of blocks to pick up the Kossuth utca, named after the 19th-century freedom fighter, a wide boulevard heading into the heart of Pest and then out to the motorway. They might be able to ditch them in the warren of back streets on either side, but Devlin doubted it. Unless they wanted to lose both their prisoner and their lives, they were going to have to stand and fight.

"Who are they?"

Devlin knew he had less than two minutes before the un-known tormentors would pick them up again. "There are six in all, two in the lead car and four shooters in the trailing ve-hicle."

"Not good."

"Up to us to make it better. Even things out."

She gave him a quick smile, then glanced back at the rearview mirror. There was no sign of the SUVs. "I think we might have lost them."

"Impossible. Even an amateur on a bicycle could follow this piece of Nipponese plastic. They're waiting for us, up ahead somewhere. Stop the car—over there."

Maryam pulled off into a side street, and circled the block three-quarters of the way. There was no place to park, but then there was never anyplace to park in Budapest, so she wedged the car perpendicularly between an ancient Lada and a new Ford and killed the lights.

Devlin climbed into the back and lowered one of the fold-down seats, keeping his HK trained on their unwilling passenger. "Farid, are you all right?" he asked his unwilling passenger in Arabic.

There was no sound from the trunk. Devlin turned the Nokia backlight on and peered in. Belghazi was relaxed, his eyes open, but he didn't look happy, and no sound came from his mouth.

"Maybe he didn't understand you," suggest Maryam. "I told you to polish your street Arabic."

"Yeah, well, let's see how you do in the back alleys of Magdeburg with that Bavarian honk," he said. "In the meantime, let's move. Pop the trunk."

Cautiously, Devlin switched off the dome light, opened the door and slid out, concealing himself between the other cars. Senses on full alert, he listened for the sound of a motor, but heard nothing. He moved around to the trunk and, standing, hoisted Farid out, and slung him over his shoulders. Maryam was already out of the car, weapons over her shoulder, searching for a place to hide.

European cities were not like American ones, full of open spaces, wide streets, and generous yards. Here, they nestled up against one other, sharing walls on both sides, and you were lucky to get a garden the size of a postage stamp in the back. Not that you entered the garden from the street: what gaps there were between buildings were closed off by high cement and stucco walls, their gates tightly locked. This part of the world had seen too many conquerors come and go to trust the good nature of their fellow man, or his benign designs.

A row of big European trash cans stood near the curb, the kind into which you could easily stuff a body or two. Devlin dumped Farid into one of them and closed the lid, marking it with a felt-tipped pen he produced from one of his pockets. He didn't care how unpleasant it might be inside, with the coffee grounds, rotten vegetables, and soup bones; that was Farid's tough luck. He should have thought ahead, before he started stealing secrets from CERN and passing them along to al-Qaeda. If that, in fact, was what he'd been doing. But with the rapid proliferation of nuclear technology, this was no time to take chances. The apocalyptic genie that had been confined to the bottle, largely successfully since the day after Trinity, was now well and truly loosed upon the earth.

Devlin scanned the street—and didn't like what he saw; at either end of the road, blocking access and egress, were the two SUVs. They were trapped.

Devlin checked the Surge. He punched a couple of buttons and the video display suddenly turned to a four-block map of the area, right down to the smallest detail. He thought a moment, then entered a series of cipher codes and hit send.

In the distance, he could hear the sounds of one of the SUV's doors opening, and voices. As they approached they would be close enough to scan, but he didn't need a device to tell him what he already knew; they were outnumbered at least two to one, and there was no way out. Softly, Devlin cursed in Italian under his breath. He liked cursing in Italian. There was music to it, and somehow the mellifluousness of the language made almost every situation seem not so bad. He was hoping that was still true.

"Over here." He turned to see Maryam in a stairwell that dipped below the surface of the pavement. There was a door at the bottom of the stairs, one that Devlin knew would lead into the old building's ancient cellar. Devlin dashed over to her and spoke rapidly in French. "They'll be here in a less than a minute. They're going to find me. They are not going to find you, but that's okay. Trust me, they won't have time to think about it. Now blow the lock on this door, get in and get out."

He took a quick look at the area map; her instincts, as usual, were impeccable. "There's a garden in the back, which connects through to the buildings on the other side of the street. You can crawl out the cellar window, sprint across. The fence on the other side shouldn't be a problem and then you're out on the *utca* and away. Now ditch the wig and get out of here."

"What about you?" There was no worry in her eyes, just professional curiosity. That was part of their deal.

"I have to wait for Duke Mantee." He sensed, rather than saw, her look of incomprehension. "An old friend," he explained. "Now get out of here. Seriously."

She hesitated, for just an unprofessional instant—

"Arnaud's, just like we planned. Bienville Street."

"Order for me," she smiled. And then she was gone.

Devlin slipped back into the car. "Duke Mantee" had his instructions. It was all going to happen very fast, it was all going to happen all at once, and it had better damn well work.

They were almost upon him now. He could hear voices, speaking in different languages. There was no point in listening to what they were saying. It would be over soon, one way or another. But, even though he'd never met him, he trusted "Duke Mantee" more than he trusted anybody else, except her.

He strained his ears above the voices, listening for the Duke.

The men came closer to the Prius, weapons drawn. They wouldn't be expecting to see him sitting there, big as life, which is what he was counting on. All those crazy spy books and their Rube Goldberg plotting devices—he'd trade them all for the element of surprise. Naked was always the best disguise.

They'd have suppressors, of course, and a silencer was something he lacked, but if the Duke was punctual, he wasn't going to need one. It was like trying to unwrap candy in a movie theater: never make a series of little noises when you can make one big noise and get it over with.

There—now he heard it. The *thwack* of a helicopter, approaching rapidly.

The men heard it, too. They stopped for a moment and looked up at the sky. Budapest was not Los Angeles, and the sound of a helicopter in the middle of the night was not a normal occurrence. They were amazed when the chopper roared over the buildings, dipped down, and hovered just over their heads.

Now—

Devlin opened fire with the shotgun, bringing down two of the men with one blast as the other two scattered and returned fire. He could hear the *pock* marks as the bullets slammed into the Prius, but he was already out of the car, rolling, the shotgun abandoned now in favor of the HK and one of the Armalites. He got off two quick rounds, heard one of the assailants groan. And then an extraordinary thing happened.

A lifeline descended from the chopper. But no ordinary lifeline. Instead, it was more like a grappling hook, rocketing down a winch and heading straight for—

The trash can. It latched on and began winching the thing up.

Devlin shot the fourth man with the HK and sprinted away, in the opposite direction from Maryam. Op sec came before everything else, and he had planned the operation with multiple outcomes in mind.

One of the four was still alive as Devlin passed him, but there was no time for mercy. He shot him as he ran, heading straight for the other SUV at the end of the street, the two-man team. He could see they were out of the car now, firing at the helicopter. Devlin said a quick prayer that none of the rounds would clip Farid, but he kept running, staying on the sidewalk, in the gloom of the old 19th-century blocks of flats.

Now one of the men spotted him, redirecting his fire. Bullets gouged out chunks of the buildings. Devlin somersaulted twice and came up shooting. He dropped his man with two shots, even though it should have only taken one, and dashed for the SUV. He had time for a quick glance back, and saw that the trash can had disappeared into the chopper's interior, and the big bird was already whirling away.

He was in the driver's seat of the Benz before the last man standing knew he was there. Devlin popped the clutch and squealed into first gear as a bullet clanked off the rear window. Bulletproof. Good—he didn't need to be driving around Budapest in the middle of the night with a rear window punched out. The man was still pursuing him, firing. Devlin caught a glimpse of his face in the side mirror—it was the Hungarian he had seen with Farid up on Castle Hill.

One more thing to do.

Abruptly, he slammed the big car in reverse. Before the man could react, Devlin ran him over. He never knew his name, never would know what crime, if any, the man had committed. But he had been trained to understand that it didn't matter, and it didn't. The back alleys of central Europe were littered with the bodies of nameless ops, who had vanished unknown and unmourned. That was his tough luck. Operational security was everything.

CHAPTER TWO

In the air

Emanuel Skorzeny did his best to relax into the leather seats of his private airplane. For the past nine months, he had been a veritable fugitive, airborne, fleeing the wrath of the U.S. government. Until last year, that had not been a thing worth fearing, not for a long time, not since Americans had landed on Normandy Beach, bridged Remagen, and came close enough to Berlin to let the Soviets and Zhukov hurry up and take the prize. So much for the bromide that violence never solved anything. It certainly sorted Hitler and the National Socialists out.

More—not since the Americans had cleared the Pacific islands from Tarawa and Iwo Jima to Okinawa, firebombed Tokyo, and dropped the Big One on Hiroshima and Nagasaki. Oddly enough, that was the end of Japanese militarism, *finis* to the Empire, the rude termination of the Greater East Asian Co-Prosperity Sphere. Thank God the Americans didn't fight like that anymore.

Still, here he was, a prisoner of his own wealth and ambition. Airborne in his private 707, outfitted and retrofitted to his exact specifications, a home away from home, a flying

living room if indeed he would ever have stooped to anything so vulgar as a living room. Free to fly the world, but
never land, a contemporary Flying Dutchman, a Wandering
Jew, the desolate hero of Schubert's *Winterreise*—the living
embodiment of a hundred European tragic heroes, but without the heroic deeds that had accompanied their ineluctable
fates.

That devil, Devlin, had done this to him. The boy he had
failed to kill when he had the chance, a latter-day Hercules,
who had turned the tables on the snakes sent to throttle him
in his cradle. And now, after all these years of waiting and
plotting and planning, Devlin had defeated him again, defeated him and his most potent operative, Milverton, killed
him with his bare hands in his own house, as Hercules had
strangled the serpents. Broken his back, stopped his plot,
razed his house, and nearly killed Skorzeny himself. He had
underestimated his enemy. It was not a mistake he would
make again. The next time they confronted each other would
be the last time.

"Is there anything else, M. Skorzeny?" asked Emanuelle
Derrida. Since the unfortunate demise of M. Pilier, Mlle.
Derrida had taken his place as his most trusted assistant. She
was younger than Pilier, and certainly prettier. She was also
unmarried and seemed entirely uninterested in men. Which
meant that, luckily, he was almost uninterested in her.

Mlle. Derrida was, like Chopin, half French and half Polish. From her French father she had inherited her Pascal-like
rationality; she never bet, unless it was on a sure thing. From
her Polish mother she got her blond good looks. The first
time he had seen her, at a concert in Singapore, he had been
struck by her willowy figure, the way the breeze moved over
her dress and sent it clinging to her body, hugging her in a
way that every man desired but no man would ever obtain.
No matter: he had hired her on the spot.

Not that his was any life for a young person. Under his

arrangement with Tyler, he had escaped the full wrath of the USA, but only under the condition that he stay confined to his home in Liechtenstein, or to those countries without a politically controversial extradition treaty with the United States. And yet she had accepted his offer unhesitatingly, as if there was something that she, too, was fleeing. Not that he had asked—other people's troubles were none of his business, only his opportunities. But Mlle. Derrida needed the handsome salary he paid her, and he needed her, and that was that.

But not, he confessed to himself privately, the way he needed Amanda Harrington.

In these past nine months, he had thought often of Amanda Harrington. Of all the women in his life, of all the women he had known, she was the acme. When he heard that she had survived the poisoned chalice he had offered her, he had spared no expense on her treatment and recovery. He saw to it that, every day, her rooms were filled with roses, that she wanted for nothing, that as she progressed everything would be provided for, that her home in London would be taken care of. He gave her everything. The only thing he could not give her was the child she had loved briefly, and then lost. But, then, he could always try again. He was still potent, and in every respect. And now he would see her again. Things would be as they once had been.

"We are approaching Macao, sir," she said.

Next to Dubai, Macao was one of his favorite places in the world. For an internationalist like Emanuel Skorzeny, the world really was pretty much his oyster, even if that oyster had been severely limited by the informal, unacknowledged sanctions Tyler had imposed on him in the wake of the EMP fiasco. Macao was the old Portuguese settlement on the southwest coast of China, dating back to the early 16th century. Along with the Portuguese foothold in Nagasaki, Macao was where the West had begun in its penetration of the East. Now, of course, it was the East that was penetrating the West.

"Thank you, Mlle. Derrida," he said. "Please ensure that everything is in readiness for our arrival."

"Indeed, sir," she replied. She gave him a little smile—was it of encouragement? Advancement? Impossible to tell. He smiled back, neutrally, he hoped. Everything was a lawsuit these days; it was getting to be that a man couldn't make an honest living as a pirate anymore.

Which is what both perplexed him and animated him. What had happened to the secure world he had once known? True, it had never existed, except in his own idealistic imagination, but that did not make it any less real. From his boyhood in a *Sippenhaft* camp in northern Germany near Lübeck—Sieglinde's aria, *Der Männer sippe* was for him the most resonant part of Wagner's *Ring*—through his *Wanderjähren* as a young man, to his arrival in Paris, to his first million on the trading floor of the DAX, he had held fast to his vision.

"Music," he said, and as if on command, Elgar's *Enigma Variations* came over the aircraft's loudspeakers. One of the things he most liked about Mlle. Derrida was that she could read his mind. Something Pilier could never quite do.

The Boeing 707—the kind of planes they used to use for long-range international travel back in the early '80s, when the Aught Seven was the last word in aircraft—bumped a little, then settled down. In its original configuration, it was basically a flying cigar tube with two rows of three seats on either side of a center aisle; in his specially outfitted version, he had reserved the entire center section of the aircraft, the safest part over the wings, for his own private quarters.

Toward the front, between him and the pilots, was the communications headquarters. Despite everything that had happened, he had maintained most of his agreements with international air controllers and national satellite systems, which meant that he could still monitor the position of every aircraft in the Skorzeny fleet, no matter how temporarily diminished in numbers. To the rear were the sleeping quarters, both his and the staff's, and behind them, the galley and his personal chef's quarters. He hadn't yet made up his mind about Mlle. Derrida; she might prove to be more trouble than she was worth. But, fortunately for him, there were no sexual harassment laws at 40,000 feet.

Skorzeny let the music wash over him. A "riddle wrapped in a mystery inside an enigma." That about summed it up. Most of the idiots who had inherited Western culture thought of Elgar—if they ever thought of him at all, which was doubtful—as a kind of Sherlockian Col. Blimp, a weird *doppelgänger* of King George V, the clueless monarch who torpedoed his country, his Empire, into the trenches of the Somme, with results that were now distressingly visible.

Enigma. The Morse Code of the principal theme. Two shorts, two longs. Followed by two longs and two shorts. In code: *I am. Am I.* The question mark practically screamed its presence. Man's existential dilemma, made aural in music. "I am. Am I?"

Emanuel Skorzeny was a confirmed atheist, and had been since he watched his mother and father executed in the late winter of 1944. A God that could kill one's family was capable of any enormity, and was one not worthy of worship. Just as the West, in its present incarnation, was not worthy of redemption.

The ninth variation sounded throughout the airplane. No matter how he steeled his heart, it always moved him. *Nimrod*, the Hunter. So appropriate. And followed by Dorabella, Elgar's secret love, to whom he wrote coded communications, both musical and literary. What was he trying to say to "Dorabella," Miss Dora Penny?

"Sir?" Mlle. Derrida startled him. "Are you quite all right?"

"I'm quite all right, Mlle. Derrida, yes, thank you," he said, in a tone that warned: never interrupt me *en rêve*.

"We're preparing for final descent."

"I am always prepared for final descent, Mlle. Derrida," he said. "You would be well advised to do the same."

The plane's wheels touched down at Macao International Airport with as little disturbance as possible. Skorzeny prided himself on being able to find and hire pilots who made landing an art form. Instead of proceeding to the main terminal, however, the plane diverted onto a secondary runway, heading for a small collection of hangars well away from the main flight paths.

Mlle. Derrida rose and began to prepare the cabin for exit, but Skorzeny remained seated, still listening to the music, and relaxed even farther back into his chair. "You know the old saying, don't you?" he inquired idly.

"I'm sure I don't, M. Skorzeny," his attendant replied.

"If Mohammed will not come to the mountain, the mountain must come to Mohammed."

Mlle. Derrida froze. Any talk of Mohammed made her uncomfortable. Being relatively new, she was not sure exactly what Skorzeny's religious views were, or whether he had any at all, but she was young enough and educated enough to know that, these days, one did not lightly discuss the Prophet. Bohemond, Charles Martel, Sobieski, and the rest of them were moldering in their graves, and yet the Messenger of God lived on; one spoke of the Prophet at one's own peril. "Sir?" she inquired.

"I mean, Mlle. Derrida, that Mr. Arash Kohanloo will be meeting with me here, in my aeroplane. Chef, I believe, will have the meal ready in 15 minutes." He let the look of surprise wash over, and then away from, her face. "Did you have an appointment here? Something, someone, to see? I hope I have not disappointed you, but the blandishments of Macao will have to wait for another time."

"No sir, not at all, sir," she replied quickly. "Might I inquire where—"

"You may not. Now please get ready to greet our guest and see that all is in readiness in the meeting room. I will need full communication capability, and please instruct the pilots to activate the mobile-phone jammers. I want and expect complete privacy."

"Yes sir." There was a new look of respect in Mlle. Derrida's eyes. This was the first time she had really seen Emanuel Skorzeny in action, and he could sense that her opinion of him was rapidly undergoing a transformational change: not the doddering old rich fart with time on his hands and money to burn that she had thought him; but then, that was the point.

"Very well, then, sir," she said, backing away and out of the private quarters. "All will be to your satisfaction."

"Thank you, Mlle. Derrida," he said. "Please ensure that it is." And, with that, he dismissed her.

There were no briefing books or any electronic screens where Skorzeny sat. He had no need for them. He had long since committed to memory the particulars of the man with whom he would be meeting. Arash Kohanloo came from one of the first families of Qom, the holiest of Shi'ite Iran's holy cities. Qom was where the Iranian nuclear program had been secretly developed for years, built impregnably into the side of a mountain. But, more important, Qom was also the city and redoubt of the 12th Imam, the long-awaited Mahdi, whose imminence would be presaged by a time of troubles that made Christian Revelation look like Eve at play in the Garden of Eden. He was, in other words, just the fellow Skorzeny was looking for.

Skorzeny rose and moved toward the front of the plane. As expected, everything was ready in the conference room, including a repast of *nan-e dushabi*, *panir*, dates, eggplant, lamb, and *faludeh* for desert, washed down with *doogh*. Off to one side, several computer screens blinked with rows of raw numerical data.

The door to the aircraft opened. "M. Kohanloo," Skorzeny greeted him, "I bid you welcome."

The Persian was short, wiry, with what looked like a month-old beard. He was dressed in Western garb, and he bowed to Skorzeny rather than kissing him. He, too, had been briefed: Skorzeny did not like to be touched.

The meal passed with only the basic exchange of pleasantries. Of the current geopolitical situation the two men said absolutely nothing. Skorzeny partook of the meal with the addition of a small glass of Shiraz wine from Australia. He had no intention of insulting his host, but neither did he wish to seem weak; for him Islam was just another human superstition, albeit more useful for his purposes at this moment than Christianity, Judaism, Hinduism, or any of the Far Eastern faiths.

When the plates were cleared and the palates cleansed with some aniseeds, Arash Kohanloo looked at his host and said: "You are an infidel, an unbeliever. You mock me with your wine, and insult me and my family; worse, you insult both the Prophet, blessings and peace be upon him, and the immanence of the Twelfth Imam, Abu'l Qasim Muhammad ibn Hasan ibn 'Ali, who from the time of the Occultation has waited with infinite patience for the day of the troubles, when he will come again, accompanied by Isa—Jesus, to you—to bring peace and deliverance to your world."

Skorzeny looked at him for a long moment, and then said: "Pick up your mobile phone." Kohanloo extracted an iPhone from a suit pocket. "Look at it. Try it."

The Persian ran his thumb over the screen, trying to access an application, then punched up a number. Nothing.

"We are in a completely controlled environment here,

M. Kohanloo. Nothing we say leaves this room, and only those communications which I wish to receive can enter it. You may speak frankly here, without fear. So let's cut the bullshit, pardon my Farsi, and get down to business, shall we?"

Now Kohanloo smiled—a broad smile of recognition that he was with a kindred spirit. "Deep packet inspection," he said.

"The key to your success. In fact, the thing that keeps your government operating. With the enthusiastic cooperation of suicidal Western telecommunications companies, you are able to monitor all Internet traffic going into and out of your country. There is nothing you cannot eavesdrop upon and, should you so choose, you can selectively block, record or disrupt, as the case may be. For a primitive nation in the grip of an imported and imposed superstition, you have adapted remarkably well to the 21st century, M. Kohanloo. I congratulate you."

Kohanloo's lips formed the simulacrum of a smile, although his dead eyes gave nothing away. "What was it your Lenin said? 'You will provide us with the rope with which to hang you'? So it is written, so shall it be done. If you will pardon my misquotation of sacred scripture—in this secure environment, of course."

"The Americans' National Security Agency can only look upon what your nation does and weep that they have not the moral strength to engage in such ruthless activity. For there is a genius in that, a moral liberation. The higher ends must always be served, no matter the immediate cost. This I learned as a child in Germany. One must set one's heart against all emotion, against all entreaties, to let the cries of both the innocent and the guilty fall upon your deaf ears, that the greatest good for the greatest number be served."

Kohanloo's visage took on a conspiratorial mien. "But

what of the Black Widow?" he hissed. "Cannot the Americans do the same thing?"

Skorzeny suppressed a laugh by disguising it as a cough. "They could, but they won't. One of their whiny little senators in our employ would make a speech, calling upon his countrymen to 'defend the Constitution' or some such. Or one of their media captains, who draws a considerable sum from our exchequer monthly, would lead a secular crusade against the government, challenging it to live up to America's highest ideals."

"Which apparently includes suicide," Kohanloo said. "Still, I worry about the Widow. . . ."

"Let me worry about her," consoled Skorzeny. "And now, to business." He pointed to the dancing computer screens, on which a very large sum of money had appeared on the screen, expressed in various currencies: dollars, euros, yen, yuan. "Take your pick," he said.

Kohanloo barely glanced at the screens before turning back to Skorzeny. "How dare you insult me with money?" he said, and rose to leave.

"M. Kohanloo." Something in Skorzeny's voice stopped him in his tracks. "What you believe or don't believe is absolutely immaterial to me. I myself, as you note, am a proud unbeliever in many faiths; all of them, in fact. But I see that you are a man of principle, and I like that. So I will make you a new offer."

"And what is that?"

"Nothing. Absolutely nothing."

Kohanloo thought for a moment, and then a big smile broke over his face. "Under the present worldwide economic circumstances, recruitment has been going exceptionally well, especially in your prisons. By constantly harping on the iniquities of your society, our friends in the media have prepared the people for revolution—a necessary precondition for the arrival of *al-Mahdi*. As for our Sunni brothers, apostates though they may be, they need to know nothing of our larger purpose, and only wish to fight and die as martyrs for Allah."

Kohanloo opened his briefcase, took out a manila folder, and placed it on the polished table. "So do we have a deal?"

Skorzeny looked down at the dossier and smiled. Then he stuck out his hand. "We have a deal," he said.

DAY ONE

Begin each day by telling yourself:
today I shall be meeting with interference, ingratitude,
insolence, disloyalty, ill-will, and selfishness.
—MARCUS AURELIUS, *Meditations*, Book II

CHAPTER THREE

Manhattan

Francis Xavier Byrne had a choice: the .38 or the 9-millimeter?

It was the same choice that every senior officer in the New York City Police Department had to make every year, a choice not given to the grunts, to the junior officers, to the rank and file, but to only a select few, those with seniority and experience.

He had earned that right. Earned it long ago and continued it every day he spent on the force. And every year, when this moment rolled around at the Police Academy on E. 20th Street, Captain Francis Xavier Byrne made the same choice:

He took the .38 Colt Detective Special.

As he raised the weapon into firing position, sighting on the first of the targets, he took a moment to reflect. He was 51 years old now and most definitely old school. No matter how many times he fired the various 9 mms. the department authorized, he still preferred the security and heft of a revolver. The Glock 19 was a plastic piece of shit with a six-pound pull—not the thing for some frightened rookie to be wielding in a crisis—and even retrofitted with a twelve-pound-pull "NY-2 Trigger," it still felt like a lethal toy gun. The Smith & Wesson 5946 and the Sig P226 were improvements, although not by much. Byrne and his men also had the option of carrying the Kahr K9s as backup pieces or off-duty weapons, but in his opinion, unless the brass was willing to admit the past century of semi-automatic firearms technology was a mistake and get some old-fashioned Colt 1911s, he was going to stick to the trusty revolver as his sidearm until they pried it from his cold, dead hands.

He slid his right index finger down the frame from just below the cylinder toward the trigger. That was the way they taught it now at the Academy: no fingers on the triggers until you were ready to fire. Until you were ready to shoot. Until you were ready to kill.

Byrne brought the Colt up to eye level. He used a one-handed, full-frontal stance, right eye closed, his dominant left eye sighting down the barrel. Not for him was the sideways stance, in which you were essentially aiming over your shoulder. Not for him was any flashy, muzzle-waving, sideways-pointing ghetto grip: throughout his career, he had several times staked his life on the proposition that the safest place to stand between a gangbanger with a Glock and whatever he was shooting at was right in front of the target.

Fuck it: it didn't feel natural. The whole "finger on the side of the gun" crap was a "safety" rule—for the perp's safety, not the cop's. He dropped his finger onto the trigger, let it curl around the trigger in a lover's caress. There was next to no chance of a double-action revolver going off accidentally, or even of a bed-wetting patrolman jerking the trigger hard enough by accident to fire the weapon.

Byrne let out his breath, then held it. Despite the noise of the range all around him, only partly muffled by his protective ear wear, he always felt at peace here. It was so unlike real life: just you and the target, standing there motionless, a big bull's-eye at its center, dangling twenty feet away, just begging you to shoot it. Of course, it wasn't really shooting. It was just punching holes, very quickly, through a piece of paper. But it still felt good, and the fact that there was no return fire was a bonus.

Byrne pulled back the hammer: *now* the weapon had a hair trigger. He fired and punched a hole near the center of the target, just slightly to the left. Each year, as he requalified, his astigmatism got a little worse, and each year he had to learn to compensate for it a little more. Some of the men—Vinnie Mancuso, his old partner back in the days when they were both young and hungry, now working in Commissioner White's office and about ready to start pulling his pension as he counted down the days—suggested that he wear his glasses to the range, but to Byrne that was like making love with them on. You didn't really need to see what you were doing as long as you knew what it was and how to do it.

He compensated a little to the left and fired again. Closer; good enough for government work. Not good enough for him. Another slight shift, another shot: perfect.

"You're getting old, Frankie," shouted a voice off to his left. With his headgear on, the voice to Byrne was like a whisper. He didn't have to turn or look to know who it was.

"Move 'em back another fifteen, Lannie," he barked. "And this time make it hard."

Aslan "Lannie" Saleh stifled the crack he almost made. Something about "old" and "hard." After all, Capt. Byrne was his boss, the man who had given him his break, and even though the unit operated more or less full-time in politically incorrect mode, Lannie Saleh knew that for Frankie Byrne the shooting range was the next best thing to St. Michael's on Easter Sunday. He knew better than to break the boss's sacramental concentration.

Lannie said nothing as he hit the control button and

dragged the shredded target forward. Everybody kidded everybody in the Counter-Terrorism Unit about their marksmanship, but over fifty or not, Capt. Byrne was still the best shot in the department. There were all sorts of stories about him; about the time when he had caught a burglar in his mother's apartment in Queens and, without even looking, had put a bullet in the man and knocked him through a window.

Lannie pinched up a paper bad guy and sent it fleeing into the distance. Twenty-five feet, thirty, thirty-five—

"Keep going."

He stopped at fifty. Byrne was reloading. Lannie admired the way the boss so smoothly, so effortlessly, slipped the .38 cartridges into the cylinder, then snapped it into place with a flick of his wrist. That was something you weren't supposed to do; you were supposed to politely shut the cylinder with your free hand. But Frankie Byrne was at heart an Irish cowboy, and his men loved him for it.

"What did you say?" shouted Byrne. Saleh shook his head: nothing. Jesus, the man really was a mind reader, just like everybody said.

Byrne turned back toward the target and let out his breath. Instead of holding it this time, he kept exhaling; instead of cocking the hammer and firing single-action, he fired double-action, each pull of the trigger doing double duty, each pull cocking the hammer and then releasing it. Six shots. Lannie didn't even have to look at the target as he reeled it back in to know the extent of the damage.

The first shot, he knew, would be right in the bad guy's head; the other five were just for show. Or, knowing Byrne, to make a point. In the CTU, setting a good example and, from time to totally unreported time, creating an object lesson for the mother of some son of a bitch back home in Amman, was simply good manners.

Byrne grunted as he looked at his handiwork. Head, heart, stomach, spleen, balls, and, for good measure, a knee-cap. Mission accomplished. "Your turn," he said.

Lannie felt his heart drop into his shoes. He hadn't come prepared to shoot, and certainly hadn't expected to perform in front of the boss. Byrne slapped the protective earmuffs on his head and thrust the Glock into his hand. "You're good to go," he said.

The new target rocketed out. The book said that most side-arm confrontations took place from point-blank range to no more than twenty-five feet, but Byrne had just sent Osama bin Laden flapping in the breeze at least ten meters.

Lannie took the pistol and tried to steady himself. Even though he had already qualified this year, it didn't matter: Byrne could fire him at any moment for any reason. The CTU was the most highly regarded and hard to get into unit in the NYPD, and the most top-down in its hierarchy; its members didn't have to answer to any civilian review board, fat-bottomed top brass, or even the mayor. Once, shortly after 9/11, some deputy chief had tried to insert one of his stooges into the CTU's secret headquarters, which in those dark days were in Brooklyn. Byrne, or so the story went, marched down to One Police Plaza and threatened to put the dope's head through one of the double-glazed windows on the fourteenth floor; and since Frankie and Commissioner Matt White had been partners in the old days, that was the end of departmental interference in the CTU.

Lannie took a deep breath of pride—pride in his unit and pride in what he had already accomplished just getting into it—and squeezed off nine shots in lightning succession. Three hits, six misses, but at this distance that was pretty good, good enough for government work.

"You shoot like a sand nigger," said Byrne, inspecting the target. "No wonder you guys always lose."

Had anyone else said that to him, Lannie would have brought him up on charges; from Byrne, it was a compliment. "You know, I could have your badge for a crack like that, Captain," he ventured.

Byrne laughed. "Which is one of the things that's wrong with this country today. In the old days, in New York, that's how we used to talk to each other, the Irish to the Italians to the Jews. Nowadays, you foreign pussies go running to the U.N. if somebody looks at you askance."

"Askance? What does that mean?"

"It means you're in America now, Buckwheat, so learn American." Byrne slipped the .38 he had been using back into the holster that he wore on his right hip. He popped the clip—there was another term they didn't want you to use anymore—out of the Glock and left both pieces of the weapon on the shelf.

They walked together out of the old Academy and into the glorious sunlight of an afternoon in New York City. Almost instinctively, Lannie turned east, toward Second Avenue, but Byrne took him by the arm and headed west, toward Gramercy Park, instead. "We're in Chelsea, remember?" he said.

The corpse of Cabrini Medical Center lay directly across the street. The century-old Catholic hospital had closed down in the spring of 2008. Byrne could feel Lannie's gaze on him as he reacted to the sight. "What is it?" said Saleh.

"It's an old hospital."

"I know that."

"Cabrini Medical Center. One of the oldest Catholic hospitals in the city. Not financially viable, the state said. And now it's gone."

Lannie shrugged. "So what? New York's got plenty of hospitals."

Byrne put a hand on his shoulder: gently, but firmly. "It's

what we were just talking about. It's the past, old New York. It's what used to be. And now it's not."

Lannie still didn't get it. Byrne kept his hand on his shoulder as he spoke:

"It was named after Mother Cabrini. Frances Xavier Cabrini, an Italian nun from Lombardy. She was the first American citizen ever canonized as a saint of the Roman Catholic Church. In 1946, every wop in this town went apeshit when Pius XII punched her ticket to heaven. If you don't believe me, ask Vinnie."

"So I guess that makes her pretty special." Lannie hoped his tone came off as encouraging, but knew it didn't.

Byrne seemed to let it slide. "I'll say. I was born there. I was named after her. And one other thing—"

Byrne still hadn't moved. His hand was still on Lannie's shoulder, his eyes still focused across the street, at the back of what used to be Cabrini Medical Center.

"My father died there."

Lannie felt his cell phone buzz in his pocket, but he didn't answer it, or even glance at it. He didn't want to break the mood, even though to him this was all ancient history, and foreign ancient history at that. "I'm sorry, boss," he said.

"It was a long time ago," replied Byrne.

They started walking. "You know," said Lannie, "not all Muslims are Arabs."

"So the Iranians tell me," said Byrne. "But you're not Persian. Hell, you're not even Irish."

"And not all Arabs are Muslims," Lannie said, undeterred. "Some of us are Christians."

"And not all Christians are Catholics, but all Catholics are Christians. So what does that prove?"

Lannie had no answer. He was 24 years old, and even though he knew pretty much everything about life that was worth knowing, like computers and girls, he also knew that he knew almost nothing about anything that actually mattered. He was on the CTU thanks to Capt. Byrne, especially considering he couldn't shoot for shit.

Byrne buttoned his overcoat against the raw spring wind. "So, is that your own personal .38?" Lannie asked. Walking with the boss was awkward, and it helped to have some neutral conversational topic.

"Yes, it's mine. And no, not originally. It belonged to my dad. He was wearing it the day he was killed in the line of duty."

Byrne got that faraway look in his eyes that everybody in the department knew so well. It was a look that said: this far and no farther. There are some lines not to be crossed.

Byrne had picked up the tempo now, barreling west past Teddy Roosevelt's birthplace and across Fifth Avenue. It was as if he knew something was up, was responding to some unarticulated urgency, and it was all Lannie could do to keep up with the old man . . . on any level.

They had crossed Seventh Avenue, into Chelsea, and were heading north when Lannie felt his cell phone buzz again. Involuntarily, he stopped and pulled the phone out of his pocket. It was one of those shitty departmental phones, standard-issue, not his BlackBerry, which he had left back at his desk in case something really important happened.

"What is it?" asked Byrne. If it were really important, whoever was on the other end of the line would have called him. On the other hand, if it had anything to do with computers, Lannie would be the go-to guy. And that was, after all, the reason Byrne had hired him. Certainly not for his marksmanship.

Lannie glanced at the display: URGENT. He picked up the pace. They didn't have to say anything. Byrne got it. That was one of the things that made him such a good chief.

They hit the intersection of 20th and Eighth, nearly running now, and headed north.

They rounded the corner. Up ahead was an old, nondescript warehouse, one of the few buildings that hadn't been converted into artists' lofts or art galleries. Actually, that was not quite true: most of it had in fact been converted, but there was still a big chunk of the giant building, which occupied a full city block in two dimensions and rose five stories into the air, that had been given over to the CTU. Not that any of the other tenants knew about it.

That was one of the things that still made New York New York, thought Byrne as he spied the building: not making eye contact with neighbors was still considered a virtue.

They pulled up in front of the building. "Mother Cabrini—Frances Xavier Cabrini—is the patron saint of immigrants," said Byrne. His cell phone was buzzing now, too.

Lannie beat him to the punch. "We're here, right in front of the building," he said softly.

Byrne watched his younger colleague's face fall. "What is it?" he asked, but Lannie was already sprinting through the front door.

CHAPTER FOUR

New Orleans

"Archibald Grant" had a choice: to finish his speech or to react to the urgent message now coming across the face of his wristwatch.

This was no ordinary watch he wore, but then nothing about Mr. Grant was ordinary. As one of the RAND Corporation's leading experts on international terrorism, he was in great demand, not only back at the home office in Santa Monica, California, but worldwide. RAND maintained divisions in Boston, Pittsburgh, Washington, D.C., Jackson, Mississippi; Cambridge, England; Brussels; and Doha, Qatar.

His attention from the message was distracted by the blonde in the front row. She was a reporter, one of the few the RAND Corporation allowed into policy addresses such as this. Most of the time, RAND hid its global activities behind its anonymous name, Research ANd Development.

This was a special occasion: a conference organized by RAND's Gulf States Policy Institute, which had been formed post-Katrina to aid three of the most benighted states in the union, Louisiana, Mississippi, and Alabama. The topic of his lecture was: "Terrorist Opportunities in a Devastated Environment: Some Thoughts on Media Responsibility," but the reporter seemed more interested in him than in the subject of his remarks. Even in his guise of "Mr. Grant," he hated inquisitive people, and blonde network reporters were right up there with the worst of them.

It wasn't that Grant was so good-looking: balding, overweight, slightly buck-toothed, he was no woman's idea of a prize. But he was brilliant, and a compelling speaker, which in his experience was more than enough to interest a certain class of women. Luckily for men, brains often counted more than looks when it came to the fair sex.

". . . and so, ladies and gentlemen, let me conclude with this thought . . ." His mind raced, trying to finish his remarks and at the same time process the information he was reading surreptitiously. Silently, he cursed himself for taking this gig, for being so far away from Washington and New York at a time like this. Maybe it was just an early yellow flag, but in his experience the National Security Agency didn't issue SCI alerts—Sensitive Compartmented Information—on a whim. And besides, these days, there were no yellow flags, only red ones. He'd have to wrap it up and leave as quickly as possible, without incurring suspicion. Especially from the blonde.

"The days of so-called 'separation of church and state,' whether we want to admit it, are over. A new media environment, brought on first by the emergence, and by the dominance, of the Internet, coupled with the severe economic downturn of the past 48 months, has finally brought the relationship of the press and the government into a new era of cooperation and, dare I suggest, symbiosis: no longer natural adversaries, but partners in the brave new world of the 21st

century. Our shared land, our common patriotism, demands
no less.

"America is unique among the world's nations in more
ways than simply the political, the military, or the economic.
Three other countries—Russia, Canada, China—may be
larger, territorially speaking, but none is subject to the kinds
of climatological and ecological disruption. Blizzards, earthquakes, wildfires, floods, tornadoes, hurricanes; had civilization tried to arise here, rather than the Indus Valley, it surely
would have perished in short order. Far from being a land of
milk and honey, America has always demanded the survival
of the fittest. Lest we forget, the 'shining city on a hill' was
bought with the blood of patriots."

There was a slight stir in the audience; nobody used the
word "patriots" anymore, nor referenced Jefferson's famous
Tree of Liberty, however obliquely. What they usually forgot, of course, was Jefferson's exact formulation in his 1787
letter to William Smith, written from Paris, of which Mr.
Grant now reminded them:

"Or, to quote Jefferson directly, 'the tree of liberty must
be refreshed from time to time with the blood of patriots and
tyrants.'"

The buzz grew louder as he entered his peroration:
"Against all odds, America defeated the world's other
superpower through a combination of willpower, tactical su-
periority, and a consummate knowledge of the battlefield—
virtues we sorely lacked on September 11, 2001, and in its
aftermath, and in many ways continue to lack. When the
next terrorist attack comes—notice I said when, not if—our
first line of defense will not be the government, or even the
first responders, but will be the media. How the attack is
framed, and explained, will determine in large part the will
of this nation to fight back. In a sense, we were lucky on
9/11. The attack came so suddenly, and without warning,

that the usual collection of nervous nellies, naysayers, National Public Radio eunuchs, and nabobs in the 'loyal opposition' took several months before they were able to regroup and begin the counterattack. But when the next blow comes, they will be ready, appeasement on their lips and terms of surrender already signed and sealed in their pockets. I just hope that we—the tip of the tip of the spear—will be ready, too."

There was a smattering of weak applause, which is about what Mr. Grant had expected. He let it almost subside before finishing.

"Of the abilities of the men and women employed by our counterterrorism agencies I have no doubt. Nothing the media says or writes or broadcasts can or should or will affect them. Rather, I am thinking of the civilian population, the people who get their news from the networks and the cables and from what few newspapers and magazines anyone still takes seriously. I am thinking, in short, of ordinary, average Americans. People who once knew how to deal with extraordinary events and overcome them or endure them, secure in the knowledge that *Der Wille zur Macht* would see them through adversity. The very people whose will to fight has been eroded by half a century of guilt, defeatism, analysis, and Hollywood. For, when the time comes—and come it will—it is they who, more than anyone else, must once again summon the courage of their forebears and seize the day."

He paused and looked out over the sea of faces. It was time to go. "Thank you for your kind attention."

Through the perfunctory applause, a question: "So you're advocating vigilantism?" It was the blonde. "And a follow-up—if so, then why do the American taxpayers spend billions of dollars each year on the military and the intelligence services? Are you saying that, in the end, all of our vaunted technology and martial prowess can't guarantee our safety? And finally—"

"Would you kindly identify yourself, please, Miss?" Mr. Grant asked.

"Principessa Stanley. National-security correspondent, People's News Network."

There were a couple of titters in the audience from the Europeans. That was to be expected. The Americans were too ignorant and uneducated to get the operatic reference, while the Europeans got it at once. She had spent most of her life trying to live up to the implications of her name, to be as regal and beautiful and as cold as her namesake, the Princess Turandot. She turned briefly and flashed her famously telegenic smile: "My father was a big Puccini fan," she explained.

"You understand, Ms. Stanley, that we are on Chatham House rules. Off the record, on deep background, however you care to phrase it. In any case, not for attribution." He took a small sip of water to delay her answer, giving him time to glance down at his watch once more. The news had not gotten any better. Luckily, she was waiting for him just outside, and they would be at the airport in short order.

Principessa smiled her famous network smile again. A cable network smile, but still a network smile, and one that had, along with her pretty face and killer figure, taken her a long way from Bloomfield Hills, Michigan. If she played her cards right, pretty soon she'd move up from the mid-morning slot to the late-afternoon slot and after that, there was no telling what might happen when one of the prized evening gabfests suddenly found itself in need of a host. She had been hearing rumors, and doing her best to spread of few of her own, and in her opinion a couple of the anchors were only in need of a little push—or a gossip item dropped in the right place at the right time—and the way would be open to her. Besides, Jake Sinclair liked her, a lot.

"Yes, I do." She rose, letting everyone in the audience get a good look at her. Like all the interchangeable blondes on the cable newscasts, she was leggy, bosomy, brash, and the proud possessor of a law degree. One more button on her blouse was unbuttoned than absolutely necessary. "And finally . . . what do you have against the news media? Wasn't it also Jefferson who also said that given a choice between a government without newspapers and newspapers without government, he would happily choose the latter?"

Mr. Grant smiled; she had walked right into his trap. "Yes, Ms. Stanley. To which George Washington replied, 'I consider such vehicles of knowledge'—that's newspapers to you—'more happily calculated than any other to preserve the liberty, stimulate the industry, and ameliorate the morals of a free and enlightened people.' And by 'industry,' of course, he meant—"

"I know what he meant by 'industry,' Mr. Grant," she retorted.

His return glance indicated that he very much doubted that. "What Washington meant, Ms. Stanley, was that vigorous political opposition was a good thing, but that a news media, to give it its current favored term, that saps the will of the people, that reduces them to pleading, whining petitioners and diminishes the morals of the public is not one to be admired. The First Amendment does not protect sedition."

"But it sounds to me like you're arguing in favor of American exceptionalism. Isn't that a form of elitism?"

"On the contrary. I'm arguing in favor of results. Which, in my world, are the only things that count." He shuffled his papers, reassembling in an unmistakable sign that the talk was over. These days, all of the reporters' questions emanated from a mountain of moral certitude, which crumbled the second it was assailed.

Principessa reddened, sat down, seethed. "This all sounds rather jingoistic to me," she said.

Mr. Grant looked at her with all the pity in world. "Who cares what it sounds like to you?" he said, and left the stage.

That went well he thought to himself as he stepped into the wings, to the sound of applause. He moved swiftly, glancing down at his secure BlackBerry. A quick glance at the screen caused him to double his speed. He exited by an emergency door.

There was a car waiting, a nondescript black sedan with four tinted windows. He got into the back seat, closed the door and hit: AUTO-START.

Driverless, the car started up and moved forward. He could control the steering from a console on the back of the driver's seat. He wasn't going far.

He glanced in the rearview mirror: a door was opening, and he could see a woman's head peeking out. It was Ms. Stanley, eyeballing the car and talking into her cell phone. It was too bad he couldn't treat reporters the way he treated enemies of the Republic . . .

As the car moved, Mr. Grant underwent a remarkable transformation. His teeth fell out of his head; his midsection slid away, a hairpiece came off. And all the while he was wondering whether the raw data he was receiving was as sinister as it seemed, or worse.

The car reached the far end of the parking lot and slid into a reserved, covered space. He ran a brush through his hair, popped a pair of brown contact lenses from his eyes. He had to hurry.

He opened the door and, keeping low, slid into the adjoining Mercedes, its engine purring, as the front passenger door opened.

"Not bad," came a voice from the driver's seat. He didn't

turn to look at her, but he didn't have to. He knew every line of her lovely face. "But that reporter sure was a bitch."

"You were watching?"

"And listening. Every word, every gesture . . ."

Jealous. He liked that in a woman. Especially one he hardly knew, but trusted with his life. "You know there's—"

She turned toward him and, as usual, he fell in love with her all over again. His mouth covered hers.

"Really, Frank, I think you're slipping," she said, breaking away. "Why put yourself in—"

He reclined and, for the first time in two hours, stretched. They both knew the answer to that question, which was: there was no answer. "My name's not Frank."

"You're telling me." She pulled the car out of the lot and into traffic. "How bad is it?"

"Hard to say. Cyber attack, maybe a security breach."

"Against us?"

Mr. Grant shook his head. "Worse—NYPD. Fort Meade is still monitoring, but the situation is unclear. And you know how tough it is to get any information out of the cops. They'd rather see the city nuked than share anything with us. We need to get to Teterboro A-sap."

"So I guess Arnaud's is out of the question."

He smiled. "Arnaud's, Galatoire's Brennan's, Congo Square, Exchange Alley—the whole nine yards."

Maryam hit the radio button twice and nodded to Devlin. He took the cigarette lighter out of its holder and pressed it against his thumb. The biometric reader vetted him, and suddenly the navigator screen leaped to life. He punched in his instructions.

"Go."

The car leaped forward, speeding west out of town and toward Louis Armstrong Airport. There would be a private plane there, fully equipped, on the director's orders. In no time, he and Maryam would be fully up to speed and, if possible, already fighting back. There were contingency plans for something like this, but plans went out the window as soon as the first shots were fired, and from the looks of this . . .

No matter. He was doing what he was born to do. He was himself again.

He was Devlin.

CHAPTER FIVE

Los Angeles

Jake Sinclair had a choice: to stay sober or to get drunk?

Not just drunk, but, like Elmer Gantry, eloquently drunk, lovingly drunk. Elmer Gantry was one of his favorite characters in literature—not that he had ever read the novel, but he had seen the movie many times over, and he loved Burt Lancaster's performance, even if the movie left out most of the novel. He loved it so much that he owned a print of it—not a DVD, but an honest-to-God movie print—and had it shown in the screening room at his house in Loughlin Park whenever he wished. It was easy; he owned the studio.

From his custom-built, body-contoured easy chair, Sinclair looked longingly across the room at the built-in wet bar, a relict of a time when real men not only drank but also smoked.

Loughlin Park was the Beverly Hills of Los Feliz. Sinclair was very proud of himself for living in Los Feliz. Los Angeles had moved as far west as it could go without actually trying to build houses in the Pacific Ocean—although there were more than a few movie industry types of his acquaintance who were convinced they could walk on water—

so now the smart money had begun to move back east, or at least as far east as Griffith Park Boulevard, where houses that might go for twenty million dollars in the bird streets above Beverly Hills could be snapped up for two or three, and yet you were still dozens of blocks away from the nearest Mexicans. Now that was what he called smart shopping.

Now, about that drink . . . after all, it was always five o'clock somewhere.

The house had been built by W. C. Fields when he decided to follow Hollywood's path westward and move in next door to Cecil B. DeMille. Although Sinclair had "modernized" the place, Mrs. Sinclair had insisted on sparing a few of the period touches, and so the wet bar still stood, its hidden refrigerators filled with designer waters like Saint-Géron, which was supposed to be a prophylactic against anemia. Mrs. Sinclair was enamored of the distinctive long-necked Alberto Bali–designed bottles. But there was no booze in the wet bar, nor anywhere else in the house, in keeping with Hollywood's new, healthy, raw-foods-and-Brita-filtered-water lifestyle. Thank God tennis and sportfucking were still allowed.

The reason Sinclair wished he was drunk had to do with business. Almost everything in his life had to do with business, including the current Mrs. Sinclair. She was, of course, not the first Mrs. Sinclair; Jake Sinclair eagerly subscribed to the Hollywood custom in which every man of significance is or was married to some other man of significance's wife, and every man owned, at one time or another, a house that had formerly belonged to one of his rivals, colleagues, or mortal enemies, and then either totally remodeled it or tore down. As the saying went: Hollywood is a relationship business. And, as far as relationships went, he'd had quite a few.

Luckily, the current, although soon-to-be-ex Mrs. Sinclair was Jennifer, just like the first Mrs. Sinclair, which is why he thought of her as Jennifer II or Jenny the Second. Like some arranged marriage between European potentates in the 16th century, she had come to him as a kind of reverse dowry. Jennifer Gailliard was the daughter of one of the biggest investors in the country, an investor Sinclair had been wooing with even greater ardor than he would later woo the man's daughter. The three-day celebration of their marriage on the island of Corfu was in all the gossip magazines—the photo rights alone went for more than $2 million to *People*—and it was quickly followed with the news that the bride's father had invested upwards of $500 million in Jake Sinclair's media company for acquisitions, with which money he partly financed his hostile takeover of Time Warner and thus now owned *People*. So the two million bucks was money well spent, especially since it had landed back in his pocket. Plus he had some really great family photos.

He liked Jenny the Second well enough, but he would have liked her more had she allowed him his favorite Scotch at a time like this. Which was the closing of yet another deal. For even by Jake Sinclair standards—Sinclair often thought of himself in the third person, although he rarely slipped into that particular locution, at least in public—it was a big deal. As his father often told him, it was a stupid man who could not make financial hay in an economic meltdown, and Jake Sinclair's father had not raised a stupid child.

Which was why, at this moment, he had just decided to divorce her.

Since he had been a kid, he had anticipated this day. Not just to own a major newspaper chain, a major newsweekly, a major television network, and even a major Hollywood studio—but to own all four. The superfecta of media, made possible by other men's blind greed, blinkered overreaching, and sheer sightless stupidity. During the 1980s, when corporations were merging faster than actors on a movie set, Sinclair—then a junior executive in a media mini-conglomerate—had watched, listened, and learned. Watched as one moron after another, so fearful of being left behind in the tsunami of M&As, had yanked the cord on his golden parachute and sold out his company for a mess of pottage and a face-saving seat on the board, which was soon revoked. One dope after another had fallen for the snake-oil salesman's charms of "high tech" whispers and "transformative transaction" pornography. Most of them, like his principal rival, had ended up padding the beach at Santa Monica with their New Age replacement wife in tow, spouting some holistic bullshit and telling *Us Weekly* how glad they were to finally be out of the rat race and living on a mere million dollars a year.

Well, fuck them. They were out and he was very much in, and glad to be here. For it wasn't an honor just to be nominated—for Jake Sinclair, the only honor that counted was to see his face on the cover of as many magazines as possible, to have his minions chart how many hits his name garnered on Google every day, to ferret out references to himself in novels, television shows, and movies, where he often appeared, thinly veiled as an Important Tycoon or a Media Mogul.

Well, fuck that, too. He was not just an important Media Mogul. He was *the* Media Mogul. He could afford to divorce Jenny II and get seriously involved with the Other Woman.

That was another thing. Most people laughed at him when, during a time of collapsing "old media" value, Sinclair Holdings, LLC, had snapped up failing properties like Time Inc. and the *New York Times*. Well, they were as dumb as the people who bailed on New York City during the Abe Beame administration, when Gerald Ford famously told the city to drop dead.

He could taste the Scotch. The cigarette, too. And, if he tried real hard, he could taste her.

Jake Sinclair rose and padded toward the bar. He pressed a switch under the sink, recessed behind the garbage disposal. The false back of one of the cabinets slid aside,

revealing his private stash of Oban Scotch and Balkan Sobranie cigarettes, the ones with his initials monogrammed
on each coffin nail.

Houses were like wives, he thought as he sipped his
Scotch and sent the smoke from the Sobranie cigarette spi-
raling toward the extractor fan, in that you didn't hang on to
them for the memories—you tore them down, rebuilt them,
or replaced them with somebody's else's. Memories, good or
bad, were noxious.

He was glad he didn't have any children. This was an evil
world, and it would be criminal to bring an innocent life into
it. The thought hadn't occurred to him that perhaps, in the
instant before conception, his own parents had thought this
way, and their parents before them. That if, going back to
Adam and Eve at the Fall, every prospective pair of parents
had thought this way, there would be no human race all.

*Of Man's First Disobedience, and the Fruit of that For-
bidden Tree, whose mortal taste brought Death into the
World . . .*

"Yum." He looked around the room for the voice and then
realized it was his own. That's what often happened after a
drink or two, and for that he blamed Jenny II. If she let him
have a nip every now and then, this wouldn't have happened.
Yes, he definitely was going to divorce her. He made a mental note to call his personal attorney in the morning.

Anyway, fuck Milton. Sinclair had hated it when they
made him read *Paradise Lost* in school, mostly because he
found the sentences hard to understand.

In fact, it was *Paradise Lost* and its lit-class ilk that had
set him on his current path. For Jake Sinclair believed two
things: that he was always the smartest guy in the room, and
anything he couldn't readily understand would be too hard
for his fellow citizens to grasp. Therefore, in the name of humanity, he had made it his life's work to "dumb down" all of
his publications and broadcasts and movies and television

shows, so that people less fortunate then he would not have to be confronted on a daily basis with the proof of their own ignorance.

He was so wrapped up in thoughts of his own magnanimity that it took him a few seconds to realize the phone was ringing. He downed the last gulp of scotch and jacked the extractor fan to High. Jennifer would be home from her tennis game at any minute. "Hello?"

The caller ID revealed the identity of every one of his callers and, on the off chance that the ID was blocked, he simply refused to answer: in fact, the phone company bumped it immediately to voice mail heaven. Which he never checked. If it was a solicitor, they could call his business manager; if it was someone trying to evade security, the hell with them; if it was a petitioner, then fuck him.

It was none of the above.

A brief beat as switching and relay systems from Los Feliz to Mars did their thing. This was another perk of the office: a massive security system that, once having identified a legitimate caller—especially this one—encrypted all voice communications into something that nobody, not even the National Security Agency, would be able to readily decode.

Finally, the voice came on the line. As agreed, the chatter was kept to under 2.3 seconds, so as best to avoid the tender mercies of Fort Meade. No matter which political party you bribed, in the end, they were both going to fuck you. But there was no mistaking the sweet sound of her voice:

"They took the offer."

Sinclair hung up, poured himself another drink, and looked at the clock. What the hell was he worried about? Jenny II wouldn't be home for at least another half hour. He made it a double. Now he wouldn't have to calculate how much a divorce would cost him. He'd just made half a billion dollars by answering the phone, and that would be more than enough to take care of her.

CHAPTER SIX

Byrne and Saleh rode in silence up the elevator, Byrne slumped back against the lift's wall, watching his subordinate's agitation. "You know the old joke, right?" he said. "About the old bull and the young bull?"

"Huh? Joke?"

"Yeah, joke. Don't they tell jokes in Ragville?"

Lannie got that aggrieved look on his face so characteristic of young people these days. "You know, Chief, I could—"

Byrne finished the sentence for him. "Bust me down to buck private for hate speech? Maybe. But I can bust all your teeth down your throat first, so the choice is yours." They went through this all the time, half-joking, half-serious.

"It's always the Irish way with you, isn't is, Boss? Punch first, ask questions later?"

The elevator shuddered to a stop. "It's the only way that works," said Byrne, getting off first.

As long as he had been on the force, Byrne had never quite gotten used to his new digs. He was used to shit-ass quarters in precincts around the city, at Police Plaza, which even to his office had just enough room for one desk, two chairs, and a window. Even the city's best detectives were lucky if they had access to a computer that worked only slightly more often than a civil servant.

This was different. In the aftermath of 9/11, the NYPD had spared absolutely no expense in outfitting the CTU with the finest equipment available, and if it wasn't available, to create it. How the brass had managed to conceal the vast expenditures it took to get CTU up and running was beyond Byrne. But, over the years, his former partner and permanent friend Matt White had mastered bureaucratic infighting to an extent that Byrne never would have thought possible. Matt was the living reincarnation of the old Irish Tammany bosses—John Kelly, Richard Croker, Charlie Murphy. Not bad for a black guy from Houston.

Byrne and Saleh badged their way in. This was no ordinary cop shop; you couldn't just waltz past a metal detector, plow through the busted hookers, and get to some sad-sack sergeant to report that your car had been stolen. Instead, a scanner read a microchip on your special NYPD badge, a second scanner zapped your eyeballs, and a third made sure you were not carrying any unauthorized weapons—even Byrne's daddy's .38 had to pass muster.

"What is it?" barked Byrne.

"DoS," came a reply from somewhere in the room.

DoS was the last word any computer operator wanted to hear, much less utter. Denial of service. A call on the system's resources so great that its servers failed, overwhelmed from the sheer volume of access requests. "Standby main, alternate packets," barked Byrne. "Secondary servers . . . what does Langley say?"

"Langley OotL, sir," said somebody. Out of the Loop.

"NSA ditto," said somebody else. There were new faces, and voices, all the time; the burnout rate was tremendous. Staring all day at computer screens was no job for a real cop, in Byrne's opinion, but a lot had changed since September 11, including him.

"NSA is never ditto," said Lannie settling into his chair. Of all the aces in the room, Lannie Saleh was the ace of aces. That was why he was on the team. "Even if we think they're ditto, even if they promise us they're ditto, they're never fucking ditto."

Byrne knew exactly what he meant. Chiefs past and present had fought hard to make the NYPD's CTU a stand-alone operation, answerable to no one but the residents of New York City. The attack on the Trade Center had happened in their city; the CIA, the NSA, and every other federal agency had let his people down, badly, and they paid for it with their lives—along with the cops and firemen who died alongside them when the towers shuddered and fell. NYPD was often accused of making 9/11 personal, to which their answer was: *Damn right it's personal. And it's never going to happen again.*

To that end, Byrne had cops stationed all over the world. One was based in Lyons, France, to liaise with Interpol; two more worked with the Israelis in Tel Aviv and Jerusalem. Byrne himself had done a stint in Belfast and Dublin, sharing information and techniques with both the Royal Ulster Constabulary and the Irish Gardai. As needed, officers headed to Bombay, or whatever the hell they were calling it today, to the Philippines; even Australia—wherever and whenever a terrorist incident occurred.

The point was, NYPD did not trust the CIA, nor any of the other dozen-plus intelligence agencies the federal monster had spawned, including the FBI. Byrne had his own, very good reasons for never trusting the FBI, all of them named Tom Byrne, but in general when the Langley Home for Lost Boys told him they weren't interfering with the CTU he believed them; most of them, in his estimation, were too dumb to tie their own shoelaces, and the thought of them getting a jump on his boys was laughable.

The National Security Agency, on the other hand, was something else. The former "No Such Agency" had seized an inordinate amount of power in the wake of the terrorist attacks, and even under the reformist President Jeb Tyler, it still wielded a hell of a lot of clout. Was it eavesdropping on their eavesdropping? Of course it was, if the Black Widow was doing her job.

Lannie was making clucking noises under his breath as he punched the keyboard, which Byrne knew was actually Arabic. He'd learn Arabic someday, he promised himself, right after he learned Irish Gaelic, Urdu, and Esperanto and maybe even French. "Speak English," he commanded.

Lannie stopped clucking and wrapped his tongue around words everybody could understand. "Not good. We have a major DoS coming from"—he punched in a blur—"coming from, it looks like . . . Bulgaria and . . . Israel . . ."

"Typical Arab," said a good-natured voice Byrne recognized as Sid Sheinberg's. "Always blaming Israel first." Sid was Sy's nephew, a smart lawyer who had dropped his fledgling practice and joined the force when Frankie recruited him for the team. The former Medical Examiner, Sy Sheinberg, had been Byrne's friend, mentor, and rabbi, and he still missed him after all these years. Almost enough time had passed for Byrne to be able to forget the last time he saw Sy, when he found the body after the suicide . . .

"In this case, Sid, I'm blaming Israel second," Lannie snapped. "And then Uzbekistan and Azerbaijan and . . ."

Byrne ran an emotionally loose ship. The CTU was no place for hurt feelings; you checked your resentments and entitlements at the door and you elbowed your way to the table like everybody else. Festering grievances were the worst—if anybody had a beef, let him air it out. Byrne and

Matt White had worked that way for two decades, and were not about to change now.

"What have we got—are we blind?" Instead of answering, Lannie turned to Sid. "Gimme a hand here."

Sid slid into the seat next to Lannie's and for the next five minutes, neither of them said a thing. Instead, they worked furiously, in some kind of mental rapport, their agile minds leaping to the same hypotheses almost at once.

As they worked, the playfulness fell away, to be replaced by a grim, serious look that played around their lips. The CTU computers had been fucked with before—that much was SOP in this business—but something told Byrne that this time it was different, that this time it might be very, very bad.

"We've got a shitload of traffic going across the core switches—forty gigs a sec minimum," shouted Sid Sheinberg.

"We've got timeouts . . . we're out of CPU on the core switches . . . impossible," barked Lannie.

"What's this 'multicast' shit?" said Sid. "Come on, you fuckers!"

"Is it a virus?" asked Byrne.

Neither man turned to look at him. "No, external," said Lannie. "Incoming ports are swamped by 'bots.' What the fuck?"

"Rebooting the cores," said Sid, and one by one the machines went down. For all practical purposes, the CTU was now blind, if only for a few moments . . .

The screens blinked on again. "Fuck," said Sid. "We're still greened out, to the max."

"Impossible—"

"Connections dropping like flies off a camel's ass—"

"Origination point?"

"Dunno. Cabinet switches . . . ten gigs apiece. Fubared."

"Isolate."

"Isolating now . . . gotcha suckers!" Sid was nearly out of his seat.

"Kill the downlink ports."

"Killing . . ."

"Rebooting now . . ."

Everyone in the room held his breath and the screens winked out again . . . and then blinked back on. One by one they came back up—and held.

Lannie never took his eyes off the screen. "T1 and T2—quarantine those motherfuckers," he said. Sid shut the switches down. The crisis was over.

"Jesus fucking Christ," said Lannie.

"You can say that again," said Sid.

"Watch your mouth, boys," said Byrne, "especially seeing as how neither of you believes in Our Lord and Savior in the first place."

Applause rippled through the room. Lannie and Sid stood up to take a bow. Byrne cut their end-zone dance short.

"My office, now," he said. "On my father's immortal soul, everybody else, back to work."

He didn't have to say anything more: the older guys in the squad knew, and the newer ones would hear about it soon enough. How Byrne's father, Robert, a detective first grade, had been shot in the back on the Lower East Side, killed on Delancey Street along with his partner, in 1968. He had lived long enough to draw his service revolver—the same .38 Byrne still used—and might have shot his assailant, but the street was too crowded with innocents. So he died, bled to death on the street in front of the pushcarts, taking the identity of his killer to the grave with him, but sparing the lives of others.

Like everything else on the floor except for computer operational security, it was informal. Byrne's office was not one of the glass-walled fortresses the brass had over at One

Police Plaza, with the views of Brooklyn Bridge and, if you looked hard enough and used your imagination, into the borough where half the cops in the city had originated. Flatbush. Bensonhurst. Brownsville.

"Fingerprints?"

Lannie looked at Sid, then spoke. "Hard to tell until we take a closer look, but first guess is the Chinese."

"First guess is always the Chinese," Byrne said. "Continue."

"But upon further review," began Sid, who was a big football Giants fan, "it looks like somebody's just trying a little deflection, a juke and okey-doke."

Byrne hadn't heard those terms since O. J. Simpson was playing for Buffalo. "A flea flicker?" he asked.

Lannie was thoroughly confused. "I thought you said to speak English," he said.

"Football," said Byrne. "It's as American as baseball."

"But there are no feet in your football," said Lannie.

"Sure there are," said Byrne. "You use 'em to kick the other guys in the nards when the refs aren't looking. Which is what I want to do to these people. So who are they?"

Sid shuffled through some notes. "They might be Indians. There are some indications of a redirect via Mumbai—Bombay to you—but now that I look at it, I think this is a flea flicker too. So I—we—are going with Azerbaijani. Baku, probably."

That was a new one to Byrne. The Chinese were always probing the American cyber-defenses—hell, they attacked the Pentagon every chance they got—but because they bought our increasingly worthless bonds, whichever administration was in power in Washington generally let them skate. And that pussy Tyler was not about to let a little thing like cyberwar interfere with his we-are-the-world foreign policy. Byrne despised everybody in Washington.

"What happened in the window?" he asked, referring to

the moments that their defenses were down. There were times, he swore, when he felt like Captain Kirk on the deck of the *Enterprise,* shouting to Scotty about the shields being down. Another reference they probably wouldn't get.

"Running a recap now," said Lannie. "And it's not Baku. It's Budapest."

"Let's worry about that later. Right now, we need to know how blind we were."

Hopefully, the window was as short as possible and their redundant systems and fail-safe backups would have worked. Hopefully, this was not a one-two punch. But as Byrne well knew, hope was never an option, much less a plan. Hope was for losers.

Lannie stood there for a moment, transfixed as he consulted his secure PDA. It was a knockoff of the ultra-secure BlackBerrys the NSA had developed for the President; supposedly, it was unhackable, but Byrne knew enough about computers and personal digital assistants to know that nothing was unhackable.

The window was crucial. From this location in Chelsea, the NYPD monitored all its cameras and sensors installed·in the wake of 9/11—not just the ones in the subways, but surreptitious monitoring devices at either end of every bridge and tunnel connecting Manhattan either to the Bronx, to Long Island or to Jersey. Not only that—there were also cameras and radioactivity sensors underwater, below river level, on every pier, dock, and jetty. New York had been born a water city and a water city it still was, even if commerce now came by train, plane, and truck. But an island cannot afford to be without its seawall defenses. Pirates had roamed the East River well into the 19th century, and it was up to the NYPD to make sure they never returned.

Lannie's brown eyes remained impassive as he completed his readout. "Not good," he said at last. "Down three, maybe four minutes."

"Where?" asked Byrne.

"Everywhere. City-wide. Somebody just crawled in our ass and shoved a sharp stick up it."

"What about overlap?" There was a certain amount of fail-safe built into the system, so that if any one part of it went down, a nearby camera would cover for it. But fail-safe didn't even kick in until they'd been down for five minutes. A system-wide failure would mean no coverage.

Command decisions came easily to Byrne; he'd been making them ever since his father was killed and he realized that he, not his older brother Tom, was going to have to be the man of the house. "What do you think, Sid?" he said, requesting the only other opinion that mattered.

"Think it might be time to liaise with NSA," he said.

That did it. If Sid was recommending outside assistance, the shit really must be hitting the fan.

"We've been breached," barked Byrne. "Go red."

CHAPTER SEVEN

Manhattan—late afternoon

"Mom! Look at this!" Emma Gardner squealed like the child she once was, not the freshly minted teenager she had so recently become. Standing there on Broadway in SoHo, in front of shops she had only ever dreamed about back in Edwardsville, Illinois, she was again her mother's little girl, the ghosts of her horrible ordeal for the moment cast off, gone.

"Yuck!" exclaimed Rory. He was about to turn eleven, and still had no use for girls, much less girlish things. But such was his love for his sister that even he managed to feign interest in the latest fashions that almost entirely occupied the minds of girls.

"Say cheese!" shouted Hope. Rory and Emma struck a mock-pose as she snapped the picture with her cell phone camera. She didn't care if she looked like a dumb tourist. She was a dumb tourist, in New York City for the first time in her life, and loving it. "Now, who's for some lunch?"

"I am!" "I am!!"

They walked up Broadway to Houston Street. The plastic

map she was consulting indicated that the mysterious and wonderful place called Greenwich Village lay to the west, and a brisk walk should bring them into that legendary land of hippies, gays, poets, and painters in just a few minutes.

"I like New York," said Emma. "And I'm getting real hungry."

"Me, too," seconded Rory.

They crossed Seventh Avenue and soon found themselves in the maze of the West Village. The angles of the streets confused Hope. She was determined to show her kids that she was in charge, but when they crossed the intersection of West 4th Street and West 10th Street, she was sure her world had turned upside down.

"Mom, are you sure you know where we're going?" asked Rory skeptically, scratching his head. He didn't know much about Manhattan streets, but he knew what a grid looked like, and this wasn't it.

Hope looked at the map in her hands and realized it wasn't there. Rory had snatched it away and was studying it like an expert cartographer charting the coast of Malabar. "This way," he decided, and off he went, heading north by northeast, with Hope and Emma trailing.

Hope took Emma's hand as they walked past the rows of brownstones and red brick houses, so unlike her notion of what New York City was. This was one of the oldest surviving parts of Manhattan, and as she walked she began to understand what it was that had attracted so many people to Greenwich Village over the centuries. It really *was* like a little village, if you didn't count the whizzing yellow cabs and the trucks rumbling down Seventh Avenue and the . . . unusual . . . people on the street.

They passed restaurant after restaurant, but didn't stop. Although none of them would admit it, there was something forbidding about Manhattan eateries. It was almost as if they

were a series of private clubs, with admittance only to famil-
iars; Hope was sure that the minute she entered one the people inside would immediately spot them for the tourists they
so obviously were, and would make fun of them behind their
backs, or take advantage of them. Besides, the prices . . .

Emma clutched her mother's hand tightly. It wasn't that
she was afraid—the nightmares had finally stopped a few
months ago, and she knew she was as safe here, in the middle of the largest city in the country and the greatest city in
the world, as she possibly could be. But there was something
reassuring about the physical contract, a warmth that helped
dispel the lingering fear.

Suddenly, she shivered and stopped. "What is it?" asked
Hope, and then she heard it: *Thwack thwack thwack* . . . The
sound of angels' wings. The sound of a helicopter.

Hope turned and craned her neck. Emma looked down at
the dirty pavement. Rory felt, rather than saw, that they had
stopped, and was rushing back to his sister. *Thwack thwack
thwack* . . .

Then Hope saw it: high over the Hudson, a police chopper was describing a lazy arc in the sky as it surveyed the
area along what the locals still referred to as the West Side
Highway, even though the highway was long gone. It was
not threatening, not alarming, but the sight and sound
brought back unwelcomed memories for both Hope and
Emma.

"Food!" shouted Rory, rushing ahead.

In their ignorance, they had wandered north of 14th
Street, where Rory had spotted a Sabrett's hot dog vendor
wheeling his pushcart north. A hot dog was far from haute
cuisine, but it was certainly better than nothing.

The vendor, however, didn't seem to want to stop. From
time to time he glanced down at his watch, and then cast a
look at the sky, but he kept pushing the cart north on Seventh

Avenue, Rory on his heels. "Hey, mister, wait up! We wanna buy some hot dogs."

The pushcart vendor, however, didn't stop, but kept up his steady pace. He wasn't exactly running—you couldn't really run with a pushcart, Rory noticed—but his pace was quick, almost double-time, and he either didn't hear Rory or wasn't inclined to stop.

"Hey, mister!"

The man looked over his shoulder: "Off duty!" he shouted and kept right on moving.

Hope watched her son chase the man up the avenue. She had already learned the hard way that, in New York, when people said they were off-duty, they were off-duty. A couple of fruitless interactions with yellow cabs and the mysterious dome-light signals had taught her that.

Still, Rory was not about to give up. When the vendor had to halt at a light, the boy caught up with him. "Three hot dogs, please," he said, brightly.

The man turned to look at him. Rory wasn't much good at guessing grown-ups' ages—they all looked old to him—but he figured the guy had to be somewhere between 20 and 50, African American, with close-cropped hair and a small mustache. He noticed the man had a couple of tats on his big arms. He looked like he worked out pretty regularly, and you wouldn't want to mess with him.

"Off duty," said the man and started up the pushcart again. Then, suddenly, he changed his mind, flipped open the top, and pulled out three dogs as Hope and Emma approached. "What d'you want on 'em?" the man asked.

"One with ketchup, one with mustard, and one with sauerkraut," replied Rory.

"You got it," said the man, much friendlier, coming up with the three hot dogs.

"My name's Rory. Rory Gardner. What's yours?" For a

moment, Rory thought the man was going to snap at him, but instead he smiled a nice smile and replied, "Ben. My name's Ben."

Ben stuffed the hot dogs into buns, added the condiments, and handed them over.

"Thank you so much," said Hope, handing him a $20 bill as Emma and Rory tucked in. "Please forgive my son. He's just curious, is all."

Ben smiled again. "First time in New York, huh?" he said. "Have a nice day." And then he was gone.

"People sure are weird here," said Emma. Rory made a face at Emma as they walked and ate, just like real New Yorkers. Hope was glad to see them laughing and kidding . . . and then she remembered the hurt and the void at the center of her heart. She took a bite out of her hot dog and looked up at the sky. The noise had distracted her: not just one helicopter now, but two, three, more, circling in the clear blue sky.

A taxi slowed to turn the corner. It was available. "Come on, kids," shouted Hope, signaling to the cab. Astoundingly, it rolled to a stop. "Who's up for a movie?" Gleefully, they all piled into the backseat."

"Times Square, please," said Hope. The driver hit the pedal, sending them tumbling back into the seat cushion. This was going to be fun.

CHAPTER EIGHT

New Orleans

Maryam noticed the car behind them before Devlin did. "Seven o'clock," she said. They were driving up Canal Street, past the ghost of Ignatius J. Reilly and the clock.

"Bogies?"

"What is bogies?"

Sometimes he felt older than he actually was. Why would she know what "bogies" were?

"Bad guys. Like Bogey, before he became a good guy."

"Right—who is Bogey?"

Devlin took a deep breath. "He was a bad guy before he became a good guy."

She moved the car ahead faster, but not too much faster. Maryam was an expert. She knew that too sudden a movement would indicate they had something to hide, or, worse, something to flee from.

She swerved around a low-riding Chevy and a Prius, then cut in front of both of them as she took a hard right on St. Charles Avenue. The Howard Avenue roundabout was coming up fast.

"Where are you—"

"Shut up," she said. "And hang on." She floored it.

The car behind them picked up speed. Whoever was tailing them was inexpert and obvious. But he was a good driver.

They shot under the Pontchartrain Expressway. The Garden District was dead ahead, served by the famous St. Charles Avenue streetcar, which trundled down the middle of the boulevard from Canal Street to the terminus, thirteen miles away. "Slow down," said Devlin. Maryam obeyed instantly, knowing he would have a reason.

Devlin used the darkness of the underpass to flip over into the backseat, where his briefcase was. There were weapons in it, but he didn't need a weapon at the moment. A special hand-held would do just fine.

Most drivers didn't realize it, but today's cars were basically computers attached to a drive train, and topped with a home entertainment center. The days of "driving" a car were long gone; the computer drove it and you just steered it. There was no need anymore to shoot out tires of a pursuing vehicle, or run it off the road; all you had to do was knock out its computer and a $50,000 Mercedes became just another expensive piece of immobile junk. And the jalopy behind them was no Mercedes.

Devlin punched the make and model of the car into his PDA. It was a little something of his own devising, which he had developed in his spare time in his office at Fort Meade. At close enough range, it could access a car's onboard computer and get a complete readout of the vehicle, including its VIN; via a satellite uplink, Devlin could then take control of the car, jam it, disable it, or even wreck it if he so chose. All he had to do, once the readout was complete, was push a button.

Sam Raclette was enjoying the ride. It wasn't every day that he got a call from a big-shot network correspondent to "follow that car," but today was his lucky day, in more ways than one. For one thing, he had just happened to be hanging around RAND when the call came in, hoping to squeeze off a shot or two of somebody famous, but idling in the parking lot having coffee, all he saw was some dumpy guy get into a car. Then Ms. Stanley stuck her head out as if she was looking for him, so naturally his curiosity was aroused and he decided to grab a couple of pictures of the Principessa when she saw him and started to chew his ass out until she had a better idea.

"Follow that car," she said, just like in the movies, and slipped him a couple of hundred fresh simoleons. Well, as it turned out the damn car didn't go anywhere except into the parking garage, but he never saw the dumpy guy get out and when the car next to it pulled out, he decided what the hell, especially after he got a load of the babe behind the wheel.

And now here he was, chasing a woman into the Garden District and enjoying it. He'd catch up to her soon enough, somewhere at a light on St. Charles, and try to calm her fears. All he wanted to do was talk to her, ask her a couple of questions, maybe get her number. He heard cops did that sort of shit all the time, pulled over a hot chick just for the heck of it, pretend she was doing 50 in a 35-mph zone, check out her license and registration, let her off with a friendly warning and then give her a call a couple of days later.

There she was, just ahead. The damn tinted windows made it hard to see through the back windshield, which was really pissing him off. He was going to have to get closer, but she kept pulling away from him.

Suddenly, the car in front of him slowed. Maybe she was getting tired of the game. Maybe she'd caught a glimpse of him in the rearview mirror and liked what she saw. He was known to have that effect on women, if he did say so himself. NOLA was a pretty easy town to get laid in, especially if you didn't mind big girls, but Sam liked a challenge, and who didn't?

Something caught his eye, something he hadn't noticed before. There was somebody else in the car with her: a man. A man who had just climbed into the backseat. Damn! Suddenly his whole fantasy of scoring with the hot chick didn't seem so plausible anymore. Now it was back to business, try to flag them down and—

What if the guy in the car was the dumpy guy? Then he'd really be on to something. There was an underpass below the Pontchartrain Expressway just ahead. If he sped up now he might be able to catch them in the darkness.

He gunned it.

Something was wrong. The readout on the car came through okay, but that was part of the problem. It was an ordinary, off-the-lot Taurus from a few years back, nothing at all special. If the guy following them was really on to them, he would have been driving something up to the challenge. If he really suspected something or if he were sent by somebody who did, he would be driving a lot differently. If it really was an enemy and not a random dope, they wouldn't even have spotted him until it was almost too late. Something was definitely wrong.

It can't be, thought Devlin, his finger on the button. What were the odds of a civilian picking them up and giving chase? None at all. Plus the handoff in the garage had been clean, of that he was sure. His mind raced, trying to spot the flaw in his argument, but he couldn't find any. Not on short notice.

And the guy *was* following them.

Still . . . what if the guy was an *amateur* . . .

Too late. He pushed the button.

* * *

Sam Raclette was closing fast on her when all of a sudden his car stopped.

Except it just didn't stop. It went from 40 to zero almost instantly. The engine shut off, the brakes locked, and the steering went out. There was a sharp jerk and then the back of the car came up off the ground and flipped over. The car's windows exploded outward from the impact, the airbags popped and the theft-alarm system went off. In the gloom of the underpass, it spun on its roof once or twice, then settled. Tires screeched, horns honked, as the other cars tried to avoid the wreck.

Inside, Sam followed it head over heels in its tumble, and found himself hanging upside down by his seat belt. *This fucking piece of shit* he thought to himself. Outside, he heard the screech of tires as the cars behind him braked and squealed around him. All he needed was some idiot to smash into him now, before he could get out.

The noise inside the car was deafening; it was hard for him to hear any of what was going on outside. Still, the first thing was to get the hell out of there. With some difficulty, he released the seat-belt catch and slid down the seat. He was covered with broken glass, and there was blood running down his face, but nothing seemed to be broken except the damn car. Although he was stunned from the impact, Sam could still think clearly enough to understand that he had to get out fast, and that he was going to sue the ass off Ford Motor Company once he did.

And then he heard the klaxon of a semi, right behind him.

Devlin had a ringside seat as the truck clipped the Taurus. "Shit!" he exclaimed.

"What's wrong?" Maryam glanced in the rearview mirror just in time to see the aftermath.

The Taurus spun crazily, a lopsided top sent careening toward one of the stanchions that held up the highway. The truck driver delay-reacted, swerving only after it was far too late, which caused several other cars to leap out of the way as best they could. Unable to stop, the truck righted itself and continued to plow on until the driver could bring the vehicle under control.

"We've gotta stop. Go back," said Devlin. Unbidden to his mind came the memory of that FBI agent he'd killed in his home in Falls Church. The woman he'd shot in his bathroom—

Evalina Anderson. That was her name. He had found it out later, and had made sure that her family would never want for anything again. They were told *you won the lottery* and then they were whisked away from a modest home in Prince Georges County and resettled in northern California. They thought good fortune had at last smiled on them. But it was not good fortune. It was the Angel of Death.

Did he have to kill everything he touched? That was the way he'd been trained, practically from birth, and certainly from childhood. Raised by the man he most loathed in the whole world and condemned to this horrid existence as an operative of Branch 4 of the Central Security Service, the most secret intelligence unit of the United States government. Although the work of the CSS was fundamental to the overall mission of the National Security Agency, it was the CSS that had remained anonymous from the day it was ordered into existence by President Nixon on Dec. 23, 1971, his little Christmas present to the nation, courtesy of National Security Decision Memorandum 5100.20.

On paper, the CSS looked like a million other government agencies—how they had grown, until it was now they, rather than the elected officials, who ran the country—hiding behind a bland exterior and a mission statement that concealed rather than revealed. He could recite it by heart:

"The Central Security Service (CSS) provides timely and accurate cryptologic support, knowledge, and assistance to the military cryptologic community.

"It promotes full partnership between the NSA and the cryptologic elements of the Armed Forces, and teams with senior military and civilian leaders to address and act on critical military-related issues in support of national and tactical intelligence objectives. CSS coordinates and develops policy and guidance on the Signals Intelligence and Information Assurance missions of NSA/CSS to ensure military integration."

The CSS was so secret that it didn't even get its own emblem until 1996; the insignia showed five service emblems balanced around a five-pointed star; each emblem was that of one of the armed services' cryptologic elements, including the United States Naval Network Warfare Command, the United States Marine Corps, the United States Army's Intelligence and Security Command, the United States Air Force's Intelligence, Surveillance, and Reconnaissance Agency, and the US Coast Guard. That ought to tell you nothing.

In fact, what the CSS was, was the muscle arm of the NSA. Nixon had originally intended CSS to be equal in stature with the other armed services—the "fourth branch," which is where his unit got its in-house name—but the services are good at nothing if not turf warfare and so CSS took refuge at NSA, where it could take its creation as an "armed service" literally. As the focal point of interservice liaisons, and with the weight of the NSA behind it, there was nothing it could not do, nowhere it could not go.

As thus Devlin had been born. "Devlin" was not his real name. His real name had died long ago, along with his real parents, at Rome's Leonardo da Vinci airport, Christmas 1985, when Arab terrorists shot the place up, as well as Vienna's Schwechat Airport. The eight-year-old Devlin had survived when his mother threw herself on him, but both she and his father—intelligence service professionals—had died in the attack.

The man who was not there that day had raised him from that moment on. He had taken him away, taken him off the grid, taught him, trained him to follow in both his parents' footsteps, but stronger and tougher than even his father had been. His new father had had an apt pupil, one equally adept at combat and weapons training, at languages, and in ELINT and cryptology. He was Mime to Devlin's Siegfried, trying to create and hone a fine, burnished weapon but unable to put on the finishing touches. Only Devlin could do that, and he had: completely anonymous, like his service, he was the CSS's most valuable asset, his existence above SCI—Sensitive Compartmented Information, which was above top secret—and known to only a handful of the highest officials in the U.S. government: the President of the United States, the Secretary of Defense, and the Director of the National Security Agency.

And the man who had raised him, who had whisked him away after the death of his parents, the man who had been having an affair with Devlin's mother, the man who had betrayed them to their worst enemy . . . that man was General Armond Seelye. His boss.

His worst enemy was the man who had financed the Abu Nidal operation, as he had financed the operations of the terror network across Europe in those days. The man who posed as a great benefactor of the people, the man who used his suffering at the hands of the Nazis as both a sword and a shield, the man whose philanthropy—although a pittance compared with the huge sums he'd made as a rapacious financial genius—was celebrated on the covers of magazines around the world . . . that man was Emanuel Skorzeny. Who, Devlin fully understood, not only wanted him dead but needed him dead.

Skorzeny had escaped the last time they met, in France. He wouldn't be so lucky the next time.

"What are you going to do?" Maryam's worried voice brought him back to reality.

He had to make this right. He *had* to. If the man in the trailing vehicle was still alive, he had to rescue him. "I'm going to save him."

Maryam turned right on Erato Street and doubled back on Carondelet and turned right again on Clio, which brought them back to the scene of the accident. The cops had not arrived yet and, knowing the New Orleans cops, it would be hours before they got out of the donut shops or the bars. Before they got to St. Charles, he jumped out, fully outfitted for the task, and ran. He gave a tug on his Tigers cap, making sure it obscured as much of his face as possible. In a situation like this, no one would remember anything but the truck hitting the car, but no point in taking chances; he'd had enough bad luck for one afternoon.

The Taurus was shoved up against the side of the underpass, and traffic had slowed. Good. This would make things a lot easier.

The first thing he had to do was stop traffic. A couple of smoke grenades rolled down the street accomplished that in a hurry; traffic, already crawling, simply came to a stop as it neared the underpass.

He tossed a couple of flares to mark the car's location. Good Samaritans did that all the time. Psychologically, they would further serve to keep nosy civilians away.

He shone a light into the car, a powerful beam that he activated from his key ring: nothing fancy, the kind you could buy commercially to use both as a flashlight or as a distress signal, but amazingly useful.

The driver was alive but unconscious. His face was covered in blood, but Devlin could see at a glance the blood was coming from a cut forehead. He pulled up an eyelid and directed the light into the man's eyes. The pupil reacted: good.

Maryam had the car right where he needed it, backed into the underpass, trunk opened. Devlin got the man into the trunk, closed it, and hopped back in. Then they were around the corner and up onto Highway 90, the famous Gulf Coast Highway that soon enough would turn into I-10 and get them to the airport.

Devlin lowered the rear seats and slid the unconscious man into the back of the car. He could give him some first aid, but they'd be at Charity Hospital in five minutes, and he'd never remember a thing.

CHAPTER NINE

Washington, D.C.—late afternoon

President John Edward Bilodeau Tyler slumped back in his chair in the private quarters, alone. As the first unmarried president since James A. Buchanan, he had the ultimate bachelor pad. If you couldn't get chicks to come home to the White House, you were a sorry-assed loser for sure. But that was just the problem—even had he wanted to, he couldn't get chicks to come back to the private quarters of the White House because, in a time of heightened security, the Secret Service would blow them out of their high heels. So he was a sorry-assed loser after all.

There was a soft knock at the door, which he at once recognized as Manuel's. Manuel Concepcion was his private steward, bartender, shrink, priest, and rabbi all rolled into one short Filipino whose English was still inflected with the cadences of his native Samar. The Concepcions had been fighting on the side of the Americans since the Philippines insurrection of 1902; even in an age of ethnic grievances, there was no question where his loyalty lay. Since the death of Bill Hartley, Manuel was, in fact, the only person the president of the United States really trusted. "Come in."

The door opened a crack. "May I get you anything, sir?"

Tyler's first instinct was to say no and then he decided to hell with his first instinct. "Bourbon and branch," he ordered. The door opened and Manuel walked in carrying a silver tray upon which was a bourbon and water, fixed just the way he liked it. "You're a mind reader, Manuel," said Tyler.

"No, sir," replied Manuel, setting the drink down in front of the president, "but I am observant."

As Tyler reached for the liquor, Manuel straightened and reached into the interior breast pocket of his steward's coat. "I brought you a cigar, too," he said. Already, he had the cutter out, deftly sliced off the closed end, and handed it to Tyler at the same time producing a lighted kitchen match. Tyler accepted the cigar gratefully and leaned forward into the flame, which jumped as he breathed it in until the tip of the cigar glowed ruby red.

"I'm going to lose, aren't I?" Tyler finally said.

"Probably, yes, sir, if you believe the polls," Manuel replied. "She looks unstoppable."

Tyler took a long sip of bourbon. This was not how he had envisioned the end of his presidency, tossed out after one term, not because the people despised him, as they eventually did all presidents, but because they liked the other guy better. It wasn't as if his polls were in free fall. Instead they read like the chart of a slowly dying patient whose condition was terminal and it was just a matter of time before he was carted off from the hospital to the hospice, to make room for some son of a bitch who actually had a chance.

Four years ago, Angela Hassett had been the first-term governor of Rhode Island, of all places, a state barely bigger than one of Louisiana's larger parishes and even more corrupt. But when you stopped to think about it, it all made perfect sense. Providence was a wholly owned subsidiary of Beacon Hill, a kind of farm team for the gangsters and criminals who had turned Massachusetts from the cradle of liberty into what was, in effect, a criminal organization populated by suckers, easy marks, and robots, who regularly return the Party in Power to power no matter how many Speakers of the House got indicted.

Hassett and her handlers, however, had taken the unholy conjoining of politics and crime to a whole new level. In her, they had the perfect front woman: a Harvard-educated lawyer (were there any other kind?) with a thousand-watt smile, impeccable but understated taste in clothes, a way of mellifluously stringing an endless series of platitudes together, and absolutely ruthless political instincts. The media loved her as well, finding everything about her fascinating; the lockstep editorial pages of both the *Boston Globe* and the *New York Times* hailed her as the perfect, sophisticated antidote to the hillbilly regime of Jeb Tyler. The funny part was, Tyler had been hailed in exactly the same way when he first ran for the Senate, but the Zeitgeist had evidently tired of his rustic good looks, folksy ways, and cracker-barrel delivery. Just as black was the new white, Angela Hassett was the new Jeb Tyler.

Then there was that son of a bitch, Jake Sinclair. . . .

That Skorzeny business hadn't helped, either. Tyler's administration had foiled an EMP attack on the east coast that would have plunged America into a hundred years of dysfunction and darkness, but he couldn't take any credit for it; in fact, he couldn't even let anybody know how close they had come to the abyss. Instead, he was blamed for the death toll in Los Angeles and Edwardsville, Ill.

True, he had struck an onerous deal with the fugitive financier. In exchange for his relative freedom, Emanuel Skorzeny had become, in effect, a combination of debtor and confidential informant, forced to pay an enormous sum to the United States in compensation for the Grove bombing and the attack on the midwestern middle school, as well as to Her Majesty's government in London, where the bombed-out London Eye had been transformed into affordable housing and a mosque for the capital's burgeoning immigrant population.

That was not all. Skorzeny also had been forced to surrender all his domiciles save Liechtenstein and use his continuing influence in the world's stock market to restore some of the lost capital his machinations had stolen. In exchange for his cooperation, and to prevent him from going completely stir-crazy, Skorzeny was free to fly on his private jet. But it could not land anywhere in the world that the United States of America had any political, economic, or military influence. All Skorzeny could do was go for a ride in his custom 707, refueling in the air if he could manage it, and occasionally stopping off in Chad, Vanuatu, and Lapland. Even Switzerland didn't want to see him anymore, although the Swiss were still happy to take and harbor his money.

Even so, Tyler had nearly blown one of the nation's most valuable resources—the Central Security Service's Branch 4 clandestine operation, and in particular the agent known as Devlin. And then there was Bill Hartley's suicide, which had left him without a single Senator he could either trust or reliably bribe. The presidency thing was a lot harder than it looked. No wonder Caesar had nudged the Roman Republic toward the Empire.

"Sir?" Manuel's question brought him out of his fog.

"Yes, Manuel?"

"Will there be anything else this evening?"

Tyler looked at his manservant; funny how here, in the heart of the world's greatest democracy, the president still had manservants. He was about to say something when the phone buzzed softly. That was Manuel's signal to leave. He bowed and backed out of the room, closing the door and leaving the president alone with whatever problem was now announcing itself.

It was Millie Dhouri, his private secretary, calling from the Oval Office. "Yes, Millie, what is it?"

"Mr. President, I have Director Seelye on the line. He says it's urgent."

Tyler wished that Manuel had made it a double. Calls from Seelye could never be good news. "Patch him through, please."

"Yes, sir." There was a short pause, with a faint crackle on the line, as the security of the connection was verified and the scrambling devices activated, and then Lt. General Armond "Army" Seelye—the Director of the National Security Agency—came on the line.

Tyler spoke first: "How bad is it?"

Seelye did not seem surprised in the least by the president's opening gambit. "Unknown at this time. Apparently, there's been a major security breach at NYPD CTU. They were blinded for several minutes by a coordinated DoS attack, most likely Chinese in origin."

"The Chinks are always doing that sort of thing," Tyler interrupted. "They've been in our shorts for years: at DoD, the Agency, even the power grid and water supply. I thought you guys were supposed to be doing something about that."

"Yes, sir," replied Seelye's voice; even scrambled, the sting was audible. "We are, sir. But as you know, despite the reorganizations post 9/11, interservice agency cooperation is still a reformer's fantasy and a bureaucrat's nightmare. And, in any case, NYPD acts alone."

That much was true. The New York Police Department had become a stand-alone, off-the-shelf operation, completely independent of the nation's intelligence establishment. How exactly that had happened was unclear, but it didn't really matter at this point. The clannish Irish—and every cop on the NYPD was at heart Irish, no matter what his or her ethnicity—were deeply suspicious of the Washington outsiders and, after Atta & Co. punched two huge smoking holes in the ground of lower Manhattan, were in no mood to trust Langley, Fort Meade, or the Pentagon ever again.

"Who's in command of the CTU these days?" asked Tyler.

"Captain Byrne, Francis X. Byrne," replied Seelye. "Old-school to the end. Father was a cop, KIA. Plenty of write-ups and citations. He's also been best buds with the commish since they were young detectives together. He's bulletproof."

"So we know nothing about their operation."

"Not really, no sir."

Tyler sighed. What the hell was the point of having multiple intelligence agencies under the vague aegis of the Director of National Intelligence and the cumbersome Department of Homeland Security? The whole thing was a giant cluster fuck. If he survived the fall campaign, it was something he was going to have to fix. Especially when a city cop shop could tell all of them to go pound sand.

The hell of it was, the CTU was probably the best-equipped counterterrorism operation in the world, even better than the Israelis'. They had the latest equipment, state-of-the-art computers, and the top techies, including a cadre of former hackers who had been persuaded to join the force in lieu of a stretch at Auburn or Dannemora. By contrast, the FBI was making do with the un-networked equivalents of the old Trash 80s and Kaypros, and even the vaunted NSA was still behind the WYSIWYG curve on some of its older terminals. It was a wonder, Tyler reflected, that given the determination of America's enemies to strike and strike again that there were any buildings standing in Washington and New York at all.

". . . and there's a reason for that, which goes beyond their insularity," Seelye was saying.

"What's that?" Talking to Seelye exasperated Tyler, but given their shared past, there wasn't much he could do about it. Seelye stayed until he quit, or until Devlin asked for his resignation. That was part of the deal, too.

"Byrne's brother, Tom."

"Go on."

"As in Deputy Director of the Federal Bureau of Investigation, Thomas A. Byrne."

"Oh, shit. Don't tell me that asshole is our guy's brother."

"That's what they say the 'A' stands for, yes sir."

How and why Tom Byrne was still with the Bureau, not to mention how and why he had risen as far as he had, was one of Washington's great mysteries. Not since Hoover himself had a SAC been as roundly and as cordially despised as Tom Byrne, and yet he had continued his unimpeded rise through the ranks. "Haven't you got anything on him?"

There was silence on the other end of the line for a moment as Seelye chose his words. "Plenty of stories, mostly about something that went down years ago. Something that seems to have involved both Byrne brothers. But if anybody knows anything, they're either not talking or sleeping with the fishes. Which is weird, because . . ."

"Because?" prompted Tyler.

"Because the two brothers hate each other's guts. They're like two guys, each with a loaded gun at the other one's head, knowing that no matter who pulls the trigger first, they both get their heads blown off."

Tyler saw the outlines of a possible play. As Seelye had told him in the middle of the Skorzeny business, he really was getting the hang of the intelligence game. "Sort of like you and me, in other words."

"You could put it that way, yes, sir," Seelye said.

"Not to mention Devlin."

"Let's not, if you don't mind, Mr. President."

"You don't like him very much, do you?" asked Tyler. "Is it because he's hard to like?" Tyler was still smarting from his confrontations with Devlin.

"It's not that he's hard to like," replied Seelye. "He's *impossible* to like." He wondered if the president would get the reference to the original *Manchurian Candidate* and immediately decided he would not.

He did. "The first version really was much better," said Tyler. "Did you know I was one of the Chinese workmen who laid the track on this stretch?" This president was always full of surprises.

"Nonetheless, Maryland is a beautiful state."

"So is Ohio, for that matter—so level with me. Where's Devlin?"

The thought crossed Seelye's mind that somehow Tyler had found out about his true relationship with the man known as Devlin—how he had in fact raised him after his parents' death in 1985, trained him to be the perfect operative, kept him off the grid and in his pocket until . . . until the Skorzeny business came out into the open. The only other person who knew was Howard Rubin, the former Secretary of Defense, but he had retired to his farm in Maryland six months ago. Seelye and Rubin had never been particularly friendly, but he felt for the man when Rubin had called him up one afternoon to tell him of his impending resignation. "When a couple of guys with a suitcase nuke can take down a whole country," Rubin had wondered, "what's the point of a Defense Department?" Especially one that, for reasons of political cowardice, wouldn't fight back.

The new SecDef was Shalika Johnson, the former governor of Tyler's home state, Louisiana. There were plenty of folks who thought Johnson was simply an affirmative-action appointment by a floundering president looking to shore up his minority base, but Seelye had already learned the hard way that Ms. Johnson was one of the toughest human beings in Washington, which was saying something. If the country were ever really to go on a war footing, she would be the fiercest, most uncompromising warrior since Scipio Africanus. He dreaded having to have the Devlin discussion with her, when and if the time came.

"He's in the air."

"Where is he going?"

Seelye hesitated. "He . . . he didn't say sir?"

"The fuck you mean, 'he didn't say'?" At the other end of the line, Seelye could feel the temperature rising inside the White House.

"He was supposed to return to Fort Meade, but—"

Tyler exploded. He hadn't yelled at anyone all day, and it felt good. "God fucking damn it, I don't give a rat's fucking rear end what he was supposed to do. I'm in the goddamned fight of my life with this phony from Rhode Island, even my bought-and-paid-for pollsters and TV pundits are telling me there's no way I can win, and after all I've done for this goddamned country, and if something goes tits up in New York, well, this job won't be worth a plugged nickel. And neither will yours, General. Do I make myself clear?"

"Perfectly, sir, yes." Seelye was used to dealing with Tyler, had even come to almost like him, and he reached for the right words to say. The last thing he wanted to see was Angela Hassett—untested, untried, a creature of the media and mostly of Jake Sinclair, who was probably fucking her or was thinking about fucking her—in the Oval Office. Especially since her one qualification for the office was that she was not Jeb Tyler. "Devlin has an instinct for these things, Mr. President. He's probably on his way to New York right now. That's where I'd head if I were him. Teterboro, most likely—no commercial traffic." Seelye paused, the telephone equivalent of a shrug. "Anyway, you know his deal. He does what he wants, when he wants."

"I know it," said Tyler evenly, "but I still don't like it."

"It's the only deal we have."

"It's the only deal *you* have," Tyler reminded him. "And he can pull the plug on it any time he wants. So you'd better make damn sure that, whatever he's up to, it goes smoothly."

"Yes, Mr. President," said Seelye.

"Now make sure he gets wherever he's going, on the double."

"Er . . . sir?" Seelye got his question in just before Tyler hung up on him.

"Yes, General?"

"It's not just him, sir. It's her, too."

"Who?"

"The woman he's taken as his partner in Branch 4 operations. You remember, the Iranian. You authorized it, at the meeting at the Willard Hotel."

"I don't remember anything about an Iranian." That part was probably true. Tyler only remembered things that were important and, of course, grudges. "Who is she?"

"We don't know, exactly. Only Devlin knows who she is. That was part of the deal. We haven't even been able to vet her, and here she is—"

Tyler didn't feel like arguing. The U.S. Government was so endemically riddled with moles, sleeper agents, old Soviet illegals, and various other burrowed and semi-dormant creatures that one more wouldn't make any difference; it was a miracle the Republic had lasted this long, what with all the enemies, foreign and domestic. And, these days, it was impossible to tell them apart . . .

"Whatever. Defend your country, General Seelye."

"Yes, sir. Thank you sir."

Once again, the President of the United States was alone. Tyler leaned back in his chair. He'd only been president for three years, but it already seemed like a lifetime, and as he looked back on that much younger man who had sought, and won, the office, he hardly recognized him. From the outside, running a presidential campaign might look hard, and of course it was, but it was nothing compared to actually having the job itself. All the political bullshit went out the window the minute you walked into the Oval Office for the first time and, unless you were really stupid or arrogant or both, that's where it stayed, fertilizing the Rose Garden until either you were ready to leave or the voters sickened of you and threw you out.

If anything happened, he could pretty much kiss his re-election chances good-bye. Even if the country rallied round the flag, there was just enough time from now to the election to make them forget. Maybe. Unless it was really horrific, in which case a century wouldn't be enough. The patriotic shock would turn to outrage, and the second term of a Tyler presidency would be toast. He had to figure out an angle . . . of political survival.

Instinctively, Tyler reached for his bourbon, then remembered he'd finished it. But when he brought the glass to his lips, he saw to his astonishment that it was a fresh one, as if delivered by a ghost. Manuel must have brought it to him while he was on the blower with Seelye. Nothing like a man you could trust, even here in the White House.

CHAPTER TEN

Fort Meade, Maryland

General Armond "Army" Seelye put down the secure phone to the White House and typed out an encrypted message to Devlin: FRANCIS X. BYRNE, CHIEF OF NY CTU. He'd gotten his orders, which was the easy part. Executing them was something else.

Whatever was going on in New York was plenty troubling. Not that it was exactly a surprise. The Chinese, the Russians, and all sorts of other "frenemies" were constantly engaged in a relentless probing of America's cyber-defenses, so much so that the President had recently appointed a "cyber-czar" to war-game possible responses to a takedown of, say, the electrical grid. Not that they were going to stop there. Over the past few years, the number and the severity of the probes had been growing exponentially, which told him plenty. For one thing, it meant that the Chinese were no longer afraid of the Americans, and why should they be? They were holding a huge amount of American paper, notes they could call in any time they wanted to wreck the currency or take down the economy. Not even Emanuel Skorzeny at his most powerful could take on the once-almighty dollar.

For another, they had millions of men under arms and, in the coming years, that number would only swell. One of the unintended side effects of the Peoples Republic's one-child policy and the preference of Chinese families for boys was the creation of a lopsided generation in which males outnumbered females in a ratio 1.25 to 1. That was a lot of horny, frustrated boys, more than a quarter of whom were born losers who never would get any girl at all. The English used to deal with this by having one boy inherit the estate, the second son join the army, and the third take the cloth, but the Chinese had no cloth, and so droves of young males were heading into the army every day; if they couldn't fuck they could damn sure fight.

Worse, it told Seelye that even countries like Bulgaria and Israel and the lesser 'stans of the old Soviet Union had no fear of the American eagle, either. Al-Qaeda had taught Americans that a handful of zealots armed mostly with the element of surprise, ruthlessness of will, and the sheeplike nature of modern *boobus Americanus* could easily overpower a crew and turn the morning flight to Los Angeles into a guided missile; all it took was the audacity of a bunch of dopes who thought they were ticketed for paradise instead of a fiery inferno or a farmer's field. Everyone, it seemed, felt free to poke the old lion.

But even a czar wouldn't be able to pry anything out of the NYPD if they didn't want to give it up. New York City was its own country, and just as unafraid of Washington as everybody else.

He pressed a buzzer on his desk, which connected him immediately to his assistant. In the old days, she would have been called his secretary, but somewhere along the line someone had decided this wasn't politically correct.

"Ms. Overbay?" he said. "Please ask Major Atwater to come up, please."

"Right away, Director," replied Ms. Overbay. If someone

put a gun to his head and demanded that he describe Ms. Overbay, he wasn't sure he could do it. Everything about the modern workplace had become distant, defensive, protective, impersonal. If he could get through the day without interacting with anyone face-to-face, he would, and Seelye suspected that a lot of managers and office workers around the country felt the same way.

It would take Atwater only a few minutes to hustle to the DIRNSA's office. Seelye let his eyes roam over his desk, which was always kept as tidy as possible. But on this day there were a few items laid out on it, simple enough individually but disturbing when taken as a whole. Someone was trying to send him a message.

Regarding the first, there was no doubt about its provenance. It was a letter, an old-fashioned letter, from Moscow, bearing the unique postal stamp of the Kremlin:

"My dear Seelye," it began, in English, obviously painstakingly translated in its writer's head from the original Russian thoughts. And then, just as obviously, not. It read instead as if it had been passed through one of those Web translation programs, which rendered the most elegant original into snarling gibberish. "Long time I am retired but fashion change so I write tell you danger. Illegals program of course you know but what don't know is that continued long after Soviet Union demise, people in place already, what else to do, nothing. But still election danger. Yours, N——."

The old Soviet "illegals program" was a long-running attempt to recruit, or insinuate, native-born sleeper agents into the U.S. government at the highest levels. Throughout his career, Seelye had monitored and tracked them, taking them out where he could—that was a real problem, since so many of them had graduated from elite prep schools like Hotchkiss and Choate, or from Harvard and Yale; there really were no traitors like old-money traitors, and the nouveau quota babies who aped them. But this note took the illegals program to a whole new level. Was an "illegal" now running for the highest office in the land?

If the information was true—a big if—then this was a problem that no one in the U.S. government had ever before confronted. For nearly three centuries, it was assumed that both political parties were acting in good faith, that the candidates they offered were Constitutionally eligible, and beholden to no foreign power. But, aside from Article II, Section One, there was no check on eligibility. The people had to take the word of the parties that the candidates they offered up for consideration were, in fact, eligible. It didn't matter whether the Constitution was "living" or "original," the language was plain. And from that trust in the system flowed all else, including the military's tradition of absolute deference to duly constituted civil authority, which most certainly included his own deference to the President of the United States, whoever might be currently occupying the office. Still, he was going to have a run a thorough background check on Angela Hassett—and on Jeb Tyler, for that matter, just to be fair.

That task was certainly much easier today than it ever had been. There was a world of personal information about nearly every man, woman, and child in America available on the Internet and the amazing part was that—through Twitter, Facebook, MySpace, LinkedIn and the other social-networking sites—the American public had made such information freely and publicly available.

Which was why Government 2.0 had been such a success, depending on your point of view, of course. The executive branch didn't need the NSA or any of the other intelligence agencies to compile their rosters and lists of the voting public, didn't need spooks and FBI agents going door to door to inquire about people's loyalty or sexual predilections or political persuasions: the public had already volunteered such information, even if it didn't yet realize it. The thought of all this information in the wrong hands some-times kept Seelye awake at night. It was all right if such ma-terial stayed relatively safely in the hands of professionals like himself, but now every political hack, twenty-something ideologue, and freelance double agent had access to it. It would, he knew, all end badly. He just hoped and prayed that he wouldn't be around to see it happen.

The note from the "Russian" was only one of several puzzling things on his desk. Spread out before him were several pieces of paper he had not yet shared with the president or anybody else. They were printouts of a series of anonymous e-mails that had come not through channels but directly to his in-box. His secure e-mail addresses—he had several, depending on the usage—were known to only a handful of staffers both in NSA/CSS and at the White House. They were classified Top Secret. And yet someone had at least one of them.

"Dirnsa Seelye," began the first one. "What are the Thirty-Nine Steps?"

"Lt. General Armond Seelye or To Whom It May Concern," ran the second. "Edgar Allan POE. (signed) the Magician."

The third was a bit more complex: "UG RMK CSXH-MUFMKB TOXG CMVATLUIV." It was unsigned.

The fourth was a series of numbers: 317, 8, 92, 73, 112, 79, 67, 318, 28, 96, 107, 41, 631, 78, 146, 397, 118, 98, 114.

The fifth was a series of 87 characters, squiggles based on the letter "E," arranged in three rows:

The sixth was the briefest of them all: "Masterman. XX."

All were, of course, ridiculously easy to recognize, if not to understand. The real question was what, cumulatively, did they mean? Were they a game? A warning? A threat? And did they have anything to do with what was going on in New York? In the wilderness of mirrors, everything was related and nothing was connected.

Seelye spread the printouts on his desk and looked them over. How he longed for the days when written communications were actually written, or at least typed, and the paper could be subjected to various forms of analysis. In the old days, each typewriter had its own distinctive signature, like a fingerprint, and many was the criminal who went to jail, or the spy who was exposed when the papers came out of the pumpkin, or executed when his machine was found and identified. Not anymore. Today almost everything came electronically, even bills and junk mail, and thanks to the infinite permutations of ones and zeroes, anything could be encoded within anything else. Churchill's famous comment about Russia, that it was a "riddle wrapped in a mystery inside an enigma," could now properly be applied to everything. Even e-mail.

Well, that was part of the NSA's brief, too. No Such Agency was founded by President Truman in 1952 to both collect and decode foreign signals (SIGINT) and to protect America's codes from hostile code breakers. The Second World War had made both encryption and cryptanalysis boom industries, and a wide variety of codes had been employed, everything from the Germans' "Enigma" machine—named after the series of musical variations by the British composer, Sir Edward Elgar, to the Navajo "code talkers" who had worked for the Marine Corps in the Pacific theater.

Still, in the end, code-breaking was all about patterns, even if those patterns were sometimes so deeply hidden that they resembled wheels within wheels, whose sprockets had to be carefully aligned for the message to be read and understood. Today, the volume and the magnitude of the threat was infinitely greater than it had been 75 years ago—one missed pattern and the next thing you knew there was a smoking, radioactive crater where midtown Manhattan or the Washington Monument had once stood.

Which is where the Black Widow came in.

The Black Widow was the in-house nickname of the NSA's Cray supercomputer at Fort Meade. Forget privacy—no matter what the sideshow arguments in Congress were about the FISA laws or civil liberties, the Black Widow continued to go remorselessly about her job, which was to listen in on, and read, all telephonic and written electronic communication, in any language, anywhere in the world. It was the old Clinton-era "Echelon" project writ large, able to perform trillions of calculations per second as it sifted and sorted in its never-ending quest for key words, code words, patterns. The ACLU had screamed, but presidents from both parties had surreptitiously embraced it. The Black Widow was here to stay if only she could be heeded and translated in time.

Wiretapping had come a long way. In the popular imagination—and in the minds of the media, which, to judge from the op-ed pages of the *New York Times*, now viewed everything through the lenses of bad movies and show tunes— "eavesdropping" still conjured up images of fake telephone repairmen in jump suits, shimmying up phone poles or cracking open service boxes in the sub-sub-basement and applying alligator clips to the switching machinery.

None of that mattered anymore. It was all for show. the Black Widow not only heard all and read all, she could sense all: the technology had advanced to such an extent that the Widow and other Cray supercomputers like her—including the Cray XT4, known as the Jaguar, and the MPP (massively parallel processor) housed at the University of Tennessee—

could read the keystrokes of a given computer *through the electrical current* serving the machine. And all linkable. If the Singularity wasn't here yet, it would be soon.

"Major Atwater is here, sir," said Ms. Overbay's disembodied voice. Seelye punched a button on his desk that unlocked his office door—security was everything here—and in came the major as the door closed behind him.

Kent Atwater was from Thief River Falls, Minnesota, a place more celebrated for its evocative name than for any particular attraction, other than its mind-numbing winter weather. He had graduated from the Air Force Academy in Colorado Springs with high marks in math and cryptography, and had distinguished himself with the 91st Missile Wing at Minot in North Dakota, first with the Gravehaulers of the 741st squadron, then with the Security Forces Group. In that capacity, he had caught the eye of NSA brass, been transferred to Fort Meade, and bumped up the chain in Seelye's direction. Blond, strongly built, in his early 30s, he was a practically a caricature of what the world used to think of as a typical American but was now the vanishing remnant of a bygone ethnic archetype. Seelye liked and admired Atwater, although his demeanor never showed it, but the young Air Force officer had promise, which is why Seelye was grooming him as a possible deputy.

"Sir?" said Atwater, saluting.

"At ease, Major," said Seelye, gathering up the sheaf of papers and handing them to Atwater. "Please take a look at these and give me your first reaction. Don't think, just react. And please sit down."

Atwater was already through the papers by the time his rear hit the seat. He said, "Anybody who knows anything about the history of cryptography knows what these are. Someone with a literary bent."

"Indeed," replied Seelye.

"I mean, *The Gold Bug*, Dorothy L. Sayers, the Beale

Treasure. The only thing missing is the Voynich Manuscript. What is this, sir, a treatment for the next *National Treasure* movie?"

"You tell me, Major."

Atwater thought for a moment. "Well," he began, "obviously it can't be as simple as it looks."

"Does it really look that simple? And what if it is? Sometimes the best codes are the simplest." Seelye suddenly flashed on those ridiculous "Dancing Men" from the Sherlock Holmes story, the substitution cipher that he had overlooked, but that had unlocked Devlin's past, and thus given his most potent agent complete power over him, the nominal boss.

Which brought today's events full circle. President Tyler had just ordered Devlin into action, and Seelye had no choice but to obey. And yet, under his agreement with Tyler, Devlin could terminate Seelye at any time, for any reason. That was something that was going to have to change.

". . . me to do, sir?" Atwater was saying. Seelye looked up—

"Sorry, Major, say again?"

"I said, what do you want me to do, sir?" inquired Atwater.

"I want you to track down the sender—that shouldn't be too hard—and I want you to tell me what all these references to bygone codes—"

"Some of which have never been cracked," interjected Atwater. The man was evincing just the slightest signs of borderline insubordination, which was another thing that would have to be addressed. As if he'd read Seelye's mind, Atwater immediately apologized. "If you'll pardon the interruption, sir."

Seelye ignored the mea culpa. "Just give me your best assessment on this, Major. It goes without saying that, since this directly affects the operations of DIRNSA, your report is eyes-only."

"Yes, sir. Of course, sir."

"That's all."

Atwater shot to his feet. "Yes, sir," he said, saluted once more, performed a crisp about-face, and pushed the door open the instant he heard Seelye unlock it.

"Fail me not," said Seelye as the Major left. Or maybe he said it to himself. It wasn't clear, even to him.

Chapter Eleven

In the air

Emanuel Skorzeny was so absorbed in the numbers dancing in front of him on a computer screen that he almost forgot his manners. "Would you like a drink, my dear?" he inquired, reaching out to pat her on her knee. "A gin martini, ice-cold, just the way you like them? All you have to do is ask, and Mlle. Derrida here will be more than happy to fetch one for you. Isn't that right, Mlle. Derrida?"

Whether she was happy or not didn't really matter. Emanuelle Derrida swallowed both her tongue and her pride as she awaited a request—no, an order—from the woman who had boarded the plane in Macao and who was now on her way with them toward their next destination. Where that was, exactly, Skorzeny had not told her, but it didn't really matter: wherever he went, she went, no questions asked or answered.

Amanda Harrington stiffened at his touch. That he was insane, there could be no doubt. After what he had done to her in London and in France, and now here, as if nothing untoward had occurred. And there was nothing she could do about it. She hated the evil bastard, and dreaded whatever it was he now wanted from her. Maybe a martini would help. She nodded assent, and Ms. Derrida went to fetch it, leaving them alone.

Skorzeny gazed at her with those relentless eyes, so used to command, to fulfillment. Then he spoke:

"It seems that we underestimated the opposition," he began, without preamble, as if the past nine months were but a single day. That was Emanuel Skorzeny's secret of success, an indefatigable focus, a refusal to accept defeat. "And of course the loss of . . ."—here it came—"the loss of Mr. Milverton was regrettable. But here again perhaps I over-estimated his powers."

Amanda had never fully learned the whole story of her lover's last moments in London, and she had no way of knowing how much Skorzeny knew of her relationship with the man called Milverton. *That* he knew, of course, was in-disputable—she was barely living proof of his jealousy and malice. "How did he die?" she managed to ask.

"But here is Mlle. Derrida with your libation," he said. The assistant set the drink down in front of her and awaited further instruction. "That will be all, Mlle. Derrida," he said dismissing her. The woman shot Amanda a look as she left.

"Happy days," said Skorzeny.

Amanda took a tentative, flinching sip. The last martini she had accepted from his hand nearly killed her. But if he had wanted her dead in Clairvaux, in that horrible prison he called a country retreat, he would have killed her. Instead, he'd paralyzed her as punishment for her love for Milverton.

"I trust the libation is satisfactory?"

Amanda knew that had she replied in the negative, Mlle. Derrida's days in Skorzeny's employment, if not upon this earth, would be numbered. She decided to let the girl live. "Yes, sir," replied Amanda, setting the drink down on the spotless table.

"Excellent. And now to work." Skorzeny produced a

manila folder, extracted a few papers, and spread them out on the desk. For a man addicted to computers—a facility remarkable in a man his age—he still preferred real paper for important things.

The papers were a curious lot. One was a map, with a series of international destinations. One, she could see at a glance, was Macao, so presumably the others would be places at which Skorzeny planned to call. Others appeared to be gibberish—rows of numbers, nonsense letters, childish scribblings. "What is the point of chess, Miss Harrington?" he asked.

"To win?"

Skorzeny shook his head. "No. Not to win. That is the inevitable effect of the point of chess. Please try again."

Another of his infernal Socratic puzzles. "If not to win, then what?"

"Think."

She knew how his mind worked. She got it. "Then, not to lose."

He smiled a reptilian smile that, at some point, someone must have told him was as close to a simulacrum of pleasure as he was ever likely to display. "Very good. Not to lose. In fact, no one every really loses at chess. There is no killing blow, no coup de grâce, no severed head to exhibit to the throngs and multitudes, as the Mahdi's men severed General Gordon's head at Khartoum and lodged it in a tree branch, so that the birds could peck out its eyes, and the tree would be watered with the last of Gordon's lifeblood, what little might remain."

Amanda shuddered: Skorzeny had lost none of his taste for the grisly and the macabre. Whatever had happened in London, whatever had transpired at the old monastery while she lay in her drug-induced coma, he had been defeated and yet somehow he had escaped, determined to fight on. That was a quality in a man she usually admired, but in him it was only hateful.

". . . not to lose," he was still rattling on. "Instead, the lesser player resigns, turns his king over, surrenders, the way the smaller and weaker of two fighting lions eventually gives up his pride of lionesses and slinks off into the veldt, there to displace another lion weaker than himself, or to die. To fight on, or to give up: those are the only two choices life offers us. As you can see, I have made my choice." This, she knew, was as close to admission of temporary failure as he was ever likely to come.

He pointed to the map. The places circled were far from his usual civilized haunts—remote parts of Asia, the Subcontinent, sub-Saharan Africa. "Are these the places we're going?" she asked.

"No, those are the places I've been," he replied. "Countries without extradition treaties with the United States. Gruesome places, without a modicum of refinement and, in most cases, evidence of civilization of any kind. In short, the only places that savage, President Tyler, would let me visit. But I turned it to my advantage. Preparing for this day."

"And which day is that, Mr. Skorzeny?" It was amazing how quickly she fell back into her old role as his advisor, confidante and, when necessary, executrix.

Instead of answering, he asked: "What do you know of the End Times, Miss Harrington?"

"The End Times, sir?" she asked. "The Last Trump, you mean?"

"Indeed, I do." He seemed very pleased with the prospect of this conversation. "Apocalypse. Armageddon."

"Have you had a religious epiphany, then?"

Now he laughed out loud, a horrible barking laugh. "I should say not. Organized superstition is hardly my line, but adherents to the millenarian faiths often prove helpful. Useful idiots, as Lenin deemed them. And it is a fact that many cultures foretell the end of the world. Both Christianity and Shi'a Islam anticipate the day when Jesus will come again, although our Muslim brethren consign the Nazarene to a secondary role in the final drama. Still, they share a vision of turmoil, of war, until the end finally comes in a rain of quenching fire."

"And then what?"

"That's what we're going to find out."

"What do you want me to do?" she asked. She wasn't sure he would answer, but his mood seemed temporarily expansive.

"You'll learn out when we get there."

"And where would that be, sir?"

Abruptly, startlingly, his hand landed with a thump on the desk, his right index finger pointing to a place not highlighted on the map. "Do you believe in God, Miss Harrington?" he said.

CHAPTER TWELVE

Manhattan

The screens that kept Manhattan safe stayed on. But Byrne already knew it was too late. Something had happened, something more than a probe, and now it was simply a matter of finding out just how bad it was. Silently, he cursed under his breath. This was not how he liked to fight. Byrne's natural impulse toward hotheadedness he had outgrown with age, but he still liked to play offense, not defense.

This was no ordinary breach, that much he already knew. He not only knew it, he felt it. Like a lot of Irish cops, Byrne trusted his Celtic instincts, the little voice that whispered you'd be okay when you crashed through that apartment door in the Bronx or the one that warned you not to dash around the corner just this instant. He had gotten this far, and stayed alive this long, by listening to those little voices. Now he had a job to do.

It was the job he never wanted and yet was now closest to his heart: protecting New York City. If over the years he had earned a reputation as a cowboy, well so be it. A cowboy was what New York needed now, not some by-the-book bureaucrat, not some IA weasel or desk jockey who had never pulled his piece or fired his weapon. When Byrne got into trouble, as he had a couple of times, Matt White had had his back, and when this job opened up there really was only one man in the entire department White trusted with.

"Now what?" said Lannie.

"Let's brainstorm this thing and try to figure out what we're up against before the shit hits the fan."

"You think it will?" asked Sid.

"Your father would never have asked such a dumb question."

"That's because the people he worked with couldn't talk back to him."

Byrne smiled. "That's where you're wrong, Sid. Nobody could make a dead man talk like Sy Sheinberg. Anything about a cause of death that Sy didn't know or couldn't discover wasn't worth knowing or discovering. That's what made him the best medical examiner I ever worked with.

"But our job is different—it's the opposite, in fact. We're not like normal cops, who basically show up to cart away the stiff and interview the witnesses. We're here to stop things before they happen. Remember what the president said years ago: we have to be lucky all the time; the terrorists only have to be lucky once. Well, on 9/11 they got lucky, if you call shooting an unsuspecting man in the back lucky. I call it cowardly. But on my watch, lucky ain't got nothing to do with it. So let's stop some shit, whatever it is. Lannie, what've we got?"

Aslan Saleh tapped on a terminal and brought up the camera feeds, displayed on a large screen on the wall across from Byrne's desk. It was like a fly's-eye view of midtown, fractured into dozens of individual CCTV scans, but they were all virtuosos at reading the images, able to sense hinky body language before they could see it. And not by accident. The Department of Homeland Security had spent a fortune developing something called Project Hostile Intent, a kind of vaguely practical version of "pre-crime" that moviegoers saw in *Minority Report*. Lannie, in fact, had been recruited from DHS by Byrne himself, when he was looking for a native Arabic-speaker/computer geek to join the CTU, and Lannie had brought some of the principles of the program over with him.

Byrne thought much of Project Hostile Intent was typical Washington bullshit, the kind of gee-whiz crap that got gobs of money thrown its way, but at its core was simply good old-fashioned police work, the kind that used to be SOP across the country before the ACLU and its fleet of lawyers sank their teeth into the cop on the beat. In a normal civilian setting, "pre-crime" would be laughed out of court, dismissed on all sorts of procedural grounds, with the racism flag fluttering ominously in the background. The program relied heavily on facial expressions and body language, but also employed a battery of sensors that could read body temperature and brain waves; it had even developed a laser radar to monitor pulse and breathing rates from a distance. Now dubbed FAST, for Future Attribute Screening Technologies, the program was still in development, but was being discreetly deployed at various airports and other ports of entry around the country.

Byrne had simply stolen it. Lannie and his handpicked crew had installed advanced prototypes at key points around Manhattan—at Wall Street, City Hall and the Tweed Courthouse, Brooklyn Bridge, Gracie Mansion (the mayor, who took everything personally, had insisted on that), and, of course, in Times Square. It was mind-numbingly boring to spend half your life watching people go about their daily business, or lack of it; but it had to be done, if only as a complement to the computers that never tired of monitoring human beings, finding them as endlessly fascinating as cows watching traffic on a country road.

The CTU's computers were outfitted with advanced

facial-recognition software, in part developed right here in Chelsea and—not being hampered by the strictures of political correctness or probable cause—the CTU was empowered to act on whatever information, leads, and hunches the combination of men and machines developed. Byrne had drilled into his men that they were to stay out of the courts if at all possible, which was why dead-solid takedowns never got reported, either into the main NYPD database or, God forbid, to the media. Terrorists had rights in every court and police precinct in America, except here. Sure, there were mistakes from time to time, but they either were hushed up, paid off, or buried in unmarked graves.

"Okay, let's play catch-up," said Byrne.

On the screens, everything was as it had been ten minutes earlier. Out in the command room, teams were busy retrotracing the DoS tracks, piecing together a model that would help prevent future blindsides. But that was barn-door stuff; right now, Byrne was more interested in what was going to happen next.

"What's your hunch, Captain?" asked Saleh.

"Times Square." It was less a hunch than a wager he would take to Vegas. Nothing would shout maximum impact more than an attack on Times Square. Nobody in America cared about the mayor, or even knew where Gracie Mansion was.

Brooklyn Bridge was iconic, but would be plenty tough to bring down, especially with the unadvertised but very real police boat presence on both sides of the East River. If a dog so much as took a dump on the bridge, the likelihood was that the cops knew about it before the pooch's owner did.

All at once, sixteen different angles of Times Square jumped onto the screen. Nobody said a word as they scanned the crowds. The usual: tourists gawking, theater crowds milling, a few hookers trolling, pickpockets sniffing the wind.

Gazing at the human comedy day in and day out, Byrne often thought that it was a miracle that cities existed at all, that citizens were not constantly at each other's throats, the hunters and the prey, but in this jungle the ratio of prey to predator was thousands to one, and so ignorance, and the law of averages, was bliss.

"What's that?" said Byrne, pointing. "Gimme a zoom."

It was a pushcart vendor. Normally, no big deal. There were pushcart vendors all over the city and had been for two centuries. But this guy was different.

For one thing, he was running. Vendors paid the city for their allotted spaces, but these were general licenses. There was no need to rush to your spot, like a homeless guy who had dibs on a certain step of one of the West Side Protestant churches, which now functioned as impromptu shelters for those too proud or too strung out to enter a real shelter. But this guy was out of breath. He was also doing something even fishier—he was looking at his cell phone like his life depended on it.

"Nobody's in that big a rush to sell hot dogs," said Byrne. "Let's snuggle up a little closer to this baby." Lannie zoomed in. Although the cameras shot in black and white, they could clearly relay facial features, skin tone, even hair color.

Now the man was doing something hot dog vendors didn't usually do. He put down his cell phone and opened up his cart, but didn't appear terribly interested, for all his haste, in the presence of customers. Instead, he was fiddling with something under the cart.

"Who's in the area?" asked Byrne. "What units, foot, horse—what've we got?"

Sid was already punching up the data. NYPD cops in Manhattan never went anywhere without GPS locators on them, which really cut down the time they could spend with their girlfriends and mistresses, but which meant that One

Police Plaza brass and others could find them instantly. At first the cops had bitched about it, but after a couple of lives were saved in officer-shot situations, they quickly came around.

"Couple of Tacs over on Eighth, Johnson, Guttierez, Adderly and Kemp between 42nd and 45th, and Bradley and Petrovich on the ponies."

"Converge," said Byrne, rising. "On the double."

Byrne was already through the door of his office and into the command center by the time Lannie and Sid saw what he had seen.

Protruding from the hot dog vendor's waistband as he got up from underneath his cart was the unmistakable grip of a .45 automatic.

CHAPTER THIRTEEN

Times Square

Jake Sinclair's face was forty feet high on the JumboTron above Times Square, smiling at some joke only he was privy to. Since he pretty much owned the media in the U.S., that was not an outrageous supposition. Underneath his picture, the Zipper was proclaiming to the world: WITH BLAST AT TYLER, SINCLAIR HOLDINGS SELLS MANHATTAN HEADQUARTERS TO GERMAN MEDIA CONSORTIUM. CORP. HQ TO RE-LOCATE TO LOS ANGELES.

Those who looked up at the JumboTron at that moment would have seen Sinclair, speaking now, praising Tyler's rival in the upcoming election. "The Tyler Administration," he was saying, "has forfeited all claims to credibility. The attacks last year on the homeland proved that this administration is not to be trusted with our national security. Despite his gross and flagrant violation of civil liberties, President Tyler has not kept us safe and, in my opinion, it's time for a change. That's why every patriotic American should send a message to Tyler and his party at the polls this November. Not just 'throw the bums out,' but *hell yes, throw the bums out.*" He smiled the oleaginous smile that had made him a favorite of most of the media, for Jake Sinclair had long ago learned the first and most important lesson of Hollywood, which had since translated to journalism: if you can fake sincerity, you've got it made.

"I hate that sonofabitch," said Morris Acker to his wife, Shirley, indicating Jake Sinclair on the JumboTron as they traversed the new pedestrian zone and waited to cross over to 42nd Street. They were heading for the New Amsterdam theater, where *Mary Poppins* was still playing. Once upon a time, this had been the crossroads of the world, the place where Broadway and Seventh Avenue intersected, collided, and then split to go their separate ways. In the old days—the *very* old days—it had been a mass of pedestrians, pushcarts, horse-drawn vehicles and motorcars, but gradually order had been imposed upon civic chaos. Now, where traffic once had rushed, pretty girls sat and gawked at the buildings while the boys sat and gawked at them. Meanwhile, cars fought for space in the few lanes still allotted to them. It was a typically lunatic idea of the former mayor, a nasty little busybody who had finally been driven from office when he attempted to raise the price of pizza to prohibitive levels on the grounds that it would improve the health of the average New Yorker. Then he raised the subway fare, on the grounds that people would be even healthier if they had to walk forty blocks instead of spending five bucks for a subway ride.

"We should have parked closer," said Shirley. "If we had, we'd be there by now."

Morris shrugged. He hadn't gotten this far in life by wasting money. The parking garages around here were insanely expensive. For a few bucks a trip uptown to the cheaper lots on the Upper West Side was well worth it, even with the new subway fares. The Ackers were in from Rye for the day to catch a matinee on Broadway, have an early dinner, and then return home to Westchester. Mr. Acker was a recently retired employee of Time Warner, who over the course of his career had managed to upgrade his life by two neighborhoods, four automobiles, one boat, and zero wives from his humble beginnings on Long Island. If he never set foot there again, it would be too soon.

As he stepped off the curb, Mr. Acker looked down so as not to miss the step. His eyesight wasn't what it used to be, and nothing would be more ridiculous—or would kill him faster—than a stupid pratfall. When you got to be his age, what was once funny was now lethal. "Schmuck," he said to himself.

Across the street, a pushcart vendor was just setting up at the corner. The man was slightly out of breath from his sprint uptown, but he had arrived in plenty of time, and now all he had to do was wait for his customers. His cell phone buzzed silently in his breast pocket, and he took it out and looked at the display. It was not a caller, but a text message. He read it, then began his preparations . . .

At that moment, Marie Duplessis, a recent immigrant from Haiti, was trudging up the subway steps at 42nd Street, and heading for one of her three jobs. She had taken the train in from LaGuardia Airport, where she worked cleaning the bathrooms at Terminal Six, and was now headed to the Condé Nast building to perform the same task for the journalistic princes and princesses still lucky enough to have paying jobs churning out copy that instantly outdated long before it achieved print. Luckily, she had had just enough time to stop off at her apartment in Jamaica to check on her pregnant daughter, Eugénie, who was all of thirteen years old.

Eugénie's pregnancy had broken her heart. True, life in America, even in Queens, was preferable to Port-au-Prince, but there were trade-offs, differing social mores being one of them. At the Catholic girls' school back home, Eugénie at least had a fighting chance to retain her honor, but here . . . The boys had found her quickly, like predators on a domestic creature that had suddenly been released back into the jungle, with predictable results. Back home there had been community, family, language, religion. If you stayed within those boundaries, there was still a chance that a girl wouldn't have to go to the altar with child. Here in America, the only certainty for people like Eugénie was a trip to the abortion clinic, and that was something her mother was simply not going to allow. To Marie, every life was sacred, even this as-yet unborn offspring of her only daughter and some gangbanger, the kind of boy who would never have been admitted into her society back in Haiti. America might still be the land of economic opportunity but the trade-off in social dysfunction was not worth it. Which is why Marie had just made up her mind to take Eugénie home to Haiti to have her baby. She'd tell Eugénie just as soon as she got home this evening . . .

Stranded in the middle of the great intersection of Broadway and Seventh Avenue, Uwe, Helga, and Hubertus Friedhof watched the crossing signals carefully, awaiting the green light. They had been to the movies, where, despite all the years of English they had taken in school in Germany, they had hardly understood a single word of the dialogue, which bore not the slightest resemblance to the English they were used to hearing back home.

They were discussing this strange new language of the New World as they crossed the street, heading for one of the chain restaurants they had heard so much about back in Wiesbaden, one of those places that made Americans so amazingly obese, which they simply had to see and experience for themselves.

"Look!" exclaimed Hubertus, who was nearly 19 and about to leave for university. With any luck, under the German system, his parents would only be financially responsible for him for another seven to ten years.

Hubertus pointed up at the JumboTron and Jake Sinclair's face. Everybody knew Jake Sinclair's face, even foreigners, and in point of fact the movie they had just seen and hardly understood a word of had been made by Jake Sinclair's studio. ". . . we betray our real values, the values that made this country," Jake Sinclair was quoted in the electronic crawl—in real English—across the bottom of the giant screen, "the values that made this country the greatest country on earth . . ."

Uwe was just about to ask Helga why the Americans were always banging on about being the greatest country on earth when the light changed. The crowd moved forward, in that impatient New York way, but Uwe's path was blocked by a young man standing stock-still. Being German, Uwe's instinct was to plow ahead. He was sick of these Americans and their uncivilized ways, and it was high time he showed one of the natives how things were done in Germany. Back home, if somebody was standing between you and wherever you were going, you simply knocked him aside, whether you were a pedestrian with the right of way or a bicyclist zipping down a marked bike path onto which some hapless tourist had inadvertently wandered, or even a speeding motorist, exercising his God-given *vorfahrt vom rechts*.

The pedestrian signal had already turned to the blinking red hand, and the numerical countdown begun. Uwe pressed forward in that familiar way that Europeans have and that

Americans, with their greater need for personal space, invariably resented. The young man, however, did not budge. Instead he barked over his shoulder. "What is your fucking problem?"

Uwe stopped, taken aback. In Germany, nobody spoke back. They simply got out of the way. But these rude *Amis* were a different tribe. Well, their days of strutting around the globe as if they owned it with their no-longer-almighty dollar were over. "*Ja, okay*," said Uwe, "so now we can go, yes?"

Ali Ibrahim al-Aziz had come to America on an express visa from his native Saudi Arabia. It amazed him that, even after 9/11, Americas were still so friendly, so trusting. Part of that friendliness, true, was owing to the country's desperate need for oil, which ensured that the old partners in Aramco would still have need for each other's goods and services, and a little thing like 3,000 dead people and a gigantic hole in the ground in lower Manhattan would not be allowed to come between them. As long as America ran on oil—and as long as the Americans, unaccountably, tied both hands behind their backs by not drilling for it in their own country—Saudi-American friendship would go on and on.

It felt good to be standing here, just a few miles north of where his holy brothers had accomplished their spectacular act of martyrdom. Before he embarked on his own martyrdom, he had made sure to tour the holy site, still essentially empty after all these years. It was typical of the degenerate state of America and its inhabitants, he thought, to still be squabbling about something unimportant like a memorial when there was work to be done. They could have shown the world that even a grievous blow such as 9/11 would not stop them in their godless pursuit of commerce and harlotry, but instead they reacted just as the sheikh had predicted, in sorrow and fear.

When the Towers fell—something not even the sheikh had predicted—there was much joy across the *ummah*. But in the succeeding years, as blow after blow was plotted and then failed, the opportunity to bring forth the tribulations was slipping away. What was needed now was a killing blow. Beneath his breath, he began to pray.

And then he felt a tap on his back, more of a bump, and he began to fear that his prayers were not sincere enough, that he had been discovered by the enemy. He slipped his hand inside his jacket and felt the grip of the gun as he turned to see what was the matter.

The taxi let Hope and her children off at the corner of Eighth Avenue and 42nd Street. To the east, a series of multiplexes beckoned. They weren't the kind of theaters she was used to back home—for one thing, there was noplace to park—but she'd heard that once you were inside, it was like being at an especially nice shopping mall. Behind them, the ugly monstrosity that was the Port Authority bus station loomed.

"What's that?" cried Rory, pointing across Eighth Avenue at something called the Adult Entertainment Center. "Never mind," said Hope, grabbing him by the arm and dragging him east along 42nd Street. He would learn about porn soon enough, if he hadn't already. Up ahead, the theater marquees beckoned . . .

The man blocking the Friedhof family had still not budged. Instead, he was staring at his cell phone, as if waiting for a call. He was also cocking his head to one side, as if listening for something, but the only thing he could possibly hear, besides the traffic, was the rumble of the IRT subway under the ventilation grate beneath his feet. In any case, he wasn't moving.

His patience exhausted, Uwe pressed forward again, deliberately bumping into the man. Pedestrianism was a full-body contact sport in much of Europe, especially in Germany, so what Uwe was doing was, by his lights, a perfectly reasonable way to show one's displeasure and to remind the fellow to get a move on. Unfortunately for Uwe, the man did not see it that way. Ali Ibrahim al-Aziz turned back to him, but instead of speaking he pulled a revolver from beneath his Windbreaker and shot Uwe Friedhof right in the face.

At that moment, Byrne was on the blower to all available patrolmen in that part of Times Square, and was calling in reinforcements from elsewhere in the city. If his hunch was right, there was no time to lose.

"I want a cordon around Times Square. Nobody in and nobody out. Shut down all the West Side subway lines, including the IND, the BMT, and the IRT. No need to be subtle about it: I want the full surge. But this is not a drill. Repeat, *this is not a drill.*"

Lannie and Sid caught up with him. "What is it?" asked Sid.

"It's a go, isn't it?" said Lannie. If this was for real, it would be his first taste of action.

Byrne turned to his two protégés. "Not for you—I need the two of you right here. Lannie, check all the communications monitors and see who's been calling into Times Square on cell. Sid, go back over the SIGINT files for the past 48 hours and see if you can get the slightest lead on whatever the hell it is that's going down."

A voice from the back of the room—"There's a report of

shots fired, somewhere in the pedestrian zone. That's all
we've got right now."

Mentally, Byrne gauged how long it would take him to
get from Chelsea to Times Square. With the surge already
under way, there was no point in taking a car—if he hustled
he could get there on foot in ten minutes. He wasn't as fit
as he used to be but, damn it, he could still run down a perp
if he had to.

"I'm going in," he shouted, heading for the door.

Uwe Friedhof never had time to realize what had happened as he toppled and fell. Helga started to scream and
then she, too, dropped with a bullet in the chest. Hubertus,
who had dreamed of studying the law in Munich, had just
enough time to register a dark beard and a pair of piercing
brown eyes when the next shot hit him in the gut. He collapsed into the street, where he was hit by a speeding taxi anticipating the change of the light. His body flew into the air
as the cab stopped, then landed on the windshield and rolled
off and onto the ground.

The cabbie, a recent immigrant from Bangladesh,
jumped from his taxi, recoiling in horror as he realized what
had happened. Three young women dropped their ice cream
cones as the enormity of what they were witnessing over-
took them. Others screamed, cried, fled. The gunman, however, never moved, but instead seemed to be talking to
himself, muttering really, as the roar of the Seventh Avenue
express train approached. As the brakeman slowed the train,
the roar changed to a screech, and Ali held his cell phone
aloft in the air for all to see, and bear witness.

At that moment, Marie Duplessis decided that her Metro-
Card needed a refill, and that as long as she was here, she

might as well go back down the stairs and put some more money on it. She hated running for a train only to realize she was short of funds, so while she had money in her pocket and plenty of time to get to her next job she could take care of it now and not have to worry about it later. She turned and headed back down the stairs. She stuck her card into one of the addfare machines, punched in how much she wanted, and inserted a $20 bill.

Hope and her children were moving east on 42nd Street, savoring the marquees of the theaters on both sides of the broad crosstown street, trying to decide what to see. This was not like even the big cineplexes back home. This was a veritable feast of cinematic choices. There were a couple of vulgar sex comedies, which she was under no circumstances going to allow them to see, along with the usual assortment of full-length cartoons, vampire movies, gruesome slasher flicks, and movies about giant robots that could turn into cars and other heavy machinery. She had not been to the movies on a regular basis for years, and from the choices available, she could see she wasn't missing much. Why couldn't they make movies like *Tender Mercies* anymore? Well, she supposed those days were long gone; not enough sex, and nothing to blow up. It was going to have to be the talking cars.

They went inside the AMC Theaters complex on the south side of the street and bought their tickets. Even though she was expecting the worst, Hope was still amazed at how expensive they were, twice as much as back home. How in the world could people afford to live here was beyond her.

They took a series of endless up escalators, higher and higher, until she was sure they were heading for the top of the Empire State Building, which she knew was around here somewhere. At last, they got to the top floor, where a giant candy counter practically begged them to spend some more of their money, but Hope steered Rory clear of temptation and pointed him and Emma toward the theater. She was about to wonder what had happened to grownup culture when suddenly the whole building shook and everything went dark.

A car bomb is no ordinary bomb, nor even an enhanced Improvised Explosive Device (IED). In fact, it is three bombs in one. The first bomb is the one packed tightly in the trunk or under the vehicle—Semtex, or C-4 plastic explosive. Detonating with the force of 150 pounds of TNT, it will destroy everything within a 100-foot radius, shattering glass, penetrating and exploding brickwork and masonry, tearing and rending flesh. Its fireball will incinerate everything it touches, and as the blast radius extends outward, it will singe all living creatures within a tenth of a mile. But that is just the beginning.

The second, and worse, effect is the air-blast shock wave, which causes devastating failure in exterior walls and interior columns and girders, resulting in floor failure. The third effect is shrapnel. For, packed tightly into the plastic explosive, is an array of common objects—nails, screws, ball bearings, washers—that turn suddenly lethal when propelled at several hundred miles an hour. They rip through flesh and bones effortlessly, hurtling outward like some ontological recapitulation of the phylogenic Big Bang. And, in a confined space such as a movie theater or a New York city street, the amount of damage they can do to human beings is almost incalculable.

The United States military calls them "VBIEDs," or "Vehicle Borne Improvised Explosive Devices." When there is someone at the wheel, willing to die for his cause, they are referred to as SVBIEDs, the "S" standing for "suicide."

They are often referred to as "the poor man's air force," for they accomplish on the ground what cannot be managed from the air. But the effect is the same.

Byrne's mind raced as he ran. He'd seen the gun on the man's hip, but worse, he had seen the assault weapons beneath the pushcart. A man might carry a gun in Manhattan, even legally, but there was no way that a brace of AK-47s was ever going to be allowed. And what did he have two of them for? A lone nut with a semi-automatic weapon was high on the list of things that every cop worried about, but a lone nut with two of them was capable of anything.

His radio crackled. The cops on the scene were converging. In the distance, he could hear the sirens as the surge charged toward Times Square. The surge was something the NYPD had practiced since 2004—the sudden, unannounced arrival of dozens of squad cars on a single area, up to 200 heavily armed and flak-jacketed cops bursting from the vehicles. It was meant not only for tactical practice but as a very visible show of force designed to put the fear of God—or Allah—into anyone witnessing it. Police work had changed dramatically since Byrne was a rookie—instead of the kind cops on the beat, the NYPD had become a paramilitary force, with some of the best tools and tactics in the world.

He listened up ahead, trying to detect the sounds of gunfire. A single shot might be lost in the noise of the city, but multiple shots would be unmistakable. Even with the exertion, he started to breathe a little easier. Maybe his men had already taken the perp down, pre-crime.

Then he heard the explosion, and he knew this was going to be a very long and shitty day. There was more to come, and it was his job to be in the middle of it. If he could not save those people, it was at the very least his duty to die trying.

Ali Ibrahim al-Aziz also heard the explosion. In fact, he could see it, across Times Square to the west. That would be the signal to the others, the sign that the glorious strike was beginning. They had planned this martyrdom operation for years, since right after 9/11, but the Americans had been too quick for them, had reacted too fast. They had instituted all sorts of safeguards, been aggressive in their counterattack, disrupted the domestic cells, shut off much of the funding. What the movement had hoped would be a killing second blow had been on hold, first for months, then for years.

But then they had learned how to penetrate the defenses, how to hack the security codes. Not on their own, of course, but with the help of their friends in Russia and central Europe. Left to its own devices, the *ummah* would never be able to create even a single computer, much less a network. The only proper study in a university was the study of the Holy Koran, the divinely revealed word of Allah to Mohammed, his Messenger. But al-Aziz and the others were no longer students, they were holy warriors, *jihadis*; no longer dwelling peacefully in the *dar-al-Islam* but fighting the infidels in the *dar-al-Harb*, the territory of war and chaos, where the final battle against the West would be fought and won: on its turf.

It was true: so decadent had the West become that there were many who actively supported the jihadis and their networks, not men of Islam but men of no faith at all. Men who would be among the first killed when the final triumph was proclaimed, men who cared so little for themselves, their wives, their families, and their decayed culture that they would rather submit to the holy blade. They deserved nothing less than scorn and death.

The subway train beneath his feet had stopped. He could hear the conductor's voice over the loudspeaker. He said a quick silent prayer and then pushed the talk button on his cell phone just as he shouted *"Allahu Akbar!"*

Marie Duplessis waited for the machine to spit back her card at her. She was old enough to remember the days of tokens, and she guessed that, on balance, the present system was better than the old one. But still, it was a racket, since a lot of times you never quite managed to use every dollar of your fare before you bought a new card. Marie, who had a head for figures, reckoned that the MTA made millions a year in unused credits on the fare cards, but somehow it was still always broke, always asking for fare increases, and usually getting them.

The card snapped back out at her and she took it. There were plenty of rides on it now, and when she got home she would give it to her daughter to let her take a ride out to Coney Island to get some sea air and some exercise before the baby started weighing her down. Then, before she really started to show, before the other kids in her school started making fun of her, before the boy who had knocked her up started bragging all over Jamaica about how he'd treated this "ho," they would catch a flight home, maybe leave the child with her mother to be raised properly, maybe put it up for adoption with the church. It would all work itself out, and they could get on with their lives.

Alas, Eugénie would never learn of this plan, because these, as it turned out, were the last thoughts Marie Duplessis ever had.

At the sound of the explosion Ben, the hot dog vendor, pulled out his AK-47 and opened fire. God, but it felt good to finally be able to strike back. All the years in Green Haven and other prisons had hardened him, made him even more vicious and relentless than he had been growing up in Brownsville/East New York, Brooklyn. Guys from Brownsville prided themselves on how tough they were, how relentless, how remorseless. They had to live up to the standards of the old neighborhood, the place that had given America Murder Incorporated, guys who would put your eyes out with ice picks, who would hang you from meathooks and leave you there to dangle until you finally died.

The only rules Ben Addison ever knew were the rules of the street, the law of the jungle. School held no interest for him, and when his mama managed to scrape together enough scratch to send him to that Catholic school one year, he never got along with the other kids, mostly Latinos; never liked having to wear a uniform; and seriously disagreed with the turn-the-other-cheek tenets that they preached there.

One hot summer night Ben and some of his crew had gone into the city—gone into New York, as some Brooklynites still said—to see what was up. Even after one of the former mayors had cleaned up the place, there were still parts of Manhattan that outsiders were well advised to stay out of, and when they found a group of smashed college kids bar-hopping along the old gangland main drag of Allen Street, near Rivington Street, they decided to mug them. The boys gave it up quick, but one of the girls had mouthed off to him, called him out, dared him to do something, and so he did. He shot her in the head and then, because the guys had seen them, he shot the rest of them too. One, though, had lived, and it was his testimony that had sent Ben to the slammer. The mouthpiece had managed to negotiate the beef down to manslaughter, on the grounds that the kids had provoked him, and that they reasonably should have known that a man with his underprivileged background might react violently to any perceived assault on his manhood. At sentenc-

ing, Addison's court-appointed shrinks made the pitch that
"black rage" had contributed to the events of that night, that
Ben was not solely responsible for his actions, and the judge
saw it their way. Ben got eight-to-twelve years, was out in
seven.

And that had been the only break he had ever caught in
this life until he got to Green Haven, which was where he
met the Imam. It was not until then that he learned what the
words mercy and compassion truly meant—not weak weasel
words, the way the Christians used them, but strong, muscu-
lar language that befits a warrior race. Courtesy of the people of New York State, and cheered on in the editorial pages
of the *New York Times*, the Imam came regularly to minister
to his burgeoning flock. He was so much more compelling
than the pallid padre and the timorous rabbi, both of whom
spent their time trying to understand the men and their
crimes, to "work with them," to tell them that God forgave
them. The hell with that.

Most of the converts were, like Ben, African Americans,
but there was a smattering of white boys as well, guys looking
for something better than passivity and forgiveness toward
others, cons who regretted their time but not necessarily
their crime. In Islam, they found a new way of looking at the
world, at their society, and at themselves, and they liked what
they saw. The Imam Abdul never forgave anybody; forgiveness jive was not what he was selling. Instead, the Imam was
selling punishment, misery, pain. The Imam didn't want to
understand the old you: he wanted him to die, and be reborn,
not as a Christian but as a fighter. You died in Christ, but
arose again in Allah, whose plan for mankind required
killers, not healers. "We love Death as you love Life," the
Imam taught them to chant in Arabic, after he had trained
them in the recitation of selected verses from the Holy
Koran. Ben's childhood Christianity, what little there was of

it, had sloughed away like an old skin, to reveal the proud Islamic warrior beneath.

And so Ben Addison, Jr., had become a new man, with a new name. He was now Ismail bin-Abdul al-Amriki, Ishmael the American, son of Abdul, and his vengeance on the society that had spawned him would be terrible.

Once he had nothing to live for; now he had everything to die for.

"You know how I hate that word, *schmuck*." said Shirley Acker, just as they heard the shots behind them. Not that they recognized them as shots. Like most New Yorkers, the Ackers lived in a gun-free world, at least as far as their social circle was concerned. They were against firearms in all forms, didn't see why a little thing like the Second Amendment couldn't easily be ignored, failed to understand why anyone would hunt for food when you simply buy it at Fairway, and were quite sure that, were they ever to possess a gun, one of them would quickly kill the other, or perhaps him- or herself, entirely by accident. And should there ever be trouble in a post-Giuliani New York (they hated the sonofabitch, but had to admit that fascist had cleaned up the town), they would simply call 911 and the cops would come running.

"Look, Morris, there's a Sabrett's guy," said Shirley. "I could use a nosh. How about you?"

With a muzzle velocity of 2,346 feet per second, and a 40-cartridge magazine, you could fire 600 rounds per minute and pretty much hit everything within 300 meters. Unless you were a sniper, in combat you were basically firing at a man standing right in front of you, and the Kalashnikov was designed to be operational in all kinds of weather and under all kinds of conditions. There might be better assault rifles—and there were—but none could touch it, even today, for ease and reliability.

Death from a weapon like the AK-47, even the cheap Chinese-made imitation of the Soviet original, was not like it was in the movies. The impact of the bullets did not lift you off your feet and knock you back 25 feet. Instead, they put you down, hard. One shot might shear off the top of your skull. Another might drill a hole in your forehead and blow out the back of your head like a pumpkin, but in either case you dropped, dead.

At the training camps in Pakistan, Ismail had learned to shoot. Not for him was the gangbangers' spray paint job, stylin' as they shot and pretty much missing everything except babies in their carriages and nuns on their way to Mass. With the AK-47, you fire either semi-automatic—one trigger pull, one shot—or full auto, but Ismail had learned to husband his ammo and make every shot count. Besides, he wasn't alone. From all over midtown Manhattan, Chelsea, the Flatiron District, and Hell's Kitchen, more holy warriors had converged and were in place, freshly armed. In fact, he could hear them firing now.

The first people the former Ben Addison, Jr., killed were an elderly couple who were heading for him, right in the line of fire. The old man never saw him, so intent was he on not falling on his face as he stepped into the street, and the woman only had time to allow a fleeting look of understanding flit across her face and then she, too, went down.

Then he opened fire in earnest. At first he fired single-shot, semi-automatic. It was fun to see how well he had been trained, to watch the enemy—he didn't think of them as "victims," since everybody was a victim these days, most especially himself—fall, ripped apart, just as first the paper targets had shredded and then the metal targets had clanged and finally the live-fire captives, scrambling desperately for their worthless lives, had been cut down in a burst of well-placed fire.

Now people screamed and ran. But withering fire came from everywhere, from all directions, high and low—the Brothers, activated by the sound of the explosions. Gunfire came from everywhere, from several stories high in some of the surrounding buildings, from the streets, even from the storm sewers. Screams rent the air as bodies dropped. Panic broke out. Nobody knew where to run, where it might be safe. There was noplace to hide. Vehicles collided, pancaked. And still the gunfire continued, a rain of fire from hell.

Phase one was now well and truly under way. And then the ground beneath his feet rippled, buckled, and exploded.

The No. 3 train was just starting up to leave the station for its run uptown to 72nd Street when Ali Ibrahim al-Aziz pressed the talk button on his cell phone and activated the bomb that had been stowed away on the train in the few minutes the sensors had been down. The resulting explosion sent several cars of the train hurtling skyward, ripping apart the street where the ancient cut-and-cover was at its shallowest. Immediately, the signal shorted out all along this stretch of the line, which meant that the trailing No. 2 had no way of knowing that the station wasn't clear. The resulting collision forced the cars from the demolished No. 3 train up and out into the street, carrying a load of incinerated corpses into what had become a running gun battle.

The force of the car bomb that had struck the AMC Theatres on 42nd Street was nothing compared to this. Triggered by the cell phone call, more than 1,000 kilos of plastic explosive had obliterated much of Times Square. A giant sinkhole yawned across the famous intersection, swallowing up cars, buses, and small buildings alike. The military recruiting center above the station was one of the first to go, collapsing in upon itself and tumbling into the abyss. Beneath the ruined train, tunnels fell in upon themselves, then plunged down, into the network of other tunnels—electrical, steam—that had run beneath the streets of Manhattan for more than a century.

The ripple effect was devastating, as electrical systems failed, manhole covers were blown 50 feet into the air dozens of blocks away and scalding steam flayed alive anyone unlucky enough to be near a vent when it sundered. Chunks of pavement became lethal weapons, buried electrical wires became snaking, spitting instruments of death. Worst of all were the ruptured gas lines, which quickly ignited and set ablaze the buildings directly above. The air quickly filled with acrid, lethal smoke.

And still, gunfire from all directions continued to rake the killing field that had once been Times Square.

CHAPTER FOURTEEN

Teterboro Airport—later

Technically, Teterboro was a township in New Jersey, but it was basically an airport and not much else. As Van Nuys was to Los Angeles, Teterboro was to New York—an unglamorous location for the very glamorous private airplanes of the moneyed set.

"What?" said Devlin. "Say again?"

Maryam looked at him as he spoke softly on the secure phone. Throughout the flight aboard the custom-built Gulfstream C-37B, he had kept his own counsel, remaining mostly silent as he absorbed real-time information streaming over his direct connection to Fort Meade. Since she was not, officially, an employee of either the NSA or the Central Security Service, it was none of her business to inquire. He would tell her soon enough, if he chose to.

Secrets. They were the basis of their relationship. Even though she knew it was not his real name, she still called him "Frank," because that was how he had first introduced himself. She had since learned that "Frank Ross" was one of a series of operational pseudonyms he had used, never to be repeated, but Frank he first was to her and Frank he had remained. Perhaps, someday, she would learn who he really was. But then, she supposed, he would have to kill her.

As for herself, there were plenty of things she hadn't told him. Most things. In fact, everything about their relationship—even their love affair—was based on indirection, misdirection, or outright lies. And neither of them would have it any other way.

They both had jobs to do. Thrice already in their lives their jobs had intersected, the first time in Paris, the second last year in Los Angeles and, later, in France. They had been there for each other, when they needed each other, and in their business that was just about the highest compliment one could pay to a colleague—or a lover.

And she did love him. Whatever had been the original impetus for her assignment, it didn't matter. Iranian politics, especially since the revolution, were impenetrable to outsiders, even to him. But she had been raised in them. For more than thirty years her country had cried out for justice and vengeance. She only hoped she could give it a little bit of both.

Most Americans over the age of 50, she understood, had zero sympathy for Iran. As young people, they had had their senses assaulted by the hordes of Iranian demonstrators on the streets of America's cities, shouting about the Shah and his secret police force, the SAVAK. Then Khomeini came back to Tehran from Paris and the Shah fled and the ayatollahs took over, and suddenly the most Western country in the Middle East, a Persian culture that had existed for millennia, with great art, literature, poetry, and music, had succumbed once more to an alien, fundamentalist oppressor and was taking American hostages and shoving its women into burqas. In less than a decade, the glorious Peacock Throne had degenerated into another totalitarian dictatorship.

Then the demonstrators took the streets again, this time

against the Ayatollah. With hundreds of Americans being held hostage in the embassy, in violation of every international diplomatic protocol, they found no shoulders to cry on. If, in 1980, President Carter had nuked Tehran, he would have won reelection in a landslide, thought Maryam. But he was too weak, and the rot that had taken over America had first revealed itself; despite Reagan's tough talk, his primary focus was breaking the Soviet Union, which he did. And after him, the deluge of mediocrity that resulted from warring political families, neither with the best interests of the nation at heart. Which is why Tyler had been elected as a breath of fresh air, a plague and a pox on both their houses.

". . . ready?" he was asking her.

"Sorry, what?" she said, coming out of her fog of remembrance.

Devlin looked at her. Every instinct, every bit of his training told him that he shouldn't trust her, that he didn't really know anything about her, and yet he did. It was Milverton's last question to him as they battled to the death in London: "Do you trust the bitch? You don't even know her real name." But he had ignored that, instead taking a page from Milverton's old outfit, the SAS-22's: "Who Dares, Wins." All his life he had trusted nobody, but he trusted her.

"New York is under attack. We have to move. Now."

Maryam tried not to let her alarm show. She was, after all, a professional. But an attack on New York was the nightmare that had been waiting to happen for a decade. "Then we go in together," she said.

The plane was rolling to a stop as he replied: "No. I go in. You go on."

"Where? When?"

"As soon as I tell that idiot Tyler what we're going to do. Right now you're going to tell me how bad it is."

"But—" She caught herself. She knew it was no use to remonstrate with him. Neither love nor guilt played any role in his psyche, and on some level she felt that he would willingly sacrifice her if the mission ever required it. Just as she knew, deep inside, that if the day ever came when she had to choose between her mission and their happiness . . . She let the thought trail off, not wishing to finish it.

"There's some kind of incident going on in Times Square. Whether the police are up to handling it, we'll soon find out. Probably not, but they'll never admit it. That's why I need you to crack the CTU unit and find out what they know."

"With what?" Even though they were aboard an NSA plane, which was as well equipped with computers and surveillance equipment as anything in the air, including Air Force One, they still might not be up to the challenge. The New York Counter-Terrorism Unit was famously secure.

"With your head," he replied. "Now get cracking."

Devlin pulled out his secure BlackBerry and opened up a direct channel to Seelye. This was not his preferred method of communication, because he felt a wireless device, no matter how well designed by the NSA engineers at The Building, could never be as safe as the hard-wire he'd had back at his home in Falls Church, but at this point he didn't have any choice. This would get him straight to Seelye, which meant straight to Tyler.

IN PLACE SIT UPDATE ASAP

The scrambled and decoded text came flying right back at him. There were a lot of things he hated about Tyler—almost everything, in fact—but one thing he had to admit, the man was always on the job. Tyler had taught him a lot of things Devlin wished every night he could forget, but a work ethic and a sense of duty was not one of them.

HANDS OFF THIS END. YOU ARE SOLO. NORMAL ROE. CONFIRM

CONFIRMED. ACCESS?

NONE. LOCKDOWN. NYPD SHOW.

TOOLS?

IN PLACE, SAFE HOUSES. STAND BY. REVOLU-
TION

Devlin had to wait only a beat or two before a series of
numbers flooded the secure computer screen. In a few minutes, they would be sorted out into street addresses superim-
posed upon enhanced-imaging maps provided by the National
Reconnaissance Office, another of the many U.S. intelligence organizations few Americans had ever heard of. The
NRO was attached to the SecDef, and it was responsible for
collecting and coordinating aerial imagery from airplanes
and satellites. In other words, the NRO was Google Earth on
steroids, and it could send you a picture via nearly instanta-
neous transmission that could show you the Iranian nuclear
installations at Qom or the tramp stamp on the girl on the
beach at Ipanema.

"Revolution" simply meant that the vetted safe houses revolved on a daily basis and the secure information he was receiving would sort out the active flops from the dummies
and the poisoned pills. Assuming he could get to one of
them, it would be outfitted with just about any kind of
weapon he might need, short of a low-yield nuclear device
and he wouldn't put that past NSA, either. Devlin glanced at
the computer, which had identified three safe houses in
Manhattan; one in midtown near the United Nations, one
downtown near Wall Street, and one at the northern tip of the
island, in Inwood.

ROGER THAT. COOP?

ASSUME NONE.

EMERGENCY LIAISON BYRNE, FRANCIS X, COR-
RECT?

UNDER ROE ONLY, YOUR CALL

Devlin clicked off. He memorized the locations of the
safe houses and committed the floor plans to memory as
well, noting all entrances and exits. There would be codes at
each of them, security death traps for the unwary, the too-

curious, and the sacrificial pawns, but he could handle that sort of thing in his sleep. He only hoped that the situation would not get too far out of control before he could in and get fully equipped.

Maryam's voice nearly startled him: "It's him, isn't it?" He didn't need to ask who "him" was. They both knew and they both knew it was him. Hope was not a plan.

Devlin turned to Maryam. There was no point in lying to her. Instincts had kept them both alive for years, and to try to deny them was suicidal. Nevertheless, Devlin preferred to base his conclusions on evidence, which right now was in short supply.

Maryam saw it in his eyes, saw the lack of the comforting lie. "I know it. It's him." Her eyes flashed and, for an instant, changed color from deep brown to something more akin to gold. "He'll never leave you alone. He'll never leave *us* alone. Until we kill him."

"Or he kills us. But right now this isn't about us."

"Of course it is. You're going in. That makes it about us, whether it began that way or no." He loved that, "or no." There was a slight British quality to her speech that he would have to expunge if she ever really had to pass for an American overseas, but they could work on that later.

She placed her hand on his wounded shoulder, into which Milverton had plunged his killing knife. How close the thrust had come to severing an artery she would never know, and he would never speak of it. She only knew how close to death he had been when she got to him in that horrible cell in France. To watch the sight of his life's blood draining away was a vision she never wanted to see again. "How do you feel? Are you fit enough?" It was not a question she should have asked, but one that she had to ask.

"Fine. In the pink. Never better." He smiled. "Any other clichés I can lay on you to make you think twice about asking a stupid question?"

She gave him that look, that mysterious Oriental glance that women of the region had been giving their men since the days of Darius. The one that is at once challenge, taunt, reproach, and exhortation. He returned the glance as best a Westerner could, then glanced down at the computer. The safe house information had already been atomized and now only the screensaver—an animated gif of a bobblehead Alexander Graham Bell doll doing handsprings and backflips while rushing for a ringing telephone—now visible.

"This might tell us something while Washington figures out what's going on." He punched a few keys, and Maryam saw that he was tapping into the live Echelon II feeds across Manhattan. ATM cameras, CCTV cameras, bodega cameras, building security cameras—their cyclopean images floated across the tiny screen, stupefying in their uneventful reality.

"Nothing much—Jesus!"

Times Square. Something was happening there. It was hard to make out, but one of the rotating CCTV cameras was on to something . . .

A streetscape and then smoke. Flames. Even in grainy low-res, it was clear that something was happening. Devlin called up the cable news nets and divided the screen in four quadrants.

"We have to do something." Maryam's eyes were still glued to the unfolding disaster. Devlin turned to look at her, and then, once more, the voice of his old enemy sounded in his ear:

"What is she to you? She's a dream, the dream of the prisoner in the condemned hold. You think that this time it's going to be different, but when they string you up and drop the trap, you'll realize as your neck snaps that it was all a fantasy."

Milverton's voice, in his head. Not the voice of his conscience, but of caution. The caution that, as the saying went, had been thrown to the winds in his desire for her, and in his desire to be free—from Seelye. Free of the past that had entrapped him and refused to let him go. But freedom was not a gift. It had to be won, and hard-won. Milverton had been there at the beginning, in Paris, and he had been there at the end, in London. He haunted them still.

Devlin's hand shot out, grasped hers. The horror remained on the screen. "Are you real, or only a dream? Who are you?"

"What?" She pulled back a little, frightened by the intensity in his eyes. She knew that look. She was one of the few—perhaps the only one—to have seen it and lived.

Best not to show fear. "Who are you, Frank?"

"You know who I am," he replied calmly. His touch was like ice. "I am the Angel of Death."

CHAPTER FIFTEEN

The White House

Tyler had all the TV screens up and running as Seelye entered the private quarters. He was surprised to find Tyler alone. At the beginning of his presidency, Tyler would have been in the Oval Office, jacket off, sleeves rolled in his faux-populist style, hands on hips, barking orders to a room full of acolytes and subalterns, trying as hard he could to look presidential. Now, after nearly four years, he looked simply old and tired and in disbelief at what was occurring in New York.

"Where's Secretary Johnson?" he asked, coming through the door. "Where's Celina Sanchez? Melinda Dylan? Pam Dobson?" Sanchez was the National Security Advisor, Dylan, the Director of Central Intelligence, and Dobson, the press secretary. All of Tyler's top security officers were women.

That wasn't quite true, of course, even in this time of female ascendancy. The Chairman of the Joint Chiefs of Staff was Marine Corps General Lance Higgins, the Director of National Intelligence was Lamont Sutton, and the head of the Department of Homeland Security was Bob Colangelo. But, in Seelye's opinion, their input was pretty much negligible. Tyler came into office with a pronounced aversion to military men—he hardly ever laid eyes on his military attaché, Col. Al Grizzard, the man who controlled the nuclear football—which ruled out Higgins's input. Sutton, in a politically incorrect opinion he kept exclusively to himself, was an affirmative-action appointment, and Colangelo was simply an idiot whose lack of organizational talent or intellectual acumen was perfectly suited to running the country's most useless bureaucracy. So maybe Tyler was right to trust the women; after all, just about the only job in the U.S. government women hadn't taken over was that of chief executive and that was just a matter of time—maybe a matter of months, if the polls were right. A President Angela Hassett meant the end of his career, the end of a lifetime of work. The end of Devlin as well, after which Devlin would be looking to cash in his chips. And that simply could not be allowed. He had to save Jeb Tyler's ass to save his own.

"Sit down, Army, and give me what you've got."

Seelye was ready with the numbers. "It began with a denial-of-service attack this afternoon on the Counter-Terrorism Unit of the New York City Police Department. A complete wipeout that lasted nearly five minutes, so bad it rang the alarm bells from Manhattan to Fort Meade."

The president gestured at the television screens. "Best guess?"

Seelye hated to have to say what he was about to say. It represented a complete failure of all the safeguards that had been put in place since 9/11. It was the last thing a reeling Tyler Administration needed, and when the word got out, there was going to be unholy hell to pay. He took a deep breath.

"Best guess is that they've been planning this for months, maybe years. First they probed our defenses—and, as you know, despite all our best efforts, despite our crack Department of Homeland Security, our state of the art ain't so great, especially as you travel down the bureaucratic food chain—set off a series of feints, hinted that they might strike the electrical grid, the water supplies. And then . . ."

"And then?" Tyler was in no mood for coy. He was watching midtown Manhattan burn live on national television.

"And then they rammed it right up our ass. How they smuggled the stuff into the city . . ." His voice trailed off. This was exactly the kind of thing all those sensors and hidden cameras were supposed to help prevent. All those city, state, and federal dollars. The networks of HUMINT. "We can only hope that the sensors were not down long enough not to detect anything fissionable."

"You mean nukes. A suitcase nuke?"

"Or two. Or four. Or, God willing, none."

"How could they get them into the city so fast?"

Tyler wasn't going to like this answer. "Maybe they didn't. Maybe they were there all along, waiting. You know how patient these people are. They're still fighting battles from a thousand years ago, nursing grudges, plotting. For them, revenge is a dish that cannot possibly be cold enough."

"I don't understand."

"Maybe the devices—if they've got them and that's a big if at this point—were already in Manhattan, secreted there and then activated before all our shields were back up. There's a lot of places they could hide them: in hospitals, swimming pools—"

"Not a lot of swimming pools in Manhattan," said Tyler, reddening. Seelye braced for what he knew would be the eventual eruption of Mount Tyler. Maybe this time, he thought, the president would keep his cool. Maybe this time he would control himself and his fiery temper. Maybe this time, he'd act like an adult. If not, they were all doomed.

"You'd be surprised, sir. There are lots of indoor swimming pools in the city. Any Y will do just fine. But that's worst-case scenario, and the rest of it is barn-door stuff. The real question is, what are we going to do about this?" He gestured at the televisions.

From every angle, on every network, the extent of the destruction was awesome. Half the great intersection was afire, and 42nd Street was burning as well. Down the block, the wreck of the AMC theaters was plainly visible. Across the expanse of the square itself, heavily armed cops were engaging in a running firefight with an unknown number of assailants, and they were taking casualties.

"Has the governor sent in the National Guard yet?" asked Tyler. Hurricane Katrina had taught every succeeding president that one could stand too long on ceremony and chain of command.

"NYPD hasn't yet called for military assistance, so the answer is presumably no. We're monitoring the governor's office and the official police communication channels, of course."

"Of course." Another bourbon and branch had materialized on a side table, but as much as he wanted another drink, this was no time to lose his faculties. "What's the SIGINT chatter?"

"Nothing out of the ordinary. If this was an al-Qaeda operation, they'd be shouting from the tops of their mud huts already. But everything's quiet. Which means . . ."

Tyler arched an eyebrow.

"Which means," continued Seelye, "that we're not up against a group of terrorists. We're up against something that can keep a secret, that holds absolute operational security. In other words, one man."

"In other words, Emanuel Skorzeny," said Tyler, one eye glued to the TV screens.

Seelye chose his words carefully; there was a play for him here, a chance to settle the oldest and most personal score in his book, but he had to be careful how he laid it out. "No, sir, I think not. He's old, he's taken a terrific financial beating, and he's content to fly around all day in that airborne fuck palace of his, trying to put the pieces of his empire back together. I don't think we have anything to worry about from Skorzeny at this point. Besides, he knows he exists at your sufferance, so why go out of his way to attract unwelcome attention?"

"Simple," said Tyler. "Best reason there is: because he can. Look, he's old, he's mean, he's ornery, and he's guilty as sin. He's already got his ticket punched straight to Hell, whether he believes in it or not . . ." Tyler thought for a moment. After all, it was he who had let Skorzeny off—in order to protect the CSS, Branch 4, and Devlin, to be sure. "Who then?"

Seelye tossed a couple of dossiers in front of the president. "This man," he said. "Arash Kohanloo."

Tyler's heart sank as he picked up the first manila folder, stamped SCI, eyes only. "Please don't tell me he's Iranian."

"With a name like that, of course he is," replied Seelye as the President leafed through the folder. "But he's no ordinary Persian. He's not one of the mullah's thugs. He's older, for one thing. He remembers a time before the Islamic Revolution. He attended the Hotchkiss School in Connecticut, and went on to Yale. How the CIA missed recruiting him with that pedigree, I'll never understand. Got a doctorate at the London School of Economics, then another degree at the Sorbonne. Speaks six languages fluently. For some reason the ayatollahs seem to trust him, and pretty much let him have the run of the planet, which means that whatever scam he's running is enriching all of them and clearly serves their geo-political ambitions. He spends as much time looking after his private business interests in Macao, Goa, Dubai, Los Angeles as he does in Tehran. In short, he's a sophisticated man of the world. Just like . . ."

Tyler put the folder down, took his eye off the TV, and gave Seelye his full attention. "Just like . . . ?"

"Just like Emanuel Skorzeny, with whom he met in Macao within the past twenty-four hours."

Tyler took a deep breath through his nose, held the air a moment, then expelled it slowly. Good; breathing exercises might keep him calm, at least for a while. "You're sure?"

"Yes, sir. Skorzeny uses some pretty sophisticated hamming equipment, and of course he's bought off half the air-traffic control systems in the world, but we can still track the old goat. Just waiting for the word from you for him to have an unfortunate aeronautics accident."

"Well, just don't let him have it over Iran, for Chrissakes," said Tyler. The United States was still having trouble living down its wipeout of an Iranian civilian airliner in 1988, near the end of the Iran-Iraq war—a purpose pitch and small payback for the hostage crisis that still inflamed anti-American sentiment, as if Iran needed any more reasons to hate the Great Satan. "Two questions: what's this Kohanloo's weakness?"

Seelye had been expecting those very queries. "I wish I could tell you he had some exotic vices, Mr. President," he said. "That he raises tropical fish and uses them as an aphrodisiac for the little girls he kidnaps on school playgrounds, but no such luck. He's a good Muslim. He doesn't smoke or drink, conducts his financial affairs in accordance with Islamic principles, and in general lives according to Shari'a law."

"So what's his vice?" Tyler certainly knew from vices; in his view a man without a vice wasn't a man at all.

"His vice is that, outside the caliphate, in the West, he does as the Romans do. He gambles at all the best London clubs, and there isn't a reasonably attractive woman in the Western world he hasn't tried to seduce."

"And the Iranian security services let him get away with that?"

"I think the question answers itself, sir. He's still kicking."

"So how do we get to him?"

"At the moment, we don't." Seelye pointed back at the screen. "We have to see how this plays out. It might be a co-ordinated attack—and I think the evidence is clear on that point—but it might also be sheer coincidence, the timing of the DoS attack and the bombing. Probably it's not, but stranger things have happened. But we're not without certain, er, weapons."

Tyler was already mentally calculating the amount of money the feds were going to have to send to New York, even assuming this incident got resolved quickly. He was also weighing the hit his reputation was going to take, and how much political hay that bitch Hassett would be able to make out of this once the fires were out and the victims were buried. "What weap—?"

Tyler was cut off by the sound of the intercom. It was Millie Dhouri, his private secretary. "Deputy Director Byrne is here, Mr. President," said the disembodied voice.

"Read the other dossier first," advised Seelye.

"Ask Director Byrne to wait just a couple more minutes," said Tyler, opening the dossier.

One thing you had to admit about Tyler, Seelye thought, the man was a quick study. A lot of lawyers were, especially trial lawyers, but Tyler was exceptional. He could speed-read the densest page and absorb it in one gulp. Not only could he sell igloos to Eskimos, carry coals to Newcastle, and hawk oil burners in the Sahara, he could sell himself to the American people as something other than what he was: a millionaire trial lawyer who had made his reputation and his fortune putting doctors out of business with crippling lawsuits, all the while posing as a champion of women's reproductive rights. It was either a commentary on Tyler's political skills, or the stupidity of the American public, or both. And yet . . .

And yet there was no question that he had a knack for the presidency, in a way many of his predecessors didn't. Maybe you really could grow in office.

Tyler tossed the dossier back onto the table. "Show him in," he said.

A knock at the door, and in came Byrne. At sixty-two, Tom Byrne had lost neither a hair on his black Irish head nor his good looks, and he moved with the confident grace of a man who held an awful lot of secrets. Like his brother, Frankie, Tom had grown up in Woodside, Queens, when it was still a Paddy stronghold, and even though New York had long since ceased being the city of the Irish, Italians, and Jews, nobody had had the guts to tell him that. Tom Byrne believed passionately in George Washington Plunkitt's dictum that "the Irish were born to rule."

"Mr. President," he said by way of acknowledgment. "General Seelye."

Seelye rose and shook hands. Despite all his years in Washington, this was the first time he had ever met the fabulous creature in the flesh. Stories about Byrne were legendary, particularly his Kennedyesque appetite for women, but NSA and the FBI had very little to do with each other, and both sides endeavored to keep it that way.

"Sit down, Mr. Byrne, and tell me what you make of the situation in New York. You know why I've asked you to come here, I'm sure."

Byrne smiled. "Because my little brother, Frankie, is head of CTU."

"Precisely," said Tyler. "What do you hear from him?"

"Hear from him?" replied Byrne. "Nothing. We haven't talked in years, except through official channels."

"You two don't like each other very much, is that it?"

"No, sir. But that's no secret. We've hated each other since we were kids."

"May I ask why?"

Byrne smiled. "It's complicated, Mr. President. And, with all due respect, I think we have a lot bigger fish to fry at the moment."

"Where do you suppose your brother is right now?"

Now Byrne laughed. "Not at his desk, that's for sure. Frankie's got this big mick, first-through-the-door attitude, so if I know my bro, he's out there right now, in the middle of the sh—in the middle of it."

"Are you in contact with him?"

"No, sir," replied Tom. "Frankie speaks only to God and his squad. Mere mortals like us need not apply."

Tyler looked Byrne over closely, trying not to let his distaste for the man show. He'd read the files, heard all the stories. But Washington was a tough, unforgiving town, and sometimes you had to climb into bed with people you'd otherwise cheerfully strangle, just to get the job done. This was one of those times.

"Director Byrne, let me be blunt. I need to know what your brother knows, in real time, and I don't much care how you do it, so long as that information pipeline is up and running A-sap. No matter how much you know, or think you know, about me, Director Seelye, members of my cabinet, or the dog I had when I was twelve, it doesn't matter to me a bit. Your job depends on opening up a channel of communication for me to Captain Byrne. Do I make myself clear?"

Seelye expected to watch with satisfaction as the wind went out of Byrne's sails, leaving him becalmed on the shoals of 1600 Pennsylvania Avenue. Instead, he looked as if Tyler had just handed him a present. "Rat out my own brother? The pleasure's all mine. I'll need your authorization though—in writing."

Seelye saw the play right away, even if Tyler didn't. What

Tyler had just done was crack the wall of separation that the NYPD had so assiduously erected between it and the feds; by ordering the FBI, in the person of Tom Byrne, to breach NYPD security, he had effectively just delivered the New York City cops to their ancient enemies, the Bureau: the street Irish versus the Notre Dame Irish, pigs in the parlor vs. the lace curtains. The same fucking tribal animosities, imported from the Ould Sod to the New World, most likely with the same sad results. Both sides would lose.

"Director Byrne," replied Tyler, coldly, "I am the President of the United States. My word ought to be good enough for you. And Director Seelye is your witness. Now get out of here and get me an inside channel to the CTU. I don't give a rat's fucking rear end how you do it, whose toes you have to step on, or whose balls you have to break. Are we clear about this?"

"Yes, sir."

"Now give me your assessment before I have the AG fire you right now and give the job to somebody else."

"Yes, sir." Byrne collected his thoughts. He was pretty sure Tyler was bluffing about firing him. After all, it was he who had successfully transformed the FBI from a bunch of lawyers with guns chasing bank robbers in Omaha into a pretty fair imitation of Britain's MI5, the domestic security service, and the front-line counterterrorism soldiers in the ongoing war against the *jihad*. Not to mention the fact that the Director was a moron, and the AG couldn't indict a ham sandwich even if he caught it standing over the dead body with a smoking gun between two slices of rye bread. On the other hand, Tyler was known to do some pretty strange things, and with a tough election fight coming up, Tom's scalp might just turn out to be a campaign collectible.

"From what we can tell," he began, "there are at least a dozen terrorists on the ground in New York at the moment. There may be more. There may be sleeper cells, waiting to go into action after we tip our hand. In fact, I would say that is entirely likely. But right now, that's our best guesstimate, and they're armed with some pretty formidable firepower."

"Can the NYPD take them?" asked Seelye.

The intercom buzzed. "What is it, Millie?" barked Tyler, annoyed.

"Pam Dobson on the line, sir. She says the media is clamoring for a statement."

"Tell her to keep her panties on," said Tyler. "And I didn't say that."

"Yes, sir," said Ms. Dhouri's voice. "I'll phrase it more artfully."

"See that you do, thanks," said the president. He turned back to Byrne. "Well, can they?"

"Of course they can. And if they can't, the Guard is on the way, and with those reinforcements—"

At that moment, a terrific explosion could be heard from the TVs. All three men turned to look.

A huge plume of smoke was rising over the Hudson and lower Manhattan around Canal Street on the west side. It looked like half the city was on fire.

"Oh, Jesus," said Tom Byrne. "They bombed the Holland Tunnel."

CHAPTER SIXTEEN

Los Angeles

Even in his semi-buzzed state, Jake Sinclair was on the phone in a flash when it vibrated in his palm. He had seen the first news reports—sketchy, incomplete things born of panic and fallibility and gossip and rumor, full of the mistaken details that would later give rise to a thousand conspiracy theories—and was clutching the instrument even before it rang. He pushed the talk button and spoke: "Flood the zone. Everybody in the field. I don't care how dangerous it is."

The voice on the other end of the line crackled with something very like fear. It was Bill Connolly, the head of his cable news division. "We're on it, Mr. Sinclair."

Sinclair tossed a glance at one of the video feeds. Huge billows of smoke were ascending into the sky from what had once been Times Square, and farther to the south, another conflagration had started. The only question now was how much worse it was going to get. A lot worse, was his guess. "Status report," he commanded.

"Times Square is cut off. Looks like some kind of bomb just sealed the entrance to the Holland Tunnel on the Manhattan side. Jesus Christ, what are they doing, taking out all the—?"

"That's your job to find out," snapped Sinclair, "so get to it. Put Principessa on the air—let her anchor. People like to see a pretty girl when the shit hits the fan."

"Um, sir? Principessa's just getting back to the city now. She did a hell of a job just getting to within a hundred miles of Manhattan."

Sinclair's mind raced. He would have preferred to have that magnificent rack front and center on America's TV screens; she wasn't terribly smart but she was pretty, had a great body and was absolutely unafraid of her own stupidity. In fact, she was stone-cold brave, a quality you didn't find in many women.

"Okay, then track her. Get another crew with her. If she starts to mix it up in the shit, we need to be there to cover her." He'd hate to lose Stanley if anything happened to her, if she caught a stray bullet or got clipped in an explosion, but hey, this was war. Ernie Pyle made a great career move when he bought the farm in the Pacific, and as far as Sinclair was concerned, today's reporters were a bunch of pussies anyway, covering stories from the studio or, in a pinch, from their satellite vans. Good to see the girl on the streets.

"I've got another call." He punched the talk button again. This time it was Ben Bernstein, the editor in chief of the *Times*. "Give it to me straight, Benny," he said.

"We're under attack," shouted Bernstein—

"Calm down," he soothed. The man sounded like he was having a heart attack. "It's happening right in your own backyard. Chance of a lifetime. Who've you got on it?"

"Everybody—"

"Good. See that they stay there. Tear the paper up and get ready for a Pulitzer."

Bernstein was practically sobbing. "But, Jake, it's . . . it's terrible."

"Of course it's terrible. It's news. Forget 9/11—we *own* this story." He rang off. Alert now, he punched up Firefox. Almost immediately, the tabs to his principal websites popped up so he could watch what was happening in real time. Under the guise of providing "traffic cams" and "beauty shots" of various cities, Sinclair had been one of the first to install and link a series of private spy cams around the country. Gradually, *sub rosa* and through discreet bribery, he also managed to install "news feeds" in Europe, the principal Asian cities, and a couple of places in South America, precisely against moments like these. People didn't trust the news much anymore—not that he could blame them; after all, *he* didn't trust it much anymore, and the reporters were mainly employed by him—and they were more likely to believe the evidence of their own senses than some silly blow-dried mouthpiece doing a standup from a safely secured "war zone." This way, the anchors could perform their voice-overs while the remotely controlled cameras gave the viewers a grunt's-eye view of what was really going on. Needless to say, the viewers loved it, even if the reporters didn't, and his network's ratings soared. Besides, who cared what the reporters thought? He had fired half of them already and looked forward to the day when he could fire them all and use 3-D animated avatars, just like in the movies.

One glance was enough to tell him this was very, very bad—which meant for the news business, it was very, very good. It mattered not if he lost a day, or a week—hell, even a month's worth of revenue. He would make it up in the numbers of eyeballs delivered to advertisers down the line, and in prestige by his Nielsens. And he would make it up on the back end when he eventually drove his competitors completely out of business, leaving the field entirely to himself.

Too big to fail was just fine by Jake Sinclair, and, if anything, he planned to get even bigger.

Which was why he had left New York, and wasn't that looking like a smart idea? Not like the poor guy who had leased the old World Trade Center a few weeks before the nineteen holy warriors leveled it. Part of his considerable fortune had been based on smart real-estate deals, and the close of the sale of the New York corporate headquarters to some European interests was his smartest deal yet. The building he had purchased quietly in Century City—the retrofitting was almost complete—would be a beacon for all other corporate moguls, and with better weather.

"Oh, my God—have you heard?" That would be Jenny II, coming in the door from the porte cochere. He could hear her rustling around in the kitchen, dropping her Maxfield's bags and her keys; in a few seconds, she'd be in the room, and then he was going to have to feign shock and horror at what was transpiring three thousand miles away instead of gloating about how he'd just made a fortune, and that his network's rating were sure to soar. "Yes," he shouted, hoping his voice had just the right amount of concern. "It's terrible. I've got it on right now." Sinclair linked his computer's screens to the huge flat-screen television that dominated one wall of the room.

"I thought the president was supposed to keep us safe," said Jenny. The look on her face was so real and so sincere that for just a moment Sinclair felt a little embarrassed at his own conflict of interest.

He put his arms around her and held her close. It was at times like these, when she was the vulnerable girl he had first met playing tennis at her father's house, that day he had come to consummate his business relationship with the father and eventually wound up marrying the daughter, that he actually enjoyed her company again.

"What can I do? What can one man do?" he whispered softly. Like most Hollywood wives, she gladly accepted the often brutal violence of the torture-porn movies his and other studios made, yet in the face of the real thing became completely unglued.

"You can fight him," said Jenny, softly. "You fight him with everything you've got. With everything *we've* got." She pulled away and gestured around. "I mean, why have you worked so hard to acquire this business, your newspapers, your whole media empire, if not to use it to save our country?"

Sinclair pulled Jenny II close to him. It was at moments like this that he was grateful he didn't have to remember a new name. Over her tender, soft shoulder, he could see New York burning.

It was surreal, a sight he had seen hundreds of times before in his studio's movies. Disaster movies were ten cents a dance these days, when filmmakers looked for any excuse to blow up the White House and the Vatican (but never anything Muslim), but that was only because nobody ever expected their cinematic visions to actually happen. Fiction was only fun when it stayed fiction.

There wasn't much left in Jake Sinclair other than greed and a vague, free-floating animus against various wrongs, both real and imagined, but whatever it was welled up inside him, and he found himself once again making promises that he could not keep. Still, as always, it felt good to make them. "I'll get them," he said.

Jenny II pulled back, her face still turned away from the disaster unfolding in New York. He would try to shield her from it as long as possible; holding fast to progressive belief meant denying reality as long as one could. "Will you, Jake?" she asked, her face streaming. "Promise me you will."

Still holding her in his arms, Sinclair maneuvered her as far away from the flatscreen as he could. "You know I will," he whispered. "When have I ever lied to you?" From this angle, he could just manage to reach out and hit the computer, shutting off the video feed to the other twelve televisions in the house.

They had moved toward the French doors, which led out to the patio. Sinclair spent most of his life indoors, in a car, or on an airplane; the fresh air felt good.

"You can do it, Jake," Jenny said. "You can get them, those bastards." Somewhere, on somebody's TV, Manhattan was still under attack, but that was not what Jenny meant. "You can get them, hold their feet to the fire, make them live up to our American ideals."

The relaxation of monopoly rules under a succession of presidents and congresses had given men like him an opportunity. Most Americans never thought at all about where their information was coming from, how it was filtered, interpreted, refashioned, and corrupted until it landed on their computer screens, BlackBerrys, iPhones or, diminishingly, in newspapers. Sinclair's genius was that he owned them all. In fact, some of them he had purchased from a man named Emanuel Skorzeny, a well-known financier who had mysteriously gone missing the year before after selling off many of his media assets at fire-sale prices.

"Get in the game, Jake," Jenny was saying. "Use your empire. Take that bastard Tyler *down*."

Jenny II or no Jenny II, he had just about had it with the party in power. The man had been elected on an "anti-" platform. Anti-everything that had come before, most especially his predecessor, whose invincible ignorance and smug moral certainty had enraged every almost segment of society except Flyover Country. And yet, something had caused Tyler to turn away from Blame America First. Once in office, he had disappointed many of his supporters and enraged others by refusing to move his social reforms along as quickly as he had promised, and they had hoped. Some devil had snuck into the White House in the dead of night and climbed under the covers with the Bachelor President. Sinclair wondered who it had been.

There were plenty of stories about Tyler on hold. Stories in the newspapers, the magazines, stories ready for broadcast, awaiting just the pushing of the "publish" buttons on the net. But progressives weren't supposed to attack their own, certainly not the matter of sexuality, or even of speculative sexuality, and certainly not when they were supposed to take the side of the "anti-" party, whatever its current positions were. It was unseemly to attack any member of the party, any potential ally, any useful idiot, which Tyler had always been. But now, with New York aflame, it was time to take the gloves off.

Gently, he released Jenny II. Thoughts of divorcing her had fled his mind; his field of vision had room only for the devastated heart of midtown Manhattan and her father's bank account, most of it still unplundered, ripe for the taking. "I'll get the bastard," he told Jenny II. "You can count on me."

As they moved toward the pool, he unfastened the halter top of her simple shift, which dropped to the ground. As he stroked her bare back, he guided her toward the spa.

She slipped into the water like a sleek mermaid. It was amazing how much better, how much sexier, naked women were in the water, so smooth, so unencumbered, their skins glistening as they cut through the water like seals. It was their natural element.

He sloughed off his shirt and slid out of his trousers. One thing left to do.

He punched a single key on his Surge, the one that connected him directly to the newsroom of his flagship paper in Manhattan. He was getting ready for another round of downsizing, but they didn't have to know that now. All they had to think about at the moment was the Pulitzers they were going to win. Might as well live it up.

"Endorse Hassett. Yes, tomorrow morning. No, I don't care how this ends, it's not going to change my mind. You have my standing editorial. Set the agenda. Do some damage. It's the American way."

He turned to Jenny II, so seductive. His hand brushed the button for the spa. The bubbles leapt to life. So did he.

By God, he still had it. He still had it.

CHAPTER SEVENTEEN

Manhattan

In his heart, nearly bursting from the exertion of his sprint, Frankie Byrne had always known he would be too late, but he didn't know what else to do. "First through the door" was the motto of New York's Finest, Irishmen to the core no matter what their ethnicity. He had lived by this motto for his entire career on the force, and he was not about to give it up now. Not even when the danger was greatest, which made the urgency all the more fierce. First through the door meant first through the door, whether the door was real or figurative, whether a shithole in the Bronx or a Park Avenue apartment, whether the door opened onto a swanky restaurant, an East Village head shop, a Queens crack house, or the Archbishop's fuckpad across from MoMA. It was all the same to him. You went in to sort the situation out, or you died in the attempt. There was no sense rationalizing it. You just did it, and if the devil got you, well, you hoped you'd be in heaven long before the cocksucker knew you were dead. That was the Paddy way, and it was the only way he knew.

Why this was true was a mystery, but it was departmental lore and so every cop on the force abided by it. For Byrne, however, it went deeper. His father had died in the line of duty. In a firefight, you shot first or you died, and Robert Byrne had had been shot in the back, and even though he managed to turn on his unknown assailant he had not fired his weapon, out of fear of hitting a civilian. And so he died. Byrne honored his father's memory, but he had no intention of ever letting that happen to him.

The explosion at the AMC movie theater practically hit him in the face. Luckily, he had not yet rounded the corner, or else he would have been instantly as dead as all the other pedestrians in the vicinity, from the Port Authority to the Great White Way. Instinctively, he fell to the pavement, rolling as close to a nearby building as he could manage, waiting for the shitstorm to stop.

He had never been this close to a general disaster—personal disasters had been enough for him—but he found himself strangely calm in the midst of it. In all his other encounters with the forces of evil, he had been a lone man, facing another lone man, both of them holding a sidearm. The romance of the movies was that men fired at each other from great distances with pistols, but Byrne knew from bitter personal experience that in urban confrontations your opponent was usually standing right in front of you, so it was not a matter of marksmanship but alacrity. Despite the caterwauling from the sissies and the nancy boys on the city council and the Civilian Complaint Review Board, an officer's first job was to go home safe every night.

Even as an NYPD officer, Byrne had never experienced anything like this: a rain of fire, of molten brick and steel and plastic. When he was finally able to peek around the corner, a stunning sight met his eyes: shredded bodies, some of them headless, many of them limbless, all of them dead.

Despite the increasingly militarized nature of urban police forces, cops weren't supposed to be soldiers. They kept the peace up close and personal, not from a marksman's dispassionate remove. They fought one-on-one, like the street fighters they had once been, battling the thugs, grifters, and second-story men their forebears knew so well. In the old days, back when Byrne's grandparents had come over from Ireland and settled first on the Lower East Side and later in Queens, you grew up with the criminals you would eventually put in jail. Today, they came from thousands of miles away, disembarking at Kennedy Airport, their support staff already in place along Atlantic Avenue in Brooklyn, just waiting for a signal, whether from their controllers or Allah.

Right now, what he had to do was get to the AMC Theater and figure out what the hell was going on.

All thoughts of the hot dog vendor guy were lost. Given what was unfolding in front of his eyes on 42nd Street, Times Square was a million miles away. The uniformed officers in place would have to deal with it, and the reinforcements that were undoubtedly already on their way. Although it was clear that this was an attack on the order of 9/11, Byrne found himself hoping that the feds would let the NYPD handle it—this was their turf, and nobody knew it better. It was already a blow to the department's pride that something like this was happening, but in fact this is what they had trained for, prepared for—it was not their fault that geopolitical developments had intervened. The job of a New York City police officer was to protect and serve, and that was exactly what he intended to do.

The AMC, or what was left of it, was only a couple of hundred yards ahead.

"Dinner at the Four Seasons it's ragheads," said Sid Sheinberg.

Lannie Saleh piloted the unmarked police car at top speed through traffic. From time to time, he skirted the shoals of the sidewalk, expertly navigating around rogue parking meters, illegal sidewalk cafés and the usual urban flotsam and jetsam that wouldn't have known the city was under attack if the Last Trump was being sounded by the New York Philharmonic. "You don't know that."

"Sure I do," said Sheinberg. "It ain't nuns or Norwegians. Probably al-Qaeda."

"Now I know you're an ignoramus," said Lannie, negotiating around a couple of BMWs with New Jersey tags. "And probably a bigot, too."

"What makes you say that?"

"Because *if*," began Lannie, "and this is a big *if*, this is some kind of Muslim assault, it's far more likely to be Twelfthers than Sunnis."

"Who cares? What's the diff?"

Lannie downshifted, even with the automatic transmission, and nearly threw Sid into the windshield. "If this is as big as I think it is—as big as we both think it is—then this isn't al-Qaeda. All they want to do is kill us."

"As opposed to—"

"As opposed to starting the apocalypse." Lannie glanced over at Sid and saw that he had no idea what he was talking about. "Look," he said, "Christians and Shi'as believe in the Last Days. The rest of us, not so much. If and when they come, they come, but we have no intention of hastening them. When al-Qaeda attacks, it's because they're pissed off, refighting some fucking battle against El Cid or whatever. Let's face it, since Mohammed swept out of Arabia and Islam conquered everything to the east, including Persia, India, and Indonesia, we've been on a hell of a losing streak."

The street buckled. "Holy shit!" shouted Lannie.

The force of the blast knocked the car sideways, then up in the air. It sailed for just a moment, hit the pavement, spun. Lannie tried desperately to control the vehicle, its siren still wailing, but the Crown Vic was being tossed around like a skiff at sea. The car hit a mailbox, rebounded, and caromed off a fire hydrant. The hydrant ripped a huge gash in the passenger's side and exploded, water geysering straight up. They clipped several parked vehicles, flipped, and came to rest, upside down, in the middle of street.

A couple of miles to the south, Lisa Richmond was headed home to Jersey after a lunch in SoHo. She didn't come often to New York anymore, even though she had been born in the Bronx. What had once seemed close now seemed so very far away, what with a family and all, and despite everything she had believed as a young career woman working on Wall Street twenty years ago, Jersey had turned out to be not such a bad place to live and raise a family after all. Sure, the taxes were a killer, although the new governor was making noises about reducing them—yeah, right—but the air was a bit cleaner, parking was less of a problem, and the schools were a heck of a lot better.

The approach to Holland Tunnel was always a pain. It was as if the city planners hadn't reckoned on the population of northern New Jersey mushrooming, so they decided to cram it in down here where Canal Street met Varick and Hudson streets. No matter how you approached it, or what time of day, you were practically guaranteed at least a twenty-minute wait to enter the tube. Lisa shuddered at the memory of the old days, when the squeegee men had lurked around the tunnel entrances, wielding their spray bottles and their dirty rags and their threatening countenances as they shook you down for a quarter. A lot of her friends paid them, just to make them go away, but she never did. For one thing, she was too frightened to open the window, and for another she felt instinctively that the service they offered was an indirect form of assault. Her husband, Adam, always gave them money, explaining that it was safer and easier to pay them off rather than to risk their probably drug-addled wrath. It was one of their many areas of disagreement.

At least there were no squeegee men anymore, not in New York and certainly not in Montclair, New Jersey.

Lisa's mind was still on the squeegee men, inching her 2010 Jeep forward toward the mouth of the tunnel, when she felt the earth tremble. At first she thought it was just the rumble of the subway, the vibrations, but then, as she began to take notice, she realized that the car was moving—not forward, but from side to side, as if it were in an earthquake. The next thing she knew she was looking down at lower Manhattan from a very great height, and screaming to earth at the speed of gravity.

Raymond Crankheit was a tourist from Wahoo, Nebraska, or so he had told everybody he met, especially the girls. New York City girls were not like the girls back home, which in fact was not Wahoo, Nebraska, but that didn't matter at the moment. Contrary to popular myth, or at least what he saw in the movies, New York City women were harder to get than the tramps back home, snooty and stuck-up; they could smell a rube like him a mile away, and their noses visibly crinkled as he approached, so Raymond Crankheit had decided to get even. Which was why he was here, standing by the Central Park Reservoir, waiting for a call on his cell phone.

For a long time he had wondered precisely how he was going to go about it. New York City had tough gun laws, and he didn't own a gun himself, you couldn't take one on a plane, he was too scared to drive across the country with a heater in his glove compartment. Originally, the family named had been spelled Krankheit, but that meant "disease" in German and his father had quickly had enough of such jokes back home in Pullman, Washington, and so in partial homage to the host of the CBS News program, he'd changed the spelling, although he still got it wrong, and moved the family across the Cascades to Seattle, where they left unspoken the implication that they were related to the famous newscaster.

Luckily, the flat accents of Wahoo were very similar to the flat accents of Pullman, so Raymond had to work only moderately hard to be able to pass for a Nebraskan. For some reason, he had decided that for this mission to succeed—"Operation Revenge," he had dubbed it in his own mind—his cover story was going to have to be perfect, and he practiced like Travis Bickle in front of a mirror, holding a broken broom handle instead of the gun he didn't have, and coldly shooting down every woman who had ever refused him a date.

Raymond Crankheit wouldn't have said that he hated women, exactly. He was not a mishshogomast or whatever the term was that one of the crazy shrinks his parents had sent him to after the second incident, the one with the neighbor's dog, had used, but on the other hand, it really pissed him off when some cunt blew him off and called him a dork or a geek or an asshole or any of the other unladylike terms girls were using these days. Yeah, those same girls that tattooed themselves up like the cheap whores working the old Skid Road back in Seattle. It was payback time for a life of rejection.

Pullman, Washington, was just across the state line from Moscow, Idaho, and for a time as a kid Raymond had fantasized about running away from home by "defecting," as he thought of it, to Idaho. Eastern Washington State was a pretty dreary place, apple farms where there was water and alkaline deserts was there was not, and in his youthful imagination Idaho was a land of green mountains and secret communists. Then he got uprooted and transplanted, and that was the end of that notion, although he kept his lifelong fascination with the Soviets, the heroic protectors of the Third World and of people of color everywhere. There weren't many people of color, except for the odd Mexican migrant worker, in Pullman, Washington, and so in the absence of people at whom to direct his compassion, Raymond's sense of injustice burned even fiercer.

And so Raymond left home without telling anybody, not the 'rents or the parole officer or anybody. He hitched his way down to Frisco, and that had pretty much been the extent of the plan except that he never actually made it to Frisco. Instead, he wound up across the bay, in Oakland, where his money ran out, and he decided to find a place to crash in the Oakland flats. Everybody told him the Oakland flats were no place for a white boy like him, but by chance he had wandered into a little bakeshop not far from the Berkeley border, a Black Muslim bakeshop, the kind of place that attracted big black tough guys and those hot little white girls and Asian tramps from the UC campus, the ones that liked to walk on the wild side and pretend they were fucking for social justice when in fact they were just fucking.

The place was called the Malik Shabazz, Jr., Bakery and Book Store, and it was a place where you could bum a halfway decent, if halfway eaten croissant if you promised to help with the washing-up, and there was always plenty to read. That's where Raymond encountered the Holy Koran, which at first he found hard to understand until one of the Brothers explained some of the more interesting suras to him. It was one of those moments he had wished for all his life, when a flash of knowledge, of revelation, comes and all at once he could see exactly what he had to do and how to do it.

The Brothers saw the flash of light in his eyes and knew they had found a soul mate. Instruction had begun immediately. Raymond was an apt pupil.

And now here he was. He glanced around at the cityscape, a 360 maneuver that rotated him from the top of the park to the residential towers of Central Park West, south to the wall of 59th Street and then back around again, east, across Fifth Avenue.

His cell phone rang. It was one of the Brothers, telling him that all his dreams were about to come true.

Even though he knew everything was A-OK, Raymond checked the backpack that had been stashed for him, as promised, in a trash can behind the National Academy. All the tools were there, everything he had trained with. He'd never be readier. He slung the backpack over his shoulder and stepped across Fifth Avenue. If he had any regrets for what he was about to do, it was that, despite what the Brothers had preached, he personally had nothing against the Jews.

Janice Gottlieb left her office at the 92nd Street Y to nip around the corner for a quick coffee with a cultural critic for the *New York Times*. Ms. Gottlieb had been at the Y for almost five years, having landed a plum job as assistant director of public relations for the Y's ongoing series of concerts and speakers. Out-of-towners were always amazed when she told them that she worked at the Y, helping to put on concerts. For most of them, gentiles, "the Y" conjured up visions of indoor swimming pools and basketball courts, but she always patiently explained that this was a Jewish Y, the Young Men's and Young Women's Hebrew Association, one of New York's foremost cultural institutions since its founding in 1874.

One of the best things about her job, thought Janice as she stepped onto Lexington Avenue and headed for a little Greek coffee shop, was that it made her parents so proud. Unlike most of the Jewish women who worked at the Y, Janice hailed from Omaha; New York was more than a thousand miles away, a fabled land that stood as a living monument to Jewish achievement in America.

Her head was still full of these thoughts as she left the building. The fresh air felt good. It was hot today, but not as hot as it was going to get. Janice had already been through a few New York Augusts, when the steam rose off the pavements and the garbage reeked and the city's denizens stripped down to the bare minimum of clothing that decency, or what was left of it, and New York City's public lewdness laws allowed. Which was almost nothing.

She didn't mind. It was something you didn't see back home in Omaha.

There was a young man trying to cross the street, from the look of him obviously not a New Yorker. Instinctively, Janice recognized a kindred spirit, a fellow midwesterner, baffled by the city and intimidated by the traffic. Against the light, he'd gotten halfway across, then chickened out and dashed back to the safety of the curb on the west side of the street. That was how she could tell: a real New Yorker, once committed to jaywalking, would proudly continue carrying out the crime.

"Come on, you can make it!" she shouted at him. The lights on Lex were synched, and even though the crossing showed red, he had plenty of time before the taxis came flying down from Spanish Harlem.

The man looked at her and smiled. Definitely a non–New Yorker. New Yorkers, even transplants, just didn't look like him, or dress like him, or give off that vibe. In fact, as he approached, Janice thought he seemed a little weird, and was briefly sorry she had encouraged him. Out-of-towners had strange ideas about New York and New Yorkers. Instead of waiting to greet him, she turned away.

"Hey, miss!" he shouted and now she really was sorry.

And ashamed of the—what was it? Could it be called big-otry?—what she felt. It wasn't danger, probably, it was just difference. Diversity. Yes, that was it. Diversity.

The man was pointing at the Y, smiling. "Is that the 92nd Street Young Men's Hebrew Association?" he asked and then she knew. But it was too late. She had already nodded and words had already tumbled out of her mouth—

"Yes. I work there."

Raymond was still smiling when he produced a machine pistol and shot her in the chest and in the head, just the way the Brothers had taught him. One Jew down, so many more to go.

He sprinted into the Y, firing as he went. The guards, the metal detectors—nothing was stopping him. It was so easy to squeeze the trigger, and they all went down so fast.

"You okay, Sid?" From a distance, Sheinberg could hear Lannie's voice calling to him. "Sidney, talk to me!" There was a terrible pressure on his chest, which was one of the things that was hindering his reply. Sid took a deep breath and winced at the pain.

"What happened?" He tried to focus his eyes, then real-ized he was upside down, still strapped into his seat and dan-gling in midair.

"Some kind of bomb. While they blinded us."

"Eyeless in Gaza," muttered Sid, although why that par-ticular expression came to him at this moment he could not know. But he knew he was right.

"Come on."

Sid could feel Lannie's fumbling with the seat belt clasp. In the distance he could hear explosions, maybe gunfire. Aside from training, he had never used his weapon; in the parlance of the squad room, he was a virgin. "A virgin Hebe," some of the guys called him, in honor of the character in

Q&A, which was every detective's favorite movie, but he didn't care: the virgin Hebe had been the guy who, at the end, took down Nick Nolte's rogue Irish cop.

Sid hit the top of the car with the thud, but didn't feel a thing. "I think my legs are fucked, Lannie," he said, but Lannie wasn't listening. Instead, he was pulling Sid through one of the shattered windows, out of the car and into the street. The pavement was burning hot. Lannie hauled him to his feet.

"I can't walk, Lannie. I can't." The pain was excruciating.

"I don't give a shit," shouted Lannie. "You walk, I carry you, it doesn't matter. We gotta get out of here."

The two men were face-to-face. Amazing how all that had divided them didn't matter anymore. Not ethnicity, not religion. It was a cliché, but it was true: right now, they were both Americans, fighting for their lives and their country.

"Whoever these fuckers are," Lannie was shouting, "I am personally going to fuck up their shit two times."

Through his pain, Sid Sheinberg smiled. Lannie was such a Brooklyn boy.

Byrne managed to grab his radio, but he knew before he tried that he wouldn't get through. Everything around him was on fire, and he knew enough from all the war-gaming they'd done that Times Square probably wasn't the only place in the city that was burning right now.

What was it Sid Sheinberg had said about the cyber-attack—a redirect through Mumbai. Byrne's mind raced, trying to intuit what was going on. In 2008, a group of ten Pakistani-trained terrorists had attacked Mumbai and held the entire city hostage for nearly three days, killing nearly three hundred people before the Indian police managed to take them down, killing nine and capturing one.

As Byrne tried to shake some sense back into his head, he

repeated that to himself: ten gunman had held one of the world's largest cities hostage.

Oh, Jesus.

A Mumbai-style attack was one of the CTU's worst nightmares. A handful of killers who didn't care whether they lived or died could do tremendous damage, not simply in human terms, in the number of lives taken, but in psychological damage. The Indians had been used to it, since their country, with its huge Muslim minority, had been subjected to ongoing horrific attacks of terrorism for years. Mumbai had been hit repeatedly, including a nasty series of train bombings in 1993 that killed more than two hundred and fifty people and wounded seven hundred others. True, periodically the Hindu majority wreaked its terrible revenge, but even bloody retaliation hadn't stopped the ongoing conflict between two irreconcilable beliefs and political systems.

And we thought it couldn't happen here, thought Byrne. Secular America was beyond such petty religious squabbles; nobody, not even the twelve nuns left in the United States, took their faith that seriously anymore; we mourned Michael Jackson, not Jesus, and suffered along with the contestants and judges on *American Idol.* And yet we worried. Which was one of the reasons why, in the wake of 9/11, Manhattan's defenses had been hardened and strengthened. And what good had it done?

He realized he had his .38 in his hand, his father's gun, and was running toward to the destruction now, east, toward the wreckage that could only have come from a car bomb, and toward the gun battle he could hear in the distance at Times Square.

And then he heard the explosion behind him, to the south, and he knew they were in for it now.

CHAPTER EIGHTEEN

Washington, D.C.

Tyler's reeling presidency couldn't take much more of this, thought Army Seelye as they gathered in the Oval Office: the president, Seelye, and Byrne; plus the SecDef, Shalika Johnson; Celina Sanchez, the National Security Advisor; the DNI, Lamont Sutton; Colangelo from Homeland Security; and General Higgins from the Joint Chiefs. Even Col. Grizzard, the man with the football, was present.

Seelye felt a sense of despair wash over him. These were the best minds of the Republic, or should have been. They owed that, at least, to the American people who were paying their salaries and trusting in them to do the right thing, which was, first and foremost, protect them. Instead what the great American people got was this collection of hacks, time-servers, and affirmative-action appointees, most of whom couldn't get a job in the private sector unless it had something to do with their brother-in-law or a government contract. It really was pathetic when you thought about it: that more than two centuries of American History had come to this.

The old Tyler's first instinct would have been caution,

wait and see; the new Tyler, emboldened by his success last year in stopping the EMP attack on the east coast, would want to hit back, strike out. But this Tyler was already a different man—one who saw his political death staring him in the face. There was no way out of this. No matter how much worse things got in New York, the damage was already done. Hassett might as well start measuring the Oval Office for new drapes, especially with the endorsement that sonofabitch Jake Sinclair already ringing over the airwaves.

"What's the situation?" asked the president, as if he didn't already know. He looked at Seelye to begin the briefing.

"A short while ago, the Counter-Terrorism Unit of the New York City Police Department came under a coordinated denial-of-service attack from various points overseas," Seelye began. "As you know, NYPD has been given extraordinary latitude in defending the city, especially after we all let them down so badly on 9/11. And, as you also know, they've been extraordinarily successful in preventing further attacks—at least fourteen that we know about." On the silent TV screens, images of a burning New York danced to the unheard words of the network anchors' professional, dispassionate concern.

"But today was different. We've seen coordinated cyber-assaults before—hell, the DoD gets them on a daily basis, mostly from China. Our infrastructure is also routinely probed, including the electrical grid, computer networks, and the water supply. While we're sleeping, our enemies are awake, trying to take us down, and no amount of kumbaya is going to change that. You'd think we'd all learned that by now, from 9/11."

That part was bureaucratic ass-covering. Seelye knew that Tyler would now turn on Sutton and Colangelo, and he was right.

"God-fucking-damn it!" exclaimed the volcano, exploding from his chair behind the *Resolute* desk. "Ladies and gentlemen, the American taxpayer spends a hellacious amount of money on us annually, and the only thing that John and Jane Q. Fucking Public expect in return is that we keep their asses safe. And now," he gestured at the TV sets, "we've let them down again . . . *I've* let them down again."

"Sir," began Colangelo. This was not going to look good for Homeland Security, and the Secretary was leaping to the defense of his turf. Would that he would leap to the defense of his country with such alacrity. "With all due respect, my department has done everything in its power to—"

"Shut the fuck up, Bob," shouted Tyler and Seelye flashed back to the late Senator Bob Hartley, Tyler's friend from across the aisle, whom he had left to hang out to dry in the interests of state, and so caused his death. Seelye wondered how heavily that weighed on the man behind the desk.

"If I may, sir," interjected Sutton. The Director of National Intelligence was another accretion from the aftermath of 9/11, part of the defensive political reaction to the disaster: the creation of yet more bureaucratic bullshit, sold to the American public as a great leap forward in the defense of democracy.

"You may not," snapped Tyler. "I know what you're going to say, what you're all going to say. We don't have the right equipment. We don't have enough manpower. We don't have enough money. Nobody in this town ever has enough men and matériel; nobody ever has enough money. The American people throw it at you like women throwing their panties at a rock star, and still it's not enough. It's never fucking enough. I sign the budget authorizations and yet we still have secretaries that don't talk to each other, crap-assed equipment that sucked back in 1984, and a metastasizing bureaucracy of vampires that hoovers the life out of our countrymen while it fucks them in the ass and doesn't even give 'em the courtesy of a reach-around."

"So," Tyler concluded, "what are we going to do? And

don't give me any bullshit. Give me your best recommendations and make sure they're good, because if they aren't I am going down. But before I do, I am taking you all with me."

The usual boilerplate. Homeland Security wanted to send in the Army. General Higgins pointed out that sending in the Army was basically unconstitutional. The Director of National Intelligence had no particular intelligence. Defense Secretary Johnson kept her mouth shut, waiting for Seelye's turn. But Tyler turned to Byrne first.

"Deputy Director Byrne, what do you say?"

Tom Byrne looked around the room. He'd had long experience with the Soviets and their surrogates and cutouts, and while everybody else's attention was directed to the Arab world by the spectacular example of the crashing Twin Towers, Tom had kept his eye on the ball. He knew that the old enemy was not really dead, just sleeping, reconstituting, lying in wait. The Soviets had had extensive dealings in the Islamic world. People forgot that the Tudeh Party, Iran's communists, had allied themselves with the Ayatollah against the Shah as the Soviets sought hegemony both in the Iranian oil fields and in the Caspian Sea—only to see the whole thing fall apart in the wake of mass executions as Khomeini turned on his erstwhile allies and liquidated them.

All this Tom Byrne laid out in a calm and rational voice. He had always been the calculating one; emotion he left to his brother, Frankie, the hotheaded cop, who at least once too often had shot first and asked questions later. Frankie still had plenty on him, but in this world, where every e-mail was read and every phone conversation was recorded, who didn't? Lack of privacy was just something the world had to live with. Brass balls would have to see him through.

"So what's your recommendation, Director Byrne?" asked Tyler, who seemed impressed. If Byrne's reputation as a major-league asshole had preceded him, today's appearance severely diminished it.

Tom welcomed the attention. It wasn't often he got to tell off the brass, and he was going to make the most of his moment. And get back at his brother, although that was incidental at this point. "My recommendation is nothing," he began. "First, you can't send in the Army, not just for legal reasons but for political ones. You send in the Army and it tells the country that you've lost all control of our borders. You think that fight over illegal immigration was bad? It was nothing.

"Second, you have to let NYPD handle this. We don't know how many gunmen there are, or—"

"What the hell difference does it make?" shouted Colangelo, manning up. "We've already lost Times Square and the Holland Tunnel, and for all we know they might have smuggled a nuke or two into the city while our pants were down, so—"

"That's precisely correct, Mr. Secretary. We don't know. We should but we don't. You send troops in there and you're going to have an even bigger catastrophe on your hands." Byrne wished he could light a cigarette, but in the new fascist-friendly America, everything that was not expressly allowed was forbidden. "I grew up in New York. The city's never been part of America, not really. We rooted for the Brits during the Revolution, faked patriotism during World War II, when half my Irish people were working for the Germans, and have supported every commie notion since before they fried the Rosenbergs. A lot of New Yorkers hate America, more or less, which is why God gave us the New York Yankees to beat the crap out of the rest of the American League. Whatever happens, happens. But let them handle it."

"Director Byrne's bother, Francis, is the head of the CTU of NYPD," interjected Seelye, hoping to sound like the voice of reason. For his own purposes, he had no desire to see Tyler send in the caissons; as bad as this thing was, they had to let it unfold, to find out who was behind it. Not that he had much doubt and neither, he suspected, did Tyler. "I think we should listen to him."

"Let me get this straight," said Shalika Johnson. Over the past few months, Seelye had gradually been sizing her up, and he liked what he saw. He could work with her. "You're telling me that the National Security Agency is seconding the motion to let New York fry?"

" 'Fry' is not the way I'd put it, but—"

"Well, how do you put it?" retorted Johnson. "I mean, it's *your* agency that's supposed to ensure cyber-security. It's *your* agency that reads every e-mail, listens in to every phone conversation. It's *your* agency that's supposed to—"

"You're talking about classified information, Madame Secretary," responded Seelye, coolly.

"I'm talking about the damn Black Widow," said Johnson. "That's what I'm talking about. And I want to know why it didn't work, why it failed us at this crucial moment and why New York City's on fire right now." She gestured empathically toward the televisions and then turned back to Tyler. "With all due respect, Mr. President, please don't give us some song and dance about the Kaypros in the Commerce Department and the Trash-80s at IRS. We all know that NSA gets whatever it wants, and a lot of times it gets it under the table, off-budget and off the books. That's why NSA has stuff like the Black Widow while we make do with whatever." She paused, and then, almost as an afterthought, added: "And God only knows what CSS gets."

Well, there it was: the Central Security Service. Tyler wondered if she knew; certainly he had never told her. He glanced over at Seelye, but the longtime NSA chief was his usual impassive self. Well, if the Sec Def was ignorant, she wouldn't be for long. He would see to that, right after this meeting was adjourned. Which would be very soon, since he had made up his mind.

He liked this Tom Byrne character, found him a man after his own heart. Sure, he'd made his career faking both sympathy and empathy, whereas Byrne had clawed his way to the top despite everybody's loathing of him at nearly every step. To get that far, Byrne either had to be ruthless, or have something on everybody in town or, more likely, both. In any case, they could do business together.

Why Byrne seemed to want to abandon Manhattan to its fate was still a little puzzling, but he assumed the man had his reasons. Being from Louisiana, Tyler only knew New York the way the rest of the nation knew it, as a tourist. Byrne was the genuine article.

Which meant his brother was likely to be as well. In fact, if what he'd read and been told was true, his brother was even tougher than he was. Frankie Byrne was nobody's idea of the kindly cop on the beat, but he'd caught the nastiest assignments on the force and distinguished himself in every one. Oh, there'd been trouble along the way, but F. X. Byrne—the altar boy's name hardly seemed suitable—had been both tough and smart, tough enough to get out of tight spots, with firepower when necessary, and smart enough to hitch his wagon to the only star brighter than his in the department when they came up together: to J. Arness White, the Commissioner of Police. The man who sat where O'Ryan and TR once sat, the man who was the odds-on favorite to be the next Mayor of the City of New York and was goddamn sure to be even now figuring out a way to salvage this situation from the shit. What Tom Byrne knew, what he felt, Frankie Byrne knew and felt, too. They'd been through too much together, and Tyler instinctively grasped that neither of them was likely to let the other go down, and sure as hell not without a fight. If he'd had a brother, he'd want their relationship to be exactly the same.

"Cut off the island of Manhattan," said Tyler. "Seal all the tunnels and blockade the bridges—all of them, not just the toll roads. Railroad bridges, too. Nothing and nobody goes in or out of the island until we get our arms around this thing." He had to pretend to get the others involved and so he looked at Colangelo and Sutton. "Keep your ears to the ground. Use every asset you have, HUMINT or ELINT. I want to know what the world is thinking and saying about this. Every little detail, no matter how innocuous, could potentially be helpful. And, for God's sake, keep NORTHCOM out of this until I say so." That would keep them busy for a while.

"Otherwise, we let NYPD play this one out. I want to let the American people know that politics has nothing to do with this. The easy thing, the telegenic thing, would be to send in the Army or the National Guard. But that's probably exactly what they're expecting us to do—and then who knows what will happen, or what they've got? For too long we've worried about the death of a single soldier or civilian, and let hundreds, thousands of our people die for our prissy precaution. Well, as Harry Truman said, the buck stops here. May God have mercy on the souls of the people who will die, that others might live. God bless America. Thank you, ladies and gentlemen," said Tyler, rising and signaling that the meeting was over.

Puzzled looks were exchanged. "Secretary Johnson, Director Seelye, will you kindly remain after the others leave?"

Nobody said a word as the room emptied. Byrne lingered a little, as if half-expecting to be spoken to. In this, he was not disappointed. "Thank you, Director," said Tyler, shaking his hand. "I'm sorry that your brother is in the shit, but—"

"Frankie can handle it, Mr. President," said Byrne. "In the shit is where he lives."

"I don't know your brother, Byrne," replied Tyler, "but from everything I've read he's a hell of a guy. I look forward to welcoming him to the White House when this is all over."

"I'll be sure to tell him that, sir," said Tom.

"I'm counting on it," said Tyler, ushering him out. Once the door was shut and Ms. Dhouri signaled that the coast was clear, Tyler spoke again to his remaining confidantes.

"Army, I think there's something you need to tell Secretary Johnson?"

CHAPTER NINETEEN

Los Angeles

"Dad?"

Danny Impellatieri heard the voice of his nine-year-old daughter, Jade, as if in a dream. It was not that he didn't hear it—no parent can ignore the sound of his own child's voice—or that he didn't care, but he was riveted to what was going on in Manhattan.

Jade stuck her head around the corner of his study and made a face at him. He was sitting at his desk, several computers going at once; instinctively, he minimized the video feeds on one of the screens, and turned toward her as she spoke: "Did you know that operating two computers at once is one of the telltale signs of nerd-dom?" she asked playfully. "It is. You can Google it. What are you watching?"

Danny tried not to let the concern he felt, both professional and personal, show in his face. Jade had already been through a lot in her young life, and there was no point in putting her through this, however remotely, unless he absolutely had to. She'd find out soon enough.

"Just some stuff for work."

She didn't fall for it. He didn't expect her to. "I thought you were off work. You just got home."

"I am," he lied. "Or, rather, I was. But, you know . . ."

"Duty calls, right?" She was a sharp kid, with sharp eyes and ears. It hadn't been as hard raising her by himself the past nine months as he thought it was going to be, as everybody had said it would be. Although they had both taken Diane's death hard, they had also realized that the only way to get through the grief and the loss was to do it together, and so they had made an unspoken pact: Diane would live, forever, in their hearts, and life would go on.

Jade stepped into the room, a little hesitant as she crossed the threshold and stopped. This had always been his inner sanctum, a place she had been trained to stay out of, not from fear of punishment, but because it was her father's private space. The big house on Hobart Street had plenty of places for a kid to play in, to get lost in, and when all else failed there was always the swimming pool and the big, overgrown yard beyond it. "What is it?" she said, with that tone in her voice. The tone that said: *I know something is wrong.*

"Nothing."

"Don't nothing me, Dad." She was right: he should never *nothing* her again. He owed her that much. He owed Diane that much.

"There's some trouble, back in New York." There, he said it. He knew it wouldn't take long for her young mind to make the leap, the leap straight toward his heart.

"New York? That's where Mrs. Gardner is, right?"

He nodded. "Yes. And Rory and Emma."

"Are they okay?"

"I'm sure they are. New York's a big city, bigger than L.A."

"You should check." She was right. He already had.

And nothing. Cell service was spotty and was likely to be for a long time. That was one of the lessons of 9/11, the instant disruption of communications not simply by a terrorist act, but by the sheer volume—a kind of self-inflicted denial-of-service attack. The Emergency Services units had learned from that disaster and had developed relatively secure methods of communication, but theirs would be just about the only signals working reliably on the island of Manhattan. He was going to have to hack into them to find out what the hell was going on.

He looked at his iPhone, as if expecting it to say something. Why hadn't he called? If the hostage situation in Edwardsville had been enough to activate Danny and a hand-picked unit from Xe, the old Blackwater group, then surely an assault on Manhattan would—

"Have you reached her?" He shook his head. "But you've tried?"

He nodded. He hadn't expected things to move this quickly, felt there was something unseemly about it and had resisted. But the heart did what the heart did, and although neither of them had so much had hinted at it, he suspected that not only did they know, but that their children did, too.

He looked at Jade. You could hardly see a trace of her injuries, except for a few scars on her face. In a city filled with great plastic surgeons, Dr. Kamin had made all the scars disappear; you practically had to look at her face under a microscope to see the tiny pitting caused by the flying glass in the Grove bombing. The bombing that had taken Diane's life and changed his world forever. Nine months on, the Grove's rubble had long since been carted away and a new and better high-end shopping center was going up on the site. But the hole in his heart had only just begun to mend. Hope had lost her husband as well, not at the Grove but during the Edwardsville school-hostage crisis that had immediately preceded it; that was the act of war that had brought them together, and that was the bond that was pulling them ever closer.

And now he couldn't reach her. Where the hell was "Linus Larrabee" when he needed him?

Not that "Linus Larrabee" was the man's real name. Danny had worked with his mysterious colleague for years, most recently on the Budapest snatch, where they had both used Humphrey Bogart character aliases. But that didn't mean he knew who he was. They had always engaged each other only through cutouts, with "Larrabee," or whichever randomly generated alias he was using for that particular mission, always initiating contact.

He stared at his iPhone. That was how they communicated with one another. The most compromised popular technology on the planet, and at the same time the most useful.

Most people didn't realize that every time they used their iPhone, the SKIPJACK chip gave the NSA access to everything the phone users generated: phonebooks, websites visited, photos, the works. As the so-called "warrantless wiretapping" program had proven, the telephone companies, such as AT&T, were in bed with the government, and despite all the lawsuits that the American Civil Liberties Union could bring against what was left of Ma Bell, in the end it didn't really matter. In the sacred name of national security, the National Security Agency was going to get its way. Devlin would have nearly instant access to any message on the iPhone that rang the bell back at The Building, even while the Black Widow was still chomping down on the data.

The Black Widow. Not the fastest supercomputer in the world anymore—that honor probably went to the Cray XT5 Jaguar at the Oak Ridge National Laboratory in Tennessee, one of the principal birthplaces of the American nuclear program during the Manhattan Project, which boasted a processing rate of 1.759 petaflops. Home computer users had gradually accustomed themselves to bits and bytes and megabytes and even gigabytes, but supercomputing took speed to an astronomical new level. FLOPS—floating point operations per second—were the new benchmark, measured in teraflops (10^{12} flops) and petaflops (10^{15}), or one quadrillion flops. But the dreaded Widow was still plenty fast enough, and she never slept, on guard against America's enemies throughout each dark, dangerous night.

Most of the bed-wetters at the *New York Times* and elsewhere in what was left of the American establishment took it as a given that the Black Widow and other components of the "illegal eavesdropping" program were listening to them. In the solipsistic world of the Good Gray Lady and other pillars of the Democrat-Media Establishment, everything was about them. They woke up in the morning and went to bed at night believing in vast right-wing conspiracies; in forces bent with hostile intent on depriving them of their civil liberties; of the presence in America of a huge, inimical mass of people who were only a beer and a shot away from joining the KKK and the Michigan Militia. From dawn til dusk they shook with terror at the hidden—but so transparent!—motives and emotions of their fellow citizens, and fled to the embrace of their shrinks and grief counselors and the hosts on MSNBC at the first available opportunities. It was so much easier than facing the reality that people they didn't even know—enemies they hadn't met yet—were out to kill them. Much more comforting to suspect the couple down the street, the ones with the New Hampshire flag on their car bumpers: "Don't Tread on Me."

For his part, Danny and the rest of his old crew from the 160th SOAR had learned from bitter experience to fight the battle in front of them. And then hit the bars instead of the psychiatrists' couches. Easier that way, cheaper, and if the medical reports were to be believed, healthier all the way around. He wished he could have a drink, but it was still too early and besides, his daughter was standing right there in front of him. Not the enemy, but the person he loved most in the entire world.

He punched in the magic words. "Now I have," he said.

She was wiser than he, and probably smarter. She had had to do a lot of growing up fast in the past nine months, part of her rude and premature confrontation with the everyday horrors of the world. No matter how you tried to protect your child from reality—and wasn't that what parenting was, in the end, all about?—reality had a way of intruding whenever it wished, as if God or the universe of whatever was hell-bent on reminding mere puny human beings that they controlled the ongoing nihilist narrative, not the snarky screenwriters, not the smarmy politicians, not the small-minded editorialists who left downtown Los Angeles and went home not to Angelino Heights, which would have been a five-minute drive, but to Brentwood, or West L.A. or Flintridge or Pasadena or even Montecito or Santa Barbara.

Jade declined to follow his thoughts. Instead, she stood there in the doorway, waiting. Finally he understood. He opened his arms to his daughter, and she ran to him.

For a long time, they held each other, no words necessary.

He made up his mind quickly. "Honey," he said, "we have to go now."

Jade was young, but she was smart. She didn't have to ask where they were going. All she knew was that, this time, he was taking her with him.

CHAPTER TWENTY

Teterboro, New Jersey

Devlin felt the pingback before he heard it. "Showtime," he said to Maryam.

He took out a PDA, a special, modified BlackBerry just like the one the president used. Tyler famously did not want to give up his mobile device, and so rather than go without he'd asked some of the best minds at the agency to come with an uncrackable device. Whether it was in fact uncrackable was open to conjecture, and in any case Devlin assumed that the NSA could crack it anytime they wanted to; if Tyler thought no one would be monitoring his conversations he was probably very much mistaken. The point was, Devlin had one just like it, but insofar as he could make it, it was better and even more secure.

The message was from Seelye, officially authorizing him into action. Not that that really mattered, since he'd already decided on his course of action, knew they had no other choice. Under the terms of his deal, he could do what he wanted when he wanted and if the government didn't like it it had two choices: terminate him or live with it. It was not a privilege he abused, but rather insisted upon, and there was no one to gainsay him. As long as Seelye held his job, Devlin was both his boy and his master.

"Punch up every point of subterranean access to Manhattan," he told Maryam, who was already working the computers, calling up every map the NSA and other governmental databases had on file.

Few civilians realized it, but the island of Manhattan was riddled with tunnels: automobile tunnels, steam tunnels, train tunnels, subway tunnels, water tunnels, electrical tunnels; it was a wonder that the island hadn't collapsed into New York Harbor of its own weight. But Manhattan bedrock was stern stuff.

"That's how we get in, huh?" she said. Her eyes were aglow with an eagerness to get into the fight, an eagerness that nearly matched his own, although he would never let it show. The Angel of Death had no emotion when it was time to wield his sword.

"That's how *I* get in," he corrected. "The zone is red hot, and you're more useful to me elsewhere." Her face fell, but she said nothing. There was nothing to say: he was the boss.

At another computer, Devlin took stock of the situation: Times Square was a battleground, with the cops engaged in a running firefight with an unknown number of assailants. Inwardly, he shuddered. This had been one of the planners' worst nightmares for years, but the attack on Mumbai a few years back had upped the stakes significantly. Conventional wisdom had been that a suicide bomber or two might self-detonate near the TKTS booth, killing scores of tourists and causing panic. But the Pakistani-directed attacks on Mumbai by members of the *Lashkar-e-Taiba* terrorist organization, changed everybody's thinking: Mumbai, like New York, was surrounded by water, and it was by water that the attackers had come, putting ashore in small boats and bringing death with them. And now they were here.

He punched in Seelye's secure number on the computer

and waited for the randomly generated redirects to conclude. "Are you ready?" came the voice from the computer speakers.

"Assessment."

"The attacks are still coming; they're not just limited to Times Square as we first thought. There's been reports of gunfire on the Upper East Side, at the 92nd Street Y. We've got all the bridges and tunnels sealed, except for the Holland, which has been bombed."

"How bad?"

"The Manhattan side; otherwise, the structure is intact. Remember they plotted to do this at least once before, back in 2006, when they thought they could flood lower Manhattan by taking out the tunnel. The FBI broke up that plot, and the sensors, plus the no tractor-trailer rule, have kept the bad stuff out."

"Mission objective?"

There was a pause as the man who had raised him after the deaths of his parents at the 1985 airport massacre in Rome considered his next words. "I don't know. Tyler thinks you're a miracle worker."

"Why hasn't the National Guard been called in?"

"The president thinks the cops should handle it. And for what it's worth, so does the DD of the FBI, Tom Byrne Seems his brother, Francis, is the chief of the CTU. One of the city's top cops, and a real Irish warrior."

"Great," said Devlin. "We've got family pride being brought to bear on a major emergency."

"Or family rivalry, I can't tell. The point is that you're to get in there, assess the situation for us without being made, take out as many of them as you can, and get the hell out. You know the drill."

He knew the drill. As the lead operative of the Central Security Service's Branch 4, Devlin lived a life on the edge, not simply of danger but of existence itself. Branch 4 ops were unknown to each other, and their existence was known only to three officers of the U.S. government: the President, the Secretary of Defense, and the director of the National Security Agency, or DIRNSA. A loss of anonymity was a death sentence, whether carried out by an enemy agent or, cruelly but necessarily, by a fellow member of Branch 4. That was the blow you would never see coming.

For a moment his mind flashed back to Milverton, the most potent adversary of his career, lying dead in his small house in London, put in his grave by Devlin himself, with both relief and regret.

"You want me to clean them all?"

"For starters."

"But what you really need to know is who's behind it. How much time have I got?"

"Not much. You can imagine the firestorm we're in the middle of. The President's—"

"—ass is in a sling, mostly of his own making. Hassett is going to hammer him no matter which way this thing shakes out, and he'll have the faces of the dead staring at him right through the election. He doesn't want to invoke the *Posse Comitatus* act and get the military involved if he doesn't have to. This is law enforcement, not war. Otherwise it's just what the terrorists want. If we call in the Marines, the terrorists win; if we don't call in the Marines, the terrorists win. Who thought up that play? The Marx Brothers?" Devlin paused. He was urgently aware of the need to bring the situation under control as quickly as possible, but he couldn't let himself be distracted by emotion. Somehow, he was going to have to get into Manhattan, identify this Byrne guy, and work with him without ever giving himself away. "What about NORTHCOM and the Rock of the Marne and the Sea Smurfs? The rules don't apply to them."

NORTHCOM—the United States Northern Command—was the Army command created after 9/11, and explicitly tasked with the defense of the homeland. Few Americans knew anything about NORTHCOM, and fewer still knew that since 2008 it had controlled the Third Infantry Division's First Brigade Combat Team, which was charged with controlling the civilian population in the wake of civil unrest or a terrorist attack. Based in Fort Steward, Georgia, the Third Division, known as the "Rock of the Marne" thanks to its valorous service in World War I, had seen its 1st Brigade essentially seconded to the feds to deal with domestic disturbances. The brigade, which now also included sailors, airmen, and Marines, had been renamed the "Chemical, biological, radiological, nuclear, or high-yield explosive Consequence Management Response Force (CCMRF), which was immediately dubbed the "Sea Smurfs."

"So far they're staying out of it. But if things go south . . ."

Now Devlin understood. He had to give it to the man: Tyler got smarter and more devious every day. "So you're sending me in to keep Tyler looking good on his left while I'm supposed to keep him looking good on his right."

"That's about the size of it—secondarily speaking, of course."

"I don't know which of you I hate more."

"It's a tough choice, I'll give you that. We can sort it out later. In the meantime—"

"They're communicating by cell phone."

"*Were*," corrected Seelye. "We bubbled it down."

"Then bubble it back up—we need to know where each of these clowns is, so locate them and start tracking them. In the meantime, they're probably using something like BBM, so tap that net, too. I'll want a real-time map once I'm in. Weapons?"

"Everything you can need, including a judge. Sending you the code now." An instant, and then the unlocking codes for the armory appeared on his screen. "What about your partner?"

Not for the first time, Devlin felt like reaching through the ether and throttling Seelye. As secure as their communications were—and they were as secure as the best minds in NSA/CSS, including his, could make them—they were still not secure enough, could never be secure enough, for him to safeguard Maryam the way he wanted to. He had brought her into this, and she had willingly joined him, but her safety was now his prime concern—more so than his own and, God help him, maybe even more so than his country's.

"Who?" he said. Point made.

Devlin glanced up and caught her look. Silently, he shook his head at her: *it's not what you think.* Her eyes stayed liquid, reproachful as the voice went off inside Devlin's head:

"Do you trust the bitch? I don't see why you should. She was on to you in Paris before I was. You don't even know her real name, do you?"

Devlin shook his head, trying to clear the webs, to get a dead man's voice out of his consciousness, trying to ignore the question, the first question, the only question, about her that really mattered, and the one question he didn't want an answer to: not because he didn't want to know, but because he didn't want to have to face the consequences of his knowledge.

"Right," said Seelye. "So off you go. Good luck, son." He rang off, if you could call disconnecting from a nearly infinite network "ringing off."

Maryam looked away as he tried to meet her eyes. "Why don't you trust me? I mean, what else do I have—"

"I do trust you. That's just the problem. If I didn't trust you I'd take you inside with me, and maybe get you killed. If I didn't trust you, I'd miss you, I'd mourn you, but it wouldn't be the end of the world. But I *do* trust you. I don't know why, but I do."

"Which is why—"

"Which is why I'm sending you elsewhere. Somewhere important. Somewhere where you can help me . . ."

". . . find the source of the DoS attack." She'd got it in one. That was another of the reasons why he loved her, and trusted her.

"We find that, we know who we're up against." She was already punching keys as he continued: "And that's another reason why I have to go in and you have to get out. You're never going to be able to hack into the CTU's computers from here. Oh, you might be able to take them down for a stretch if you had enough typing robot monkeys, but they're off our grid. So I'm going to have to find this Byrne character and check it from the inside."

"Where should I go? I can't stay here."

For the first time, Devlin smiled. Outside, the world might be going to hell, but in this last quiet moment, it was just the two of them.

"We've got one clue." Devlin punched some keys and then, to her astonishment, Maryam realized she was listening to conversations recorded inside the Counter-Terrorism Unit of the New York City Police Department that very day:

"Hard to tell until we take a closer look, but first guess is the Chinese."

"First guess is always the Chinese. Another reason to hate Nixon . . . never mind. Continue."

"But upon closer review, they might be Indians. There are some indications of a redirect via Mumbai—that's Bombay to you, buddy—but now that I look at it, I think this is a flea flicker too. So I—we—are going with Azerbaijani. Baku, probably."

"What happened in the window?"

"Running a recap now . . . And it's not Baku. It's Budapest."

Maryam looked up with a half-smile of disbelief on her lips. "You bugged the NYPD?"

Devlin shrugged. "Fuck 'em if they can't take a joke."

"Budapest," she said.

"It's as good a place to start as any. Besides, you know your way around that town, as I recall."

Devlin stood and punched in some codes on one of the overhead storage compartments. He could have opened it with the latch, but that would have gotten him nowhere. It might even have gotten them both killed. Any plane authorized for use by the Central Security Service came fully equipped with extreme-prejudice countermeasures should any trolls or doubles be aboard. The easiest and most effective preventative measure was the sudden injection of poison gas into the passenger compartment, on the theory that once the mission was compromised there was no point in trying to preserve any of the operationals; all had been lost and all must be liquidated in the name of Op Sec.

Codes were a good thing.

The latch opened and the compartment door popped open, but instead of revealing pieces of luggage and presents for the kids, the rear of the space opened up and moved forward, offering Devlin a wide choice of personal weapons.

He outfitted himself the way he liked to fight. Throwing knives inside each of his back pockets, a KA-BAR in its scabbard down the back of his jeans, and a couple of grenades in his jacket. Twin Glock 37s with ten-shot magazines under each armpit, with a pair of Colt .38s revolvers for the special pockets that were always sewn into the front of his pants. Anything else he needed, he could pick up in combat. The bad guys always came armed, and one of his first orders of business was to disarm them with extreme prejudice and appropriate their weapons as necessary. Most often of Chinese or old Soviet manufacture, but beggars couldn't be choosers.

And then, just as promised, there was the Judge.

The Taurus Judge was, at its cold little heart, simplicity

itself. Most of the time you used a handgun, the target was standing nearly directly in front of you. Sure, the movies showed cops trading shots with .38s from distances of several hundred feet, but in real life that hardly ever happened—and besides there were better weapons for that sort of killing. A handgun was more like a sword, a weapon best wielded as close-in distances; marksmanship was less important than a steady hand and willingness to pull the trigger. It so happened that Devlin was a marksman with a handgun, as he was with every other weapon he had ever trained on or been instructed in. But the Judge was something different.

Originally invented for outdoorsmen who spent a lot of time in snake country, or at least quickly adopted by them, the Judge was a five-shot Tracker .45 revolver with a lengthened frame and cylinder, which meant that not only could it take a standard .45 Colt round, it could also fire a .410 shotgun shell, buckshot, or rifle slugs, and in any combination. Even the best shot sometimes found it difficult to nail a sidewinder on the first shot, which is why the dispersing firepower of a shotgun shell came in mighty handy at close quarters. So whether you were shooting at something fifty feet away or just about to bite you on the ass, the Judge made a perfect defensive weapon. Even the most appeasement-oriented State Department official couldn't miss with one of these, although whether he'd want to take the shot, even in the interests of self-preservation, was another matter. Devlin briefly wondered at the suicide cult the American diplomatic establishment had become. Sometimes he felt like he was fighting a civil war against his own government, and half his own people.

"What about you?" Maryam's voice intruded upon his lethal reverie. Devlin turned to look at her. Standard-issue saucer eyes, deep dark brown. Light olive skin that allowed her to pass for almost anything: Indian, Italian, Spanish,

American Indian, Afghani. A generic Third World woman, if you viewed her that way. He did not. She was the woman he loved.

Perhaps, by any rational analysis, not a woman worth dying for. She was short and compact, like most Iranian women, and eventually she'd run to fat and turn into a little Persian butterball, able to spout Hafiz as well as Horace as she whipped up some *champa, naan, beryani,* and *chai,* and woe betide any son of a bitch that interrupted their repast. Hafiz, after all, had stared down Tamerlane, and she could do no less. In Devlin's world the future was as ever-receding as the horizon, but not half so trustworthy.

"*Bulbul zi shakh-i sarw be gulbang-i pahlavi / Mikhwand dosh dars-i maqamat-i ma'navi.*"

"What did you say?" He never ceased to surprise her. It was one of the many things she loved about him.

"*Last night, from the cypress branch, the nightingale sang—*"

Without hesitation, she finished the couplet for him. "*In Old Persian tones, the lesson of spiritual stations.*" Although we could translate 'spiritual' as 'meaningful,' which sort of ruins it. Poetically, I mean."

"Hafiz is never ruined, only misunderstood."

"Like Horace?" She never ceased to surprise him. It was why they were perfect together even if they could never really trust one another . . .

He moved to kiss her, then refrained. It might, after all, be their last kiss, and he wanted it to mean something. Wanted it to mean more than any other kiss they had ever exchanged, whether in Paris or Los Angeles or Budapest. Whether in passion or friendship or love or opportunity or greeting or good-bye. No kiss could mean more than the next kiss he would give her. Unless it was the one, *inshallah*, that he would give her when they next met. Whenever and wherever that might be.

"Time to go," he said, punching a last few keys on the computers. He grabbed a few things and made ready to leave.

"What about me?" she asked.

"You know what to do. I'll contact you there." She didn't bother to ask how. She just knew he would. If he was still alive.

Devlin rose and handed Maryam the computer. She was going to need it more than he was, and besides, he'd have others waiting for him on-site. "Use this. It's got a secure link to anyplace you'll need to go. Guard it with your life. If anything happens, make sure to get this before they get you."

He was about to go when he got another pingback, this one on his iPhone. He glanced at the screen. It was a message relayed from The Building. Devlin smiled as he looked at the screen.

"Who is it?" asked Maryam.

"Martin Ferguson."

"Who's that?"

"Someone who lived and died in 1951," he replied. "He used to be somebody. In fact, he used to be an assistant district attorney in New York. Now . . . he needs a friend. And that would be me."

He kissed her like it was the last time. And then he was gone.

CHAPTER TWENTY-ONE

New York

Hope lay amid the rubble, listening for the sounds of her children breathing. She had no idea what had happened, only the knowledge that something terrible had occurred, another manifestation of the evil that had visited her and her family back home in Edwardsville. Lightning never struck twice in the same place, except when it did. Some people went for years without an automobile accident, then had two of them in the space of a week. The law of averages held except when it didn't, and that was when it was evening things out for someone else, somewhere else in the great wide world. We were all prisoners of numbers, and of ruthless dispassionate Nature. And of such singularity were religions born.

This Hope knew as she lay there in the choking blackness. How many stories had she read in which someone—a survivor—had said that God had singled him out for protection, even as others died? Such items were staples of the media because, after all, the dead could not speak, whereas the lucky among the living were there to bear false witness that Somebody Up There cared for them, had saved them, preserved them, from the fate of their comrades. Until, of course, they met the same fate, as eventually everybody must. Hope's faith, never very strong, had now entirely evaporated.

"Mama?" A voice out of the bleak, endless darkness, soft but not weak. It was Emma. She was alive.

"Where's your brother?" Hope asked. "Rory? RORY?"

For a moment, silence. Then—

"I'm over here, Mama. I'm okay."

"Can you walk? Can you move?" Even in asking, Hope realized that she herself could not move. Gingerly, she tested her legs. They seemed to function, but they could not get herself up off the ground. Something was pinning her to the floor.

Hope tried to stay calm. Losing it now would help neither her nor the children. She tried to collect herself. Tried to think.

How could this be happening to her, again? What she had gone through in Edwardsville was nothing put up against what her children had gone through. What Jack had gone through . . .

She felt herself starting to break down. No: stop. Crying wouldn't bring Jack back, wouldn't erase what had happened. Jack was gone, and yet she was still here, and so were Emma and Rory. That was the way he would have wanted it, she was sure. No, she knew. That was the kind of man he was.

So why was she thinking of Danny?

Hope had often read of characters in the chick lit novels she sometimes glanced at, when Janey Eagleton slipped them to her, because she would never buy that kind of trash when Jack was alive, the kind of women that would forget their man the minute they met Fabio, or whatever name he was going by in this particular incarnation, how they would be literally swept off their feet, caught up in his strong arms, smothered by his kisses, their bodies thrilling to his harsh touch and his soft caresses, driving them crazy with the combination of tenderness and violence, sending their minds into paroxysms of confusion, torn between modern shibboleths and ancient passions and with everyone, author and reader, and character alike, knowing which side of the equations they were all about to come down upon in politically incorrect unison.

"Mom?" It was Rory. He had been brave before, not just once but many times, and now her young hero had come to her rescue once more.

The air was filling with smoke from what Hope knew was a raging fire below. They had to get out of here, and fast, or they would suffocate. But she couldn't let on. She had to stay calm. If only she could get free . . .

"It's okay, Mom," Rory was saying. "I can handle it, I think." She felt something move, something scraping across her legs, an awful weight being shifted, rearranged but not lifted.

"Try again, Rory."

"Emma! Help me."

In dread, Hope waited for Emma's assent. Please, God, let her be able to move. Otherwise, they were all lost . . .

"I'm here, Rory," said Emma. "I'm right beside you. Come on—push."

Hope bit down hard as the heavy weight slid across her legs. Something warm and sticky ran down her calves. She could feel the fabric of her skirt rend, her flesh tear—but it was worth it to finally get that awful weight off her limbs.

No matter the pain, she managed to stand. "What was it?" she asked.

"The popcorn machine, Mom," replied Rory. "Now let's get outta here. I think the whole place is about to blow."

At the moment, the building shifted on its foundations. The tilt was noticeable. They were at least ten stories in the air and while that was nowhere near the height of the World Trade Center as it collapsed, she had no wish to experience even one-tenth of the terror those poor souls felt as the Port Authority's underpinnings failed them, and they were sped on their journey to heaven by a sudden, irrevocable plunge toward hell.

"Fire escape," she managed to breathe. The air was getting heavier now. In a couple of minutes, they would have to crawl along the floor, searching for the outside exits.

"But where is it, Mama?" cried Emma.

She had no idea.

"Try your phone," shouted Rory. "Get a map."

Hope had no idea how to do what her son was suggesting. She could barely make him out in outline as she handed the instrument over. "You find it."

Rory slid his fingers over the display. You no longer need to punch keys: now everything was touch-screen, the lighter touch the better. No need to hit anything anymore, no keyboards to pound. No longer even any need for the clicks that IBM once electronically tethered to its keyboards, just so the typists could have some sort of audible feedback. The digital world had replaced the analog, cause and effect were now irretrievably disconnected. It was a metaphor for the brave new world of nothing they were entering: a world in which everything mattered, and nothing caused it.

"Nothing, Ma. We're shut down."

"Then let's get out of here. Any way we can."

There was a great groan as the building shifted again, this time distinctly listing to one side. Hope didn't know much about architecture, but she knew enough about the groans she was hearing to understand that the structure was in great distress, and was soon about to give up the unequal struggle. The building was going down, and the only question was whether they were going to go down with it.

"Come on!" shouted Rory, grabbing his sister's hand. Hope would just have to fend for herself, but that was her generational role; she had done her duty to the species, to the culture, to the country. Now it was up to her children to survive, live on, fight on.

And then the floor fell out from beneath them.

It could have been worse. They could have plummeted four, five, six stories down as the huge structure collapsed upon itself. Instead, they dropped only a few feet, although the creaking of the structural steel continued to resonate throughout the theater complex.

"Mom—what's happening?" screamed Emma. Hope knew her girl was the weak link. They had spent so many hours with the shrinks back home, making sure that she would be okay, no matter what, not that they or anyone could have foreseen this, but even so, Hope always knew that Emma would be the first to break should anything ever happen again, and now here it was, happening again, and so soon thereafter, and there was nothing she could do about it except reach for her baby and hold her and, if necessary, die trying to protect her.

"Come on, Emma—come to Mama!" she shouted She reached . . . reached . . . reached.

The AMC Theaters groaned, shifted, settled. Whatever had caused the explosion had happened on the ground floor, and it was only a matter of time before the entire building entropically headed to the source of the derangement. The scream of the wounded metal was terrifying, but to the Gardner family, it was as from a distance, a call to death that they would not heed.

Hope reached in the dark—and realized that reaching in the dark was all she had ever done. At the moment she had determined to do something about the Edwardsville hostage situation, she had begun to grope her way toward her ultimate goal. When she had crawled across the frozen blacktop on her hands and knees, she began to see it more clearly. When she had come up and fallen into the arms of that horrible man, when she was so close to her children, could prac-

tically hear them calling out to her, when she realized that
she could only save one, that somebody would have to help
her, when that somebody turned out to be her husband, Jack,
and when he died . . .

Somebody else had to save them, then— Danny . . .

And in death there was life. In death for both of them
there was life. And in death they had found each other, amid
blood and misery and grief and loss. Oprah would have
wept, but her audience would have understood—you took
love where you found it, and damn the circumstances, the
only principle of life was, after all, life itself, and no amount
of death, or death cults, or people who loved death more
than they loved life could defeat life itself.

And fuck everybody who didn't understand that simple,
fundamental principle of America and Americanism.

Again, Hope felt violence welling up inside her—a violence that she thought had long since been bred out of her,
beaten out of her, beaten out of the America she had been
born into, an America she had grown up with, an America
she had been raised to think of as good and noble and true
and honorable. And yet for years, they had been telling
her—they, the impersonal they that ran the media, that ruled
in Washington, that she saw every night on her TV set, the
chirping anchors and the serious graybeards, the snarky
commentators who celebrated what she had grown up to
think of as deviancy, shoved it right in her face. She had
often wondered, sitting at home with Jack watching the TV,
why they let them get away with this, when she finally realized that the "they" she had long assumed were in charge of
the America she had once known were no longer the "they"
in charge, that the moral rules had changed, without even an
election, that the rules were new, that the snarky commentators were on the other side, that without even so much as a
press release, the power structure had changed, and she and
everybody else she knew had suddenly come up on the short

side of the equation. How did it happen, and how did it happen so fast?

Had her country gone from American dream to nightmare in her lifetime?

That was a question for another time. Right now, she had to figure out how to get out of here and how to get her kids out of here. It didn't matter if she died, it only mattered whether she could save them

And, by God, she would—no matter how much "they" tried to drive God out of her life, and the life of a country whose money proclaimed "In God We Trust." At that moment, Hope swore to herself that, if she lived, she would contest every local seat, every county board, every state house and senate sinecure, every national office, even the presidency itself. From now on, she would be their worst enemy. And they had no one but themselves to blame, because, finally, they had driven her to it. What a mighty force the American people could be, once aroused.

Emma's hand was in hers. The pain was suddenly gone. Nothing could stop her now.

"Atta girl, Ma!" shouted Rory.

They ran. Not caring what was in front of them in the darkness, not caring whether it was popcorn boxes or movie posters or even dead bodies. The only thing that mattered now was to get to the exit, still vaguely but bravely illuminated against the carnage they knew lurked below.

If only they could make it before the building totally collapsed. If only they could cross the few short yards, no matter what her physical condition. Hope knew she could do it, and prayed passionately that her children could follow. She had never prayed much in her life, beyond the pro-forma Protestantism she had grown up with, a religion that didn't much matter, like any religion, in times of peace. But now they were up against a religion that very much did matter in times of war, a religion that welcomed war, no matter if it was only a tiny minority, as the newspapers kept telling her, no matter if it was only a fraction, a fraction of a billion was a very large fraction and it was that fraction, she knew, that was causing them all this trouble.

The exit sign—

"Come, on Emma!" shouted Rory. "Come on, Mom!"

They ran. The building groaned once more. They ran faster. A small amount of ground, which on the outside you could leap over in a flash, not less than a heartbeat away. A heartbeat, one tick missed and you were gone, one tick missed and you were meeting your maker if Maker there was to meet.

Hope didn't want to find out. She was not yet ready to put her faith to the test. Not ready to be able to answer Abraham's challenge, not disposed to be confronted by an altar upon which she was supposed to sacrifice her children, not even one of them. They would all get out, or they would all die trying.

And then, against all odds, her phone rang.

CHAPTER TWENTY-TWO

Under the Hudson River

Few civilians knew that the Hudson River was criss-crossed by tunnels, those both successful and in use, and those failed and long since fallen into desuetude. The old North River—that had been its name until the mid-20th century, reflecting its origins as part freshwater river and part brackish estuary, like the East River—had been the object of man's desire to simplify the crossing from Manhattan to Jersey for more than two hundred years. The Hudson and Manhattan Tunnels dated back to 1874, when the first attempts were made to dig beneath the silt of the river bottom and snake a tube across to the west side of the island. Because the technology was not up to the task, those early efforts collapsed, but they remained beneath the water today, unfinished and unused. Until now.

Devlin approached the edge of the water. He had committed to memory the old maps Maryam had showed him aboard the plane and, triangulating with his GPS device, knew precisely where they were.

He would have less than two minutes to find the old opening, long since buried in the river and under about ten feet of water. When the tubes eventually were successfully built—the railroad they had once served had become the PATH trains from New Jersey, operated by the Port Authority of New York and New Jersey, which also controlled the other bridges from Jersey, as well as the late World Trade Center—most of the aborted tunnels had been simply left to rot. But bits of them had been incorporated into the design and, if the maps were correct, there was still access. All Devlin had to do was dive down, locate the ingress, and try to hold his breath long enough to get in.

There was no entry from the Jersey side. When Tyler had issued his order to close off the city, all trains had immediately stopped running. Both the passenger vehicle tunnels had been choked off at the Jersey end as well. And, since he did not officially exist, there was no use trying to pull rank on the PA cops. He was going in, and he was going in invisibly.

Diving was something else few people knew anything about, except divers, of course. What seemed like just a short distance—say, a hundred feet—might as well be a mile to a diver. The pressure grew exponentially with every few feet down, and while man may well have originated in the primal soup, he had long since accepted his fate as a breathing biped. Water might be fun at the Jersey shore sixty miles south of where he was standing, but at this point, it was an enemy.

Across the river, Devlin could see the smoke rising from where Times Square would be, to the north of where he was now standing. The prevailing winds were from the west, as usual, so he couldn't smell anything, but he knew from his survey of the situation aboard the Gulfstream that the world's most famous intersection was now very likely uninhabitable. The acridity of the smoke, the ongoing gunfire, the rapidly spreading fires were sure to destroy the place, and not even the best men in the NYPD and the Fire Department were likely to be able to stop it. How many times did this have to happen, he wondered, before the United States was ready to go on offense? To hit back, hard, to lay waste to its enemies without the albatross of the lawyers and the JAGs perched on its shoulder, warning, hedging, caviling?

He took a deep breath, then exhaled. Then another, deeper breath, expanding his lungs, prepping them for what was to come.

But whom to attack? In the world of asymmetrical warfare, it was impossible for the leaders of nation-states to make their decisions. There were no diplomatic establishments to deal with, no ultimatums to be issued and then either accepted or ignored. The country was fighting a shadow army, led by invisible commanders, troglodytes who could issue their commands from cell phones and sat phones in far-off caves in countries that only existed as diplomatic fictions. Sometimes it seemed that most of the world was a giant Potemkin village, a simulacrum of a country; only kick down the false front to reveal the savage beating heart behind it, so filled with jealousy and hatred.

And behind those cave dwellers? Who financed them, manipulated them, stroked them, plied them with fake understanding? Devlin had already met one of them, a man so implacable and hate-filled that their one, brief, unfinished encounter had chilled him to his soul. He—a man famously without a soul—had looked into the ferocious eyes of nihilism and had recoiled from the void. Pray to God that he would never end up like that, that he could hold on to just enough of his humanity to keep him on the other side of the line from well-educated beasts bent on an apocalypse far beyond anything that Wagner had dreamed of at Bayreuth.

Skorzeny. It had to be him.

They had come so close to him in Budapest. But even the tender ministrations of an Egyptian rendition stint had not been enough to get Farid Belghazi to talk, and so he had died, his body dismembered and fed to the crocodiles that still could be found along the Nile. President Tyler had given them permission to take Skorzeny out, but they had failed. And now, here he was.

The mission was simple: get into the beleaguered city and terminate each and every one of the terrorists the NYPD had not yet captured or killed. As usual, he was to remain invisible to the locals at all times, tracking and killing without ever revealing his presence either to friend or foe. To any NYPD officer he encountered, he was just another endangered civilian, and should they make him, he would have to kill them. That was the part about the job he hated. It was easy to kill the other side. They had richly deserved their fate and, in fact, many of them actively sought and embraced it. Devlin's dispatching them made no difference to either of them, and it had the salubrious effect of creating one less dirtbag in the world. But the good guys didn't deserve it.

Get Skorzeny and get out. That's what the voice inside his head had been telling him for months now. Get out and take Maryam with him. Retire, and take your money with you— let the government take care of you for a change, the way it took care of so many these days, instead of you taking care of it. Take this woman, even though you know next to nothing about her. Have never allowed yourself to run so much as a cursory investigation on her. Never bothered to check her cover story with the NCRI, the National Council of Resistance of Iran, or even the scattered remnants of SAVAK, half of whom now lived in Los Angeles. Didn't care. If she was right she was right.

And if in the end she was the one who had his name tattooed on a bullet in her gun, well, that was a fate he was gladly going to accept. It would put an end to all this, to this life he saw vanish anyway, before his eyes, at the airport in Rome, to the lie he had been living for so long. It would be the end of him, but it would be the end of Seelye, too, and half the NSA. If this was martyrdom, then so be it. Perhaps he had something in common with the scores of men he had killed. In the end, when your turn came, there was nothing left to do but take it, and like it.

Get in, get out.

Get into the tunnel. Once inside he would find a change of clothes in a utility station, adjacent to one of the early monitoring posts that constantly measured the conditions in the tunnel for air quality, radiation, minute increases in humidity—anything that might signal the approach of catastrophe. In the locker he would find any other weapons he needed, in case any of his became unusable after the submersion, along with some heavier firepower beyond what the Gulfstream had provided.

He cleared his mind. He had done this many times before, although never under such hostile conditions. But at root the job was as simple as it always was.

Get in, get out.

Rely on his superior training, his instincts, and the vast emptiness at the bottom of his soul to get him through. Above all, don't think of her. She was on her way back to Europe. She was already dead to him and should by chance she be resurrected after this was over and they were together again, well, it was just another of the miracles that life held in store for a man in his profession.

He stepped into the water. Nobody saw him, nobody noticed him. What eyes there were nearby were focused on what was going on across the river.

Ten feet, twenty at the most. He stayed in the bathtub longer as a kid, head at the bottom, pretending he was a hero, a treasure-hunter, a deep-sea diver about to come up with rare pearls for the naked Japanese girls admiring him from the shore. For men like him, there were rewards in both heaven and hell.

He filled his lungs with air and slipped beneath the surface of the Hudson.

Chapter Twenty-three

Times Square

Francis Xavier Byrne had waited his whole life for a moment like this. It sounded horrible to say, but it was true. Every cop, every politician, every reporter, dreamed of such a moment. Not death and destruction, but opportunity. That was the way they saw it—opportunity to prove what they were made of. Unfortunately, it most often included violent death.

The country had so devolved, and heroism had been so devalued, that it was politically incorrect for little boys—and some girls—to imagine themselves the heroes of their own dramas. Peace might seem like a good idea to the ninnies of Code Pink and MoveOn, but it took a real crisis for the men to separate themselves from the boys and the cable news anchors and to step up. It was something they lived their lives for, hoping it would happen. Not for blood, but for glory. And if the two were intertwined, well, so what? The entire course of human history up until the 1950s had proclaimed that one simple truth, and only in a country infected with the postwar guilt-ridden moral relativism of America—the insane notion that up was down, black was white, and good was evil—could it be questioned or challenged.

In the immediate aftermath of 9/11, some of the old virtues had briefly returned. Suddenly the cops and firemen were heroes again, instead of public enemies and figures of fun on account of their lack of an Ivy League education, their Queens accents. The motto of the NYPD had long been "first through the door," a stone-brave Irish attitude that said you'd rather die than let your pals think you a coward. Cops and firefighters didn't call their lawyers when they got punched in the nose, didn't sue their neighbors or fight with them on the condo boards—in fact, they didn't even live in condos, preferring rentals in Middle Village or small houses in Orange County, which were pretty much all they could afford. Instead, they sucked it up, put their kids through school as best they could, survived their divorces without eating their .38s, most of them anyway, and got on with their lives. Although Byrne had managed to move across the East River to the city, and his place on 50th Street and Tenth Avenue in what had once been the dregs of Hell's Kitchen had turned into a very fashionable part of town, he'd never forgotten his roots, nor lost his fear of ever doing anything less than his duty.

A dying breed, he thought, that's what I am. And if today is the day that the breed finally vanishes, well, so be it. He had the .38 in his hand, drawn and ready to fire, as he hit the wreckage of the AMC.

He'd never seen anything like the destruction.

Being a cop in New York City, especially when you'd been on the force as long as he had—which meant going back to the bad old days of the Dinkins administration—meant you had seen a lot of terrible things. But those bad things were usually small family tragedies, a single point of blackness located among the thousand points of light that were the lives of the normal New Yorkers, everyday New Yorkers—in other words, those who had not gotten themselves killed on this particular day.

Most cops went through their whole careers, from the Academy to roundsman to squad cars to donuts and coffee to the desk sergeant to retirement, without every being involved in violence, except after the fact, when the crime, no matter how gruesome, had stopped bleeding and was even now bloating, swelling, and heading for the corruption of the grave. And even that was rare. Most cops only ever experienced corruption when it came to them not in the form of a popper fished out of the river or a dismembered body half-buried up near the Cloisters, but in the form of a bribe or a payoff, from a city councilman or a drug dealer or even just a two-bit hooker who offered you a blow job in lieu of a bust, and every once in a while you took it because it beat the alternative, which was nothing.

But he, Francis Xavier, would have no such luck. Sure, Mary Claire had left him long ago, and Doreen as well, and with her his entrée to the downtown Manhattan society he had always despised. But then came Ingrid and that mess with his brother Tom, and once again he had had to corrupt himself, to take a perfectly good bust and turn it, not in the direction of justice but to his own advantage, to give him power over people, over Ingrid, whom he'd condemned, and over his brother, whom he'd always loathed. He'd gotten out of that one alive and well and even prospering, just as his boss, Matt White, had, so many years ago. In that incident they both remembered all too well but which they never discussed, never could discuss, because to do so would mean the end of both of them. Behind every great fortune is a great crime, Balzac said, but far worse was the policeman's axiom that behind every great career was an even greater crime, as he understood all too well.

He could still see Rikki Marcon, holding his dead girl, Rosa, who had begged the cops to save her from her violent boyfriend, and whom he'd loved so much that he'd gone to work on her with an ice pick, and there wasn't much left of her when Matt and Frankie came upon them and without hesitation Matt had capped Enrique twice in the head with his .38 and that was the end of that. That was the reality of the city streets in those days, of bloody love and violent death, the only way these things could end when you got right down to it, which was maybe for the best. It spared everyone the happily-ever-after bullshit, the broadening of the hips, the weakening of the libido, the screaming children, the fights, the broken crockery, the sound of gunshots breaking the semi-stillness of the night in the south Bronx or Bed-Stuy or Brownsville or East New York or . . .

"RIP, motherfucker," was all Matt had said when he blew Rikki away, and as far as Byrne was concerned, that was about all the valedictory and eulogy any one of us deserved.

From that moment on, neither of them had even mentioned the incident. It was the unspoken scales of Blind Justice between them, both of them eternally complicit in what had been a righteous kill, but what had also been a crime, and the fact that one of them was now Commissioner and the other the head of the CTU was the only possible virtuous outcome in a world long ago condemned.

And now here he was, twenty years later, not as fit as he was back then but twice as smart, not as clever but twice as wise, not as amoral but twice as opportunistic, faced with an opportunity even he had never dreamed of. Not even when he and Tom were boys, sleeping in their bunk beds back in Queens, Tom the older, Tom the tougher, Tom the dominant, Tom the one he'd hated all his life. Tom who lorded it over him after the death of their father, Tom the successful one, Tom the FBI agent, the lawyer with the gun, whereas he was just Frankie the cop, the Fordham grad with the old .38, because he was too old or too dumb or too scared or simply too lazy to change.

The .38, his dad's service revolver, was in his hand as he looked up at what had been the AMC on 42nd Street.

The entire front of the building had been blown away, leaving two flanking sides with a great gap in the middle, with only the back wall of the lower floors still standing, although for how much longer was hard to tell. It was sagging, groaning with the agony of collapsing steel, a great expiring beast on its last legs, gravity about to claim it. If there was anybody still alive in there it was a miracle.

In the distance he could hear the sirens of the fire trucks. His job lay to the east, toward the gunfire that he could still discern among all the other sounds—screaming, moaning, shattering glass, the wordless voices of destruction. The voices that had always surrounded him, even back in Woodside, back when New York had been safe, when little Irish boys could sleep soundly in their beds, back before Kitty Genovese and the first World Trade Center bombing and 9/11. Back before the greatest city in the world had nearly been brought to its knees in fear and shame and guilt by 19 men from Saudi Arabia and other parts unknown. Back before invincible New York was bloodied. Back before the spiritual rot and nihilism that had long since infected the engine of capitalism and freedom had taken hold, hollowed it out, and rendered it supine before a handful of savages armed with box cutters and faith.

Twenty years ago, he remembered sitting in an Irish bar with Sy Sheinberg, Sid's late uncle, and musing that the exhausted Irish couldn't even muster one of their own as a bartender; today, the entire city couldn't even muster a single priest to give it the Last Rites, if not absolution, on its way to Hell.

A man was running toward him. The hot dog vendor. Byrne didn't have to think about the make: he *knew*.

Hope knew who it was before she looked at the display. Knew by the ring, the very same ring that announced the arrival of every incoming call. Hope didn't have the patience of her children, who somehow had managed to assign a special ring tone to each of the callers in the phone books, the better to sort them out aurally as well as visually. How long that would take, she had no idea, but it was just one of those things she was never going to get around to. When Hope was a kid, all the phones came pretty much in black and rang pretty much the same, although there were those weird pink Princess phones, but you still couldn't buy them, you just rented them from the phone company at a premium, and thought you were getting a bargain on some level. Such was the power of marketing.

"Danny?" she cried. "Help us! Oh my God, please help us!"

She knew he couldn't. Even if he were overhead in one of his choppers right this minute he still wouldn't be able to help her. But help was not really what she was after at this moment, not with the building swaying the way it was, not with hope fading so fast, not with her children clinging to her as if she were some sort of goddess, able to save them with a wave of her divine wand.

Well, why not—she had, once before. She had plucked her son out of the rubble of the middle school in Edwardsville, found her daughter in that awful prison in France when all hope had been lost.

"Hope—HOPE! Where are you? What's happening?" She could hear the fear in his voice, but more than the fear— there was something else. Something else that she herself had been feeling, but not letting herself feel. It was too soon, that's what she'd kept telling herself. Too soon for feeling, too soon after the death of her husband, too soon after the adventure in France, too soon. But Fate had a way of trumping Time, and too soon may not after all be quite soon enough.

"We're okay, Danny, but we're trapped. We were in the AMC on 42nd Street, when—"

Even in the vortex of sound, she could hear him punching a computer. "I've got you on video feed from the police helicopters," he said, and she didn't even bother to wonder how that was possible. "I've got the building on Google Earth. Now listen to me, Hope—"

Hope screamed as the building shifted and tilted. She had a flash of being on the *Titanic*, just like in the movie, when the boat began to slide beneath the waves, the elevation of the stern growing ever steeper.

"Hope. HOPE. Listen to me, baby, listen to me. I've tapped into the city building archives, so I've got the plans right here in front of me. Can you see all right? Can you breathe?

"We're on the roof, Danny. Can't you get someone here to pick us up?"

"Not right now, baby. So stay as calm as you can and listen very carefully . . ."

Ben Addison, Jr., saw the cop in front of him, made him as sure as he'd ever made any cop in his life. Cops were something he knew almost from childhood, cops were the things you'd best avoided unless you were ready to take them on, cops were the white men—even if they were black, like you—the white men who made your life miserable, the white men who were the font of all your misery, and your mama's misery and your long-gone daddy's misery, because after all he was probably in the jug somewhere, some guy you never knew whose rash action had brought you into this shitass world, and now here you were face-to-face with the Man, and it was long since past payback time.

To your left was the crackling hulk of the AMC, another evil infidel pleasure palace, where men and women could watch shameful films together, not segregated but side by side. There was a time when Ben Addison, Jr., enjoyed the company of women and, like every man, had measured his progress as a man by the number of women he'd seduced, or coerced or, once in a while, had even raped. But none of that was his fault—those were just terms, arbitrary definitions, judgments made by another culture on his culture. That was what they had taught him in the joint, the reason why the words of the imam had soothed rather than inflamed, had made him feel better about his own base appetites, although still ashamed, rather than angry. After all, he had a lot to thank the white man for, the removal of that awful guilt he had once felt, felt for so much of his life, to be replaced not by atonement but by righteous anger—by a burning desire for revenge, which had become his own personal version of atonement.

The cop was running toward him. So what if one of his AK's was gone? The other one would be plenty to take this sucka down . . .

Byrne knew he had no chance if the shooter got off more than a few shots. Even a spray-painting gangbanger like this guy could get lucky once in a while. Byrne firmly believed in the cop's adage that a single law enforcement officer with the right training and experience could take down an asshat with a single round left in the cylinder, before said asshat could blow away two little girls, an old woman, the milkman, a couple of cleaning ladies and half the side of the building, but miss his target, with an Uzi or an AK. As politically incorrect as it was to say, there wasn't a cop in that situation, facing those odds, who didn't like his chances.

Ben Addison, Jr., liked his chances. He's seen the way the people fell when he pointed and shot them. What a feeling of power—to merely wish and will and down they went, all his tormentors from childhood, defenseless and helpless, unable to fight back because they were unwilling to fight back, having long ago disarmed themselves morally and emotionally. Whereas he had found the truth in the white man's jail, where his brothers had come to him with love and mercy and the promise of justice, and then had put a gun in his hand to prove it.

The cop was his. He brought his weapon up into a firing position . . .

Byrne saw the AK: ghetto sideways, body out of alignment, weight on the wrong foot. His odds had just markedly improved. Closing fast, it wasn't about firepower now, it was about marksmanship. And aside from blind luck, marksmanship was always the deciding factor in a firefight.

Like a .335 hitter watching a pitcher's release point and picking up the rotation of the baseball, Byrne could see the shooter's finger on the trigger, could follow as if in slow motion, every twitch of the muscle ordering the cartridge into position, the firing pin to engage, the powder to ignite, the bullet to shoot down the rifling, spinning, heading straight for him—

His hand on his piece, Byrne dropped to the ground, rolled . . . came up ready to fire—

As he did, somewhere in the distance, he heard a woman scream.

Ben Addison, Jr., knew that he'd gotten off at least twenty rounds at a single pull. Fuck that bullshit they tried to teach him at the range at the mujahideen camp upstate, the shit about the deep breath and the exhalation and the slow squeezing instead of pulling or jerking—this was a right-eous piece he held in his hands, a thing that had never let him down, a death-dealer.

Which is why he missed the son of a bitch. That damn scream. Bitch threw him off. He'd take care of her right after he finished waxing this pig's infidel ass.

Addison stumbled, caught himself. But he almost dropped his AK and, instinctively, he reached out with his right hand, his firing hand, his trigger finger, to grab the weapon before it clattered to the ground and, in so doing, he forgot another of the lessons the upstate Arabs had tried to teach him, which was never grab the gun barrel after you'd fired.

His voice joined the screams of the woman as the burning gun barrel flayed the skin off his palm.

Just as a parent also knows the sound of a child's voice, a man can always hear a woman's screams no matter what the surrounding auditory noise. Byrne had heard plenty of women scream in his life, of course, both privately and pro-fessionally, and it was the one sound that a cop, even a homi-cide dick as he had been for many years, could not abide. It meant a lot of things—pain, suffering, fear, anguish, torture, death—but more than anything it meant this: you were not doing your job. Cops knew that they could barely solve crimes, much less stop them, but they went out on the streets every day hoping to do the latter instead of having to do the former. You couldn't tell how many people did not die today because of your presence, and you most certainly would never know them if you saw them, but they were there and you knew they were there. They were the good ghosts, the kind you hoped to meet someday, instead of the kind you actually did meet, every day, the ghosts of the people whose lives you were not there to save, the ghosts of the dead, their faces bloodied, their mouths open in agony, the ones who would haunt you, and rightly so, for the rest of your life. Until at last you joined them in whatever hell or purgatory was reserved for cops.

But one thing Byrne knew—the hot dog guy had put his last innocent victim in the grave.

Hope felt the dying building move, shift again. This was, she imagined, what it must be like to be in one of those California earthquakes. They were one of the reasons she and Jack had never gone to Disneyland, her fear of earthquakes. She'd seen enough movies, read enough books, seen enough articles in the *Post-Dispatch* to know that earthquakes shook buildings, sent the crockery flying, and worst-case scenario, split the ground asunder and swallowed up cars and houses and most certainly small children.

A voice in her ear: "There's a fire escape out the back." Danny. "Not on the AMC building itself, but on the one next door. You're going to have to jump for it."

Hope wasn't sure how to process the information. "You mean in the building, right? One of those enclosed things." In the distance she could hear the sound of gunfire, of wailing sirens, of explosions. This must be what hell is like, she thought.

"No, don't use them. You won't make it."

"But—"

"Listen to me, Hope." More formal now, the voice in command, in control. "You're not going to make it. The building isn't going to make it. It can't withstand the fire down below. It's going to collapse, and very soon. You've got to get off that roof or you're all going to die."

Hope looked around, trying to control her terror. Rory and Emma clung to her, hoping. "But—"

"Listen to me. It's your only chance. How far is it?"

Hope drew as much breath as she could and looked at her son. "Rory," she said as calmly as possible, "how far is that fire escape over there? You're good at these things—tell me." she whispered into her cell phone: "Hang on, Danny."

"No, you hang on, Hope. Say a prayer, and don't worry." She could hear the concern in his voice, which she knew, at that moment, was starting to turn to love.

She hadn't even realized that Rory had left her side when he was back. "That building next door, Mom?" he said, trying not to show his fear. "It's wrecked."

Across the country, Danny heard that. "Hope—listen to me. Listen to me. It's an old building. I'm looking at the plans right now. All they did was add on to it. There's an old fire escape, a few floors down. You know, the kind you see in the movies. Look for it."

"Over here, Mom!"

"Rory sees something."

"Hurry." She could hear the worry, and the urgency in his voice.

Hope ran to the spot where Rory was staring down. Much of the other building had collapsed. But there, just as Danny had predicted, was an old fire escape that had managed to survive the restoration and retrofitting. It had vanished into a disused air shaft, like the ones in the old dumbbell flats that used to populate this area, and if Hope had had time to think about it, she might have realized that it made perfect sense.

Originally, it would never have reached this high. But, in a fit of building-code observance, somebody—or, more likely, somebody's brother-in-law—had gotten a contract to extend the redundant fire escape up the side of the new addition, and then sealed it off. The contractor billed the owner for twice his costs, probably billed the city for some give-back that only a lawyer could love, kicked back to his relative, and walked away with some nice money for building something nobody would ever use.

Until now. Thank God for honest graft.

"I see it," she breathed to Danny. There was a slight roar in the background of wherever he was calling from.

"Then use it." His voice was raised, loud.

"What if it won't hold us?"

"It's got to. It's your only chance. Now go."

Hope looked at her children. They were braver than she; they knew what to do. "I'll go first, Mom," said Rory. "It'll be just fine."

And then he was over the side and gone. Hope looked at Emma. "Your turn, young lady," she said.

Emma hesitated, but only for a moment. "Well, I guess I've been through worse," she said, and then she, too, disappeared.

Now it was Hope's turn. She threw one leg over the side. "Where are you, Danny?" she said. "Please, after this is over—"

"We're on our way," he said. "All you have to do is stay safe for a few more hours."

Hope thought she would cry. But she didn't. Instead, she went over the side and down, into the smoke and darkness.

* * *

Byrne was on his feet now. The hot-dog vendor was hopping around, open, vulnerable. Byrne ran toward him, closing the distance fast.

Byrne had learned a lot on the streets of New York, streets he had known practically since the day he was born, since the days when he and Tommy had crawled around in the sewers of Queens, under the streets of Woodside and Middle Village when they were kids, playing hide-and-seek, playing sapper, playing city-bombing bad guys, playing the cops that had to hunt them down, the cops of *The Taking of Pelham One Two Three*. There was no scenario he had not rehearsed a million times in his mind, no spot no matter how tight in which he had not imagined himself, no moment that he could not rise to.

He fired as he ran, emptying his father's .38 into the man in front of him. Every shot found its mark. Each one tore through the gunman's body in a pattern that even Byrne would have been hard-pressed to duplicate at the firing range.

His first shot hit Ben Addison, Jr., in the side, not enough to kill but plenty enough to hurt. The second bullet hit him square in the chest, the center of mass, just like they taught you at the Academy, and just as Byrne had learned to do on the streets many years before. The third hit the shooter a little lower, in the groin, and Byrne knew from experience watching gut-shot men die that it would be the killing blow, only just not fast enough. The fourth shot took off most of Addison's left hand, leaving only a single finger and half a palm, while the fifth slug caught him in the right shoulder, forcing him at last to drop the weapon. But not before he got off one last shot.

Byrne sensed it coming and threw his body to one side. He may not have been as fast as he once was, but his instincts were honed and his reflexes sharp. He felt the sear as

the slug tore across his left shoulder, taking a chunk of flesh
and a piece of his suit with it. That was what worried him—
if he survived this encounter, he was going to have to get any
material out of the wound quickly before it infected him.
That was how 18th-century soldiers died, not necessarily
from the ball or even the bloodshed, but from infection. That
was why accounts of the old battlefields were always replete
with the cries of the wounded, the screams of paralyzing
agony, the gradual loss of the mental faculties, men being
driven mad by the fever was that eating them alive from the
inside.

He hit the pavement hard, landing on his wounded shoulder and striking his head against some of the rubble. He
yearned for a breather, a brief respite from the shouts and
screams and the din of war. But it was not to be.

Unbelievably, the hot dog man was still coming toward
him.

"God is great," the former Ben Addison, Jr., kept repeat-
ing to himself as he dragged himself toward the cop. Even
surrounded by the stench of death, he could always smell a
cop, and nothing spelled martyrdom to him more than this
pig's death. All his pent-up resentment—at the white man, at
the law, at the Man—fueled him, fed his rage, and kept him
moving. That and his faith. The Brothers had been right: this
faith was more powerful than any drug, stronger than anything he had ever encountered on the streets. This was a
thing of beauty, a synthesis of love and hatred, the nexus of
life and death, the portal to paradise.

The killing blade was sharp, and if, Allah willing, he had
the strength, he would carve the cop's head off like the leg of
a Thanksgiving turkey. Thanksgiving had always been Ben

Addison, Jr.'s, favorite holiday and even after accepting the call to Islam, he had found no reason to change his opinion. Carving was fun.

Byrne tried to clear the cobwebs, but even with the adrenaline rush, it wasn't going to be in time. His father's .38 lay several feet away, out of reach, and he wouldn't be able to get to it before the hot dog man would be upon him. Were he still a detective he would have carried an unauthorized piece in an ankle holster, or maybe even a drop 9 mm down the back of his pants, but Francis Byrne had been off the streets for nearly a decade. He was going to have to fight a wounded but crazed and still-powerful man, fight him long enough for his bullets to take effect, survive long enough that the man would finally die the way he was supposed to.

Funny what goes through your mind at a time like this. Everything was happening in slow motion, which gave Byrne plenty of time to think. His right hand reached out for a piece of brick or paving stone or whatever it was: this was the way his Irish ancestors had fought when they first came to the Island of the Manhattoes, with bricks and sticks and stones and lead pipes and beer bottles, whether they had been crooks or cops, pitched-battling on the west side, under the docks, in the railroad tunnels beneath the streets or on Death Avenue itself.

As shot up as the hot dog man was, something was still driving him forward, some combination of PCP and angel dust and religious fervor and God or Allah only knew what else, but whatever it was it was good enough, powerful juju, stronger than his God, and there was nothing left for Byrne to do but make a good act of contrition and get ready to meet his Maker.

The man was close to him now. Byrne rolled to face him.

A knife had never looked so big. He gripped the piece of urban detritus tightly: get it over with, he thought.

He braced himself—

And then the man disappeared.

No valedictory, no trash talk, no last words. He simply vanished.

No time to think about the miracle; the whole point of miracles was that they were inexplicable, so there was no point in thinking about them. There would be plenty of time for reflection later, back in his flat at 50th Street and Tenth Avenue, assuming he got out of this alive. Which was still at this point not at all a sure bet.

CHAPTER TWENTY-FOUR

Dresden, Germany, February 1945

As Emanuel Skorzeny awoke one morning from unquiet dreams, he found himself, in his bed, transformed into a monstrous thing, unworthy of sacrifice but doomed nonetheless.

For a moment, he wasn't quite sure where he was. Since July of last year, most of the beds he slept in were new to him, most of the houses unfamiliar. His life had been a series of courtrooms and judges, of soldiers and wardens, of prison cells. To find himself here, in Dresden, one of the most beautiful cities of the Reich, was like a dream. And yet he was having a nightmare.

The Elbe, the mighty river, was not far away, and perhaps in the summertime he might be able to smell it, but this was winter in Saxony, one of the coldest parts of Germany, and there was nothing to smell except his own breath before it froze upon exhalation. He dreaded getting out of bed, into the frigid morning air, the hot brick from the fire long since having cooled so that now he was snuggled up against something cold and unfeeling and indifferent. It was a feeling he would clutch to his breast for the rest of his life.

He fought for consciousness, trying to shake off the effects of the dream. But it stayed with him, and even though he knew it was inspired by Kafka, in a short story that he should not have been reading, in a place he should not have been reading it, he still found it hard to discriminate between fantasy and reality. His whole world, once so secure, was now one horrible, grotesque fantasy.

His father, his new father, stood in the doorway of the small attic room, looking at him with a mixture of obligation, fear, and disgust. "Get up, Kurt," he said. "Today, we seek the enemies of the people. Of the *Volk*."

Skorzeny arose and performed his ablutions as best he could. The chamber pot went back under the bed; the water with which he washed himself was practically frozen. He dressed and went downstairs, his hair plastered and stuck to the sides of his head like small brown icicles. He didn't mind being called Kurt, even though that was not his real name. When they let him go, released him from the *Sippenhaft* burden and resettled him and some of the others in new families scattered across the Reich, they had told him to forget his real name as quickly as he could, never to mention it again upon pain of death, to adapt and change and molt to his new circumstances until he became not only a man—which was fast approaching—but a new kind of man.

He would take a new name when the time came. A name that would signify something. For now, though, he would answer to whatever name they gave him, and execute whatever task they assigned to him. They had spared him, after all. Which is more than he would do to them or anyone like them when he got older, and at the first possible opportunity. This he had sworn to himself on that day in front of Freisler in the *Volksgericht*, the day his real father was condemned to death . . .

"What have they done, Papa?" asked the boy. He was still young, not yet a teenager, but already was treated as the future man of the house. After all, although he was *Sippenhaft*, he was also one of the future leaders, accepted into the *Adolf-Hitler-Schule*, the school for the best and the brightest Germany had to offer. He would show them. He would show them what a terrible mistake they had been to accuse his real father, and what an even more terrible mistake they had made to antagonize the son.

"Nothing yet," replied his new father. "That is for us to discover."

Emanuel Skorzeny respected his new father for one simple reason: he had survived. That was good enough for him. After all, families came and went but allegiances were transferable.

Unternehmen Eiche, whispered his father, and he knew what that meant. Every good German youth knew what that meant: Operation Oak. The rescue of comrade Mussolini from the red partisans and the revanchist forces of the King from the mountaintop hotel, Campo Imperatore, where *il Duce* was being held.

"And what did I say to *il Duce*?" his father asked. In just short time together, it already become a ritual with them. He liked rituals.

"*Duce*, the *Führer* has sent me to set you free!"

"To which *il Duce* replied?"

He only had to think for a moment: "I knew that my friend would not forsake me!"

His father smiled. They were out of the house, crossing the Elbe now. At times, Emanuel wondered why his father no longer resembled the photographs he had seen of him in his Waffen SS uniform, although from time to time he still wore the Iron Cross. After all, he was the man who had almost captured the NKVD headquarters in Moscow, before *den zweiten Dolchstuss*—the second stab in the back.

For Germany was finished, that he knew, even at his young

age. Germany had given to him and Germany had taken away—the way of the world, for which he bore the country no ill will. This was war, and in war people did strange things, fought for strange goals, shifted alliances and allegiances, with only one purpose in mind—to survive. Whatever his father had done, whatever his stepfather had done, and whatever he would do in the future, would be as a consequence of this war. There was nothing he could do about it, and there were no tears he would shed over it. Let the dead bury the dead and the living go on, to extract their terrible revenge on the corpses of both friend and foe as best they could.

Vater Otto moved swiftly down the street. He knew exactly where he was going. And when they came to the door of No. 17 Marschnerstrasse, he didn't wait for an answer to his knock, but instead as it half-opened, he kicked it in with one massive blow from his boot.

They caught the family unawares, still groping toward the fire for warmth, helpless when they should have been wary. Otto said nothing but walked smartly to the hearth, which had not yet begun to smolder, and brushed aside the embers. Then with one mighty wrench he pulled open the grate, the false grate, to reveal below a whole hidden room. "*Juden, raus,*" he barked.

And one by one they came up, with Otto lending a hand to haul them into the kitchen. One, two, three, four of them, a father and a mother and two children, the oldest not much older than himself, a boy and girl, standing there blinking in the light in the nightclothes, half-frozen and all dead.

That there were still Jews in Germany was an open secret. Despite the *Kristallnacht* and the Nuremberg Laws, despite the emigration of as many of the country's half a million or so Jews to Britain and America and elsewhere, there were still Jews in the Reich, living hidden among the people, some protected by powerful men, as in the Bavarian countryside, some more or less living openly, as in Berlin, the capital city that had never taken to Hitler and his uncouth Bavarian and Austrian interlopers. But Dresden was still a small town, for all its accomplishment in music, porcelain, and the arts, and the few still here had been eking out a living as craftsmen and black-marketeers, while plotting their escape up the great river on one of the ships that still plied the waters, despite the Allied bombing.

"Enumerate," said Vater Otto, and Emanuel knew what that meant. He gestured to the children, to the boy and the girl in their flannels, and without compunction asked them to turn over to him whatever fungible possessions they had. Even at this point in the war, when the sound of the British and the American planes overhead daily and nightly was an everyday occurrence, there was still business to conduct, and scores to settle.

The boy was about 15, the girl about 12. *"Wie heisst du?"* Emanuel asked them each in turn, and they replied: Heinrich and Eva. Good German names both, but there was no time for that now. He took their gold and their timepieces and their diamonds, because for some reason it was less humiliating for them to hand over the last things of value they had in the world to a boy rather than to a man. He could see by the looks on their faces that they knew they were done for, that no matter what the lies of the Reich about the mercy of Adolf Hitler, about the model camps at Theresienstadt, that somehow the word had filtered back, as it always does, to torment its future victims with fear as they struggled against the inevitable.

"Ihr Telefon," demanded Vater Otto, who made the call, and that was that. Security forces would round them up shortly, the German family who had been harboring them would be shot, and life for the rest of them would go on.

Emanuel knew better than to ask why them and why now. No matter how hard the regime, there were always cracks not only in the facade but in the floorboards. No matter how deep the hatred, there were always tasks that needed to be done, preferably by slave labor but when that was not up to snuff, then by the black market. There were always things that could be overlooked, until they couldn't. This family, obviously, had been one of them.

Which is what Skorzeny didn't understand. Why stay? Why wait? When doom is imminent, why not flee? And even at that age, he already knew the answer:

Because for most people it is easier to refuse to believe than to confront the truth.

It was not weakness, not stupidity nor cowardice nor even indolence, but the ancient human fallacy of believing that tomorrow will be pretty much like today, different in only the particulars but never in the general. Until one day it is not. And today, this early morning, that day had come for both Jew and Aryan.

He didn't care. That day had come for him seven months ago and, as far as he was concerned, it could come for the rest of humanity and he would not shed so much as a tear.

That evening, his father took him to a tavern, where they both drank beer *vom Fass* and dined as best one could under the circumstances. Despite the nightly air raids over German air space, Dresden had been largely untouched and every day that the people woke up to an intact city was another day that convinced them the Allies would leave them alone. There were no military targets here, he could hear the women say in the marketplace, we are far from the front and the fighting.

There was more worry about the advancing Soviets than there was about the Americans or the British. Dresden was safe; indeed, he suspected, that was one of the reasons his father was here, planning the next operation, the next counter-strike. Dresden was the only place left in Germany where you could think.

His father didn't drink much, but on this evening he ordered a second *Mass* for both of them. Emanuel could feel the first already going to his head, but didn't want to be thought a sissy or a coward. He was sent here to learn, and learning is what he was doing.

"*Also, Jungs,*" his father began. "*Wir müssen singen.*"

Looking back on that moment, if you had asked to him to provide a suitable valedictory for his last moment with his father, that was hardly the one he would have chosen. Although Vater Otto was a man of almost no words—garrulousness was not a quality highly prized by the National Socialists—when he did speak he spoke to the point, so this notion of breaking into song was unusual.

At that moment the dream came back to him—that instant before thought and word, before his father could open his mouth in song, before the second beer had loosened his inhibitions just enough for him to hear the music. In that moment, instead of hearing the music, Emanuel saw the thing he had dreaded seeing since last summer, the thing that had been kept from his young eyes. The thing that, in his dream, had turned him into a monster unworthy even of ritual sacrifice:

Piano wire.

A more horrible way to die could hardly be imagined. Jesus on the Cross at Golgotha, writhing in His agonies, but on a wire. It was hanging, but worse. The garrote, but worse. Strangulation, but worse. It was Death, come calling, but worse, without the smiling face brimming with the false promise of surcease and repose, without—

Wer reitet so spät durch Nacht und Wind
Es ist der Vater mit seinem Kind

Er hat den Knaben wohl in den Arm
Er faßt ihn sicher, er hält ihn warm
Mein Sohn, was birgst du so bang dein Gesicht?
Siehst Vater Du den Erlkönig nicht?
Der Erlkönig mit Kron' und Schweif?
Mein Sohn, es ist ein Nebelstreif

—the *Erlkönig's* seductive lullaby.

Everyone knew the words, of course. This was Germany, and the words were by Goethe. This was the greater Reich, and the music was by Schubert. Next to *Gretchen am Spinnrad*, this was the song by Schubert that everybody knew, and so it was no surprise when first one man, then another and then another picked up his father's tune, and then someone went to the inevitable, ubiquitous piano in the corner and began pounding out the triplets in the right hand and fingering the ominous bass in the left, the bass line that had spawned a hundred, no a thousand, silent-movie scores, the motif that signaled danger, destruction, and death, as symbolized by the Erl-King himself: lethal but seductive, and always fatal.

It brought the ghosts. To everyone in the room, the song brought the ghosts, in the form of the pleading boy, who begs his father to ride faster and faster, to escape the lullaby of the Erl-King,

"Oh, father do you not hear what the Erl-King whispers so close to my ear?"

But he could hear it. Could hear it through the singing and alcoholic haze, through the cigarette smoke. That voice that whispered so smoothly and so sinuously in his ear, the voice of temptation. He could hear. He could always hear it. It never left him. But he would be damned if it would kill him.

The men were just finishing up the song, the last verse . . .

Dem Vater grauset's, er reitet geschwind,
Er hält in Armen das ächzende Kind,
Erreicht den Hof mit Müh' und Not;
In seinen Armen das Kind war tot.

. . . when he heard the air-raid sirens, and knew that the ghosts would soon once more be walking among them, the Erl-King leading them.

Friends would forsake you, but ghosts never would.

CHAPTER TWENTY-FIVE

42nd Street

Devlin had no idea who the black man was or who the white man was, and didn't care, but it took him less than an instant to sort out the perp from the cop. As the man with the knife made his move, Devlin snaked out a hand and, with one powerful yank, dragged him into the shadows.

Deadweight was heavy, as every fireman knew. Much easier to lift a breathing 250-pound man than a dead 110-pound woman. The man with the knife was only half dead, which meant he was still slightly buoyant as Devlin yanked him into what had been a building entrance. As he'd learned long ago, you could always count on the cooperation of an obstreperous victim, who rather than resist would move toward you, to fight you, even though it would prove to be a fatal mistake, as indeed it did.

The knife was quickly knocked aside. Devlin applied the pressure of both thumbs to the base of the man's throat, in the little hollow known as the supra-sternal notch; sexy on a woman, so vulnerable on a man. A sharp wrench of the neck and the job was done.

Which left the cop.

Devlin pulled a balaclava down over his face and approached the cop. He couldn't risk exposure, but he didn't want to leave the poor bastard there, bleeding. He had to get that shoulder wound cleaned, fast.

The cop was a lot faster than he looked. In a flash, he retrieved the old .38 and had it in the middle of Devlin's chest. All it would take was a little pressure and Devlin would be gone.

He smashed the cop in his wounded shoulder, then clipped him on the jaw. From firsthand experience, he knew how much the blow to the bullet wound was going to hurt, and he counted on its causing the man to drop the gun or at least take his finger off the trigger. Thank God for double-action revolvers when the hammer was not cocked.

The cop sagged, then fell back. Quickly, Devlin got out a first-aid kit he had designed himself after years in the field. His flashlight had come in handy in New Orleans, and it was just as useful here: quickly, he cleaned the wound and tweezed out any foreign materials. Then he stabbed the cop with a quick hit of morphine, so that when he woke up, which wouldn't be long, he wouldn't hurt so much. And of course by then Devlin would be long gone.

He rifled through the man's pockets to find his ID: Francis Xavier Byrne, Captain, and chief of the Counter-Terrorism Unit. What were the odds?

Actually, the odds were pretty good. Everyone who had ever lived or visited midtown Manhattan had had the experience of looking up and seeing an old friend from high school across the bar, or encountering a former boss on the subway, which begged the question of how many times *could* that have happened were it not for fate: that you miss the old flame by a matter of minutes or even seconds; that you turned your head and so didn't see the guy who'd owed you money for ten years.

So here, in a mostly deserted Times Square, in the middle of a firefight, how unusual was it really that he should encounter the one man he needed to know, the one many who could really be of use to him down the line, either as an ally or as a decoy? Using a hand scanner, he quickly sucked up all Byrne's personal information and uplinked it to CSS. He also got the numbers of the cop's department phone and the personal cell phone they weren't supposed to carry, but all of them did. He felt around for a drop piece, but didn't find any. This guy was both very honest and very sure of himself.

Devlin cracked some smelling salts—that's what they still called them—under Byrne's nose and saw the man's eyelids flutter. He was going to be fine. He scribbled something on a piece of paper and stuck it in the cop's inside breast pocket, where he kept his shield.

Then he was gone.

Byrne took a deep breath and staggered to his feet. The noises and shouts and screams and gunfire from the direction of Times Square grew louder. There was no time for reflection, nor for wonderment at miracles. There were still ghosts who were not yet ghosts, and Frankie Byrne had to save as many of them as he could. Then he stopped—

His dad's service revolver was in his hand, although he couldn't really remember how it got there. So it was true: this really was the kind of gun they would have to pry from his cold, dead hands. Then he noticed that his wounded shoulder had been expertly field dressed, and that there was little or no pain. He had a vague memory of a man with his face concealed, a brief struggle . . . but that might have been the morphine talking.

Morphine? Since when were they dealing with terrorists

who brought their own corpsmen with them? And why would a terrorist not just kill him, but save him?

So he wasn't a terrorist then, even though, as memory returned, he was wearing a balaclava, just like the old PLO Fatah guys had worn back in the day. Which meant there was a foreign element in the city, that Manhattan wasn't truly sealed, and that he could only be a fed of some kind. FBI? No, they weren't that good . . .

Then—voices from behind. "Hey, mister," said one of them and at first Frankie couldn't tell whether it was male or female. He turned, ready for anything, gun trained—

A boy, then an older girl. Finally, a woman. All three were covered with soot and grime but no blood that he could see.

"Don't shoot, mister," said the kid.

"I'm Hope Gardner," said the woman.

"I'm a cop," said Francis Byrne. He hadn't said that in years. It felt good.

And now to work.

The passage through the PATH train tunnel had been uneventful. The cameras might have picked up his presence, but in the half-light of the shut-down tunnel, no one would be able to make him out, even if they bothered to go back and look at the grainy security films, which they wouldn't. In one of the service bays—the tunnel was lined with them every few hundred yards; they contained emergency equipment, oxygen, firefighting canisters, first-aid supplies—he had found what he was looking for: a spec-ops version of the Lewis Machine and Tool MRP semi-automatic AR rifle with a SOPMOD buttstock and firing the 6.8 SPC ("special purpose cartridge") round. The rifle was broken down into five component parts, including a suppressor and a Schmidt und Bender 3-12x50 mm scope, which meant he could shoot the eyes out of anything at ranges up to one hundred meters and beyond. The best part was that, with a hex head torque wrench, you could sub different calibers and barrel lengths on the weapon, depending on availability and necessity. There were also a few concussion grenades and some climbing clips in case he needed them, as well as a netbook with a satellite uplink, with which he could access all but the most secure NSA databases.

As in Mumbai, the attackers were coordinating via cell phones, which meant his instincts had been right. The NYPD's first reaction probably had been to shut down cell service, but his instructions to Seelye had obviously been executed, and he could read them clearly. No point in deactivating the bubble when it was going to be your best friend, and right now they might as well be wearing signs around their necks advertising their locations. As long as his uplink held, and they remained relatively stationary, he'd be able to identify and terminate any of them the cops didn't get to first.

Maybe this wouldn't be so bad after all.

In Mumbai, the cops had been hampered by a lack of technology: they could record the cell phone conversations of the attackers, but they couldn't triangulate and track them in real time. As a result, the killers had been left free to roam throughout the city, shooting up the train station, the Jewish center, and the luxury hotel pretty much with impunity until they were finally surrounded and cut down by superior firepower. It was agonizing to listen to, these conversations between the delusional young men who thought they were fighting and dying for Allah and their handler in Pakistan, who so casually sent all but one of them to their deaths. The targets had been carefully selected for maximum object-lesson value, and each gunman had been kitted out not only with armaments but maps and building plans, so as to make his deadly work go as smoothly as possible. The quality of mercy had not been strained, since there was none; Indian,

Jew, and foreign tourist alike had been gunned down without so much as a single act of mercy, since the word had no meaning in this context. With the killers on a quest for martyrdom, the victims were nothing more than means to an end, their lives as meaningless as the locks of hair and the scraps of flesh from his victims that a serial killer kept not as a memento but as proof of his own skill and moral rectitude.

The killers had gone to school on the Mumbai attack, that much was clear. The attack on Times Square had been well-coordinated, the timing of the subway explosion perfect, the sealing of at least the Holland Tunnel a masterstroke. In fact, Devlin was counting on their professionalism. Professionals were many things, but one thing above all was that they were predictable. Training had instilled in them discipline and with discipline came adherence to the rules—not arbitrary rules but rules that worked, rules that were proven to keep your ass alive in the toughest spots. Professionals could be dealt with, as he had dealt with Milverton in Paris and London; you might win or lose in direct hand-to-hand combat, but you knew the rules of the game.

Amateurs, however, were a different story. Most of them could be picked off rather easily, since their true-believer rage caused them to blunder time and again, as they hoped to make up for in anger what they lacked in basic tradecraft. Amateurs were like the guy who drove all the way across the country, took the Metro to the Pentagon, and opened fire at the guards at the civilian entrance; he managed to wound two before they cut him down and killed him. He'd made his point, but for what? He should have just shot himself back home in California and saved time.

Tyler had reacted exactly as the attackers had hoped he would, by sealing off the city and leaving the task to the NYPD. That's what he would have done, thought Devlin, play it right down the middle, leaving it to the pros without making a federal case out of it, but inserting some agents just in case. How many hands Tyler was playing, of course, was known only to him and maybe to Seelye; no doubt there would be other Branch 4 ops involved, plus any military units, probably at the platoon level, that they might have infiltrated. But there wasn't going to be any big action—even a reporter would eventually notice that, and Tyler's only hope lay in ending this fast without hyping it, mourning the dead and rebuilding the city as quickly as possible. With any luck, he could spin the entire episode to his advantage, have Americans rally round the flag, hand out yellow ribbons to his heart's content, have his Hollywood buddies organize a couple of telethons, and hope like hell the rebuilding effort didn't turn out to be Freedom Tower II. It was his only chance if he wanted a second term.

In the end, of course, none of that really mattered to Devlin. He had a job to do, and he was going to do it or die trying. The weightier issues of state were best left to the men and women to whom they were assigned, however inept or unqualified they might be; the decisions he made in the field were tactical, not strategic. His failure to kill Skorzeny when he had the man in his grasp in Clairvaux was something he was going to have to live with, and Devlin had not the slightest doubt in his mind that whatever soup he was about to walk into had something to do with that failure. Emanuel Skorzeny was a sick, twisted individual animated in equal parts by greed and hatred, and he would continue his atheist's war against God and civilization until the day somebody proved to him the reality of Hell.

They were swarming now, the enemies of America. For decades, maybe even centuries, they had lain in wait, hoping to take down the country and the civilizational ethos it represented. They had attacked from within and without. They had sent infiltrators disguised as philosophers, as artists, as educators, as clergymen, as patriots, and, the worst, as law-yers to manipulate the system, bore in, and hollow it out. They had created a mind-set by which up was down, black was white, and in was out. They had called into question every tenet of the American experiment and posited that it was illegitimate and inimical. They had used the failures of other societies as proof of the malfeasance of the American society. And now their handiwork lay all around him—the smoking rubble of Times Square.

And yet Devlin welcomed this challenge. Not solely for the thrill of the fight—that was a given. With his ticket out already punched, he could leave the fray whenever he wanted and, in the aftermath of Edwardsville, he had thought to de-part and take Seelye down with him. But she had changed all that.

But his welcoming of the challenge had roots far deeper. Devlin engaged because by the very act of engaging, he was proclaiming the best of American values. Most of the time, the debate over the soul and the future of the country came where it properly belonged, in the classrooms, in Congress, in the newspapers and the blogosphere, and on the political stump. But war was politics by other means, and so when it came to that, as Jefferson knew it must, it had to be fought with the same passionate ferocity. As Al Capone famously said, "in my neighborhood you get farther with a kind word and a gun than with just a kind word." The problem had been that, since the end of World War II, the poison had seeped into the body politic, Schopenhauer's *Wille zur Macht* had been delegitimized as the intellectually and morally absurd doctrine of "proportionate" response had gained first a toe-hold, then a foothold and finally had become, if not accepted doctrine among war-fighters, then at least the media-fueled template that framed the issue and thus limited discussion.

All of this could be argued in the pages of one of Jake Sinclair's newspapers. Devlin was prepared to argue it where the argument properly belonged: on the battlefield. Manhattan was now a petri dish of political pathology, a lab experiment into which he had now injected himself.

He stepped over some rubble and looked around. He was in the remains of what had once been a legit theater, but was now a heap of rubble. He ducked down behind a collapsed wall, popped open his netbook, and got a read on the situation. Using an advance logarithm that screened out legit subscribers, emergency workers, and governmental accounts from possible rogues, he counted thirteen separate suspicious entities in use within a ten-block radius. He wouldn't have to take them all out—the cops would take care of some of them—so he would start with the most difficult targets, the ones whose locations made them feel the most secure, and make an example out of them. Against these adversaries, there was nothing like a head on a pike to focus their attention on what was about to happen to them.

CHAPTER TWENTY-SIX

Midtown Manhattan

Alexander Stegmaier had never heard of Minsky's, nor seen the movie about the famous raid, nor had any appreciation at all of the famous burlesque house, so the irony of the fact that he was standing inside the New Victory Theater on 42nd Street, which had once proudly been the Republic and the flagship of the Minsky empire, was completely lost on him. He wasn't interested in naked women, except in the up-close-and-personal, but as he had no experience with the strange and exotic species, it was all theoretical.

Never mind. He was standing in the heart of the modern Gomorrah, the city of such wicked depravity that the Brothers had not stopped trying to take it down, and never would until it was leveled. The city that once gloried in its sinfulness, latterly become a home to "family entertainment," as if that would save it from God's wrath. This vile cesspool, from which was he was even now picking off pedestrians from his perch in the second-story window.

Alex Stegmaier was not a Muslim and would have been horrified at the thought. His alliance with the Brothers was pragmatic, not religious, but since the enemy of my enemy is my friend, it was not hard for them to make common cause, at least temporarily, until such time as the apocalypse was well and truly summoned, after which it was up to beings far greater than himself to sort out the final conflict. His job was to bring it on.

At first, the cars had been his primary targets. It was so satisfying to pull the trigger, hear the glass shatter, and watch the effects as the car veered, accelerated, or simply stopped, depending on whether his bullet had found a home in flesh or metal. It was not that he was a crack shot exactly, but his periods of training in Oregon, in the mosques of Dearborn, and in the encampments in upstate New York had given him a self-confidence that he had always lacked back home in Marin County, California. There, he had always been a misfit, a nerd, a weakling who had never been much good either at science or math, not to mention hopeless at sports. He stuttered, which left him off the debate team, and after he'd been routinely beaten by a parade of underclassmen at chess, he'd stopped competing at pretty much everything.

He leaned out the window. The main action lay to the east, but the west was a target-rich environment of cop cars and emergency vehicles, clustered around the Eighth Avenue intersection. He looked through his 8x-power scope and found an unmarked vehicle, overturned. A man was trying to drag another man, obviously wounded, out of the wrecked car. Alex decided that they would be good target practice and was lining up a shot when his cell phone rang.

Damn!

He lowered his sights and glanced at the caller ID: Control. He didn't know Control's name, but that was what they all called him, all of the brave warriors on the operation, whose names and real identities were unknown to each other and known only to him. Control was as close as he ever hoped to get to God in this life.

"Tammy." That was his code name, for Mount Tamalpais,

the sleeping Indian maiden turned into a mountain that dominated Marin County, across the Golden Gate from San Francisco. It was a girl's name, and he resented it a little, but he was not about to let on about that now. Not in the middle of the most glorious moments of his life.

"Where are you?" The man had a slight foreign accent, although being a Californian, almost everybody sounded foreign to Alex.

"Base One," he replied. "*Neuer Sieg.*" He liked to show off his knowledge of German, because he thought it made him sound more threatening; even if the grammar and the cases more often than not defeated him.

"Good. Hold in place, but get ready to fall back, to the east. A great vision of glory awaits you."

Alex tried to control his excitement. The vision of glory was something he had sought for many years, the moment of transcendence that would allow him to lord it over, however briefly, his tormentors. That was all he ever asked of God when he was at prayer: that just for one brief instant, he would not only be in command but that the others, his antagonists, would be forced to acknowledge his dominance. He would see the looks in their eyes, the worm turned, the worm Ouroboros devouring its own tail, the perfect circle of life and death.

And he knew something the others didn't, the swine. This was one of the things that was going not only to win him accolades and plaudits, but *earn* them: he knew, being German and all, that the word *Worm* didn't mean worm at all, but Dragon. He'd seen the movie and read the book and even looked up the images of the paintings online, he knew all about Blake and his *Great Red Dragon and the Woman Clothed in Sun*, and if he could not appreciate the visions for their artistic conception and execution, he could happily acknowledge their raw power, their controlled glimpse into the divine madness of Revelation.

Blake, however, was long gone, at one with the worms, small "w," returned to the earth by being devoured and shat out the assholes of other creatures, rejuvenating Mother Gaia as they destroyed one another. Just as he was doing now.

Damn that woman. Even amid all this tumult, her shrieks had been driving him crazy. Once more he leaned out the window and peered through his scope. This time he found her.

She was across the street, on the roof of what had been the AMC Theaters. The building was on fire, so it was only a matter of time before she would finally shut the fuck up and take those two mewling brats with her, but there was no law that said he couldn't hasten her demise along. It wouldn't be an easy shot, but at least it was a free throw—no one would notice, and if he bagged her, so much the better. Practice made perfect.

He fired.

And missed.

At least he assumed he missed. There was no reaction from the woman, at least not that he could notice, and the damn kids were still hopping around like Mexican jumping beans. But they weren't going anywhere. The flames were licking up the side of the building, the foundations were visibly shifting, and pretty soon their only choice would be to go down with the ship or stand there and let him put a bullet through their goddamn skulls.

He fired again.

And missed.

Shit.

He was lining up the third shot when the phone rang again. He didn't want to take the call, but he was a good soldier, this was his duty, and the kill could wait. On an island of two million people, there was plenty of time and plenty of targets.

"Tammy."

The voice again. "Bring as many souls to God as you can."

"Where do you want me after that?"

"That is known only to God. But to you, brave warrior, it is given to defend the Brothers. You will shoot them as they come from the west. Do you see them, O my brother?"

Alex Stegmaier glanced down the street; the sun was hanging over Jersey now, lowering into his eyes.

"Yes, I think so."

"Many are the police. They wish to kill you. You understand that, O my brother?"

"Of course I do. You think I am afraid?"

"I know you are not. But sometimes to a man comes fear unbidden, like a *houri* in the night, and he cannot resist her seductive beauty. You understand that, O my brother?"

"I do."

"And you are willing to confront this temptress, this whore?"

"Of course I am. As I have many times before." That part was a lie, of course, and perhaps Control knew that. But it was a brave lie, and when the time came, he knew that he would in fact have the courage to view Death's handmaiden unflinchingly.

"Then go bravely to your reward, my son."

"To the virgin?"

"Always to the virgin. Let her know pleasure only through you."

"Thy will be done."

"Not my will, but that of Allah."

Alexander Stegmaier was about to say something clever, but he couldn't think of anything. "Whatever," he knew, would simply not do, not given the high-toned and -falutin level of this discourse, which was like something out of a Sir Walter Scott novel, maybe *The Talisman*. Cleverness had never been his long suit.

He was still trying to think of something when he realized he was looking down the barrel of a gun. There was obviously a man holding it, but in the darkness of the parterre of the New Victory, he couldn't make out his face or his features.

"Do you know what this is?"

Alex Stegmaier thought hard. They had pointed a number of weapons at him during his training, and he thought he could still get most of them, but this one was a little different.

"It's a Colt .45."

"Very good."

Alex felt himself swelling with pride. "Am I right?"

"No, but pretty close."

The man lowered the sidearm a bit, so Alex could get a good look at it. He must be one of the Brothers, he thought, come to show him the way out of this place, and into the light. "Do you know who I am?"

"A Brother," replied Alex, confidently.

The man gave a rueful laugh. At least it sounded rueful, although in this environment it could have been jocular or sardonic or any of those other words he had never quite learned the meaning of back in high school in Marin County. Nuance was for chumps with time on their hands. He was going places.

"This is a Judge," said the Brother. "It is the last thing you will ever see. Do you understand that?"

Alex said he thought he did. It occurred to him that perhaps the Brother was going to give the weapon to him, for use in one final blaze of martyrdom. "Who are you?" he asked.

"I'm your angel."

Now this was something Stegmaier could understand. He would never let on, not even to this Brother, but he'd just about had it with the other Brothers, the ones who were always spouting off about Allah and Akbar and all those other guys, who in the end might as well have been Vishnu or Durga or one of those other Hindu gods, not counting the cows. Angels were in his wheelhouse. He could sing the choirs: angels and archangels, thrones . . .

This was no time for the damn cell phone to ring, not with him so close to heaven, but it did. He was about to push the talk button, to speak with Control, when the Angel took the instrument from his grasp. Instead of speaking, though, he waited until he heard Control's voice at the other end of the ether. Then he said: "*Quels est-ce que sont les noms de Dieu?*" followed by a stream of gibberish that sounded like the language the Brothers sometimes spoke, but different. Alex Stegmaier was never very good at languages, not even English.

The Angel hung up, but pocketed his phone. Well, this was war, so of course he would take it. Control had told him to kill anyone who tried to take his instrument away from him, but under the circumstances—and given that he was a Brother—there was not much he could do about it. After all, it was only a cell phone. Besides, he had more urgent, more pressing concerns.

"What kind of angel are you?" he asked. "Angel, archangel, cherubim, seraphim, thrones, powers, dominions, what? There are nine of them, you know, divided into three choirs."

"Only one kind," the angel replied. "The Angel of Death."

Alex thrilled to this news. A real Brother at last, not one of those muttering fakirs with their beads and their dirty feet, the feet they were always washing, to no apparent end. How could you wash your feet when you hardly used any water? For him, a nice long hot shower was always the answer for what ailed him.

He was still thinking about, and anticipating, a hot shower when the Brother did something entirely unexpected, at least as far as Alex was concerned. He fired.

The shotgun shell blew through Stegmaier's forehead, tearing off the top of his head and leaving behind only the mandible and one eyeball still attached to the stalk. Devlin had seen many men die before, and killed more than a few of them himself, but this death was different. This was not a wartime killing but an act of mercy, an act of deliverance. This was not a death to be mourned, or even to be received indifferently. This was a death to be appreciated.

He had the cell phone. He had the number. And now, just to be sporting, their runner knew he was on to them. What was the point of being the best at what you did if there was no one around to appreciate it? The poor boy on the floor had met his maker, and gone contentedly to his end. But something told Devlin that the man on the other end of the line—the Iranian, whom he had just threatened in Farsi—would not go quite so quietly, or happily.

Very well then. Let it be.

Night was falling, and darkness had always been his friend.

DAY TWO

*He who fears death either fears to lose all sensation
or fears new sensations.*
—MARCUS AURELIUS, *Meditations*, Book VIII

CHAPTER TWENTY-SEVEN

Geneva, Switzerland

Skorzeny's car was waiting for them as they disembarked in Geneva. Switzerland being neutral, and there being no actual warrant for his arrest, just an informal understanding between that rotter, Tyler, and countries with which the United States had an extradition treaty, they were free to enter. Switzerland would turn a blind eye to his presence in the country, just long enough for him to do what he had to do, make a substantial deposit in one of the banks, and be on his way.

Geneva was the most French of Swiss cities, which meant that despite its proximity to the French border, it was not French at all. It didn't matter whether the Swiss spoke French, Italian, Romansch, or German, at their heart they remained Swiss—insular at the top of their mountains, clannish despite their linguistic divisions, and dedicated solely to the proposition that making money and keeping it hidden was the highest goal of life.

Skorzeny's eyes roamed over the city as they approached. Here and there, a mosque caught his eye, and although the Swiss had recently voted to outlaw the construction of any more minarets, which they rightly deemed emblematic of the coming Islamic supremacy, he knew there would be more coming. Like some poor hypnotized creature facing down a cobra, the West had lost the will to resist its centuries-old challenger, and even here, in the very heart of rational, Calvinist, capitalist Europe, the green shoots of the coming caliphate were everywhere in evidence.

"You still haven't answered my question," he reminded Amanda. Wearing a fashionable black dress that extended just below the knee, she was sitting as close to him as politically necessary and as far away as propriety allowed.

Even though she was used to reading his mind, Amanda had no idea what he was talking about. "Mr. Skorzeny?" she said.

He shot her a look of annoyance, as if she had somehow let him down. And after what he'd done to her. But in her heart she knew he would not see it that way at all. A man as rich as he was could afford to indulge his sociopathy, all the while telling himself that it was his very love for humanity that made him hate people so. "About God, I mean."

She was hoping he'd forgotten, but the old reptile never forgot anything. Should he be incapacitated, chained to a gurney, his limbs cut off, his malevolent memory would machinate on, until the day the darkness he so passionately believed in but just as passionately tried to avoid finally descended. "I'm sure we've had this conversation before, Mr. Skorzeny," she dodged.

"If we have, I cannot recall it."

"Mr. Skorzeny—"

"Your former lover, the late Mr. Milverton, was an atheist."

He always knew to put her at a disadvantage, how to wound her. "I believe that had something to do with the way he was raised, sir," she replied.

"Whereas I have come by my skepticism independently—is that what you are saying, Miss Harrington?"

"I'm sure I don't know, sir."

"What do you know about the Higgs boson?"

She expected anything from Skorzeny, but this query caught her by surprise. "Sir?"

"I think I speak English passably well, Miss Harrington. So please answer my question."

"Higgs boson, sir?"

"Despite my advancing years, I am not deaf, madam."

Amanda decided to rewind the conversation to more secure ground. She could not hope to compete with him here, in the stratosphere of his psychosis. "Mr. Skorzeny, all I know about your background—"

"I have told you. Which is all you need to know. So, what is your answer?"

She never thought she would miss the icy M. Pilier. He had borne the brunt of Skorzeny's endless insane questions. She wondered what had become of him, but "no longer in service to us," was about all she could pry out of Skorzeny. He probably said that about all the dead people in his life. Somehow, just looking at him, she knew he had had a lot of experience with dead people. What was his family like? What sort of people, no matter what the provocation, could have produced this monster?

"I'm not sure I can give you one at this moment, Mr. Skorzeny," she replied.

"Which is why, Miss Harrington," he said, twisting the knife, "most likely you are childless at this moment. Because, were you not a charter member of your generation's suicide cult, you'd have five by now."

She felt herself reddening. "Sir?"

"Don't by coy with me, Miss Harrington, you know perfectly well what I mean. You know that if you truly believed in your country, in your culture, in yourself, and in your future, you'd have done what every other woman since Eve has done: have a child. Invest in the future. Have a stake in the benefits you demand of your government. Have some skin in the game."

"Mr. Skorzeny—"

"But no." He spat out his words with contempt. "But no, you cannot even be bothered to do that. A moment of pleasure, nine months of pain and the work 'twere done. That the next generation might live."

"Sir! I really must pro—"

"But you won't even give it that chance. Instead, you deny it life, or should it be conceived by some unhappy circumstance after a night of liquor and concupiscence, you throttle it—not in its cradle, like Hercules—but in your dark womb, where sins go unpunished and heroes die unborn."

Amanda felt a wave of murderous hostility wash over her. If she could have plunged a knife into his dark heart, she would have, though it cost her her life. If, like some character from a movie, she could have taken any weapon to hand—a champagne flute, a pair of eyeglasses, a pencil— and gouged out his eyes, she would have. But she could do nothing. She had to sit there, take it, and pretend to like it.

"Allow me to make myself quite clear, Miss Harrington as, at the moment, you are the only person, it seems, whom I can trust in this deceitful and slanderous world."

"Yes, sir." Might as well encourage him. "Please do, that I might better understand."

He smiled that reptilian smile of his, the smile she had learned so well, the same smile that creased his unholy visage even when he was making love to her.

"Making love." The very thought nauseated her. To him, she was nothing but chattel, a piece of ass masquerading as a piece of property, just as she had been on that day at the Savoy Hotel. She, one of the most recognizable and accomplished women in the City of London, reduced to the state of a Soho drab in one horrifying encounter. For which she would never forgive him. The fact that he didn't realize that was his weakness, his Achilles' heel.

But she did. And that was all that mattered. That realization, that knowledge, was her weapon against him. And by God, she would wield it, even though it took her last breath.

He had killed the only man she had ever loved. Killed him as surely as if he had killed him himself. Killed him by sending him up against the one man in the world he could not defeat, although his pride would never allow him to admit that. Killed him by forcing a face-off between them, even though he himself was hundreds of miles away, safe in his lair, with her paralyzed from the drug he had given her.

Killed him. A murder for which she would now have her revenge.

"The Higgs boson, sir?" she said, doing her best to steer the conversation back to its original topic. But Skorzeny would have none of her gambit. Instead, he focused his basilisk gaze out the window, at a group of buildings looming in the near distance.

"Do you know what drives me, Amanda?" he asked. It was the first time he had ever used her Christian name that she could remember. He, who hated Christianity, and Judaism, and Islam, and all the world's great religions, with a dispassionate, egalitarian, tolerant hatred that swept all before it, stooping to use a Christian name. Emanuel Skorzeny was the one man in the world who could profess tolerance, and then murder in its name.

Destroy the world, in fact, all in the name of his senseless revenge.

"No, sir, I'm sure I do not," she replied evenly. That was a lie. She had plenty of ideas, notions, about what drove him; even from the limited personal information he had imparted to her over the years that she had run his Skorzeny Foundation. His animus against the world knew no bounds. He would either be its master or nothing; he would not be God's madman. Which is why he hated God so much, and so personally.

"Because of the Higgs boson, of course," he replied, as if it were the most obvious answer in the world. "Because of the Higgs boson—not just the secret to life itself, no. Much more important than that—the secret to the origins of the universe. Not just our life, but life everywhere—anywhere."

"I'm not sure I follow you, sir," she said. They had entered the city proper now and were speeding toward their destination. Their trip would be very short, just long enough for Skorzeny to ascertain the information he required, and then they would be back across the border to France, in the plane, and off again. These days, even the Swiss could not be trusted: the Americans had put so much pressure that even the *Bahnhofstrasse* lawyers thought twice before routinely falsifying information that might be used in a court of law against them.

"It's very simple," he said. "So simple that even a girl child could understand my subtext, I am surprised and disappointed that you do not."

"I will try not to disappoint in the future," she said.

"As you have in the past."

"An aberration, sir," she said, hoping not to let her dual loyalties show.

"There are no aberrations, Miss Harrington," he said.

They rode in silence for a while, until at last a cluster of buildings presented itself to the west. They were nearly on the French border now, having doubled back almost to where they had started, but security was security, and Emanuel Skorzeny owned France.

"No aberrations. Everything is planned, thought out, organized. In a rational universe, that is. The kind of world and place you believe in. This is why your lot clings to your religions, or should I say your superstitions, because they are comforting and because they give you solace in your last, agonizing moments."

"What about you, sir?" Amanda ventured. "Don't you long for the solace of the afterlife?"

"A child's fantasy, and a bad novelist's fiction," he retorted sharply. "Had you seen what I have seen, had you experienced what I have experienced, had you been through what I have been through, you would never hazard such an absurd notion." He settled back into his leather seat. "Really, my dear, you disappoint me."

"I try not to, sir," she said, thinking furiously. Where was this conversation going? What point was he trying to make? Amanda Harrington had been with Emanuel Skorzeny long enough to know that he never asked a question to which either he already knew the answer or genuinely wanted to know the truth. The problem was telling the questions apart.

"You do," he said with finality. "And have, repeatedly. Nevertheless, I have forgiven you, despite everything."

That was the opening she had been waiting for. The lust that still coursed through the man's veins, no matter his age. Long ago she had learned the truth of the axiom that, at heart, every man was eighteen years old, no matter what the birth certificate said, and that when and if women ever learned that simple truth, the world was theirs. He had raped her once before, on that horrible day at the Savoy in London, and not only would it never happen again, but she would have her vengeance.

"Thank you, Mr. Skorzeny," she said.

He glanced at her across the plush leather seats of the car's interior.

"Sir?"

"You have more to say."

"I'm sure I don't sir." At times like this, she adopted the tone and the language of an aggrieved Victorian heroine. She had been born in the wrong century, of that she was sure. The only question now—far more pressing than any of Skorzeny's queries about money—was what she was going to do about it.

"Then I do."

She breathed a small sigh of relief. Baton passed. All she had to do now was listen. Which is exactly what she got paid to do.

"Allow me to extend and amplify."

"Please do, sir," she said. They were only minutes away from their destination, but at least this exegesis would likely take up most or all of the time.

Skorzeny yawned and stretched, as if he had given this same speech a thousand times before, in hundreds of different situations, to dozens of people. It was like talking to God, if God had no conscience.

"Do you know the *Credo*?" he asked.

"*Credo in Unum Deum*," she dutifully recited, good Anglo-Catholic girl that she once had been. Meaningless words, yet words that had once motivated not just a country but a culture, had called to war millions of men who charged off to die in the trenches of the Somme. Who would die for the Creed today?

It was uncanny, how he could read her thoughts. "No one believes such a thing anymore," he said. "Meaningless drivel, mumbo-jumbo, hocus-pocus.

Amanda forced herself to pay attention to his lecture, for she knew from long experience that he was going somewhere with it.

"And yet, it's deceptively simple, isn't it? Does evil need a purpose, an object of its animus, in order to exist? Or can it simply *be*? Iago believes in God, but in a cruel God, crueler than the Allah of the Mohammedans, and he understands and embraces the notion that, because he is a man in the image and likeness of God, he is also diabolical: 'I am evil because I am a man.'"

Here it came: "I could well say the same thing about myself. Oh, I don't consider myself evil, certainly not in the accepted understanding of the world. What I am trying to do, the grand project of my life upon which I am irrevocably embarked, would not be understood by most of the world's population. But I am, in my own way, an artist as great as Shakespeare. And do you know why, Miss Harrington?"

He turned to her, and she saw what she always saw in his eyes: greed, hatred, lust and, behind those deadly sins, a vast soulless emptiness. "No, sir," she said.

"Because I am going to destroy them. They thought that through their art they could approach God, but they were fools, and mortal fools as that, dust; to say they live on through their plays and their music is laughable. They are as dead as your former lover. And to them I am going to write *finis*." He gestured out the widow at the city. "I am going to destroy all this because the amateur Iagos who live here are not worthy of it. They have sold their birthright to men like me, not for a mess of pottage but for something even meaner: the illusion of security. They have turned their backs on God just as I approach Him. And here is where He is currently living."

The car slowed as they approached their destination: the CERN laboratory. The location of the Large Hadron Collider. Where the Higgs boson—the "God particle"—either would or would not be found. Where, if this madman was to be believed, the fate of the world would be decided in some way that she could not understand.

"What must He think of His creatures," said Skorzeny, his tone taunting. "They replicate Hell on earth and answer evil with evil. All Europe has become a suicide cult of relativism, of an unshakeable belief in nothing besides the self. It is a culture that has turned its back on its culture, a world of perpetual, petulant, resentful adolescence, a world in which young women have been taught that it is virtuous for them to kill their own unborn children. Is that sophistication? Or is it savagery?"

He glanced over at her. "And as I know how much you want a child, I think I also know your answer to my question."

It was everything she could do, took every ounce of self-control for Amanda Harrington not to explode, not to tear his hair out by the roots and gouge out his eyes. Then the famous Ice Maiden once again took control.

All her life she had pursued money to the exclusion of almost everything else, including love and children, and for a time she had been one of the richest women in London. Thanks to the lust to become even richer, she had signed on with the Skorzeny Foundation, of which she was still the nominal head, but what a Faustian bargain that had turned out to be. She had lost both the love she had found and, however briefly, the only child she had ever known—his gift. And now, looking at this thing, who had all the money in the world, however temporarily damaged financially by his first active foray into attacking America, she could feel only revulsion for what she had been, and what she had once hoped to become. At the moment, Amanda Harrington knew the cause to which she would henceforth devote the rest of her life—however long that would prove to be.

Just enough time left to think before she was once again caught up in whatever mad scheme had taken his fancy. But she had this to thank him for: after nine long months, her mind was clear now. She knew who he was and, more important, she knew who she was. Her man was dead. Her child was gone. From this moment henceforth, she was no longer Amanda Harrington of No. 4, Kensington Park Gardens, London.

She was the Black Widow. And she would have her vengeance.

Chapter Twenty-eight

In the air—Maryam

Good-byes were for fools and women who read romance novels. In the real word, there were no good-byes. Not in the life they had chosen. You parted and that was that. The rest was for the future, and to no woman was the future vouchsafed.

She'd be in Budapest in eight hours, maybe less if the tailwinds increased in speed. She needed all the luck she could get, because she had to pick up Skorzeny's trail fast. What she was learning was very disturbing, in ways she didn't quite know how to express at this point.

CSS had picked up Skorzeny in Switzerland, upon entry. That was the beauty of electronic surveillance: it didn't matter how much money you had, in any civilized country you would be photographed at a hundred different locations before you could go to ground. No matter how secure your bolt-hole, there was always a camera to catch you unawares, no matter your level of situational awareness—and Skorzeny's was preternatural. The international system as monitored at Fort Meade had evolved far beyond Echelon, to the point where the images could be read practically in real time; as long as there was one authoritative photograph, age almost irrelevant, the Black Widow could project and track just about any version of you—older, younger, with hair and without—that disguises or plastic surgery could create. In a world dedicated to personal freedom, every citizen was now on file.

The internal contradictions of the Western capitalist system did not concern Maryam at the moment. Using Devlin's equipment, much of which he had himself designed, she was busily bringing herself up to speed on every move Skorzeny had made since he entered Western ken. She knew that under his take-it-or-leave-it arrangement with Tyler, he was not supposed to be anywhere near a country with an extradition treaty with the United States. So there was something in Geneva that was worth risking however brief a visit he was planning to make. Something so important that he would risk his freedom and what was left of his financial empire for it.

He was, of course, with a woman, and Maryam knew exactly who she was. She was the women she'd seen in the prison at Clairvaux, at Skorzeny's macabre private concert, the woman with whom she'd made eye contact just before the performance had begun. Their eyes had met as enemies, but also as sisters, and in a flash Maryam had realized that Amanda Harrington could not move, could not speak, could barely even see, that she was a prisoner of Emanuel Skorzeny as surely as all the men at Clairvaux were prisoners of the French government.

And now she was here, with Skorzeny again, apparently of her own volition. That, Maryam was sure, was impossible. She had not been privy to all the details of the Skorzeny operation, having been brought on board to Branch 4 by Devlin after it was over, after the girl was rescued and after she shot the rifleman whose name she never learned, the man firing at the helicopter. As for what had happened in London, she didn't want to know. All she knew, and all she cared to know, was that her lover had come back to her wounded but alive, and with a burning desire to finish the job. He was, after all, a professional. Just like her.

It took Maryam all of five minutes to realize what Skorzeny was up to: the last shot of him was entering the secure area at CERN—the *Organisation Européenne pour la Recherche Nucléaire.* That was where this whole thing had started, she realized, in Budapest, with Farid Belghazi. Something big was going on at CERN, but for the life of her she couldn't imagine what it was.

Because, according to just about everybody, the place was a near-failure. Every time they'd started up the Collider, in an attempt to duplicate the conditions under which the Big Bang might have started the universe, it had failed. Once it had even been brought down by a bird, which had dropped something down the shaft. And now it was down for at least another year. It was almost as if God himself was trying to prevent the damn thing from working.

Maryam found herself fascinated with the history of the Collider. Her life up until now had not exactly revolved around science at this level, both technical and conceptual. The intricacies did not concern her. But the search for the origins of life, of existence, of the universe itself—that was something every human being could get behind. That was something every human being had wondered about since the dawn of time, when man first looked to the heavens and realized there was something out there, something bigger than himself, something full of wonder and majesty and mystery. Something infinite.

And now, here in the century of ascendent science, the age-old religious questions were being asked once more. Indeed, it seemed that the more science declared that the research was settled, that the questioning was over, and that all questions had been answered, the more people sought and questioned. Real science, of course, never really settled anything: Newtonian physics, as settled as anything ever could be, held sway for several centuries, and gave way to Einstein; in time, Einstein himself would be succeeded by something and somebody else. That was the course of history.

Only religion refused to ask. Only religion claimed the answers, infallibly. The problem was: which one was right? First-hand, she had seen the result of a religious state, one in which all questions had long ago been settled by the force of dogma. And not just Islam: all over the world, the Third World variants of European Christianity were awash in signs and wonders, mysterious apparitions. Whether they were Twelfthers, like the regime in Iran, or Marianists, who believed the Virgin Mary was appearing to them in places as disparate as California City, California, and Medjugorje, Bosnia-Herzegovina, or poor Mexican women who saw Jesus's face in a taco, or in a salt stain on a freeway underpass, they all had one thing in common: they believed.

And they had no need for the Large Hadron Collider.

No amount of computer linkage—and the Collider was not only linked to its own banks of computers but powered data to mainframes, desktops, laptops, and even netbooks all over the world, connected in much the same way that the SETI tapped underutilized, even dormant computing power on teenage boys's laptops all over the world to analyze data. The teenagers wanted to be a part of the Search for Extra-Terrestrial Intelligence, but many of the Hadron computers were unwitting zombies, drawn over to the dark side in the search for something far more important than life in outer space. This search was for the origins of the universe and, if possible, for the "God Particle"—the Higgs Boson.

The last time he had tried an EMP, it was delivered by weather balloon. That had had a whiff of genius about it, with first the misdirection in California and then the real thing on the east coast, where it would have done the most damage. And the weather balloon was a nice touch, because what—except to an Area 51–obsessed nut—could be sinister about a weather balloon? Maryam hadn't agreed with President Tyler's decision to let him semi-skate, but she also knew that she and Devlin had carte blanche to take him out whenever he came out of his bolt-hole, and now he had.

Because, no matter how smart or how careful he was, there was no place for Skorzeny to hide. Not in this day of near-universal CCTV cameras in all the cities of Europe, of cell phone cameras and iPhones and instant uplinks. No one, no matter how rich, was immune from the prying eyes and, unless you lived in a cave in Afghanistan somewhere, someday you would be found. And, if necessary or desirable, taken out. Nor were she and Devlin immune. His job was getting harder by the day, and it didn't matter how tough he was, one of these months or years he would run into somebody tougher, somebody smarter, somebody quicker and more ruthless—or maybe even somebody just luckier. And then it would be all over for him, and thus for her, too. She had to hurry. Double games were never easy, but they were the only one on offer for a girl like her.

So whatever had brought Emanuel Skorzeny out of his cell must be pretty damn big. And although there was no evidence to suggest it, she was also sure he was somehow involved in what was going on in New York. It made no sense to assume that it was a simple terrorist operation, not that any terrorist operation was simple. But the very technology that allowed her to monitor Skorzeny's movements aboveground could easily allow him to monitor his men's activities in the shadows. In Mumbai, the crew had been controlled by a Pakistani from his cell phone, guiding the poor, uneducated holy warriors on their killing spree and talking them through the acceptance of martyrdom so that they might have peace in their final moments—a peace not accorded their victims. There wasn't much sophisticated about that operation, just a true believer's willingness to kill in the name of

Allah, but that was really all you needed when it came right down to it: where there was a Will to Power, there was a Way.

The attendant was at her side: "We'll be landing in about an hour, Miss," he said. No name. As far as anyone was concerned she didn't have a name, and in fact this flight didn't even exist. They'd land at a private airstrip in Austria, where she'd be given false papers and then driven across the border in an unmarked vehicle. Should anyone check the manifest, the plane would prove to have been a rich Belgian's private aircraft, chartered through a company, sent to pick him up at a resort near Chamonix and ferry him home to his summer house in Austria's easternmost province, Burgenland, where he could happily continue to make life miserable for the EU's unhappy subjects from a country outside its purview. The old Soviet Union had never really died; it had simply moved to the Grand Place, where the food was better and the populace less restive.

There was no point in stopping in Geneva. The CSS had operatives throughout Switzerland, and although the prickly Swiss managed to be as unhelpful as possible, the best information was that he had left, accompanied by the woman. And, of course, there was to be no rough stuff, certainly not at the monitoring and shadowing level. The Swiss didn't mind what you did so long as it did not upset the fondue cart for everybody else, which meant leaving them alone in peace to continue to make and hide money. Which was why she was landing in Budapest . . .

Because that was where the twin strains of this case intersected. That was where they had grabbed Farid Belghazi, and Belghazi had been working at CERN. Hungary was where the name "Skorzeny" had originated, and even though the trail to Emanuel Skorzeny dead-ended at Otto Skorzeny, Maryam was a great believer in linguistic resonance. In her experience, people chose aliases that they could live with, that were not too far off from their real names, that *meant* something to them, something deep and emotional and significant. Emanuel Skorzeny may not have been any more Hungarian than she was, but there was something in that country that drew him, some identification with it . . .

Did he speak Magyar?

She realized she didn't know.

For all the work they had done on him in the aftermath of Edwardsville, that was something she had never bothered to wonder about. She had assumed no: nobody spoke Magyar, the language of Hungary, unless they were born to it. It was one of those rare languages, non-Indo-European in origin, related only to Finnish, of all things, a likely importation from central Asia and, if romance be true, swept into Europe with Attila the Hun and his conquering hordes. The Hungarians were half of the West and half of the East, on the border between Slav and Saxon, between Christian and Muslim, their language rolling like dactylic poetry, a parade of accented first syllables that gave the tongue a majesty and rhythm lacking in German dialects and Slavic variants with which it was nearly surrounded. Only on its eastern border, with Romania, did the Hungarians cede pride of historical place to the last outpost of the Roman empire.

Hungary—the nexus of Asia, the Roman legions, and the German colonists—was where the solution to the mystery lay, she was sure. Not just present-day Hungary, a shadow of its old self, but the lands that had once been Hungarian, including the Transylvanian district (the Germans called it *Siebenburgenland*, or "seven-castle land") so beloved of western Christian mythology. The land of Vlad Tepes—

Dracula.

Was that where the monster's lair really lay?

The flight attendant snapped her back out of her reverie. Even before he spoke, she'd caught him looking at her, the way men had been looking at her all her life, the unspoken and involuntary homage they paid to a beautiful woman.

American women hated such attention, or at least they professed to, which was one of the many things she despised about American women. Only in America, she thought, could women have achieved so much and enjoyed it so little. In a land of "diversity," their bland, homogenized beauty, grown so increasingly, so desperately conformist by the advent of plastic surgery, was designed to attract and yet their personalities were manufactured to repel. Maryam's American accent—learned in Beverly Hills and along Westwood Boulevard in Los Angeles—was as regionally noncommittal as possible, but unless she had to use it, she preferred the native accents of Shiraz, or the French patois she had learned at her fancy private school in Switzerland. Given the choice between *Schwyzerdütsch* and Valley Girl, she'd take the Swiss Alemannic dialect every time, unless she was buying a movie ticket at the ArcLight in Sherman Oaks.

"Was it a pleasant dream?" he asked.

She gave him her best fake smile, the kind of smile she'd been delivering on cue for years. "Yes, thank you," she replied. "I guess I didn't get enough sleep last night."

That was an opening she hadn't meant to give him, but luckily his manners were good and his training impeccable, although his eyes registered receipt of a message that, even if it were true, would never be acted on. And she acknowledged his courtesy back. So it went in the endless dance between the sexes, another thing that was lost on the American sisterhood, to their eternal loss, in Maryam's opinion.

The wheels touched down. Maryam looked out the window and saw nothing but the flat plain. No wonder they called this *Burgenland*—Fortress land. The only protection here was man-made, not nature-provided. Here you had to fend for yourself; at the interstices of not just cultures but civilizations and religions, it was every woman for herself. The Austro-Hungarian border had once been eradicated by royal fiat, but the Great War had ended that fiction and now it was back, a line on a map but always a line in the hearts of the people, and a line in the sand.

Her car rolled toward the border, crossed it, left the West, and entered the East.

CHAPTER TWENTY-NINE

New York City

Arash Kohanloo had spent a great deal of time in New York, especially for an Iranian national. Under some circumstances, his passport might have proven a bit of a bother, but the Tyler Administration had been determined to turn its back on the old ways. The fact that he was attached, however tangentially, to his country's U.N. mission facilitated matters greatly and, even if all else failed, he had multiple passports from multiple countries, including a Swiss passport that was tantamount to an international *laissez-passer*. It was amazing what the combination of money and power and fear could win you.

The hotel, of course, was in lockdown. The New York authorities were smart; they had learned from the Mumbai massacre, and knew that the fancy hotels were natural targets for gunmen with grudges. The elevators were all switched off, except for a couple of service elevators being guarded by private security. You could order room service to eat, but you had to stay in the hotel, and preferably in your room, until the "incident" was over.

All of which was fine with Kohanloo. In fact, that was

just the way he wanted it. Fewer people milling about suited him just fine, and as long as the cell phone service worked he could stay in touch with everyone with whom he needed to stay in touch, and then events would unfold as they unfolded.

At the first news of the attack he had informed his people back home. He had also made certain that a specific sum of money had been wired to several bank accounts in Switzerland, the Cayman Islands, and one of the Channel Islands between Britain and France. One could no longer rely solely on the discretion of the Swiss. In the crackdown on international money transfers that followed in the wake of 9/11, including the so-called Swift program that enabled the government to trace "terrorist" financing and thus disrupt the usual remittance channels and other mechanisms of Shari'a-compliant finance, the damned Americans had interfered with everything. This had necessitated a change in the networks that funneled money between the Muslim lands and their bankers in London and Brussels, and for a time the stream was partly dammed. But money is like water and soon enough it finds its way to its inevitable destination.

He didn't have to come here, and it was not part of his arrangement with Skorzeny that he do so. But the opportunity to strike a blow at the heart of a politically correct America and to supervise the operation right under their noses and in the heart of the greatest city as an honored guest was too good to resist. Skorzeny had warned him against taking personal charge, but Skorzeny was a bitter old man, with too many weaknesses, and whatever game he was playing was known only to him.

Kohanloo looked at the array of cell phones on the table in front of him. They were all local, off-the-shelf, no-contract communication devices—"plain vanilla," as the Americans said. To anyone tracking cell phone use—and even the Americans were not so stupid as to not be doing that—they would appear to be completely innocuous. What a pleasure it was to use the enemy's technology against him, to take the things his infidel culture had created and to turn even the simplest things into weapons. Whether the Brothers had used box cutters or knives on 9/11 was immaterial; the real weapons they wielded on that glorious day was the institutional cowardice of the Americans, especially the men. They had turned that weakness into the powerful flying bombs that, Allah be praised, had taken down the Twin Towers and nearly the Pentagon itself.

For what sort of men were these, who would not fight back? Who would not defend their women and children? Who would go so willingly to their deaths, Christian lambs to the slaughter? For all its sexuality, its braggadocio, its exaggerated cartoons of men and women, Western culture was at root exhausted, played out, expired. This was one thing that he and Skorzeny had agreed upon from the start: that what they were doing was not murder but euthanasia, the merciful thing to do when a living organism was in its terminal stages.

The idea behind the operation was simplicity itself. Either America would fight back or she wouldn't. The Holy Martyrs who had struck the Great Satan on 9/11 had succeeded beyond the Sheikh's wildest dreams, but in a larger sense they had failed. They had not precipitated the final war between the *dar al-Islam* and *the dar al-Harb*, nor had they set the Americans to each other's throats in a civil war over their precious national freedoms.

But this was different. This was a direct attack, man to man, on the streets of the Great Satan's financial capital and its greatest city. This was a challenge so direct that not even the *New York Times* could rationalize it away. This was the event that would finally force the cowardly Americans to choose sides and then, once they had, it would be the work of a lifetime or two to hunt the infidel dogs down—with the assistance of the collaborators, of course—and destroy them.

In the end, all would be well, and all would accept the Call or die.

But there was another, larger, and vastly more important reason behind the martyrdom operation. The arrival of the Twelfth Imam, *pbuh*, could only be hastened by blood; he would not come, with Jesus at his side, until the Great Conflict was well and truly under way. All was in readiness in the Holy City of Qom, where the path had been made straight and the centuries of the false Mahdis would soon come to an end. What better way to encourage Mohammed ibn Hasan al-Mahdi al-Muntazar to finally reappear than to set the *dar al-Harb* aflame?

Arash Kohanloo glanced over at the television set, another typical product of Western decadence. Who had need of such a monstrosity, when a simple black-and-white set would do? This was the problem with America: need had nothing to do with its desires, and the word "want" had transferred its meaning from the former to the latter. He was from a far older culture, an infinitely greater culture whose art and poetry before the Conquest had been unsurpassed, and while some sacrifices had had to be made in order to accommodate Revelation, the memory of the Persian Empire was imprinted on every Iranian's soul. Even the name of the country—its new name, not the old one—signified its glorious antiquity and pride of place in the human community: Aryan.

He had lost a few of the warriors yesterday, but the rest had gone to ground as per instructions, while they waited. This, too, was part of the plan. Warriors were only martyrs who had not entered heaven yet, and his job was to supply the afterlife with fresh souls.

Still, losing warriors was one thing; having one of the enemy speak to you in Farsi was another. He sounded like a Brother, from his accent, but his words had been puzzling and mysterious, beginning with his question in French about the number of the names of God and continuing on with various obscure theological questions about the *suras* and the life of the Prophet, concluding with a discussion of the Twelfth Imam. And then he had lost contact with Brother Alex, whom he now must assume was dead.

But why would a Brother kill Alex? It was possible that it had been a mercy killing, that Brother Alex had somehow been wounded and had been put out of his misery in order to enter paradise. It was also possible that Brother Alex's security had been compromised, and another of the Brothers had terminated him. It was even remotely possible that Brother Alex had been taken out by one of the New York City Police Department operatives, although the chances that the man would be a native Persian, or speak Farsi like one, were nil.

There was a fourth, and more worrisome possibility, however: that Skorzeny had double-crossed him.

Kohanloo thought for a moment. His eyes fell upon the mini-bar. It was so tempting . . . In the interests of *taqiyya* it was permitted a devout Muslim to deceive the enemy. A beer, or perhaps two, would aid in the deception.

That Skorzeny would attempt to euchre him would not surprise him in the least. The man's reputation preceded him and if, in fact, that turned out to be the truth, it would be the last time he ever did that. For while it was permissible for him, Arash Kohanloo, to deceived a Westerner with false promises, such behavior in an infidel—worse, an atheist— would not be acceptable, and would have to be punished with the utmost Koranic severity.

In fact, as he looked back on it, he realized that Skorzeny had been planning an elaborate deception all along, especially the bit about his not having to come to New York. Clearly, that had been his intention all along: to force Kohanloo to accept the challenge to his manhood and specifically ignore the advice he was being given. Skorzeny had *wanted* him to supervise the operation from ground zero, and not from the safety of, say, Canada, where the Brothers were numerous and the government almost as naive, trusting, and unsuspecting as those of Scandinavia. Islam had never laid historic claim to any of the lands of the North, not to mention the new world, but now, with so many Brothers acting religiously as an army of infiltration, taking advantage of the enemy's trusting nature, his generous social-welfare programs (which were really just an inverted form of racism, since the Brothers were discouraged from gainful employment), there would soon be enough Believers to assert Islam's historically necessary pride of place and conquer all the lands of the West, once and for all time.

He looked at the cell phone that linked him directly to Brother Alex. Should he pick it up and dial again? For one of the few times in his life, Arash Kohanloo hesitated. This was a new experience for him. Having survived multiple changes of regime in Iran, from Mossadegh to the Shah to the Ayatollahs to whatever undoubtedly was coming next, he was used to acting boldly and decisively. In the Middle East, nothing was ever to be gained by caution, except the perpetuation of the same way of life that had obtained for hundreds of years. For all his piety, Kohanloo was a man of the future, not of the past: he looked forward to the inevitable victory of the *dar al-Islam* and was doing his best to hasten it.

He picked up the phone, a basic Nokia. Then another thought occurred to him:

What if it was the NCRI? The National Council of Resistance of Iran?

That put a whole different spin on things. The NCRI, up to this moment, had been a joke. But the open rebellion against the fixed Iranian elections of 2010 had only served to encourage the diaspora of Iranians, at least half of whom, it seemed, lived in Beverly Hills or elsewhere in the Greater Los Angeles area. In the old days, poor countries used to export their most miserable people to the United States, so that the those left behind might have a fighting chance at survival. Iran had gone history one better: it had exported its best and its brightest and its richest, its doctors and its bankers and its lawyers. The Revolution had driven away precisely those people a functioning modern country needed, and sent them screaming into the arms of the Great Satan himself, to luxuriate in the southern California climate and plot revenge; they were like the post-Castro Cubans, but with more money.

Up to this point, neither he nor any of the mullahs with whom he did such a profitable, if irreligious, business, had given much of a thought to the NCRI. To put the organization in historical context, it was like one of those movements of national liberation that popped up everywhere in the 19th and 20th centuries, groups of raggedy-assed anarchists who threw bombs and occasionally got lucky in their choice of targets, but aside from Princip had very little effect upon the course of human history.

Of course, Gavrilo Princip had had a very great effect upon the course of human history. Incredibly lucky—imagine the Archduke Franz Ferdinand returning by the very same route on which he had dodged Princip's first attempt on his life earlier that same day—but also incredibly determined, Princip had rearranged the map of Europe and, all unwittingly, doomed the West, although it had taken just about a century on the nose for that fact to become so abundantly clear. The cream of the crop of the infidel had died in the trenches and at the Somme and at Verdun, and those who were not killed were removed from the gene pool three decades later when the same war broke out all over again. As an example of national and cultural suicide, it was unequalled; no wonder their enfeebled descendents wanted nothing so passionately as to terminate themselves, their offspring, and their civilization.

Well, he was here to help them with that. If the West had

become a giant suicide cult, Islam was just the death cult it was longing to meet. At last, a battle that had been waged since the seventh century was about to enter its final stages.

He still held the cell phone in his hand. In every operation, once the shooting started, there was something that would go wrong, and almost immediately. War plans were blueprints for buildings that would never get built; what emerged instead was some bastard combination of thought, luck, and happenstance, and you lived with the result until you were strong enough to overturn it, or weak enough to be unable to defend it.

He pushed the redial button.

The phone rang. Once, twice . . .

The security signal was four rings. Anything after four rings meant the connection was compromised, and that the Brother was considered compromised, whether he was in fact dead or not. A wounded Brother was of no use to him. At four rings, the order would automatically go out to the others, identifying the fallen Brother's last known location, with the orders that he or she should be terminated immediately. Mercy was an unknown commodity, for only Allah could dispense mercy.

Three times . . .

Nothing.

Arash Kohanloo's finger hovered over the Stop button. As soon as the fourth ring ended, he would end the call and send the signal.

Four—

"Hello?"

A voice, in American English. What he expected, but not at all what he expected.

"Who is this?" he found himself saying.

There was a long pause at the other end of the line—of course, there was no line, only the infidel's technology, which Kohanloo and his countrymen, although unable to du-

plicate, were only too happy to employ against the enemy—
and what sounded like a clicking noise.

"Go ahead please," came a female voice.

Now it was a male voice that spoke: "Target located.
Sherry-Netherland Hotel."

"Stand by," said the infidel woman.

Then silence.

Arash Kohanloo tried to control his breathing. His heart
rate was up, that he knew. The doctors had told him to keep
it down, keep it calm, keep it within the target range lest he
find himself in trouble. Damn that Skorzeny and his wily
ways. Here he was, in a situation he should never have been
in, and his heart rate was rising along with his blood pressure. He tried to stay calm and listen for whatever came next.
There was nothing to worry about.

The fools! They had no idea he was not in the Sherry-
Netherland.

"Shall I send a UAV?"

A few more crackles, then—

"Put the bird in the air and stand by."

"The bird is in the air."

Kohanloo couldn't believe his ears. Surely they would not
deploy a UAV—Unmanned Aerial Vehicle, more commonly
known as a drone—to blast away an entire floor of an expensive hotel in midtown Manhattan. The Americans didn't do
things like that. They were always more concerned about
collateral damage than they were about the success of a mission; why, a single snail darter could not only bring down a
dam in Alaska, it could probably stop a convoy of Abrams
tanks as well.

"Stand by to fire on my orders."

It was a bluff. It had to be. His eyes stole toward the window of his luxury suite; the curtains were drawn. With the
cell phone still pressed up hard against his ear, he moved
slowly and quietly toward the window.

Now another voice came on the line. He couldn't swear to it—and a good Muslim never took an oath except in a religious context—but it sounded awfully like that of the man he had spoken to earlier. In fluent Farsi, he said: "Go to the window."

He hesitated a moment.

"Go to the window now."

He went to the window.

"Now, open the curtains."

How did they know he even had a window where he was? Or that there were curtains?

"Open them." He didn't like the man's tone of voice, his peremptory way. An unbeliever should never talk to one of the Faithful like that. "Go ahead . . ."

He took a deep breath and opened the curtains, trying not to flinch—

"What do you see?"

The panorama of New York City. No hint of the sun yet, but on this summer morning, it would be up soon. Just the gleam of the lights and, to the southwest, smoke reflected in the wasteful glare.

He slowly exhaled. "I see exactly what I expect to see, and nothing more."

"Do you see me?"

He was feeling a little braver now, more like his old self. "Of course not. Now who are you? What do you want?"

"Do you see me now?"

Was that the sun? The sky had brightened a bit, or perhaps his eyes were simply getting used to the darkness. He switched off the nearest floor lamp in order to see better.

"Do you know who I am?"

Still nothing. It was all a bluff. Somehow they had managed to trace the Brother's cell signal. A cheap trick, and one that any Palestinian kid with a Bulgarian computer could manage. Nothing to—

"Smile, asshole." That was in English.

A blinding flash. For a moment, Arash Kohanloo was sure he was dead, and that he would soon be entering paradise. He cursed himself for a fool, that he had not had time to perform his ritual ablutions in preparation for martyrdom, and then remembered he was not expecting to be martyred this time out.

He was still alive. He could see.

The drone was right outside his window. It had him on video, and was transmitting his picture somewhere. Operational security was blown. It was time to regroup. He started to turn away—

"Stop. Don't move or you're a dead man."

Kohanloo froze.

"Look on the wall across from you."

Kohanloo looked.

A video image danced across the plaster and the reproduction of a Monet cathedral. It was the image of a man. "Look upon me," said the voice at the other end of the cell phone. Funny; he had forgotten he was still holding it.

"Do you know who I am now?"

"No. I do not."

"I am Azra'il. Malak al-Maut. He Whom God Helps."

The name sent shivers down Kohanloo's spine. *Azra'il*, the Arabic version of the Biblical *Azrael*, was not to be found in the Holy Koran, but *Malak al-Maut* was. Another of his names. It meant the Angel of Death.

"And you," the voice said, "are now mine."

CHAPTER THIRTY

The Upper East Side—morning

The dawn was breaking as Principessa Stanley cautiously made her way around the corner from Park Avenue and turned left on 92nd Street, where some of the shooting had been yesterday. It wasn't that she was afraid, exactly; indeed, she moved with the supreme confidence of a cable-network star. Nothing ever happened to cable-network stars. In fact, with the occasional and unfortunate exception of that poor girl back in St. Louis, or wherever it was last year—you know, the one they gave that posthumous award to a couple of months ago—journalists were free to come and go as they pleased in the United States of America. This was not some kind of Third World shithole, where you had to wear a sign around your neck that blared "PRENSA" in various wog tongues, none of which she happened to know. Principessa Stanley was firmly of the opinion that if information could not be expressed in English it was of no use to her, since none of her viewers would be able to understand it any better than she could.

And to think she had almost missed this "terrorist" attack by fooling around in New Orleans, wasting her time with her boyfriend of the moment after covering that useless RAND meeting—none of which she could use anyway. It had been a real trick to find a flight into New York after they shut the airports down, and so she had hopped aboard a military plane from the Naval Air Station, Joint Reserve Base about twenty minutes south of the city. It had taken her to the old Stewart AFB, where the New York Air National Guard was still operational, and from there a car service had brought her down to the city. Her press credentials had gotten her through the blockade last night and so she'd be able to freshen up in her own apartment on Carnegie Hill before tackling her latest assignment. If she played her cards right, this was an Emmy for sure.

The trick was to go where everybody else wasn't. The shootings at the Y had already been written off as isolated incidents, perhaps copycat killings. The real action was still at Times Square, where gunmen were still active, but this area had been quiet for hours. Besides, the police cordon was slowly constricting around 42nd and Seventh, and the 92nd Street Y now lay outside the zone.

Which suited her journalistic purposes just fine. The gunman—whoever he or she was—was still on the loose. She'd find him, if it was the last thing she did, and bring him in for an exclusive interview. The cops and the military, whoever, would wax the other schmucks, but she could talk a cat out of a tree, and surely she'd be able to talk this guy down and into her custody. She'd have him on the air fifteen minutes later, depending on traffic.

Raymond Crankheit woke up and stretched. He'd spent the night under a copse near the Metropolitan Museum of Art and, all things considered, felt quite refreshed. This was one of the first spots in New York City he'd visited when he first arrived, the place where Robert Chambers, the "Preppie

Killer" had strangled Jennifer Levin to death during what
Chamber had called "rough sex." Raymond had never had
sex, so he wasn't quite sure what, exactly, was the distinction
between rough sex and garden-variety sex, but he hoped to
find out someday, and today was as good a day as any. As
soon as he'd finished what he came here to do, he'd find a
girl and give it a try. Maybe he too could get lucky at Dor-
rian's Red Hand, but that was fairly far away, over on Second
Avenue, and he didn't have time for the trek just now. He'd
had have to find somebody closer and more available.

He was only a little surprised the cops had not found him,
but then they weren't really looking for him. The main action was with the Brothers; a few dead Jews far away from
ground zero would have to wait. Unless he did something
stupid, he could spend the entire day picking off whomever
he chose.

He peeked out from under some bushes. Even on a normal day, there wouldn't have been many people stirring, just
the custodial staff at the Museum, which he really should
visit someday except that he'd heard it was boring. His extra
ammo was still here, right where he'd buried it, and so he'd
reloaded before he'd gone to sleep and was now ready to go.

He'd had a chance to think a lot of things over last night,
and come to several conclusions. One was that he didn't
mind killing people at all. Upstate, during training, he'd been
deemed a little squeamish, and he found he really didn't
enjoy it when he had to saw that guy's head off with a kukri
knife. They never told him exactly whose head was being
sawed off, just that the man was an Infidel and an Enemy and
that no one would miss him. To Raymond, the poor schmo
looked like just another homeless black guy, probably some
bum from nearby Hancock or, better yet, Callicoon. Anyway,
he didn't struggle much, but it was still gross.

The second thing he'd discovered was that he didn't mind
killing women. He'd been raised never to hit a girl, but when

he saw that broad outside the Y something had just gone off inside his head or his heart or whichever, and he'd taken her out without so much as a second thought. She probably wouldn't have gone to bed with him, either, just like every other girl he'd ever met, and so she'd had to pay the price for the crimes of her sisters. And then the rest of them followed.

So, now that he was over that hump, he knew that sex couldn't be far behind. At last, it was going to happen, because—thanks to the Brothers and their endless talk about the virgins and *houris* and all the pleasures of the flesh that would be available to him in the afterlife, pleasures that may or may not be denied to him in this life—he could *make it happen*. All it required was the Will.

And then his cell phone rang—that special ring that came only from the commander of the Brothers. Good: more fun.

Principessa Stanley decided to use her head, instead of the rest of her, which is pretty much what had gotten her on the air in the first place. The days when on-air female journalists earned their face time thanks to the force of their personalities, the cogency of their reports, and the reliability of their sources was long gone. Fox News had blazed that trail, rediscovering, as if rediscovery were needed, the old adages that sex sold and that everybody, male and female, loved a pretty girl. Short skirts and a law degree didn't hurt, either.

So, instead of heading toward the Y, where there was very likely nothing to be seen anyway except a lot of police-line tape, she decided to wander into Central Park. From her youthful days at the University of Michigan's journalism school, she'd been taught the old police reporter's motto, that to catch a criminal, you had to think like a criminal. One of the reasons she was such a good reporter, in her opinion, was that it was easy for her to put herself in a psycho killer's shoes; in fact, she prided herself on thinking that she would have made quite a good psycho killer had she chosen to go into that particular line of work.

Which is why she found herself at this moment crossing Fifth Avenue. Sure, it was obvious that the park was where to hide, which is why it made such a brilliant hiding place. In her opinion, police work had become far too sophisticated, too dependent on computers; the shortest way between two points was still a straight line, and that was exactly what she making at this point as she triangulated in her mind between a possible hideout and the scene of the crime, which so happened took her at a diagonal from the Y to the Museum and thence to the infamous copse of bushes behind the Met. Like the Empire State Building, they were there for all to see, but if you lived in New York, somehow you never actually visited them yourself.

So this was the famous spot. Like every other famous crime scene she had visited—and, truth to tell, there weren't all that many, since Principessa Stanley's reporting career had been almost entirely confined to the classroom at Michigan and the news desk of a couple of low- and medium-rent boondock TV stations until the Show had finally called—this one was fairly unprepossessing in person. Like Dealey Plaza in Dallas, it seemed unworthy of such a crime.

She loved New York at this hour. Many was the time she'd gone for a run around the Reservoir in the morning, sharing the well-pounded path with a few other celebrities and some of the hoi polloi who were either decent enough not to invade her sunglassed- and baseball-capped privacy, or else too stupid to know who she was. Even at the height of summer, which was approaching, the air at least pretended to be fresh before the smell of the uncollected garbage could perfume it, before the effluence of the subways could poison it, and before the body odors of the two million people who called Manhattan home, not to mention the millions of commuters, could foul it.

"Hello, Miss," came a voice behind her.

He was not that bad-looking, for a geek or a homeless person. From the looks of him, he had spent the night in the park but had somehow remained relatively clean. True, there was dirt on both his hands, black dirt, and had she had time to think about its provenance, she might have realized that there was no black dirt in Central Park. But firearms training, like logic, languages, history, comparative religion, culture, and literature, was one of the things they didn't teach you in journalism school, and so she remained innocent in her knowledge of all those arcane and most likely dangerous subjects. She was, however, proud of her ability to craft a lede and should the occasion ever present itself again, she could no doubt develop a fine inverted-pyramid of a news story.

"Hello."

Raymond Crankheit just stood there, not sure what to do next. This fine-looking woman standing before him had caught him completely by surprise, and he was suddenly as deep into a conversation with a woman as he'd been in years. He had to think of something to say next, something that wouldn't scare her away, and send her running, perhaps to the cops. He couldn't cope with cops just now.

"I was wondering . . . do you have the time?"

Principessa Stanley unholstered her BlackBerry and consulted it. "Nearly seven," she said.

"Thank you." Raymond hoped he hadn't exhausted all his conversational gambits in one fell swoop. "I was wondering—could you tell me . . . is this Central Park?" It was lame, but it was also the only thing he could think of. He was a little agitated by what the commander had just told him . . .

Principessa looked at him with a bemused smile. Of all the lame lines she'd ever heard, and she had pretty much heard them all, this was one of the lamest. This was the kind of line a guy might use in the early afternoon on Fifth Avenue, or when he caught her coming out of her office on Sixth. In fact, it was so dumb that it just might be genuine. "What do you think it is—Coney Island?" she replied with a laugh.

Under normal circumstances, that would have been the correct answer. A real New Yorker—which Principessa had tried so hard to become—would have recognized it at once as a stock reply, the kind of answer one gave to the hapless tourists standing at the corner of 34th Street and Fifth Avenue, wondering if that tall building in front of them was the Empire State Building or, worse, the World Trade Center. It was the kind of response that said subtextually, what do you take me for, a fool? A fellow tourist? And the joke would have been on the interlocutor, not the respondent. But these were not normal circumstances. And Raymond Crankheit was not a normal person.

As Principessa realized as soon as she saw the look on his face. What she had hoped would be taken as a joke had obviously fallen flat. This hour of the morning was no time for an argument so she immediately decided to backfill. She gave him her best coquettish laugh. "Sorry, just a little joke there. Of course it is. I didn't realize you were from out of town." For a tourist or a bridge-and-tunnel guy, he wasn't that bad, and she felt a stab of compassion for him. All her life she'd been accused of being a bitch on wheels, and now here was her chance to change that image, even if it was only with a guy she'd just met.

Raymond Crankheit, however, heard the backtrack quite differently. "From out of town." What the hell did she mean by that? Had she made him? The Brothers had warned him about women like her, the temptresses who would use you and then mock you, the way the women in the United States Army had done to the *fedayeen* in Iraq. The tanks and the Humvees that had entered Baghdad had played recordings over loudspeakers, taunting the Brothers over the size of their members, insulting them in a woman's voice that Believers had little dicks. This of course had enraged the Holy Warriors and out they charged, screaming and thirsting for vengeance and prepared to put the lie to the libel with a glorious martyr's death. Unfortunately, that was exactly what they had received, as the diabolical followers of Satan had expected just such a manly reaction and shot them down as they poked their heads from windows and doorways.

Women were never to be trusted. "Haven't I seen you somewhere before, Miss?" he asked as politely as he could, trying to conceal his anger and his contempt. "You're that Princess girl, right?"

Principessa smiled. Getting recognized was one of the hazards of the profession, but it irked her when a young male of a certain age did *not* recognize her, and she took the implied insult personally. What, she wasn't famous enough? She wasn't pretty enough? She wasn't successful enough? She would show this twerp.

"Sorry," she said, not sorry at all, "but I don't have time for an autograph right now. But I was wondering whether a homeless guy like yourself might be able to tell me something about what's going on around here. Were you here yesterday? Did you see anything? Hear anything?"

So he was right after all: she was on to him. She was asking questions like a cop. That tore it. For the first time in his life, he was being nice to a girl and she was being nice back at him, but something had gone wrong—something always went wrong—and now here she was, grilling him the way some of the others did, asking him questions designed to make him look stupid.

In the old days, he would have run away. He would have endured the humiliation of being bested by a twist and being unable to do anything about it. But now he didn't have to, not any longer. As he discovered yesterday, he could do something about it. In fact, here, on this hallowed spot, he could do a couple of things, and then come back for more.

Raymond turned away from Principessa for a moment. At once, she regretted her words and her actions. The poor boy had no idea who she was. He was some lost soul, an out-of-towner, probably simple, who'd gotten caught up in yesterday's events and didn't know where to go or what to do. In fact, he most likely wasn't homeless at all. He probably had a room in one of those cheap Times Square hotels, but had been unable to get to it due to the emergency. She felt like a real heel . . .

"Sorry," she said, "that was rude. I am Principessa Stanley. What's your name?"

This was a shy boy she was dealing with, she could tell that. A lot of men went all weak in the knees when they actually met her in the flesh; she was used to that. Time for a little of the old noblesse oblige.

"Raymond," he said. "Raymond Crankheit. From Wahoo, Nebraska. You ever been to Wahoo?"

"No," she replied, because after all why in the hell would she ever have been to some nowhere dump like Wahoo, or even Nebraska, when there were still places in South America and China and India she hadn't visited yet?

However, as it turned out, "no" was the last thing she said, for Raymond suddenly wheeled and struck her with the stock of his rifle as if he was swinging a baseball bat—another thing he had never been particularly good at, but at which at this moment he was more than proficient. The woman fell hard, soundlessly, face-first into the ground, her head bleeding. But she was still moving, trying to say something but producing only muffled noises, little bleats and whimpers, just the way the Japanese schoolgirls in those porn videos he watched for free on the Internet did.

Perfect.

He trussed her up with some of the rope in his kit, just the way the Brothers had taught him, bound her tightly. He wanted her alive, for later.

He pushed her deep into the bushes and into the hole where he had buried his weapons. It wasn't deep enough to fully cover her, but he could get a lot of her into it, including her arms, and by tamping down the dirt he could effectively immobilize her. He covered the rest of her with some camouflage they had given him, and turned her face up and looked at her. She was bloody and dirty, but that didn't really matter at this point. She was still a woman, she was alive, and this was likely as close as he was going to get to a creature like this.

Raymond Crankheit kissed Principessa Stanley as hard as he could. It was inexpert and clumsy, but he got what he wanted out of it. For the first time in his life, he knew what a woman tasted like. He took one of his spare T-shirts, ripped it apart and bound her eyes with it. The remainder he stuffed into her mouth. He pulled a plastic garbage bag over her head, and left her there, waiting for him.

He picked up his rifle and made ready to go, then stopped. Something wasn't right. He'd heard that guys who were dating always liked to have a little something of their girlfriend's to remember them, a souvenir, to wear or keep in a pocket or billfold. He went back to Principessa and slowly lifted the Baggie so that he could get a good look at her.

Her ears were shapely and well-formed, and he thought about cutting one of them off but decided against it because he didn't want her all bloody when he got back. He wanted her alive and beautiful, just the way she was now. That ruled out her nose as well, and as for her fingers, they were buried and thus out of the question.

He put the rifle down and started at the back of her head, working his way around. He did his best not to draw blood, although some of that was unfortunately necessary. Just a prick here or two. Had he been a wild Red Indian, like the kind who used to roam the plains of Nebraska? Not near Wahoo, because as anybody knew, Wahoo was near Omaha, which was on the river, but farther to the west, the Wild West of cowboy movies, which is mostly where he'd seen it, except for a drive across the state one time to visit some relative out there by Scottsbluff someplace—he couldn't remember.

It took a while, but by the time was finished he had most of her hair. Carefully, he replaced the Baggie and patted her on the head, to let her know everything was all right and that he'd be back to claim the rest of his trophies later. But it was time to go.

He picked up his rifle again. There were, he'd heard, millions of people in Manhattan, which meant that he would run out of ammo long before he ran out of targets. It would not be until later that he realized his cell phone had fallen out of his pocket and was probably buried along with the woman.

CHAPTER THIRTY-ONE

Century City—morning

If he had had time, Jake Sinclair would have enjoyed being in his new offices. All the right folks were moving to the old Fox back lot these days, including two of the major talent agencies and some entertainment law firms, to go along with the usual mixture of financial-services companies and shopping malls. Everything from the marble floors to the strategically placed Persian carpets to the art on the walls and the sculptures in the halls was the result of his taste and his choice. It was amazing how much art you could buy when half of Hollywood was feeling poor.

And here he was the one—the media mogul in a declining business—who was supposed to be feeling the pinch, not the stars who used to make twenty million a picture, and now were reduced to the relative penury of fourteen million. But it all made sense. When the stars made less, then everybody made less, including the agents, producers, the co-stars, and the writers. Hollywood may be Moscow-on-the-Pacific, at least as far as its social sense of itself was concerned, but in reality it was the purest form of trickle-down capitalism in the country. Sure, it was "high school with money," but the high-school pecking order made a lot of sense in a *Lord of the Flies* sort of way; it quickly sorted out the winners from the losers, the beauties from the nerds, the popular kids from the dorks, and those lessons stayed with you a lifetime.

Show people were so easy to manipulate, it was like a vacation.

But on this day Jake Sinclair had no time for self-congratulation. He had a very important meeting with the woman who would be the next president of the United States, especially if she continued to play ball.

He moved quickly from the private elevator through the public halls, where his employees could see him—a general needed to be seen from time to time—and past the ranks of video screens displaying live television feeds, his newspapers' stories as they were in the process of being written, and the websites that had latterly become such a large part of his operations.

Angela Hassett was waiting for him, standing in his office and watching one of the video feeds intently. When she became president, it was he who would have to show up early for appointments, and get used to being kept waiting, but at the moment he was delivering a Hollywood power message, which was that the more important person in the meeting dictated the schedule and the other person took it and liked it. "Ms. Hassett," he said as he swept into the room, "so sorry to keep you waiting. You know the traffic in this town."

Truth was, traffic had nothing to do with it, but Jake Sinclair always liked to make an entrance, and so he affected that L.A. air of frazzled bemusement, as if the torture of being confined in his new Mercedes during the commute from Los Feliz to Century City was akin to spending ten years on Devil's Island, except you didn't actually have to do the time. "Can I get you something to—"

"Mr. Sinclair," she interrupted, "Neither of us has time for coffee, Diet Coke, or bullshit. So let's get started, shall we? What do you make of what's going on in New York?"

Angela Hassett was, he had to admit, a rather striking woman. Her photographs didn't do her justice, and just the way she moved and tossed her head revealed the coquette beneath the frosty exterior. Sinclair understood at once that here was a woman for whom "by any means necessary" was not just a slogan but a way of life. He liked her: they could do business together. They were soul mates.

"A terrible thing, of course," he said blandly.

"I mean about the cease-fire, or whatever it is. I want to know everything you know about it."

"Perhaps we should speak privately," he said. As his people moved toward the door, she flashed the same look at her people, who quickly got the message and similarly headed toward the exits. "I agree," she said.

The door closed. They were alone. He dropped the pretense of bonhomie. "I don't know," he said. "We're working on it. In fact, we have our best reporters in the field. But I gather the gunmen, whoever they are, have gone to ground."

"Does Tyler have anything to do with this?"

"How would I know?"

"You're supposed to be the media mogul, not me. All I'm doing is running for president."

Her tone was beginning to piss him off. "Then how can I help you, Ms. Hassett?"

She didn't like his tone any more than he'd liked hers. "There's no point in wasting any time, Mr. Sinclair," she said frostily. "We both know why I'm here."

"Call me Jake—"

"Mr. Sinclair," she continued, ignoring him. "What we have is strictly a business arrangement at this point. You have something I need and I have something you want. Need and want are not the same thing in order of magnitude, which means that at the moment you have me over a barrel, hierarchically speaking. That will change come November, but for the nonce let us simply say that thus far things have worked out well, I am here to accommodate you."

Sinclair smiled. He liked a woman—or a man, for that matter—who got right to the point. There would be no time-wasting jockeying as the two adversaries sorted out whose dog was bigger. Things were clear.

"I don't have to tell you that Jeb Tyler is weak and that he's in trouble. Neither do I have to tell you why. He's weak because he's a fool and a coward. All his life he's played it safe by playing it down the middle; he thought a smile, a shoeshine, and a nice haircut could take him as far as he wanted to go, and up until last year he was right. But events and circumstances have a way of dislodging the best-laid plans, and now he's in over his head and sinking rapidly. I can beat him. I know it, you know it, and he knows it. All he needs is a little push." She glanced at one of the televisions.

"Tell me something I don't already know."

"I can guarantee you a place at the table."

"As I said . . ."

The coquette disappeared. "Don't fuck with me, buster. You and I both know that your media empire is being held together with spit and bubblegum, and if you don't get some tax breaks and subsidies from the feds, you're screwed." She gestured around the room, with all its expensive furnishings and its panoramic view of this part of Los Angeles. "You're William Randolph Hearst minus the girlfriend and the castle, but if things don't turn around, you're going to end up just like him—bankrupt and impotent . . . So now that I've got your attention, let's talk turkey."

Sinclair wasn't used to being spoken to like this. Usually, whoever was unfortunate enough to be sitting across from him in a negotiation was the one on the receiving end of the obloquy, but this woman had waltzed into his office and taken command. Jeb Tyler was in more trouble than he knew. "I'm all ears," he said.

"Good. Here's my offer. I'm making this only once, so listen carefully." Abruptly, she rose. "Where's the bathroom?" she inquired. Sinclair indicated a door off to one side. "Will you follow me, please?"

Puzzled but intrigued, he followed her into the loo. Like any self-respecting executive washroom, it was equipped with a shower, a bidet, and a wide selection of toiletries, only some of which had been filched from various hotels in Cannes and Tokyo.

She closed the door. "Don't get any bright ideas," she said, reaching past him and into the shower. With a quick turn of her wrists, she turned the mixer on full force. The water gushed forth, a vivid realization of old man Mulholland's famous exhortation when he opened the floodgates of the dammed, siphoned water from the Owens Valley and told Los Angeles: "There it is. Take it."

"It's not that I don't trust you," she said, "but I don't trust you." She pulled him close to her. The steam from the hot water was already turning the confined space into a steam bath. Sinclair felt the beads of sweat mingle with the water vapor as it rolled down his face and down his chest.

"All my life, I've been fascinated with puzzles," said Angela Hassett. "Codes, ciphers, what have you. Not crosswords or Sudoku—real puzzles. They were my hobby as a kid and so they've remained. In another life, perhaps I would have gone into the CIA or the NSA, but I chose another path." She moved even closer, so he could hear her over the running water. "Still, my love remains constant."

They were very close now, her face close to his, her mouth near his left cheek. He thought about kissing her, then reconsidered the impulse. There would be plenty of time for friskiness later, if it came to that. Imagine, fucking the President of the United States! He was starting to gain a new appreciation for Judith Campbell and the rest of JFK's mistresses.

"So, the way I see politics, is that it's a giant puzzle. In order to win, you have to fit all the pieces together. But you don't have infinite time; you have to get it right and you have to get it right under fire. Any election can be won or lost depending on which day the people vote. On which news comes out when. Stories get timed, then launched. He's a drunk, she's a slut. She had an abortion when she was fourteen; he's a recovering drug addict who did time in that rehab clinic in Park City and the only people who knew were Hollywood types. He has a taste for little boys; she for little girls. Scandals are not what they used to be, but they can still be potent. It all just depends on how you fit the pieces together."

Sinclair was getting to be pretty uncomfortable now, but what was he going to do? Ask permission to leave the bathroom? They were in there for a reason, and that reason was, she didn't trust him, didn't trust him not to monitor their conversation, not to record it, not to keep it as a weapon against her, or at least an insurance policy, against such time as he would need it, against such time when they, like thieves everywhere, would fall out and turn on each other. He hoped that day would never come, but he was too smart and too experienced and too cynical not to allow for its possibility. And so, he knew, was she.

"So what's the deal?"

She pushed back a bit, and ran her fingers through her hair, then wiped her face. "You take him down with everything you've got. His past as an ambulance-chaser. How he put doctors out of business all over Louisiana until poor pregnant black women were hitchhiking from Lake Charles to Houston to drop their babies somewhere half-civilized. How he's probably gay."

She watched his eyes closely to see how he'd react. Surely he knew, or at least suspected. Everybody did. It was the worst-kept rumor in Washington, the first bachelor president, with his great reputation as a womanizer, the ultimate get for every single gal from Bethesda to Escondido, all a sham.

"You can't prove it," said Sinclair. "Nobody can."

"What does it matter? All you have to do is raise the question. What does he have to hide?" She moved back in closer, this time for the kill. "And what about the Edwardsville fiasco? What about that dead reporter? What about his embrace of Islam? If any of those crazy mujahideen get near him, he's as good as dead—why aren't they telling us about this threat to national security? Can we really afford such a man in the White House, in the Oval Office? It's time for a change."

She placed both hands on his cheeks, then slowly moved them up the sides of his head until her fingers were now running through his hair, gently tousling it.

"And what's in it for me?"

"You'll be the last man standing," she said. "My administration will make sure of it."

Sinclair made one last attempt to find and assert his manhood. "But the same could be said for you. Nobody knows anything about you. Your past is a closed book, your records sealed. All you are is—"

"All I am is a fresh new face. All I am is not Jeb Tyler. And considering what's going on in New York City right now, that's all I have to be."

She had him there. "I guess we have a deal, then," he said. Jake Sinclair had never met anyone quite like Angela Hassett.

"Then let's seal it." She tilted her face upward, and her lips found his. She was hungrier than he expected, and they stayed that way for a while, longer than necessary for a business deal, not quite long enough for anything else to happen, leaving the promise hanging in the air.

She broke it first, pulled back and just stood there, looking at him. He broke the awkward silence:

"What about your husband?"

She laughed, then tossed him a towel with which to wipe his face. "Don't try to fuck me, Jake," she said.

She turned off the water, turned toward him. He wasn't sure what to expect, but whatever it was it wasn't this:

A slap across the face, hard.

"If you ever keep me waiting again," she said, "I'll kill you."

CHAPTER THIRTY-TWO

Manhattan

Something was nagging at Devlin, just as it had at Edwardsville. It was too easy.

Not the killing; that was hard. No matter how good you were at it, it was always hard. He was up against trained killers, and although they were not in his class, and he was armed with superior intelligence and firepower, each of them had presented a different challenge.

Once he had blown his own cover to the Iranian, things happened exactly as he expected them to. There had been one last message, blasted from the hotel to the operatives still in the field, which is exactly what Devlin had hoped would happen. That would be the stand-down message, or the save-yourself message, or the await-further-instructions message, with maybe a verse of two of the Koran thrown in for good measure. The boys and girls back at Fort Meade would know. All that mattered to Devlin was that Arash Kohanloo had just burned his entire operation.

The face-recognition software at NSA is the best in the world, and the little UAV had done its job well. Within five

minutes The Building had processed the visual information
and had relayed it back to him via a series of cutouts:

KOHANLOO, ARASH. Iranian businessman, with many
financial interests in the West. At home, he professed to be a
devout Muslim and was tight with the mullahs, but once outside the *dar al-Islam* he could be as much a party animal as
any Saudi princeling. He was a familiar type in all religions,
a hypocrite, but why he wanted to involve himself in something like this—well, that was the mystery. Actually, it was
not all that big of a mystery; in Devlin's experience, Money
and Love, or her naughty sister, Lust, pretty much explained
everything.

Devlin opened up his netbook and logged onto a secure,
encrypted channel to Seelye:

KOHANLOO—WHAT'S THE CONNECTION?

TO WHOM? came the immediate reply.

DON'T BULLSHIT ME, DAD.

TO SKORZENY YOU MEAN?

EXACTAMUNDO

WORKING ON IT

WORK HARDER. WHAT'S TYLER'S PLAY IN THIS?

A pause, then:

NO PLAY. HE'S LETTING NYPD HANDLE IT.
DOESN'T WANT TO PANIC THE COUNTRY

LETTING ME HANDLE IT, YOU MEAN

SAME THING

LIKE BLOWING UP TIMES SQUARE HASN'T AL-
READY PANICKED THE COUNTRY. IT'S ABOUT THE
ELECTION, RIGHT?

IT'S ALWAYS ABOUT THE ELECTION. HASSETT
HAD A MEETING WITH SINCLAIR, AND HE'S BEAT-
ING TYLER'S BRAINS OUT 24/7

So that was the play. Tyler didn't want to panic America,

as he had the last time with his dumb stunt of practically negotiating with the terrorists, so he was letting the cops deal
with it. With the information Devlin could give them, they'd
be able to run them down and wrap things up pretty easily.
He could see it now, as Tyler saw it: a bunch of dead people
followed by a slew of yellow ribbons, some official boo-hoo,
and then Jeb himself standing at the center of the Square,
promising New Yorkers and the American People that a new
Times Square would rise gloriously from the ashes, better
and cleaner and safer than before, a place for families to dis-
port themselves in freedom from fear.

And, of course, that this would never happen again. If Devlin could link Kohanloo to the Iranian government, there's
no telling what Tyler wouldn't do to win the election. The
President not only had a bully pulpit, he had the combined
weight of the American armed services behind him, and taking on, or even taking out, Iran would satisfy the public's
bloodlust. Plus there was a big swath of his constituency
that had been wanting payback for the hostage crisis since
the Carter administration. Even Sinclair's media empire
would have to look the other way, as long as he did it quickly
enough.

So he'd sealed off the city, but hadn't sent in troops. Not
bad. Devlin would have played it the same way, especially
with himself as his ace in the hole. But the discovery of
Kohnaloo had just ramped up the stakes. If this was an operation financed by the Iranians and executed by Hamas, there
was no way Tyler was going to be able to keep the lid on it.

Seelye read his mind: SO GET THIS OVER WITH
PRONTO

ROGER THAT, POP he wrote, and signed off.

Thus the operation had fallen silent, the shooting had
stopped as the enemy regrouped. Depending on how well

they had canvassed the city, and how long they had planned, the surviving shooters would have gone to ground by now, each to a separate bolt-hole while the Iranian plotted the next move. And, if past experience were any guide, his next move would be to get the hell out of New York and leave his team to its fate.

Which meant things were working out exactly the way Devlin expected them to. Which was another thing that worried him.

Things never went according to plan: the first rule of warfare was that if they did, your plan wasn't working. He had lived long in the worlds of violence and deception, so long that not only could he tell them apart, he had long ago realized that deception was superior.

Which was why he had blown his surveillance. By sending the shooters scurrying—by forcing them into Plan B—he had accomplished two objectives. The first was to put the heat on Mr. Big and make him do something either expected or stupid, which amounted to the same thing. The second was to force the NYPD SWAT units to stand down; he didn't need to bump into them while he was carrying out his orders, to run the risk of exposure if one of the cops happened upon him. He needed the fuzz out of the way, and so he relied on the dead-solid-certain fact that when there was trouble, New York wanted an immediate and overwhelming response, but the instant the shooting stopped, the residents demanded flowers in the barrels of the guns and cue the defense lawyers. It had to be the most suicidal city in the nation, professing "never again," but inviting it constantly.

He had taken out six more of the shooters since his encounter in the New Victory. Three of them came before the cell phone security alert had been raised.

The first was a woman, and that always made it difficult

for him. He could not control his sentimental streak, or whatever it was, because killing a woman reminded him of his mother's death in the Rome airport, when a group of very bad men, convinced of the rightness and morality of their cause, had robbed him forever of her smile, her laugh, her presence, her spirit, her soul.

Well, perhaps not forever. On the subject, the afterlife, religion, however you named it, he was agnostic. Certainly, he had never seen any evidence of its power at the moment of death, when the Angel of Death inhabited him and he did his duty by country, if not God.

He shot her from a distance, as she was leaning out a window of the Brill Building. He hoped she had a song on her lips, but if she was like her fellow Muslims, she probably didn't; the Brill Building was Tin Pan Alley and the heyday of New York showbiz in brick, steel, and mortar, home to hundreds of music and entertainment companies. In the old days, everybody who was anybody in the music business was headquartered in Lefcourt's Brill Building. Firing from across the street, the MRP took her out clean with a single shot to the head, and she fell eight stories down, landing on Broadway with a sickening thud that he could hear two hundred yards away, although of course she didn't feel a thing.

The next man the Angel visited was more up close and personal. Moving in the shadows, Devlin had found him in a storeroom of one of the many pizza places that inhabited the square. Pretending to be a looter, he had easily disarmed him and then eviscerated him with his own kukri knife. He left the body on the pizza counter, *pour encourager les autres*.

The third was another man. At least, Devlin thought it was a man, but the only good look he got was at the back of his head lining up a night-sight shot on 47th Street as he ran east. Devlin had been triangulating his GPS signal, watched the hinky behavior, and when the guy tossed the cell phone in a trash can, he put one through the back of his skull.

The other three he had already forgotten about. Track and kill. Track and kill. The only trick to it was for him to stay invisible, but there was no place for invisibility like a battlefield that had been emptied of civilians: the only bodies moving out there were either cops, who were easy to spot, even in plain clothes, or the bad guys, who were even easier to spot. You could say a lot about the NYPD, but one thing you could never say was that the front-line men and women were cowards.

In a sense, he had been fighting this enemy since 1985, although he didn't realize it at the time, and had made it his life's work to understand how he thought and, more important, what he feared. Forget all that crap about pig's blood and ham sandwiches and unclean women and women in general; what he most feared was humiliation, especially humiliation in death. In this he was not unlike the great hero of the Trojans, who had begged Achilles that, however their battle ended, humiliation should not be a part of it. But, of course, Achilles had spurned that offer as a sign of weakness, killed Hector, and dragged his body around the walls of the city with his chariot.

In Devlin's opinion, Achilles had gotten exactly what was coming to him, divine karma, when he was killed by the coward Paris with a lucky shot to the one unprotected area of his body, his heel.

Would that be his fate? Would his pride eventually bring him down? Since his conquest of Milverton, there was no man who could take him, no man that he knew about at least. But he also knew that there were hundreds of them out there, thousands, all itching for the chance to take him on. They would not know him by name, or even by reputation, but they would all be animated, as all the best young fighters were, by the notion that there was somebody out there older and better than they, and that they would not be warriors until they had tested their mettle against his.

Very well, then: bring them on. There was only one thing he feared.

The lucky amateur. The 21st-century Paris.

Chapter Thirty-three

Fort Meade, Maryland

Major Atwater sat at his desk, puzzling over the material his chief had assigned to him. Of all the things to have do at this time, when the country was riveted by what was going on in New York City, this scut work was the worst. Sifting through ancient ciphers—what a waste of time. Stuff that had been gone over and gone over for decades, centuries even, with no one the wiser. Useless crap.

The *Thirty-Nine Steps*? Not even the figment of a screenwriter's imagination, since in the original novel by Buchan the thirty-nine steps were exactly that—thirty-nine steps leading down to the sea; it was only in the Hitchcock movie that the steps were "an organization of spies" revealed by the mentalist. How lame was that?

The second message obviously referred to the Poe Cryptographic Challenge, which had been driving amateur cryptologists crazy since the 19th century. It took until 1992 for someone to crack the first substitution cipher, and until 2000 for the second one to be solved. And these were ciphers dreamed up by a drunk living in the Bronx and Baltimore.

Substitution cipher—maybe that was the clue, and not the

cipher itself. Substitution ciphers were among the oldest and easiest to crack: Sir Arthur Conan Doyle had used one in *The Adventure of the Dancing Men*, and for some reason they were much favored by fugitive lovers, furtively communicating by means of crude stick figures. As if anybody couldn't figure out in a heartbeat that the most recurring stick figure would stand for the letter "e," and figure the rest out from there. It was nearly impossible to compose an English sentence—or a sentence in any Western language, for that matter—without using the letter "e," and even though that Frenchy Perec had managed the feat in *La Disparition* and Ernest Wright had pulled off the lipogram even earlier in *Gadsby* thirty years before.

The things that occupied the human mind. Substitution ciphers, mirror writing, inverted mirror writing . . . those damn mystery writers never knew when to leave well enough alone.

The third was a bit more complex: It was unsigned.: UG RMK CSXHMUFMKB TOXG CMVATLUIV. Any first-year student at the Wyoming Cryptography School, where he had gone as an undergraduate, could spot that: *Have His Carcase* by Dorothy L. Sayers, the creator of Lord Peter Wimsey. "We are discovered. Save Yourself." Piece of cake.

The fourth was a series of numbers: 317, 8, 92, 73, 112, 79, 67, 318, 28, 96, 107, 41, 631, 78, 146, 397, 118, 98, 114.

Beale Ciphers, not that that was much of a help. The three ciphers, first published in a pamphlet in Virginia in 1885, were said to show the way to a great treasure, but only the second cipher had ever been cracked—it turned out to be a numerological correspondence to the wording of the Declaration of Independence which, when read *en clair*, said:

> I have deposited in the county of Bedford, about four
> miles from Buford's, in an excavation or vault, six
> feet below the surface of the ground, the following

articles: . . . The deposit consists of two thousand nine hundred and twenty one pounds of gold and five thousand one hundred pounds of silver; also jewels, obtained in St. Louis in exchange for silver to save transportation. . . . The above is securely packed in iron pots, with iron covers. The vault is roughly lined with stone, and the vessels rest on solid stone, and are covered with others . . ."

Lots of luck with that. No one—not even the finest minds at NSA or CIA, just screwing around in their spare time, had broken the other two; if they had, they might have found the buried treasure and retired very wealthy men. So wealthy, in fact, that they might even have been able to afford their houses in Potomac and Great Falls.

The fifth was the familiar series of 87 characters, squiggles based on the letter "E," arranged in three rows:

Again, every first-year student knew this one. It was the secret message sent by the famous composer, Sir Edward Elgar, to his inamorata, Miss Dora Penny—"Dorabella"—one of the recipients of a dedication in the great *Enigma Variations* for orchestra. This one was tough, because most cryptographers were not musicians and most musicians were not cryptographers, although come to think of it their disciplines had a lot in common, since each was based on writing in a language that bore no resemblance to the meaning, except by fiat.

But the *Enigma Variations* were tricky, even by musical standards. Elgar had composed a series of variations on a theme that, he claimed, was never actually heard in the piece itself. That is to say, the "theme"—angular and descriptive, which led some to suggest that it was nothing more than the topographic outlines of the Malvern Hills that Elgar knew so well, expressed in music—was only the counterpoint to the Unheard Melody. Scholars had spent most of the last century trying to identify the hidden tune.

Well, Major Atwater was no musician, so he didn't much care about the mysterious melody. What he had in front of him, the famous "Dorabella" set of squiggles, was much more interesting.

For a century, amateurs and professionals alike had been trying to break the code, mostly in expectation of discovering some Victorian-Edwardian raciness secreted within, like one of the "snuggeries" that so feverishly occupied the Victorian pornographic imagination. And that the fact that Elgar had further memorialized Ms. Penny in the great orchestral work itself indicated that his affection for her ran very deep. "These are deep waters indeed, Watson," as Sherlock Holmes famously said in some adventure or another. Despite the fact that a very high percentage of intelligence professionals were Sherlock Holmes fans, Major Atwater had never quite managed to see the charm of a world in which it was always 1895.

And then there was "Masterman XX."

Work backward. Whoever assembled these ciphers had meant for that to be the punch line. It had to have some meaning. The reference was obvious—the famous "Double-Cross System" developed by the British during World War

II. It was essentially a method of doubling captured German agents, returning them home, and then using them to spread disinformation. The XX stood both for the double-cross itself and for the Committee of Twenty, which oversaw the operations. Crude by contemporary standards of HUMINT tradecraft, to be sure, but there was always a first time for everything, and after the war, as the Allies split apart to become antagonists, it became the template for every doubled and re-doubled agent, every disinformation and false-flag operation that the American and the Soviets ran against each other.

He ran his hands through his hair. Already, it was thinning, he had to admit that. Life just wasn't fair. Time to think this through again.

A series of ciphers, each one famous. Some easily solved, like the substitution ciphers, and others the object of countless efforts to crack them by amateur and professional alike. What was the common thread?

There wasn't any. Literary references, imaginary ciphers, real ciphers, love-letter ciphers . . . what were the common themes?

Love and money, unless you counted the double-cross. But weren't double-crosses always about either love or money? He felt like he was living in some kind of wacky film noir, a modern-day Philip Marlowe transplanted to suburban Washington, but with exactly zero chance of a hot blonde walking through the door with a big problem and a little piece of money.

Hang on. Follow your own damn logic. *Think.* That's what they pay you do.

No, not just think. *Associate.* That's what code-makers did, and it was up to him to reverse-engineer the damn thing, like the Japanese after World War II, trying to figure out how Western technology worked, and how they could do it better.

A code consisted not only of the actual cipher itself, but the overall concept behind it. In the Beale cipher, for example, the clues to the location of the buried treasure were hidden behind the referential numbers, but the real key was the Declaration, which obviously meant something to the code-maker. This is where it got tricky.

The Declaration might have had a primal, emotional resonance for the man calling himself Thomas Jefferson Beale—his very name would suggest that—but it also might, *might* be totally coincidental. His real name might not have been Thomas Jefferson Beale, and the use of the Jefferson's great call to arms might simply have reflected its ubiquity in American culture at that time. Correlation is not causation.

But, like master bomb-makers, master code-makers saw their work as a higher calling, an art form so special that they could not resist leaving some clue to their identity, or to the code's purpose. Like the medieval artisans who would sneak signatures onto their work, in the hopes of living forever in stone or wood, the code-writers each had a style that spoke to their purpose. *This is why I am doing this* was, at root, the code behind every code, and if the applause came decades or centuries down the road, then so be it.

So why was he doing this?

Love and money. Money and love. That the code-writer was a man was a safe assumption. Most code-writers were men, and even if it was politically incorrect, it was a safe assumption that a woman had not sent these missives to Seelye—or, if she had, she was merely a courier. Men loved numbers, codes, statistics, hidden meanings, conspiracy theories. Not every man, of course, nor was every woman automatically ruled out as a participant. But every now and then you just had to play the odds, and the hell with the feelings of some female professor at Harvard.

He looked at the assemblage again, and again. Waited for it to fall into place. Waited for it to assume shape and form and meaning. Waited for it to reveal itself, to expose itself, naked, to his gaze. It was almost erotic.

Suddenly, he saw it. What a fool he had been. What fools they had all been.

Love. The Dancing Men were about love, the kind of mad love that careers out of the past to curse the present. *Have His Carcase* was about the Playfair cipher—hell, it was practically a "how-to" guide to the damn thing—but it was also a story of discovered lovers. And who was more emblematic of the 19th century than the tortured, malevolent genius of Edgar Allan Poe?

Line them up: prelude, theme, development, deceptive cadence (the Beale cipher, although it too must have resonance), climax, and coda. And what was the climax?

Dorabella.

It wasn't about sight at all. It was about *sound*.

It was all about Elgar and Dorabella.

This was what the culture got and deserved for ignoring one of its principal senses—hearing—in favor of its default mode, sight. What if the squiggles really were what some had suggested, just a bunch of jocular shit, a goof by an older man impossibly in love with a younger woman, who had hidden his real message, his declaration of love *inside the music*?

Knowing that, even in the 19th century, when the standard of education was infinitely higher than it was today, Elgar might have counted on the once-remove that music gave him. After all, he lived in the days of the fictional Mycroft Holmes, Sherlock's arguably smarter elder brother, who often *was* the British government when he was not successfully masquerading as a civil servant. At the apogee of British society, in the days before credentialism, that quintessentially American disease of bureaucrats and apparatchiks, Sir Edward would have had a panoply of cultural and linguistic references available to him. No wonder it was in this period that Britain reached its zenith; culturally confident, a synthesis of classical civilization and Anglo-Saxon ferocity, able to subjugate the native Celts and harness their scientific and literary genius in the service of the Empire.

Morse code: *I am. Am I?* A phrase and then the reverse. A yearning, strange and ineffable. Hesitant, coy and coquettish by turns, masterful and manly by others. Everyone assumed that the work was as Elgar said: portraits of various friends. Program music, the scholars called it.

But what if that, too, was all misdirection? What if the central enigma of the *Enigma Variations* wasn't so enigmatic after all, but hiding right there in plain sight? There, hidden away in one of the lesser variations—not the magisterial "Nimrod," which had come, like the *Pomp and Circumstance* March No. 1, to symbolize the very spirit of Victorian Britain itself, but the one that *immediately followed it*.

The "Dorabella" variation.

The squiggly "eeees."

The squiggly, ornamented melodic line of the "Dorabella" Variation, supposedly meant to express the girl's slight hesitancy in her speech patterns. But listen closer: the variation does not simply depict one person, but two. The strings twitter, but the woodwinds answer.

Dora. Bella. Dora the Beautiful.

And she is having a conversation with the composer.

It was all coming together. The wife, the flighty and often amusing friends. All building on the Morse Code, on the unheard, unspoken, unarticulated, unwritten "real" theme as the music drove toward to the titanic "Nimrod" variation and then . . . the whole point of the piece, carefully and calculatedly inserted precisely at the point where the audience would still be in thrall to the majesty of the Ninth Variation and never suspect that the real declaration of love would come, dramatically, where they were least expecting it.

Match it up:

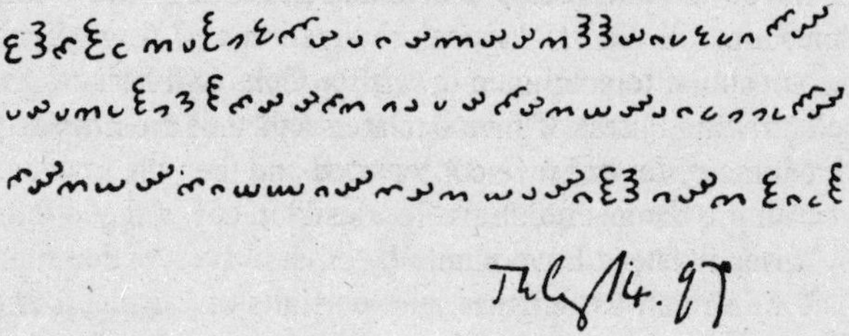

[handwritten shorthand symbols]

Tuly 14. 97

There it was, staring at him, plainly. The contrary motion of the great tune, the unanswered question of *I am. Am I?* The inverse, the mirror image. The counterpoint of existence, the yin and the yang, the harmonic balance: one door closes, another door opens. One man dies, another child is born. Perpetual contrary motion.

Look at it.

No: listen to it.

Read it. Not the way one would usually "read," but the way a musician would read:

Hearing it as he—or, in this case, she—read.

It wasn't about a code at all.

It was the unheard theme of the *Enigma Variations*, written out in Elgar's private shorthand two years before he composed his first masterpiece, and communicated to the woman he loved but whom he could not have. He had to hide his affections—after all, he was married, and he and his wife had just been on a visit to Dora, her father, and her stepmother—and so he disguised them.

Not only disguised them. Gave them voice. Orchestrated them. And then let the world hear them.

It was about Love.

In his excitement, Major Atwater leaped to his feet and began to sing. Then he stopped, caught up short—

Love was followed by the Double Cross: XX. The symbol of Death.

Not substitution ciphers—*substitutions*. Symbols of symbols. Telling a tale of love declared and love frustrated. Of love unrequited and love confounded.

"We are discovered. Save Yourself."

It wasn't about Love after all.

It was about Revenge.

CHAPTER THIRTY-FOUR

St. Clare's Hospital

"It's St. Vincent's now, officer," the admitting specialist had said last night, "for however long we stay in business"—but Lannie wasn't in the mood for a history lesson. He'd gotten Sid immediate medical attention. As it turned out, Sid's leg was broken in four places, but otherwise he was going to be okay. The doctors had shot him full of painkillers and done the best they could with the leg, but it was going to be a while, if ever, before he could resume his alternate career as shortstop for the New York Yankees.

"What's the score?" asked Sid, wide-awake, but full of more dope than Lenny Bruce.

"We're winning," Lannie lied.

"Correction," came a voice behind them. "We're going to win, but right now we are at the mercy of my least favorite people in the world."

Lannie and Sid turned to see Capt. Byrne stepping into Sid's room. His shoulder was bandaged and he was a little pale, but otherwise he appeared pretty much his old nail-chewing self. "In the old days," he said, "this was the place they brought all the gangsters, after they'd been ventilated in some dustup or other in Hell's Kitchen. They even brought the great Owney Madden here in 1912, after he'd gotten himself shot up by the Hudson Dusters. Filled him full of lead, eleven shots in all, and still the son of a bitch didn't die." Byrne pulled back the covers to take a look at Sid, and smiled. "You've got nowhere near eleven rounds in you, boyo."

Sid smiled weakly. Why did it have to be him? Everybody always made fun of him, the Jewish kid, supposedly the smart one, but not the tough one. All he'd wanted was a chance to show the boss that he was as tough and as brave as anyone in the CTU. And look at him . . .

"And show us you did, Sidney," said Byrne. It was uncanny how the man could read minds. That's what made them all love him. Sure, he was a tough, politically incorrect, mean SOB, but then so was his uncle, Sy Sheinberg, who had practically been a father to Byrne. "Think Yiddish, dress British," had been the motto of Sy's generation, but he had turned it on its head: "Yiddish think, Irish drink," was his version, and it was the way he had lived, right up to the moment he died. How he had died, and what combination of courage and desperation had driven him to, essentially, conduct his own autopsy on himself while he was still alive, Sid could not image. And Frankie had never talked about it, even though he had been the one who had found him, bottle in one hand, scalpel in the other. "You'll be out of here in no time."

Sid struggled a bit. "I wanna be in the shit, boss," he protested.

"We got plenty of guys in the shit already," said Byrne. "And we're taking them down."

Sid seemed disappointed: the kid was no coward, that was for sure. Byrne looked around the room and spoke to the nurse. "Sister," he said, even though nobody called nurses "sister" anymore except the very old-timers in the neighbor-hood, "would you please close the door and make sure we're not disturbed?"

"Of course, officer," the nurse said. She was from Haiti, but she'd been working on the old West Side for long enough to know the drill. They got plenty of shot-up cops around here and they all talked the same.

Byrne took out his departmental secure PDA and showed it to Sid and Lannie. "I got this a couple of hours ago. It gives the last known location of every one of the shooters, tracked by some GPS system I've never heard of. Which means . . ."

"Which means we got the fuckers!" exclaimed Lannie, who high-fived Sid.

"Which means that somebody in some department some-where in this great land of ours has got better toys than we do and we need to find out who they are and how we can get some for ourselves." He waited a beat. "I'm putting you both on the case, A-sap. I want you to find out who sent this to me—"

"And fuck him up?" blurted Sid, excited.

"And work with him. Or her. These guys are good, very, very good, and right now we need all the friends we can get. Just as long as they're not . . . you know who." Nobody needed to ask who you-know-who was. Capt. Byrne's an-tipathetic relationship with certain parts of official Washing-ton was the stuff of departmental legend.

Byrne handed the instrument to Lannie Saleh. "Open up a line of communication right now. We can trust these guys, whoever they are, DIA, CIA, NSA, I have no idea. I just know this." He unfolded the piece of paper he'd found in his pocket and showed it to them:

YOUR GUARDIAN ANGEL.

Lannie and Sid both looked at the note in amazement. "What the hell is that supposed to mean, Captain?" asked Sid.

"It means this guy, whoever he is, saved my life, so as far as I'm concerned he's already established his bona fides. And we're going to work with him in any way he wants us to. So get cracking"

Lannie's face dropped. "But I was going to stay here with Sid, keep him—"

"I didn't say you had to do it at HQ, did I? And if you're not smart enough to be able to make this thing sing and dance, then you're not as smart as I think you are."

"Okay, boss," said Lannie.

"But we're getting them all, right?" ventured Sid. "The bad guys." Like every cop, and certainly the men under Byrne's command, he took any attack on his city deeply personally.

"Looks that way," Byrne said. "I got our best guys—not counting you two clowns—on it, and they've registered eleven kills." He decided not to tell them that six of those kills had been made by somebody not on the team. That was a mystery that either would sort itself out or it wouldn't, so he'd keep that to himself. "So . . ." he said, looking at Sid, "just as soon as you stop goldbricking, we can get back to—"

His phone rang. His personal cell phone. He glanced down at the number on caller ID: blocked. He wondered briefly if he should take it. Normally he wouldn't, especially not on the job, since all official calls came over their crack internal communication system, the one that had so distinguished itself on 9/11. But this was an emergency, and you never knew—

"Hello?"

"Hello, Frankie, how's it hanging?" said the voice, and Byrne recognized it right away. It was his brother, Tom Byrne, deputy director of the FBI.

CHAPTER THIRTY-FIVE

Budapest

So she was back where they had started, on the hunt for Farid Belghazi, that guy from CERN, which had been much in the news lately. Despite a series of unfortunate events, the Large Hadron Collider was once again operable and going about its business. Recently, it had set a new record by colliding particle beams at seven tera electric volts as two proton beams, guided by thousands of large electromagnets, collided head-on at 3.5 TeV, registering more than half a million collision events. But that was nothing: some time in the near future, the Hadron Collider would be ramped up to reach 14 TeV.

Budapest was also, according to the NYPD, the source of the denial-of-service attack that had preceded the assault on midtown Manhattan. An hour ago, her inbox had suddenly filled to overflowing as a direct line of communication with the CTU had suddenly opened, and she knew she had Frank Ross to thank for that. Now she was directly in touch with members of the CTU, operating anonymously but under the strictest security protocols, built into the laptop and verified by relays.

It was a two-way street: she was able to transmit information relayed to her by Frank Ross and in turn they were helping her draw a bead on the source of the DoS attack that had temporarily blinded CTU and allowed the gunmen to smuggle in their weapons and get into place. Slowly but surely, she was homing in on the source of the attack: just where she had feared it might be, but the only place that made any sense: eastern Hungary, near the Romanian border. Szeged.

Szeged today was just off the motorway, but closer in spirit to Timișoara in neighboring Romania than it was to Budapest. Once one of the major border towns of the Hungarian empire, it had fallen to the Turks in 1526 and had become an important Ottoman administrative center; liberated 160 years later, it played an important role in the revolution of 1848, and was completely destroyed in the flood of 1879. It was supposed to be very beautiful, having been rebuilt in the grand Austro-Hungarian style.

In short, it fit Skorzeny to a T: once Muslim, happily radical, formerly communist, yet filled with creature comforts, good food, and the beautiful Hungarian women. Limited in his movements, he still had plenty of clout in some of the former communist countries in the old Soviet sphere of influence, and it would not be surprising if he could come and go with relative impunity, so long as nobody made a fuss. Though penetrated by German traders in the Middle Ages, the area had never really been civilized, and as one of the central battlegrounds in the war between Islam and the West, it bore the bloody scars of a millennium of conflict.

The best part, from his perspective, was that it was right on the border of Romania and Serbia, which certainly had no love for the United States, and within striking distance of both Ukraine and Bulgaria, and the ports along the Black Sea.

And across the Black Sea, of course, lay eastern Turkey

and then, Iran. Her home, still. No matter where she lived, no matter what happened, and no matter where she ended up, she would always think of it that way.

She shook off feelings, brought on by her hunt for Skorzeny and Amanda Harrington. On the flight, she had brought herself up to speed on every action the man had made since their last encounter in Clairvaux. Using both classified information and open-source material she'd been able to assemble a picture of the monster. His movements were severely restricted, but he was still allowed to operate his business interests—much reduced since the failure of his attack on America—and his Foundation, whose real purpose and activities continued to fly under the media radar.

He was a devil, she had to give him that. Perhaps as a result of his childhood, he had become a master of playing both sides of the street. He was both a rapacious capitalist and a committed one-worlder, whose largesse benefited both former communist societies and the Western poor alike. Renowned for his taste in classical music, there was hardly a symphony orchestra or an opera company on earth that did not benefit from his largesse, and until he went to ground last year, he could often be seen in his private boxes around the globe, taking in a performance of *Tosca* or *Lady Macbeth of Mtsensk*. Less visibly, he was in league with just about every terrorist organization on the face of the earth, surreptitiously funneling money to them through a variety of dummy corporations and charities, destabilizing smaller countries, then swooping in and making a killing. None of it, of course, could be directly traced to him; he had as much plausible deniability as any head of state.

Personally, he was fastidious to a fault, almost enough to make Howard Hughes at the end look sane. He chose his assistants carefully for their skills and their discretion. She had already had experience with one of them, the man named

Pilier whom she had shot on the roof of Clairvaux prison, just before he could bring down the rescue helicopter. Now, if she read things correctly, he had a woman named Derrida, Emanuelle Derrida. Maryam chuckled. She liked that. It showed a sense of humor on the old goat's part: a deconstructionist for an act of deconstruction. For she had no doubt that was what he was up to.

And now this business with Elgar. "Frank Ross" had relayed her Atwater's findings and theory immediately. For years, the Dorabella cipher had tantalized amateur cryptologists and Elgar lovers, and here was the simplest explanation of all, and one that would have presented itself immediately to any composer—that Elgar was writing out in a kind of shorthand the sketch of his plan for his first great orchestral work. Up to that point he had been a lesser composer; after it, he had taken his place among the greats. And all for the love of a woman.

It made perfect sense to her. Crazy love—random, unpredictable, mad, and often bad love—was really what made the world go round. True, institutional love with all its trappings gave society stability, provided for orderly succession of property and authority; without it, there could be no civilizations. But it was *l'amour fou* that caused the real breakthroughs, mad passion, meet one night and elope tomorrow, or throw away everything for a shot at the most inappropriate person imaginable. That was when great things happened, whether for good or for ill.

Combined with her training, Maryam set her woman's intuition to work, playing back everything she remembered from that séance in the French prison. She had insinuated herself into the small orchestra Skorzeny had engaged for the occasion—Swiss boarding schools were very good, not only for languages but for musical instruction—and she had seen, up close, the look on that woman's face: a prisoner of

Skorzeny's mad love. Skorzeny had nearly killed Amanda Harrington that day, and had they not gotten there in time to rescue the American woman's daughter, Amanda might have died. Now she was with Skorzeny again, most likely unwillingly, and there could be only one reason: *amour fou*.

Amanda Harrington would be the way they were going to get Skorzeny.

Using the laptop he'd provided her and a 4G WNIC, Maryam worked the intel network feverishly, drawing a bead on Miss Harrington. Not for the first time, she blessed Frank for having given her this, one of the most sacred and secret tools in the CSS arsenal. Innovation was the way the West could always stay one step ahead of the East.

Her thoughts flashed back to her lover, somewhere on the ground in Manhattan. Oddly, she had no fears for him. Certainly not in the realm of direct combat. There was only one thing she feared: the wild card. In his battle in London against Milverton, she might have been able to accept his death, since it would have come against a worthy adversary, a man whose skills and kills were known to her first hand; she had seen him in action. Charles Augustus Milverton had died that day in Camden Town, but it could almost as easily have been "Frank Ross." That she could have accepted and moved on. But not the chance shot, the senseless death. Then, life really would be as meaningless and random as the atheists said. And Maryam was nothing if not a good Muslim.

That night, in her room on the Pest side of the Hungarian capital, in one of those old commie-era hotels that had been acquired by a high-end Western chain, with the Danube flowing just outside to the west, she immersed herself in everything there was to discover about Amanda Harrington. Her birth, her schooling, her early lovers. Her life as one of London's "It" girls, her failed marriage, her abortion.

MI5, Britain's internal security service, had compiled a

handsome dossier on her, largely attributable to her work as a City financial wiz and later the head of the Skorzeny Foundation, and it was a treasure trove of information. Like the FBI reports in the U.S., MI5 reports contained a great deal of unsubstantiated information, even gossip, but none of this had to be provable in a court of law. That was the problem with America these days, she thought: the threshold for conviction had become the de facto standard for everything, including the court of public opinion. The populace had become cowed, afraid to think a single thought that would not be admissible under the highly restrictive and defendant-friendly rules of evidence that had evolved over more than two centuries of constitutional law.

None of that interested her. At this moment, she was not an intelligence agent, but a woman, a fellow woman. Drill down:

The abortion. Not, according to the dossier, the product of her marriage to a probably homosexual lesser peer, but the result of a fling, a one-night stand, in New York while in town on business. The prospective father never knew; Amanda had dealt with the consequences of her actions privately, personally. But Maryam knew, she just *knew*, that this had been the event that had changed Miss Harrington's life.

Suddenly, she understood everything.

The reason for the kidnapping of the American girl, Emma Gardner.

She scrolled back through the dossier: medical reports, medical reports . . . There—

As a result of the abortion, subject lost the physical ability to have children.

The girl Milverton had snatched in Edwardsville and presented to Amanda as a present. The one thing she had wanted more than anything else in the world. The one thing a lifelong career woman never had had time for. The one thing she, personally, could never have: a daughter.

So why was she with Skorzeny again?

Simple: it was he who had sicced "Frank Ross" on Milverton. He who had rolled the dice, in the realization that it almost didn't matter which of the equally matched adversaries—Hector and Achilles—won, that either way he, Skorzeny, would be the true victor. That Milverton had died that day was just as well. His death removed a rival for Amanda's hand, and the fact that Amanda, no thanks to Skorzeny, had survived her bout with the paralyzing poison—tetrodotoxin, the hospital report said, most likely derived from the poison of the Japanese fugu fish administered in a nonlethal dose—was evidence that Skorzeny still desired her and had, on some sick level, forgiven her.

She was his captive. And they were here, together, somewhere in Hungary.

Come on, girl: find her.

Search. Search for relationships, hidden relationships, the kind people used to easily be able to conceal, but now, with the aid of ERMs—Entity-Relationship Models—it was child's play to create a diagram of nearly everybody's business and personal relationships. That's the thing most folks never understood, Maryam realized as she called up the diagram, that everything they typed on the computer, every picture or piece of personal information they posted on the social-networking sites, every comment they made on a website, which could be easily traced back to their IP addresses, went into their permanent file, their publicly available dossier, there not only for everybody living to see, but for all future generations as well. If there ever was a morality enforcer—and given the understanding that morality's definition would change from generation to generation—the Internet was it.

It had to be here. It *had* to be. The one missing piece of information. The thing she needed to know. The overlooked item that would link Amanda Harrington and Emanuel Skorzeny to each other, inextricably link them in some sort of sick relationship that neither of them could gainsay, that they would assume Fate had dictated for them long before they were born.

Skorzeny, she knew, would believe none of this bullshit. Men believed in action, not in fate; they were the architects of their own desires, triumphs, tragedies, and misfortunes. Women believed in soul mates.

There had to be something between then, something that antedated Harrington's working with Skorzeny. Something in both their pasts that led them to each other, something that they would both mistake for Fate, even when it was simple Chance. You could be an atheist, and believe the entire universe was random, but when it came to crunch time, no one ever begged chance for one more chance.

And then she found it. So simple, so unprepossessing, and hiding where all good secrets, and the best intelligence agents, operated: in plain sight.

Money and Love.

When all else failed, use Occam's razor: The simplest explanation was most likely to be true.

What else was there, but Money and Love?

Money had first brought them together, and sick Love had kept them together. The sick love Skorzeny had for money and his desire for the solace, however temporary, but satisfying, of women. The love Amanda had for money; how, in the absence of a man and a child in her life, it had made her feel equal to men; and when Skorzeny tapped her—among all others!—for the leadership of his Foundation, what a proof it offered to all her detractors. With money she succeeded and with money she became equal; nay, *primus inter pares* in the world of the City.

And Love? For him, she had none. But that didn't matter to a man like Skorzeny. *Pace* the Beatles, Skorzeny believed, like most men, that money really could buy you love, and if not love, at least the simulacrum of love, which meant sex and a modicum of affection outside the bedroom.

Milton understood it. The oldest bargain there was, the source of the world's oldest profession. *Of Man's First Disobedience, and the Fruit of that Forbidden Tree, whose mortal taste brought Death into the World and the source of all our mortal Woe, with the loss of Eden . . .*

She looked back at Atwater's report, which amounted to this simple equation, this simple cipher, that not all the cryptographic machines that the CIA, the NSA, the CSS, and everybody else could muster against. The equivalent of Einstein's $E = Mc^2$. Which was this:

Money − Love = Revenge.

She took a deep breath. Were she not a Muslim, she would have taken a deep drink as well, but she only drank when she was in the West, with him, and now that she was back in the East, things were different. Even though no one could see her, there were rituals, formalities, to be observed. No one need know, but she would know and at this point, that was all that mattered.

They had to be here. They had to be here in Hungary, somewhere. There was an intersection, an interstice, and she had to find it. Because, whatever it was, it would lead her to them. Or them to her. But not right now. She had had a long journey. She needed time to think.

Maryam took off her clothes and luxuriated under a long hot shower. That was something else that was forbidden, to enjoy the pleasure of your own body, alone, to reach out and try to connect with the driving mechanism of the universe, the eternal piston engine that He had designed, which Newton had grasped under the apple tree: for every action, an equal and opposite reaction. What goes up must come down. One door opens, another closes. A man dies, a child is born . . .

A knock at the door, which she discerned only dimly as she toweled off her head. One of those intrusive hotel "welcome" packages that they reserved for VIPs, or people with money, or both. Eastern Europe still admired money, in a way the West did not. Maybe that was because the West didn't have money anymore.

She wrapped the hotel bathrobe tightly around her. By hotel standards, it was pretty darned nice; assuming that roughly one-third of the guests would steal the robes, the prices charged were fairly reasonable.

The laptop lay open and operative on the coffee table.

There was a woman at the door. Not a room service woman, not an employee of the hotel, no one she was expecting, but someone she very much anticipated seeing.

"Hello," said Amanda Harrington.

And, right behind her, Emanuel Skorzeny. "*Bonjour, mon cher*," he said. He had a gun in his hand. He looked over her shoulder, into the room, toward the laptop, and smiled. "May we come in?"

Amanda brushed past her with only a sidelong glance, but Skorzeny seemed genuinely please to be meeting her for the first time. "Really, my dear, you are as lovely as I had heard. Truly splendid." His mien darkened. "But, as you deprived me of the services of a very faithful and valuable retainer at our last encounter, I feel it necessary to introduce you to his successor."

He moved to one side. Behind him stood another woman, blond and beautiful.

She had a gun in her hand, and looked like she knew how to use it, so there was no point in arguing. Maryam ushered them into the room and closed the door.

She turned, knowing there was nothing to do. Skorzeny sat down like he owned the place—which, come to think of it, was a distinct possibility. Amanda stood off to one side, almost flinching; her eyes met Maryam's, just as they had back at Clairvaux, only this time their positions were reversed, and Maryam was now the helpless one, while Amanda was the one who might save her if she could, but not right now.

"Put on some music, please," Skorzeny commanded, and Amanda dutifully obliged. The hotel came equipped with a flat-screen TV that also carried hundreds of audio channels. In just a few seconds, Amanda had found the channel she was looking for and the music came wafting into the room.

"Turn it up," said Skorzeny, breaking into a broad smile as he heard the familiar strains of the overture: brassy, with urgent strings. He addressed his next remarks to her: "You recognize it, of course. Somehow approrpiate, wouldn't you say?"

The second woman, the one with the gun—she must be Derrida—said nothing as she started to copy the laptop files. Skorzeny noticed and jumped from his seat:

"Good God, woman, what do you think you are doing? Don't touch that. This devil poisons everything he touches."

Mlle. Derrida stopped and backed away from the machine.

"Our hostess is going to close it down, as per the safety instruction manual. And then we are going to take it, and her, with us."

Skorzeny turned back to Maryam. Out of the corner of her eye, she could see the blonde preparing a needle, with her name on it. The fugu poison again? There was nothing she could do about it.

"You haven't answered my question, my dear," said Skorzeny as Mlle. Derrida approached her. She was powerless to resist. Better to let it happen now, to learn as much as possible while she was in captivity, to try and figure out a way to escape later, to—

The needle pinched a little, and almost immediately, she felt herself shutting down.

"The music?" Skorzeny looked at her, mouthed words at her, but she couldn't make any sense of them in any language. She was so tired. Just before she went completely paralyzed, she might have heard him say:

"It's the overture to *La Forza del Destino*. What an amazing coincidence."

But then her world turned dark and she didn't care anymore.

DAY THREE

*A black heart! A womanish, willful heart;
the heart of a brute, a beast of the field;
childish, stupid, and false;
a huckster's heart, a tyrant's heart.*
—MARCUS AURELIUS, *Meditations*, Book IV

CHAPTER THIRTY-SIX

The Metropolitan Museum of Art

Principessa Stanley awoke with a start. She didn't remember much, but what she did remember wasn't good. Where was she? Where had she been last night?

Let's take them in reverse order, she decided. She had already noticed she couldn't move her arms or her legs, but right now her arms were her primary concern, if only to wipe the dirt and the goo off her face, however it got there. But she couldn't move her arms, and therefore her legs were the last of her worries at the moment.

The main worry was the plastic bag over her head and the rag in her mouth. Luckily, she could breathe, which was a *duh* because if she couldn't have breathed, she would have been dead long ago. So whoever did this to her at least had enough of a heart to keep her alive, although for what, she'd rather not think . . .

Principessa Stanley was a good reporter. In fact, she was a better reporter than most of her rivals, including those on the newspapers. She had earned her job fairly, with a high degree from a good School of Communication, which was what all the former journalism schools were calling themselves these days. It was not her fault that she was pretty and had a killer body; those assets were only the deciding factors, the extras, whenever she had been up for a gig in the past. At her level now, every woman was either good-looking or unemployed. Such was the triumph of feminism.

So why was she here, buried up to her neck in a dirt grave behind the Metropolitan Museum of Art? Who had done this to her?

She tried not to panic. That was what she always heard. Panic would get you nowhere. Worse, panic would get you killed even faster. Take deep breaths . . .

She panicked. She struggled and writhed and tried to pretzel her way out of the shallow grave, but it was useless. She was planted in the backyard of the Met, like some kind of human vegetable like Farmer Brown's victims in that ridiculous horror movie from the eighties, *Motel Hell*. Her assailant probably had seen the damn thing, which is what had given him the idea. Fucking hicks from flyover country were all the same: right-wing nuts who ought to be hunted down and exterminated. When Angela Hassett beat that horrid Jeb Tyler in the fall, things were going to change, but good. She could hardly wait, not that she would ever admit that on the air or anything. After all she was a neutral journalist.

She caught herself and stopped moving. Clearly, she wasn't going to get out all at once. She was going to have to work her way out of this, wriggle out of it, like a worm or something, a quarter-inch at a time. Slow and steady wins the race.

She tried pushing down at whatever solid ground might be below her, but couldn't get much of a purchase. The soil was soft and loamy, freshly dug; all she was managing to do was sink a little deeper, which obviously wasn't the way to go. Once again she stopped, and this time she realized she

was already out of breath. What a ripoff that gym member-
ship had been. All that cardio exercise was supposed to help
you in situations like this, wasn't it?

Think.

Then she felt something move between her legs. If she
could have jumped, she would have. Instead, she thought her
heart was going to stop, right then and there.

What the hell was in the pit with her?

Her mind raced. She was starting to lose it.

A snake? Did they even have snakes in Central Park?
There must be snakes in Central Park. There were coyotes in
Central Park now, and she had to admit that she always felt a
small thrill whenever another wild animal was sighted
within the five boroughs. It was long past time that humans
should move aside and start sharing the limited space on the
planet with animals who, afterall, were just people without
lawyers of their own species.

It moved again.

It didn't feel like a snake. It didn't feel like it was slithering, whatever slithering felt like. Snakes didn't travel underground, did they? She remembered that time when she was a
girl when she saw a sunning snake slither back into its lair,
in a hole in the ground. So it could be a snake, after all.

But what if it was a gopher, or a groundhog, or a wood-
chuck, something with teeth? Would that be worse than a
snake? Something that would start by nibbling on her ex-
tremities, get a tasty bite or two, and then set about making a
meal out of her, so that when they finally found her, when
the city wasn't in lockdown anymore, they'd reach for her
head and that would be all that was left of her, the rest having gone to nourish a colony of woodchucks the size of
Staten Island.

There it went again. That same feeling. Whatever its
source, it didn't seem to be moving, just sitting there be-

tween her knees and her crotch, buzzing, tickling her, vibrating . . . in other context, she might even have enjoyed the experience. But not now.

She tried to push herself up again, which was a dumb idea, because she moved farther south, and she also felt whatever it was slide a little as it vibrated once more.

It was a cell phone. Her cell phone, which she had been looking at when that bastard assaulted her. If she could somehow slide her hand down and grab it . . . well, that was the first half of the plan. The second half would be to somehow get her arm out from underneath the dirt and bring the phone to her face, where she would somehow manage to get the damn thing to work, even if she had to press the talk button with her nose.

She reached. It was like fighting her way through molasses, but amazingly she could make a little progress. That was the upside of the loamy soil; her hand could actually move a little. Inch by inch. Keep it simple. Baby steps. Get to the goal eventually, even if it took forever.

Wait a minute—she didn't have forever. She tried to recall what she read about people living without food and water. You could go without food for weeks—just look at those Irish hunger-strikers—but water, she was pretty sure, was a nonnegotiable commodity. Maybe a day or two, then madness set in, followed by death. What if the crisis wasn't over by then? The way the cops fought these days, it might take them a week to round up the dudes for the fair trials. She couldn't wait to cover the proceedings.

Her thoughts continued to run along these lines until she realized that she was already slipping into madness. Goddamnit, didn't that bastard know who she was? He couldn't treat her like this! The minute she got out of here, she was going to hunt his ass down, find him, and rat him out to the cops. She'd testify at the trial and hope to hell he'd get the death penalty. Normally, she was against the death penalty, but in this case she'd make an exception.

The buzzing again. Her hand moved closer. It brushed up against something. By God, she was closer to it all along than she had thought! Now we were getting somewhere.

Keep buzzing, you bastard, she thought. *Come to mama.*

She had it!

It was a cell phone!

But not her cell phone. She could tell by the feel. It was just a cheap piece of crap. WTF?

It was his. That dirty son of a bitch. She had him now. As soon as she got out of here, she could trace this sucker, ransack his phonebook. The little bastard would be sorry he was ever born after she turned the wrath of the Sinclair empire on his sorry ass. She started laughing. Revenge was going to be eaten hot and she was going to enjoy every bite.

Her arm was moving!

The dirt was falling away from her shoulder. All of that moving and shaking had loosened it just enough so that now, in her justifiable rage and anger and lust for vengeance, she could extract it.

Here it came—

Her shoulder popped out of the earth. She shrugged as hard as she could, just like she did in the gym with some light dumbbells in each hand, toning the traps, and raised her elbow. Pushing, pushing. Come on, do it. Remember the old bodybuilder's motto: *what can be conceived can be believed and achieved.*

She did it! It was coming up through the ground, her hand along with it. Which meant she could snatch the stupid baggie off her head and in just a few minutes—

"Just what I was looking for."

Somewhere in the back of her mind, the voice sounded familiar. One of the things that made her a good reporter was her ear. She had an ear for music and an ear for voices, and she rarely had to think twice before being able to attach a name not just to a face, which was easy, but to a voice, which was much harder.

This voice she knew.

No time to think about it now. The cell phone disappeared from her grip. Shit. There went her last hope. The bastard had come back for it, and now he was going to kill her.

"I was wondering how long it would take me to find you. Brave girl. Now, where is he?"

He had not taken the baggie off her head, and he was behind her. But he wasn't fondling her or anything like that, so she had to assume he was one of the good guys. Still, he didn't sound like a cop—

Hang on. Didn't sound—sound— Say, she *knew* that voice . . .

"What was his name?" The voice was sterner now. Somewhere a clock was ticking. No time for games. She'd find out who it was later.

"He didn't say."

"Sure about that?"

Something about this guy's voice said not to fuck with him. Think—there. "No, wait, he did say."

"Thought so. You weren't lying to me, were you?"

"No, why would I—"

"I can tell when you lie. I can tell when anybody lies. So be straight with me, collect yourself, and everybody will be happy."

"Yeah."

"That's yes, sir."

"Yes, sir." No point in arguing.

"What did he say his name was? Some Arabic name?"

"No, American."

"Go."

"Raymond. Raymond something."

"D.B. Do better."

"Gimme a sec. Something German-sounding . . . wait . . . it's coming."

"So's the Rapture. Hurry."

Her mind raced again. It was doing a lot of that lately. It was on the tip of her tongue . . . news business . . . anchors . . . She had it!

"Cronkite, like Walter, I think. How could I forget something like that?"

"I believe you," her rescuer said. So he wasn't going to kill her; he wasn't another sick fuck psycho. He was a kind of guardian angel.

"So? You're going to get me out of here now, right?"

No answer. She could free herself after a while, but it sure would be easier with a little help.

"Right?"

"Listen, you cocksucker," the man was saying intro the phone. "I'm coming for you. O my Brother, this will be the last dawn you will ever see." Except that she couldn't understand a word: to her, it all sounded like a variation of *haLA-haLA-haLA-haLA*. She really had to start studying languages, especially those funny foreign ones they spoke in the Middle East. "Because I am sending you to hell." That part at least was in English.

She stayed silent and listened in case he spoke again . . . but could hear nothing. Either he was still here, or he was gone.

"Hello?"

No response.

"Mister?"

Ditto.

Fifteen minutes later, covered with dirt, Principessa Stanley tore the baggie off her head and took a deep breath. The back end of the Metropolitan Museum of Art had never looked so good to her. In vain, though, she looked around for the man who had saved her, the man whose voice she dimly recognized, and would now devote the rest of her life to discovering his identity. What a story that would be.

She looked in a 360-degree circle, then ran out onto Fifth Avenue.

But he, whoever he was, was gone.

CHAPTER THIRTY-SEVEN

The Central Park Reservoir

The killing had begun again that morning. Raymond had never felt so liberated, so alive. Being a martyr was a wonderful thing.

Up to now, he had never understood the principle, of life-in-death and death-in-life. He had never understood the relationship between Eros and Thanatos, which he'd read about in a book once and never quite got. The yin and yang thing he'd thought he understood, especially if it came with those sex diagrams attached, but it was one thing to understand something intellectually and quite another to feel something viscerally.

But this was totally different. This was raw, exciting. This was what freedom felt like. Now he understood what those crazy suicide bombers felt like when they pulled the pin on their own grenades, secure in the knowledge that they were going to take bunch of the infidels with them, send them straight to hell, while they themselves would soon see paradise. He wasn't quite sure if he believed all the blather about the seventy-two virgins, or raisins, or even if there was anything on the other side, but what the hell did it matter, because he was here, he was now and—

Blam! Got the bitch with one shot.

Blam! Another one.

Blam! Another one.

He could shoot them from the bushes. He liked the bushes. This was a nice park, much nicer than any he'd seen, even nicer than Golden Gate Park, where the Brothers had taken him once on an outing, although it didn't have the same sweet smell of the eucalyptus trees, or the delicious salty taste of the fog in the late afternoons.

As usual, the chicken passersby started running in all directions, squawking. It was just as the Brother had said: no one would fight back against him. He was not only invincible, he was invulnerable. He was free to kill as he liked. He not only like God, he *was* God.

Devlin had already punched the name into the CSS database and gotten his readout: nothing. Raymond Crankeit or Kronkite or Krankheit or however you wanted to spell it, nothing. His worst nightmare: a punk with a rifle, a chip on his shoulder, and a limp noodle.

His secure PDA buzzed: MARTIN FERGUSON read the display.

"Eddie Bartlett," as he'd been known on the last operation. Danny Impellatieri, his man main, his old buddy from Blackwater, now Xe, the country's foremost PMC, or Private Military Company. There are dozens of them, and some very good ones, like Triple Canopy, but despite all the bad publicity Danny continued to work with and recruit from Xe— mostly ex-elite forces, like Danny, who knew what to do with a piece of equipment or a lethal weapon, and who also knew how to count money and keep their mouths shut.

Even though they'd never met, and operated together

under strict rules, including a rotating series of aliases that, for laughs, were generated by random run-throughs of the movie database imdb.com, they trusted each other with their lives.

LOCATION?

STEWART. NEED CHOPPER

MILITARY? XE?

NG. CITY SEALED. OFFICIAL CHANNELS OUT.

ALL BUT ONE.

EXPLAIN

NYPD

NO CONTACTS

NO WORRIES.

WHAT KIND OF RIDE?

Danny had been one of the Army's top helicopter pilots with the legendary 60th Special Operations Aviation Regiment (Airborne), 2nd Battalion, at Fort Campbell, Kentucky, known in the biz as the Night Stalkers. Danny, he knew, favored the MH-60/DAP (Direct Action Penetrator) Black Hawks, but the NYPD choppers were damn near as good.

STAND BY AND BE READY TO HOP

ROGER THAT.

He didn't care what Danny needed the chopper for; he owed him. His next message was to Byrne:

HAVE POLICE CHOPPER STANDING BY ON MY ORDERS, WITH BARRETT. ANGEL

He had to make sure Kohanloo did not get off the island, and a chopper, which could sweep from one side of Manhattan to another in a couple of minutes, was the ideal way to ensure that. With everything closed, there was only one way off Melville's Isle of the Manhattoes, and that was the way the original Dutchmen had come: by sea. Whatever other reason Danny might have for wanting a hawk, he was going to make damn sure Kohanloo stayed put, or died.

Kohanloo, if he was as smart as Devlin thought he was,

would have had a boat ready, on a jetty, anything, most likely on the East River—the Hudson was too wide, he'd be a sitting duck, ripe for target practice—and would try to slip out under the cover of darkness.

Then, over the police scanner he was picking up with his PDA, he heard the reports of shots fired at the Reservoir. And he knew, he just knew, it was Raymond.

Byrne got the message. This was crazy, but crazy was all he had time for right about now. He didn't like the tenor of his conversation with his brother—he never liked the tenor of their conversations—and he could tell the bastard was snooping around, planning something, plotting something, more likely. If it weren't for their sainted mother, Irene, still alive and still living in the flat in Queens, although Frankie had been trying to coax her into a nursing home in the Bronx for years, a nice one, but she was convinced he meant the Hebrew Home for Aged and the very thought of that agitated the old Russian lady, who had retained her reflexive anti-Semitism all her life. Although, God knew, she had been through enough horror in her life, and the life of her family, for the world to cut a crazy old lady a little slack. Rufus even continued to keep watch over her, invisible and silent as ever, as he had for more than a decade. Rufus was a successful businessman in Jamaica, Queens, but he still cruised by the old neighborhood, looking for a random game of pickup hoops and always with the intent of checking in on Irene, just in case . . .

He ordered the police chopper on standby. He'd deal with his asshole brother later. As much later as he could.

Devlin moved slowly but deliberately, cautiously but not suspiciously. With the city still in lockdown, and the other shooters rounded up there would be cops rushing to the spot in minutes, converging on the Reservoir in full force. That's what they were trained to do, and that's the way he would have responded, too, were it not for one thing:

He knew, dead-solid-fucking-certain *knew* that Raymond whatever his name was, Mr. Disease, would not be there when they got there. Not because he was a genius. There was no chance a guy like him was a genius. He was in fact an idiot. But there were idiots and then there were idiots savants, and he'd long since pegged this last of the Mohicans as a savant.

Raymond would do nothing expected. He would do everything wrong. He was, in fact, like the enemy he served: technically inept, tactically amateurish, unable to grasp the basic concepts of warfare, except for the most important one: always keep your opponent guessing.

To get Raymond, he would have to think like Raymond. This was not like taking on Milverton. Milverton was good, great even, but Milverton and he had battled according to an unspoken set of precepts, like two chess grandmasters locked in mortal combat. This putz was the Paul Morphy of gunmen, probably mentally ill, but there was a brilliance in his illness, a genius in his madness.

Where would you go? What was motivating him?

Devlin's mind raced as he neared the Reservoir. He thought back to Atwater's report: Love and Revenge.

There it was. Raymond was not a patch on Skorzeny and his crazy apocalypse, of which the attack on New York now obviously was just another piece of the overall mosaic, but just as ontology recapitulated phylogeny, Raymond was an adumbrator of the greater genius of his puppetmaster.

What did he know about the man? Nothing, or close to it. He didn't turn up in any databases, and Devlin hadn't seen enough of his MO to be able to properly formulate a—

Hang on.

The burial. The bushes. He didn't suddenly dig that grave for Ms. Stanley, he had dug it for some purpose. To bury his weapons, perhaps. But there was another reason. Jesus, it was so obvious:

He felt comfortable underground.

That was where he had slept. That was where he would go. Underground. And nowhere in America was there a more hospitable underground—if such an adjective could be used in this context—than New York City. The city was burrowed under by miles of tunnels: subway tunnels, steam tunnels, water tunnels, electrical tunnels; there was almost as much civilization under Manhattan as there was above it. Cops hated going down there, workers hated it, maintenance men hated it, and even the sandhogs, the brotherhood of blacks and Irish who were digging—and had dug—the gigantic water tunnels that flowed down from Westchester and gave life to the city—hated it.

That's where Raymond would go. He had to beat him to it.

And where was the nearest underground?

Under the reservoir. In the pump house.

Like its now-vanished cousins, the reservoir had once been the oasis of the city, not to the extent the old Collect Pond had been in the early days, which had fed the Five Points, both now buried under the concrete of the august courts of lower Manhattan. Nor was it a rival of the real reservoir that once had stood, in all its faux-Egyptian splendor, where the New York Public Library was today. Now that had been a reservoir. Still, the Central Park Reservoir could boast of something the others couldn't, which was its survival.

He had to get to the pump house. And then he had to deal with Arash Kohanloo.

He glanced at his watch. Maryam should have checked in with him long ago. Well, she was a big girl and could take care of herself. No time to worry about something he couldn't control. To think otherwise would not only be unprofessional, it would make him crazy.

Arash Kohanloo tried to stay calm. Everything was in readiness. The boat was going to leave from a private slip down the slope from River House. He was in River House, in the apartment of a fellow Iranian, who lived in the kind of splendor that he himself, for all his success, still aspired to. All he had to do was stay calm.

Calm.

The people who lived in River House were extremely rich, but while Manhattan's newspapers may articulate the glories of philanthropy and the coerced public good of tax dollars, the bitter truth was that many of them had inherited their money, not earned it in any meaningful sense, and so could make a great show of working for a dollar a year, or donating their salaries to charity, or demanding that wage slaves pay up, secure in the knowledge that their capital was not only untouched, but always growing. After all, it was called an "income" tax, not a "capital" tax.

From the earliest days of River House, there had been a private egress down the shore, which not even the construction of the FDR Highway had disturbed. Once upon a time, the East River had been awash with vessels plying the waters around Manhattan, including steamboats, pleasure cruisers and even, in the early 19th century, a brisk trade in river piracy. The ill-fated *General Slocum* had passed this way, back in 1904, aflame and doomed, rushed toward her destiny on North Brother Island, just to the north, off the Bronx shoreline, but Arash Kohanloo neither knew nor cared about that now; all he could think of was getting off the island as quickly as possible and slipping out to sea.

He made his way down the dank stone stairs, slippery

with age and shaking, in the damp and the chill, with his fear of this *Malak al-Maut*, this specter who had emerged out of the night to read his every thought, to know his every intimate wish and desire. Him he must flee; what would happen after that, after he got down to the rendezvous point in Red Hook, only Allah knew.

The boat was there, where it was supposed to be. On board were flares and firearms, maps and guidance systems, plus a communications device. He would have to run both silent and fast, but with the craft's markings, he felt certain that no one would stop him. If anyone stopped him, he was on a mission of mercy, running medical supplies downtown. After all, he was on a Red Cross boat.

CHAPTER THIRTY-EIGHT

Central Park

The Reservoir—the Jacqueline Kennedy Onassis Reservoir, to give it its full name—had not been actively connected to the city's water supply system since the opening of a massive new water tunnel in 1991, but that didn't mean the infrastructure wasn't still there. As one of the main storehouses for the water that kept lower Manhattan alive, the reservoir collected the water brought down from Westchester and in turn sent it farther south, to where the people were. The area under the Park was one vast canal, much of it still in use, but some of it now abandoned. That's where he would be.

There would be cops crawling all around the reservoir, so Devlin went in the same way the city's rats headed wherever they wished to go, via the New York City sewer system.

People who were dazzled by Manhattan and who never ventured belowground, got only half the picture. True, the city's skyscrapers, from the Woolworth Building to the late World Trade Center, had long been objects of wonder and envy. But underground, where the water tunnels, the subway tunnels, the steam tunnels, the electrical tunnels, the service tunnels and everything else all jostled for position, was a miracle of subterranean organization. Animals lived down there, and people too—the cops called them the "skells," either in colonies or as lonely, wayward, and usually crazed souls, who had nothing to connect them to the world above.

He knew exactly how they felt.

Which was why he was chasing this boy now. From his observations of the scene with the woman buried behind the Met, he had already developed a profile in his mind. This boy had kept her, not killed her, which meant either he had other plans for her, or had felt a stab of something—love? compassion?—that prevented him from acting on his natural impulses, which had otherwise been given free rein.

The shooter was not a Muslim, of that he was certain. Muslim fighters may kill women, but it is an unmanly thing to do. There was no glory in killing women, even infidel women, and however poor their combat skills were otherwise—and aside from the occasional rush of crazy bravery, they were very poor indeed—their reverent contempt for women in general had no place for their murder, unless on moral grounds. So most likely he was an American, one of these poor lost skells who had not yet found the way to his place below and beneath the earth. But now, if Devlin had guessed right, he was about to embrace his destiny.

The Angel had left most of his tools behind him. He knew enough never to underestimate any adversary, but this job did not require the LMT, or the Glocks. Instead, he brought the Judge and a KA-BAR knife. That would be enough.

When Byrne got the message, he acted on it immediately. Luckily, there were no department channels to screw around with; in his world, he was the absolute boss, and what he said, went. If necessary, he could call Matt White directly and that would be that, but he needed to have a long conversation with the Chief later, when this thing was settled, and until then he had to play out the hand and win at all costs. His invisible ally, whoever he was, was on his side, and when he said he needed the best police chopper in the fleet on standby, on the roof of the old Pan Am building, fully loaded with a Barrett, Byrne didn't hesitate.

There was just one detail that puzzled him: there was no need to bother about a pilot, because one was on his way . . .

Danny Impellatieri stood on the roof of the MetLife Building and looked around. He'd been to New York plenty of times, of course, but he'd never seen it like this, in several senses of the word. Not from the roof of this centrally located building, right around Grand Central Terminal, for one. And certainly not with a blown-out hollow just a few long blocks to the west, the old Times Square. The fires had been quenched, but the rubble was still smoldering; it was awe-inspiring to think of the damage a few determined gunners and a powerful plastic explosive could do. God forbid that these maniacs ever get their hands on something more lethal . . .

But all that had had to wait until he made the phone call. He got her on the first ring.

"Danny? Danny? Is that you?" Hope had said, even before he spoke, and he could tell by the tone of her voice that those were not simply questions, but profound expressions.

He tried to stay calm. "It's me, Hope. All you all right? Are the kids all right?"

"Oh, Danny, it was—it was horrible. We were up on the roof and then you found the way down and then . . ."

"And we found that cop," he could hear Rory saying in the background.

"And then we got down just before the whole building collapsed and there was this wounded cop, just about as dazed and fucked up—pardon my French—as we were and he helped us and they got us over to the hospital to make sure everything was okay and it was, and we're all fine and when can you get—"

"Hope," said Danny, "wherever you are right now, I want you to stay there. If it's safe, don't move. I'll come for you."

He could feel the disappointment over the line. "But why can't you—"

"There's something I have to do first. Something really important."

She got it. Good Girl. She got it. "Is it dangerous?"

He decided to laugh. "If it wasn't dangerous, why would they ask me to do it? Any schmuck could do it."

"Schmuck," she repeated. "Is this a word I'm going to have to know and use?"

"Three times in a sentence, and then it's yours," he replied. He liked a woman with a sense of humor. No, check that, he needed a woman with a sense of humor. After that, everything else was negotiable. And from what he could tell of Hope Gardner, there wasn't going to be much else to negotiate. Just the date of the wedding. Which he'd do right after he got back from this job.

"See ya in a few. Kiss the kids for me."

Flying a helicopter over the East River was not as easy as it looked, but that was the gig. Unknown whether there would be incoming. Unknown at what altitude. There would be buildings to thread and bridges to dodge, no matter what.

He knew what it was before he heard it. Not one of the old Bells, the kind they used to use, or even one of the new 412 EPs, but an Augusta A-119 Koala—not just any old off-the-shelf model, either, but a souped-up jalopy that could fly at night with no lights.

He smiled. Okay, maybe this was going to be fun after all.

* * *

Devlin passed around, over and through things he didn't want to think about. He couldn't wait to take a bath after all this was over. He needed to take out his man and then get aboveground as quickly as possible, for after he dispatched this boy, Mr. Kohanloo was next. And then make contact with Maryam. That he hadn't heard from her for a while was not worrying in itself, because op-sec was everything, but . . . He had to admit it: for the first time in his life, he cared.

There, up ahead: the connecting tunnel. Plenty of visitors, runners mostly, used the bathrooms provided above, and that effluent had to be flushed somewhere. If he'd read the plans correctly, he could go up via that passageway, break through to a utility closet, and be right where he needed to be.

If he couldn't kill his man, he could stink him to death.

There—he was out of the sewer and into the utility room, which was larger than he had expected. At some point it must have been expanded a bit, probably during one of the Park's many renovations and upgrades. There was a washbasin and a toilet even down here, and he permitted himself a small chuckle as the thought occurred to him that this wasn't much different from his office back at The Building, its entryway, anyway.

The chuckle was on his lips and the thought on his mind when suddenly he was struck from behind by a tremendous blow to the head.

Arash Kohanloo set the Red Cross boat into the waters, heading south. Occasionally, furtively, he scanned the skies above for the drone, half-convinced it would come back after him. That *Malak al-Maut* knew his every move. But the skies were clear.

The waterways, too. A few boats moved on them, but the lockdown had affected all aspects of traffic in and around

Manhattan. There would be cops about, of course, but to his
relief he saw that there were other emergency craft churning
the waters. He would glide in among them and use them for
cover. His papers were all in good order. The thought had
crossed his mind that perhaps they should have disguised the
boat with Red Crescent markings instead—the politically
correct authorities would be overjoyed to see America's
Muslim brothers helping out, and should anyone raise a fuss,
the *New York Times* would be there to take their side—but it
was too late for that now. Besides, many Middle Easterners
were Christians, not just in Lebanon, but across ancient As-
syria and into Iran itself, so he could certainly fake it and
hope the cops had other and better things to do.

For the first time since the appearance of the Angel of
Death, he began to breathe a little easier . . .

Danny climbed into the chopper and took a look
around. A-OK. The baby was fully loaded, and there was a
nasty-looking Barrett sniper rifle all greased up and ready
to go.

Two men approached him as he revved 'er up: both cops.
They made a beeline for him and hopped right in.

"I'm Capt. Byrne, this is detective Aslan Saleh," said
Byrne, pronouncing the name pretty well for a white guy,
and reaching for the rifle. Saleh was obviously an Arab, and
Danny let the question cross his mind that maybe NYPD had
been infected by the PC-virus, then caught himself. Far
more likely that NYPD had done what the useless CIA
should have done in the days after 9/11, if not long before:
start recruiting from the streets of South Side Chicago and
the tougher parts of Brooklyn, instead of among the poet-
asters of Kenyon College and the University of California at
Berkeley. Good Lord, when was the Langley Home for Lost
Boys going to learn how to fight?

"Martin Ferguson," he said. "Welcome aboard."

The chopper rose . . .

Devlin wasn't sure what had hit him; some kind of stanchion, probably, something the kid had found in the room. Whatever it was, it hurt like hell. He was good, but he wasn't Superman. He was tough, but he still bled. And he was bleeding now.

The blow to the head was followed by a power punch to the nose, which sent sparks shooting into his head. Either of the blows, had he known what he was doing, could have been killers; nobody had taught this punk, but he had the instincts of a pro. And Devlin hadn't even seen his face yet. There was no worry that his opponent should see his, because no one had ever escaped from an encounter with the Angel.

Except, of course, Emanuel Skorzeny. And that mistake would someday soon be rectified.

Devlin rolled, confidently expecting to miss the next blow, but instead got a kick that just narrowly missed the point of his chin. Good God, who was this guy?

He lashed out, but again his man wasn't where he expected him to be. The only thing he'd gotten right about this guy was his hidey-hole, and now he was beginning to think that that was on purpose.

Crash! A rusty old tool kit collided with the wall behind him, sending a shower of old, disused tools to the floor. At last, thought Devlin, he's made a mistake. And then he realized that was exactly what the kid wanted to do. He knew Devlin would be armed; now he had an array of weapons to choose from, including screwdrivers, hammers, lug wrenches, and a couple of small saws with nasty, rusted-out teeth.

No more mistakes: the kid would be on him in a flash.

And a kid he was, too, from the looks at him he could get. He had to end this and in a hurry.

"This is fun!" came the voice and a handful of nails hit him in the face, just missing his eyes.

A hammer hit him square on the back, missing the vertebrae.

Stop fighting like a pro, he thought to himself. Forget everything you know for about five seconds, just long enough to meet him in his own battlespace. Because right now you are getting the crap kicked out of you. Think; what did this punk want?

A sharp stab of pain as the point of a Phillips screwdriver slashed his pants and tore the flesh on his calf. Great, thought Devlin: I have enough toxic shit on me to poison the city, and now it's heading for my bloodstream. *Finish this.* What did this punk want?

He had it: love and revenge. Just like everybody else.

"You're good, Raymond" he said, dodging another thrust with the screwdriver. "Real good. I could train you."

"Shit," sneered Raymond. "From the looks of you, you old dog, you can't even keep shit out of your ears.

Just a little pause in the assault. That was all he needed. A little more—

"I bet back home in Wahoo everybody thought you were a dork, didn't they?" The kid threw a box cutter at him, with a wicked aim that creased the top of his hair. "Especially the girls. Am I right?"

Raymond's eyes widened.

"And the girls probably made fun of you when you showed them that little dick, didn't they? You need help, boy."

"I don't need no help to kick the shit out of you, buddy," said Raymond, and he was on him again. This time, though, Devlin was ready. His head was still ringing, and there was blood somewhere and the clock was ticking and he had to

finish his man and get the hell out of here, because Danny
would be ready by now and—

"How could you help me? What could you teach me?"

That was all the opening he needed. Just that pause.

"How about this?"

Devlin lashed out with a perfect kick to the man's throat,
which sent him tottering backward, but didn't knock him
down. The kid was tough, he had to give him that. "Ow!" he
exclaimed, and Devlin realized he was dealing with somebody who was maybe eighteen years old. Then he saw it, and
any doubts he might have harbored about having the wrong
man were gone. As Raymond tumbled, the woman's hair fell
from his belt, where it had been hanging. In a flash, Devlin
scooped it up and held it aloft.

"She's mine now, Raymond. I'm going to be the one who
fucks her tonight, not you. So you're going to have to listen
to me and take my offer if you want to tap that ass."

They were circling each other now, wary. Raymond was
having a hard time breathing, and he was gulping like a fish
on the bottom of a boat; the sort of blow he'd just received
did that to you.

"Can you teach me?" Raymond croaked. "The Brothers
taught me, but I bet you could teach me more. They didn't
let me near no pussy on account of the faith, but they knew I
wanted some and they promised me I could get me some if
I . . ." He coughed.

"If you became a martyr, is that right?"

Raymond nodded, lowering his head.

Because of its heavy handle, the KA-BAR wasn't thought
of as a great throwing knife. You could dig a trench with it,
generally fuck somebody up pretty good with it at close
range. But you could also conk them with it.

Devlin heard the skull crack as the handle of the Marine
Corps knife came down on Raymond's head; the blade cut
his hand as he grasped it, but no matter. This would be over

soon now. He just had to keep Raymond alive a little while longer. But first he had to teach him the lessons he so desperately wanted to learn.

Devlin sprang behind and caught him in a choke hold. He put the point of the knife under his chin, then releasing the hold, caught him with a hard left to the kidney. The boy whimpered but stiffened, and kicked backward. But now the fight was on Devlin's terms. As Raymond turned, under the illusion he had escaped the deadly hold, Devlin thrust a thumb into his eye socket and popped the eyeball loose. It stayed in his head, dangling from its stalk.

"I thought you were going to teach me!" he shouted.

"I am teaching you," Devlin replied calmly. "It's just that you have to use what you've learned in the next life, because you sure as hell aren't going to use it in this one."

"That's what you think, old man."

He must have pulled the gun out of his ass or something because the next thing Devlin knew the room was being spray-painted with bullets and all he could do was react. He dove behind some old paint barrels and boxes, not thinking that they would block the shots, but that with only one eye Raymond's aim would be off, that he'd be firing by instinct and that, once again, all he needed was a little time.

He must be slowing down. He'd never needed time like this, time like a dropped fighter needs when he's taking a standing eight count. He should have listened to his own good sense last year, and gotten out when he could. He could still punch his ticket, take Maryam and go live somewhere far away from all this—Argentina, maybe, or New Zealand or Mongolia, for that matter. It didn't matter. The whole world was the same damned fucking place to him, and he'd hated it since that day in Rome.

The firing stopped.

Devlin rose, the KA-BAR in his hand, grasping it by the

handle this time. The Judge was still with him, but he wanted to impart one last lesson.

The heavy knife got Raymond right below the breastbone. "Mama!" he cried.

A pro would know to lie down. A pro would know it was time to die, the way Milverton had done when he'd bested him. A pro would show some respect.

All these things young Raymond Crankheit still had to learn, and never would.

Devlin was hardly surprised when the kid, with four of the KA-BAR's six inches stuck inside him, tried to pull it out. He was not surprised when the kid tried to bite him as he approached. Nothing this punk did would surprise him now.

"Last lesson, Raymond," he said, pulling out the Judge. "When you shoot at somebody, make sure you don't miss."

Raymond's face was a bloody, grotesque mask as he spotted Devlin, looking down at him. Whether he saw the gun was hard to say, but he surely knew what was coming. "Give it back to me," he hissed.

"What?"

"The hair. My girlfriend's hair. She'll be mad at me if it gets lost."

"I'll make sure she gets it back, kid," said Devlin. He thought a moment for an appropriate valedictory. "They say there but for the grace of God, and you know what—they're right, if you don't take the God part too seriously. But when I look at you, Raymond, I don't see just another misspent youth, a life that went nowhere. I see something else. I see a kid that's going to be saved, not cursed. You've got talent. You've got moves. You've got heart."

"Thanks, pop," Raymond said. "I wish you were my dad."

"That's why I'm not going to let you grow up, so that you can be like me. So they can make you into another version—maybe a better version—of me. Look at me, Raymond. Look at me."

The boy turned what was left of his face to Devlin's.

"Here, but for the grace of God, might have gone you."

He fired two .45 rounds in Raymond's heart. That got that part of the pain over with. He'd never feel another pang of love or lust or anger or hatred again.

Devlin looked down at the mess that had been Raymond Crankheit. Some woman bore this creature, some man had fathered him, whipped him, beaten him, turned him into the sniveling wreck he'd become, a pit bull that cringed in front of its master but attacked the neighbors. Somewhere there were the two people who were Raymond's parents, and whether they still loved him or despised him, or whether they were even still alive, since Raymond might have killed them first, Devlin saw no point in having their son's final, horrific misdeeds come back to haunt them. If he could not grant absolution to the son, then let him do it for the parents.

The third round in the Judge's chamber was a shotgun shell. He pointed the gun at Raymond's head, and blew it off, in the hopes that someday, someone might do the same for him.

The quickest way to the river was back the way he came. There he could wash off both the shit and the stench of Raymond's martyrdom, cleansing himself of all the sins and getting ready for one more kill.

CHAPTER THIRTY-NINE

The East River

Kohanloo's boat slipped in and out of the traffic. He kept radio silence, which was something he didn't intend to break until the last possible second, to locate his contact in Red Hook.

All things considered, the operation had been a success. They had struck a mighty blow at the Great Satan. Certain financial investments he had placed both for himself and for the mullahs would now pay off handsomely. There was the matter of the score he had to settle with Skorzeny, but that could wait until after the hero's welcome he was undoubtedly going to get when he got back to Tehran.

He looked at the radio. It didn't look like much, but he had to assume that it was state of the art, that it would do its job, that it would make the contact as promised and planned. He almost lifted the receiver and cranked it, just to see if it was working, but decided against it. Patience was one of the great virtues, and curious, sinful man had such a hard time understanding that.

He was lost in these thoughts for a moment until he gradually became aware of the *thwack thwack thwack* of an approaching helicopter, the beats growing louder. He did his best not to panic immediately. New York was filled with helicopters—police helicopters, private helicopters, news helicopters, sightseeing helicopters, now even military helicopters. Perhaps all the Brothers had been killed; perhaps the city was being reopened.

He glanced skyward. No visual, but the sound was growing louder. It was also growing _lower_ . . .

"What a fucking moron," said Lannie Saleh. "I mean, come on, it's not like he's obvious or anything." He finished assembling the Barrett and got ready to hand it to Byrne.

"First rule of police work, Lannie," said Byrne, moving into position. "If criminals weren't stupid, the cops would never solve any crime." He shouted over at "Martin Ferguson"—"Can you take us down a little lower? I want to get a visual on him if possible."

"We'll spook him."

"I don't know what area of law enforcement you're in, pal, but I'm a New York City cop, with a real live NYPD badge in my pocket and a formerly regulation .38 sidearm. I shoot some civilian and even under a state of emergency my career is meat and I'm lucky to be pulling down half-pension on Fire Island. Lannie?"

Lannie angled the computer toward Byrne's field of vision. They'd downloaded all known pictures of Kohanloo, and their mysterious benefactor had sent them a ton of surveillance photos as well, and had kept them coming until the transmission had suddenly gone dead a few hours ago. No matter, with enhancements, they knew every inch of his face the way his mother would. With other software, they could calculate his body mass, his weight, his height, then do a full-scale mockup of what he would look like in various positions, measured against objects they all knew. There was no chance, zero, that in person he would turn out to be shorter than they thought, or fatter. They'd know him in a dark alley. All they needed was one good visual and . . . pow! He'd be sleeping with the fishes.

They had taken off from the Pan Am Building—everybody still called it that—and circled across the river, wheeling over Queens to come around over Randall's Island, with the whole sweep of the river heading south before them. They were over a place where the ocean tides and the waters of the Long Island Sound collided with and the estuarial waters of the Hudson River and its effluent, the Harlem River. Sailors had long hated this part of the riverway, with its treacherous eddies and rocky outcroppings. No wonder it was called Hell Gate.

"Take us down," ordered Byrne.

"Over or under?" asked Danny.

"The bridges, you mean?"

Danny nodded. "Under is better. You want to see his face, I can let you shake his hand."

"That's what the scope is for," said Byrne, patting it.

"You're the boss."

The chopper rose almost straight up in the air as it neared the Queensboro Bridge and both Byrne and Lannie almost lost their lunches. "Under's better. A little trickier, but leave that to me."

Kohanloo saw the chopper suddenly peel off and shoot into the air as he approached the Queensboro Bridge. He breathed a little easier when he shot beneath it and didn't see the damn thing. So it was a false alarm after all. Good. At the speed he was doing, Red Hook was less than 45 minutes away. He was going to make it.

* * *

Danny rocked the chopper hard to the left as he ascended, then leveled off and headed straight across the river for Manhattan and the buildings of the East Side.

"What the hell are you doing?" shouted Byrne. "I would have had him."

"Not under these bullshit RoEs," shouted Danny. "You want a face-to-face shot, I'll give it to you. But you boys are going to have to get used to riding with the pro from Dover, and that means no barfing, even if it is your chopper."

"Hold me down, Lannie," shouted Byrne, elbowing his way forward to get the barrel of the Barrett into position. He had no intention of dying by falling out of a helicopter over the East River, but he also had to make his shots count. The first one would go through the engine block—at a relatively short distance the Barrett could blow right through it. It would be as if the boat had had a heart attack. The next round would go through the radio, if he could locate it quickly enough, and the third, once they had a positive ID on the scanner, would go through Mr. Kohanloo.

It would have been possible, in fact, for him to have hooked up the sight with the computer and wirelessly relayed the images he saw for immediate ID, but in the rush no one had thought of that. Byrne was still old school, and trusted his eyes a lot more than pixels. Still, it was a blunder, so he'd better make the shots count and hope nobody asked about it later.

Ferguson's skills were amazing. He keep the chopper low as they barreled down Second Avenue, darting in and out of the side streets in order to catch a glimpse of the river, and of the bogus Red Cross boat they were chasing, but without letting their man get the wind up.

Byrne knew just where he wanted to take him now: between the Manhattan and Brooklyn bridges. They'd let him come out from under the Williamsburg Bridge, dodge the old Navy Yard and then trap him between the bridges, where they could dispatch him.

"You're sure you can put this crate under the bridges, no sweat?" yelled Byrne.

"Ask me something difficult," smiled Ferguson.

Byrne thought for a moment. "Okay, where's the best place to eat in Bayonne?"

Over his shoulder, Ferguson flipped him the bird. The truth was, Byrne didn't know. His old partner, Vinnie Mancuso, would have known, but Vinnie was sunning himself down at Rehoboth, ogling the pretty Delaware girls in their bathing suits, and thinking about getting fat and happy in early retirement.

The chopper dove, and this time Byrne really did barf.

You could mark your passage by the bridges, thought Kohanloo, and here was the Williamsburg, which would be followed in quick succession by the two more famous structures, the Manhattan and the Brooklyn bridges. How pleasing it would be in Allah's sight some day to see them all collapse into the river, never to be rebuilt, their destruction, like that of the rest of the city, to be celebrated for centuries in the tales of the people, in the lore of the *ummah*. Truth to tell, Kohanloo was tiring of all this Western decadence. It made him feel sinful and dirty; it meant accepting the world on their terms, with their disgusting food and their whorish women. When he got back to Iran, he would repent, whip himself bloody on the feast of Ashura, and make everything in readiness for the coming of the Twelfth Imam.

What a surprise they would get, no matter what happened to him. The fools may have been able to take down a handful of Brothers, but not unless Allah had cursed him and his work would they ever think to look for, much less find, the little parting gift he had left them, the thing that required the blinding of the cursed CTU computers for just long enough to bring it ashore and take it to the last place where they would ever think to look for it—in one of their beloved hospitals, where its low-level radioactivity would never be detected by routine flyover surveillance and where it would stay, asleep, like the Holy Imam himself in the well at Qom, until such time as the Day of Reckoning was decreed, and then it would come alive and go off in a roar and a rain of holy fire.

And to think it had been delivered to River House by this very craft, slipped into a van and deposited for safekeeping at the Jew hospital, Mt. Sinai, where they were so lax they openly allowed the Brothers to work as doctors, technicians, and orderlies. The Brotherhood of Man meant much to both cultures, but with a very different meaning of brotherhood for the Faithful, as the Chosen would soon find out. No matter what happened to him, whether he lived, Allah willing, or died a martyr, that in the end was why he had chosen to come. He had to see it, this miracle, this proof of the might and power of Allah and his divine wrath.

"Showtime, boss."

Byrne moved into position. "Sit on my legs," he said.

They had circled round and were coming back up from the south. Since the East River was not really a river but an estuary, buffeted by the Sound and the waters of New York Harbor, there really was no up or down in the traditional sense, just as the waters of the Hudson sometimes ran north when the tide was high, the salt water engaging with the fresh water coming down from Albany. New York City had always been a swirl of misdirection.

They were south of the Brooklyn Bridge, and high in the air when they saw the Red Cross boat emerge from beneath the Williamsburg. "Hang on, boys," shouted Danny, and then the chopper dropped straight down, in a controlled dive that knocked the wind from Byrne's lungs. Inside his coat, he could feel his father's .38 slipping from the unbuttoned holster and start to slide. He made a mental note never to go up in a helicopter again, not if he could help it.

Down they plunged until, at what seemed like the last possible second, Danny leveled her off and then, still heading lower but this time at a proper diagonal, darted under the Brooklyn Bridge.

With his newfound piety, Arash Kohanloo decided he didn't much care what happened. It would, however, be good to know whether his radio actually did work, whether there was as compatriot waiting for him in Red Hook. He took the receiver off the hook and cranked the ancient set—and he was, he had to admit, not terribly surprised when nothing at all happened. He was on a suicide mission after all.

He cursed himself for not having shaved his body, as the law prescribed, for not making the proper ablutions a holy warrior should make, but there was nothing to be done about it now. Perhaps he could ditch the craft on the Brooklyn shore and make a run for it. There were plenty of Brothers in Brooklyn, and not just along Atlantic Avenue anymore, but everywhere; since 9/11 the city's population of Arabs and Muslims had increased and grown more visible, in quiet celebration of the achievements of Atta and his men, and also in the anticipation of the glory that was surely to come when the crescent flew over City Hall, as someday fly it must.

There was the Manhattan Bridge. He'd land there. He steered the boat sharply to port and made for the shore. He prayed to Allah, prayed for a sign that his decision was the right one.

* * *

"What the fuck? Where is he?" In the gloom beneath the great bridge, they had lost the boat. "Lannie, find me this fucker, now."

Lannie was still hanging on to Byrne. "What do you want me to do, boss?"

"Track him on GPS, radio, whatever. He must be emitting some kind of signal. Just find the bastard."

Lannie hesitated. "Okay, but I have to let go of you a little, boss."

Byrne braced himself against one of the seats as best he could. "Make it quick, find the cocksucker and then let's get him."

Still trying to hold on to Byrne with one hand while operating the computer with the other, Lannie punched some keys. His eyes rotated as he tried to anticipate the charts, the signals, the points on the graphs, anything. There—

"I got him, boss. He's making for the Brooklyn shore."

Danny heard that and throttled forward, the chopper responding to the master's touch. But he also turned sharply to the right; Lannie lost his grip on Byrne, who slid forward. His gun fell out of his suit pocket, toward the open door.

Byrne had a choice: the shot or his father's pistol. For years he had carried that gun around with him like a cross, as a way of honoring his dad, but now he realized that the gun was just an inanimate object, something that long ago lost any and all meaning for his father, something in fact that had failed him in his moment of need. All these years Byrne had carried it in his memory, even used it in his memory, had shot his own half-brother with it.

There was the boat. There was the man. Ferguson, or whoever the hell he was, needed to make another turn and get them head-on at the target. And then he would take him out. "Get me a clean shot!" he yelled.

Lannie saw what was going to happen, but there was nothing he could do. He dropped the computer and grabbed both of Byrne's legs. If the gun went, the gun went; the Boss would just have to get used to the 9 mm.

Danny threw her into a hard turn, spun once as he gained full control of the aircraft, then dropped her down practically to the water itself. Damn, the man was as good as he said he was. Not that it was up to him to be as good as he said he was.

The miracle appeared before him, floating like an angry, evil dragonfly above the surface of the choppy waters. Allah be praised! He would now show himself worthy of this great honor that had been granted him.

Arash Kohanloo reached for an AK-47 and begin firing it at the approaching helicopter.

The windscreen was bulletproof, but Francis Byrne was not. He had to make his shot. No need for ID now. Just take him out. Byrne squeezed the trigger, aiming for the hull.

The 50-caliber round punched through the boat as if it wasn't there, tearing through the hull and exiting out the back. But he had missed the engine block itself, and so the distance between them was closing rapidly.

The shot had also given away Byrne's position within the craft. He could feel the bullet whizzing by his head as the man trained his fire upon him. "Don't you people ever give up?" he groused to no one in particular, then realized what he'd said. No time for apologies. He heard Lannie's answer as he fired—

"No, Boss—do the Irish?"

This time, the shot hit the engine block square and the

boat suddenly went dead in the water. Not motionless, though: its forward moment kept propelling it toward the chopper.

"Want me to pull out, Captain?" shouted Danny. The man was fearless, Byrne would give him that. "You can get a clean shot from any angle."

Byrne shook his head. "Evasive action, but keep me lined up."

Danny didn't bother to shout that evasive action was going to be sickening action, as he would be swinging the craft from side to side, moving her up and down like one of those low-riders the Mexican gangbangers back in L.A. used to cruise and bruise. "Hold on."

The Koala hopped. Kohanloo fired another burst. Byrne squeezed the trigger.

Arash Kohanloo felt the bullet tear off his right arm. Not go through it, but tear it completely off. The AK-47, still on full auto, fell into the river. The pain made him delirious, the blood made him happy. He smiled and cheered and yelled at the man with the rifle. "Shoot me again! Shoot again, you dog! You coward! You cannot kill me, for I am a Brother. I go to immortality!"

Lannie fed him another round. This one was greasy, slippery, and as Byrne looked down at his hand, he noticed it was bloody. "What the hell?"

Lannie held up a small vial of viscous fluid. "Pig's blood. I want you to send this bastard to hell for what he does to me and my people and my faith. I want him cursed for all eternity, the Shi'a swine."

Byrne tossed the round back to Aslan. "Save it for somebody who really needs it," he shouted. "I'm going to send him to hell the good old-fashioned Irish way. With one in the brain."

"*Allahu Akbar!*" shouted Kohanloo.

"Fuck you," muttered Byrne, and he fired the third shot.

The recoil knocked his father's sidearm to the lip of the door . . .

For less than a tenth of a second the world moved in slow motion for Arash Kohanloo, as Allah himself slowed it to a crawl. Gone was the pain, and in its place came the certainty of knowing that heaven was his, that all he had to do was reach out and embrace it, embrace his fate, embrace his destiny.

The round entered Kohanloo's open mouth, blew out the back of his head and then, on its downward trajectory, punched a hole through the bottom of the boat. Quickly, it filled with water and began to sink.

. . . and as Danny throttled forward to fly over the wrecked boat, the gun toppled out the door and into the East River.

Byrne looked at Lannie: "Get down there, right now. Hurry."

Lannie hesitated. "You mean, retrieve the gun?' He would if ordered. From this moment on he would do anything his captain asked him to do.

"No, you dumb raghead. Get on that boat before the fucker sinks and grab what you can. Martin, can you put us—"

Already done. They were right over the sinking craft. Lannie threw out the rope ladder and went over the side—

"Get papers, equipment, whatever. Forget the gun. And him," he said, indicating the corpse, "you leave for the fishes."

THREE DAYS
LATER

EPILOGUE

Falls Church, Virginia

Cautiously, Devlin disabled the security services on his old house in the near Virginia suburbs of Washington. He had not been in the house since the events of last year, had assumed in the wake of the FBI raid, he would have to blow it, which meant he painstakingly had to clear the charges to once more render it habitable.

He had to laugh. Falls Church had once been a prosperous and stable small city—the smallest in the country—but like everything and every place in America, it had changed radically. Today, naturally, it was a hotbed of anti-American Islamic activity, just a few miles from the Capitol. One thing you could say about the Americans; they were going to let their newfound fetish tolerance run free if it got them all killed. And if and when it did, the hell with them.

He moved into his secure room, which was just as he left it. He had just witnessed a boy much like himself go willingly to his death out of passion—not for some abstract bullshit ideal, but for something he believed in, during the course of which he touched something he had never touched before—not just a woman, but the Other. In his sick, twisted way, Raymond Crankheit had caught a glimpse of the other side, the side where happiness dwelled, and he'd liked it well enough not to kill Principessa Stanley. Just as he, Devlin, had caught that glimpse with Maryam and decided to gamble everything on his one chance at happiness.

"Do you trust the bitch? You don't even know her real name."

Where the hell was she? He had not heard from her since her last message from Budapest, and though he knew he shouldn't care, it was only business, she was on assignment— his assignment—and that op sec was indeed everything . . . he still cared.

Maybe it had been a mistake to bring her in. Maybe he should have killed her last year when he had the chance, after their night together in Echo Park, a mercy killing. Maybe he should have let her die in Paris, when she took a bullet for him.

Maybe . . . but then where would he be?

He'd watched the entire Kohanloo takedown from one of the safe houses on the Upper East Side, near Gracie Mansion. Using the electronic entrepôt that Byrne had given him—one that he knew would be temporary and limited to this operation—he was able to see the whole thing from the chopper's built-in cams, part of the same mechanism that gave the flying machine its night vision. He would have liked to have been part of that, but he had acted on his intuition that Byrne was a right gee, as the cops used to say back in the old days, and he'd been proven correct.

He went into the bathroom. He could still see the bloodstains on the floor, where Evalina Anderson had died at his hand. He started to scrub them, but they were old and dried, and after a while he gave up. Then he threw up.

There were too many ghosts now, piling up, even right here in his own home. At some point, one of them would reach out of the past and claim him and then that would be that.

He switched on his systems in the panic room. He'd have to update them all, of course, and run endless security checks, but for now all he wanted to do was see if there were any urgent messages sent via the private T-3 line to The Building in Maryland.

There were.

URGENT—that would be from Seelye. The man never slept.

SPEAK

MESSAGE FOR YOU, FROM YOU

That could mean only one thing—a message Maryam had sent from the secure laptop had been received.

RELAY

I DON'T THINK YOU REALLY WANT TO SEE IT

DON'T FUCK WITH ME DAD.

WE CHECKED THE IP ADDRESS.

HUNGARY, SO WHAT?

NOT HUNGARY.

WHERE THEN?

YOU'RE NOT GOING TO LIKE THIS

WHERE??

There was a short pause before the answer came: IRAN. TEHRAN, TO BE PRECISE

Devlin tried to control his panic. MEANING WHAT?

WHAT DO YOU THINK? SHE'S DEFECTED

IMPOSSIBLE

ENTIRELY LIKELY. WE GOT A DOSSIER, COURTESY OF SENDER. IT'S ALL ABOUT HER. WOULD YOU LIKE TO SEE IT? SEEMS SHE'S BEEN A DOUBLE AGENT THE WHOLE TIME

FOR WHAT PURPOSE?

WHY, BOY, FOR YOU. WHAT OTHER PURPOSE?

BUT SHE—He stopped. It couldn't be. It couldn't. RE-QUIRE PROOF. COULD BE SKORZENY DOUBLE, FALSE FLAG, ANYTHING

THERE WAS ONE OTHER THING

WHAT?

SIGNED BY HER

WHAT??

YOU SHOULD SEE FOR YOURSELF

SEND IT

I WILL. BUT YOU SHOULD KNOW THAT THIS NEGATES OUR PREVIOUS AGREEMENT. MY JOB IS NOW SECURE SO LONG AS TYLER STAYS PRESIDENT. WHICH YOU AND I WILL NOW ENSURE. DO I MAKE MYSELF CLEAR?

SEND IT AND WE'LL TALK LATER

SUIT YOURSELF.

Even before it came, he knew what was coming. A taunt, a jest? Or the truth?

It came across the screen:

It was the "Dorabella" Variation, written out in Elgar's hand. The code Atwater had cracked. The substitution for the substitution. The most visible layer of the endless palimpsest that was his world, and hers as well.

And underneath, in her hand, the words: "I'm so sorry."

He was not sure how long it was before he noticed a new sensation. It was a pain in his chest, a throbbing, searing pain—no, not pain, more like a new emotion, one that he had never experienced before, but one that brought on shortness of breath, sweats, shivers.

Then he became aware of a sound rushing in his ears, like the waters of a river, or the waves of a great ocean. There was the smell of salt in his nose, as of brine and felt himself toppling backwards into a tidal pool that splashed the world with ocean spray as the waves met the rocks on the shore.

He thrust his arms and let gravity take him, plunging down toward the sea, the primal sea, not Mother Earth but Mother Ocean, the place where blood and seed were the same, the place where life began and where death could take you any time it wanted. And all accompanied by the beating of a great drum, the *tactus* of the universe, the thing that set our rhythms, from the seconds to the minutes to the hours to the days to the weeks to the months to the—

The beating of the human heart.

The ghosts reached out, but he shook them off. Not yet. Too soon.

The beating grew louder, stronger, more urgent. Across the oceans of time he had heard her and could hear her now. Across oceans of distance, he would find her. The only thing he could not do, ever, was to doubt her.

Of one other thing, finally, there could be no doubt: at last he knew he had a heart.